Observations on the Danger of Female Curiosity

Including an account of the unnatural tendencies arising on the over-stimulation of the mind of a lady

Suzanne Moss

Aesculus
Books

Aesculus Books

Book 1 in the Curiosity Series

Aesculus Books

suzannemoss.co.uk

AUTHOR LOCAL TO
CONFORD.
Hope you enjoy!

For everyone who remains curious

Suzanne
Moss

ACKNOWLEDGEMENTS

This book has been in production for a good few years – one way or another, and I have been astonished and delighted by the generosity and talent of people who have given their time to its production. It began with a PhD funded by the AHRC at the University of York – ably and patiently supervised by Professor Jon Finch and supported by the Burton Constable Foundation. William Constable (1721-1791) and his sister Winifred (1730-74) – the occupants of Burton Constable Hall through most of the eighteenth century – have amused and astonished me for over ten years and I hope their curiosity and generosity is aptly reflected here.

As I rapidly found out, historical fiction is HARD, and so I am grateful for the brains bigger than mine who provided their insight on early drafts, notably Dr Alice Marples and Isabel Gilbert. Appreciating that 18th century titles of nobility and gentry are confusing, they would be outright wrong without the time generously given by Major-General Alastair Bruce. These people are all geniuses, and any mistakes remaining in the text are entirely my own.

Early beta readers had a lot to wade through – Clare Ashton who is both insightful and fabulous; C.Fonseca who is so delightfully encouraging; and my mum's friends Doreen and Julie who didn't really know what they were getting into (Doreen liked it, Julie thought there was too much sex). Thank you also to Milena McKay for unwavering cheerleading, time, honesty and for formatting advice that means buying the paperback edition doesn't require a mortgage.

Later beta readers were invaluable – Marianne Ratcliffe, Joan M Burda, Sam Hall, Janine C Sheehan and Kevin Wigley – thank you so much for wisdom and attention to detail. And Lili Clendinen as sensitivity reader – an important job here I am extremely grateful for.

My editor Eleanor Leese – amazing insight and historical knowledge as well as practical solutions. Patient but doesn't take any of my rubbish. Always amazing.

My mum and dad who are the most awesome people and who have both read it twice. Even the naughty bits, which I try not to think about.

Finally, my wife Milly, who has taken up new hobbies while I squirrel myself away in front of a screen and is utterly bored of reading this. Thanks for putting up with me.

Oh, and the dogs, Wilma and Pheebs. For snuggles.

AUTHOR'S NOTE

Whilst researching the history of plants and collections I realised that the clever, weird, passionate, creative and fearless people involved were the best thing about it – and that they deserved to be brought to life in more than an academic paper.

The inspiration for this book has always been the inimitable Margaret Cavendish Bentinck, Duchess of Portland who was inescapably curious from 1715 to 1785. A voracious scholar, over her lifetime the Duchess gathered a cabinet collection second in size only to the British museum, her intention being to collect every unknown species and publish it to the world. This book does not try to be a faithful representation of her life and work – we know and can know too little about her for me to be comfortable fictionalising around the sparse facts. Instead, she and the colourful characters around her are inspirations for those in this book.

Only four characters are based on representations of actual people. Dr William Withering as the populariser of *Digitalis* as a remedy for dropsy, as it would be unthinkable to attribute that to anyone else. Also William Constable, his sister Winifred and their gardener Thomas Kyle. The Constable Collection, including a ten-volume *hortus siccus* complete with walnuts, still remains at Burton Constable Hall in East Yorkshire and is well worth visiting. Despite their representation, the words and actions of these four characters are entirely fictitious and I do not claim that they faithfully represent their views.

Other than these specific instances, any relations to characters living or dead is purely coincidental.

Living in eighteenth-century Britain wasn't always easy. The text involves some difficult topics – including views on women, black people, colonialism and slavery, disability and queer people. At times it has been uncomfortable to write and I know that parts may be to read, but I hope that it tries to balance the views and experiences, both positive and problematic by modern views, of the time. The lines intersecting historical accuracy, acceptability in fiction and sensitively truthful representation rarely meet comfortably and there are always choices to be made. I hope that the book provides one, acceptable interpretation. Any errors or inaccuracies of representation are all mine.

Please note that the book contains a discussion of, but not a graphic representation of, suicide.

One theme prominently featured is queerness – inspired by the Duchess, her friends, acquaintances and others. There are plenty of instances and suggestions of eighteenth-century queer relationships of varying manifestations and intensities, both sexual and not. There was little language to describe it and, naturally limited specific evidence, but we do know that there was plenty of it about. Georgians were absolutely not as uptight as Victorians and frankly, researching for this has been a wonderful and wild ride. Presented here is one interpretation, but there are many others explored elsewhere, and waiting to be brought to life.

I hope, more than anything, that the book helps, in a small way, to shine a light on the overlooked, awesome women of science in the past. The more I learn, the more I am awed by them.

This is book one in the Curiosity Series, so not the end for this cast of characters. I really hope you enjoy reading about these amazing women. I'd love to hear what you think – you can find me at suzann emoss.co.uk.

PART ONE

CHAPTER 1

London, March 1758

The room was dark. Not completely dark – lamps lit the figure on the stage – but darker than usual for a public lecture. It was also tense. Definitely more tense than usual. The only sound was the *click, click, click* of metal on glass, gaining in tempo almost to a frenzy. A charge leapt through the thrumming crowd as the atmosphere crackled. The boy watched wide-eyed as the illuminated lady stirred and leaned further into the light. She extended an arm, flicked forward a lazy hand, then stretched out a single digit. From his position by the rail the boy had a clear view as sparks leapt from her outstretched finger and into the jar – the resulting flames flaring skywards and licking the spectators on the front row with a flash of acrid orange.

The audience erupted.

A collective exhalation filled the auditorium as the cheers rang out, feeding the palpable excitement.

Dr Gibson stepped into the light. 'Ladies and gentlemen!' His sturdy form and charismatic address commanded the audience which still whooped and hollered. As on every night, he had to shout to be heard. 'The spectacle you have been so lucky to witness, here today in this very hall, looks for all the world like magic!' He paused, the cheering confirming the crowd's view. 'However, there is no such thing as magic, there is only–' he paused again for effect whilst the lamps were turned up to their highest extent and the machine on the stage was revealed in its full glory.

'*Electricity!*'

The crowd gasped. Now bathed in light, the lady was shown to stand on a resin block, one hand grasping a sturdy chain, the end of which coiled sensuously around her arm. From her hand the chain soared into the gods and then looped back to the stage, its other end grazing a sphere with a glistening lustre, itself attached to a belt driven by a wooden wheel almost four feet across. She leaned out once more, bearing elegantly on the chain and bowing to the crowd, who cheered again. The boy gulped.

Dr Gibson's teeth gleamed. 'The electricity is generated by the friction of the chain against the rotating glass sphere. It passes through the chain and into Meg's body to the extent that she is so charged with electrical fluid that one flick of her finger can ignite any flammable liquid. This is a force which may be generated by the hand of man and wielded by the fingers of a lady. It is a physical manifestation of the forces of nature, tamed and controlled by this very machine.' He threw up his hands in enthusiasm, 'Now, which of you would you like to see the wonder one more time?!' The crowd roared their approval, and the lady obliged with grace while Dr Gibson imparted more tantalising knowledge to his patrons who consumed it with gusto.

When he judged their curiosity almost sated, Dr Gibson moved on to the closing act. 'Now, the grand finale!' The boy shifted his weight to the other foot. This is what he had been waiting for. 'Ladies, how would you like to test the mettle of your men, right here, in this room, tonight?!' The ladies in the audience enthusiastically confirmed their assent. 'Gentlemen, please form a line. You are now invited to kiss my most ravishing assistant. However, be warned, the most virile among you will receive quite a shock, and those that don't – well, I will leave it to the ladies to make up their own minds!'

As on previous nights the boy noticed the more timid gents sneak into the shadows, but the brave formed a line. He usually chose this moment to leave, but it was his last chance and he had to know. Meg. The word clung to his ears. He tried to convince himself it was the electricity he came for. As he joined the line the sphere started to spin once more, the chain clicking faster and faster over its polished surface. The first volunteer stepped onto the stage to wolf whistles and whoops of encouragement. The man liked his chances and bent to kiss Meg, but when his lips reached an inch from hers, a sharp spark arced between them, crackling blue and white and sending him reeling backwards into a fellow hopeful.

The cheers that accompanied this spectacle met each new volunteer and did not cease as the boy stepped forward. He had never been this close to a lady before, not like this.

Would she guess?

Meg looked directly into his eyes. He felt like he could fall into hers, a rich azure blending to teal at the centre with bright white streaks sliced throughout. Her pupils, wide from the dim of the room meandered leisurely around his face. He tracked their path, made lazy by the predictability of the charade she played night after night. His breath stalled as he saw hers hitch in her throat and her eyes suddenly snapped back to his with a startling intensity.

She knew.

'Get on with it!' shouted a voice in the crowd. It jolted him out of his reflection and his eyes urgently questioned hers. He was too aware of those inviting lips, her breath on his cheeks and the smell of musk, sweat and the clean astringency of spent electricity. Meg recovered her act and flicked an eyebrow in invitation – with amusement or resignation he wasn't sure. His pulse quickened as he drew in. Almost there.

The thrill surged through his body as the crack of the spark hit his lips, pulsated through his heart and earthed itself through his feet. He stumbled backwards and looked up towards her, their wary smiles now reflecting each other as she flicked that eyebrow once more and invited the next hopeful to try his chances.

The feeling of delight and exhilaration propelled the boy through London's streets, his old cap blowing in the wind and dusty shirt billowing as he weaved in and out of the evening promenade. Gasping for breath he reached Hanover Square and climbed over the railings delimiting the back courtyard of an extremely well-to-do residence. He dropped to the floor with a practiced grace and nipped sideways into an outhouse.

A short time later, Miss Thea Morell, eldest daughter of Mr Benjamin Morell and Mrs Euphemia Morell, emerged from the same door. She carried herself with the grace and elegance of a lady and smoothed her gown over her petticoats. She wasn't quite done up as it was impossible from the front, but it would do for now. Nipping through the servants' door she peered around the entrance to the scullery. Mrs Phibbs looked up from where she prepared the silver for tonight's dinner and a warm grin thawed her sharp features. 'Ah you're back, Miss Thea. I'll be right up.'

Thea smiled and her eyes lit. 'Thanks.'

She knew her eccentricities no longer surprised the housekeeper who had been with the family since before Thea was born. Going to a public lecture on her own was not something Miss Thea Morell could do, but the footman could, for half a penny. Ascending the stairs she smiled to herself as she thought of the scrapes the two of them had navigated over the years and how the housekeeper unwaveringly supported a mistress who was anything but normal. In her earlier years Thea had been terrified of the older lady – despite her diminutive size the wisdom of age gave her a dominant air, and her sharp features and scraped back salt and pepper hair lent a severity to her presence. But as Thea grew the two of them had developed a relationship based on mutual respect.

Technically, dressing the eldest Miss Morell was Agnes's job, but Thea would never have trusted Agnes with this secret. Mrs Phibbs was always called on if a quick change before dinner was required, and anyway, today Agnes had ridden ahead to the country estate at Milford with Mr Wade the butler to ready the house for the family's arrival. Thea wouldn't miss the London season and the house at Hanover Square, but she would miss Dr Gibson's lectures. Her brain told her it was because of the thrill of the electrical spectacle.

Once in the bedchamber a detailed analysis of the night's experiment accompanied the efficient lacing and buckling. Mrs Phibbs' knowledge of natural philosophy had grown along with Thea's whether she liked it or not, and she listened intently. Soon the pinning was complete.

'There we are Miss Thea, your mother will never guess,' said the housekeeper with a complicit smile as she put the finishing touches to Thea's dark tresses, piled high on her head. Thea assessed the figure looking back at her from the glass. Her hair was, as always, worn as low and natural as she could get away with, but it was still taller than she would like. She wore a little colour on her wide, plump lips, only to please her mother. She would never be as pretty as either of her sisters – she had a face that her mother liked to describe as 'expressive', or 'characterful' if she were feeling charitable. Today Thea wore the green silk dress, as usual with as minimal frill and ornament as possible.

The housekeeper was turning to get the door when Thea caught sight of her own, deep green eyes, and with a pulse in her chest was wrenched back to the lecture hall. She had meant to keep one portion of the evening to herself, but the words came out harshly, before she had time to think.

'I kissed the Electrical Venus today.'

Mrs Phibbs turned from the door and considered her for a second longer than usual. 'Did you now?' she asked, carefully. 'And how did you find it?'

Despite the fact that Thea had thought of little else since the event, it wasn't an easy question to answer. How was it? 'Slightly painful. Shocking' – the spark that had passed from Meg's lips seemed to burn so bright in her chest she was almost surprised she couldn't see it in the glass – 'Exhilarating.'

The truth was she wasn't even sure how to describe it, or which of the observations or emotions she should single out to express. She became aware that Mrs Phibbs was watching her with interest and flourished her ready smile. 'Anyway, time for dinner.'

As Thea walked the grand passage towards the dining room her father stuck his head out of the library door and beckoned her over. 'Thea! Come in.' She smiled and headed into the small room, the walls crammed with leather-bound volumes of knowledge. Mr Morell was a tall man, athletic in his youth and now slender with kind features and a grey wig always slightly askew. Her youngest sister Ursula sat with her father, helping him to pack books for the move tomorrow. She was four years Thea's junior and wore her blonde hair naturally, curled around her petite face and intelligent light-green eyes.

Mr Morell was pulling books from the shelves whilst Ursula ordered them in the travelling trunk from her wheeled chair. 'How was it today?' she asked excitedly.

'Excellent as always. I think they wound the machine particularly fast, one poor gentleman almost fell backwards off the stage when he went in for his kiss.' This made Ursula laugh and Thea bent to kiss her on the head, then one for her father. Afterwards she subconsciously touched her fingers to her lips. 'The power of the electrical fire is quite extraordinary.'

Ursula's perceptive eyes rested on Thea's for a second, but a book thrown onto the table by their father made them both jump. 'Quite wonderful!' he exclaimed, as ever only registering part of the conversation. 'Thea, Mr Valtrevers called while you were out, the ship made good time and he has left those for you.' He waved a hand vaguely towards the window ledge as he turned back to peruse the shelves. 'If you want them we can settle at the next account.'

Thea made for the window and picked up one of the two glass boxes – Mr Valtrevers, for all his effervescent disquisitions in the quest to trade his curiosities at least took note of how she liked her samples presented. 'A blue morpho,' she breathed, admiring the aquamarine lustre on the wings of the butterfly presented within. 'I've wanted one for ages.'

'Yes I think that's what he said it was,' said Mr Morell, tossing another book from the shelf into the travelling trunk, 'can't remember what he said about the other though, something to do with hippopotamuses, maybe.'

Thea put down the butterfly in its box and picked up the other. It held a large, iridescent green beetle with a horn on the front of its head. It didn't look much like a hippopotamus, at least not from the pictures Thea had seen. 'I'll have to look it up,' she said, and turned for the place on the shelf where she knew she would find the new edition of *Systema Naturae*. It wasn't there. She looked to Ursula, who was watching her with amusement, the book in front of her opened at a picture uncannily resembling the bug in its glass chamber.

'Asian rhinoceros beetle,' said Ursula, tapping the page, 'or *Scarabaeus rhinoceros* – first named in this very edition by Linnaeus himself. Looks like you have a particularly colourful specimen.'

'I should have known you'd be ahead of me,' smiled Thea.

'One of only two in the country according to Mr Valtrevers.'

'And let me guess, the other one is...'

'In the cabinet of the King, of course.' The sisters laughed together, Mr Valtrevers' sales technique was notorious in the Morell household. Despite his bluster he generally only brought them quality these days – over the years he had learned not to try to fob off the Morell sisters with second-rate curiosities. 'And a new psalter and rare courtly romance for father.'

Thea looked up at Mr Morell who beamed from the library steps in his shirt sleeves and waistcoat, his pocket watch glinting at his side. 'Uh oh,' she said, twisting her head so she could read the face. 'Dinner!'

Her father turned the watch so he could read it. 'Goodness, look at the time, your mother will be furious!'

Thea helped Ursula wheel herself to the dining room and Mr Morell followed. Ursula craned around in her chair and met Thea's gaze. 'Did you?' she whispered, both awe and anxiety clothing her face.

'Of course not,' said Thea, after a moment's hesitation. Although she and her sister told each other almost everything, she was not sure the kiss was something she wanted to share with her family. Not yet.

In the dining room, Mrs Morell and Tabitha were ready to eat. 'In the library again no doubt! Mrs Smeaton's pudding is getting cold and you know we still have everything to do before we leave tomorrow.' Mrs Morell stood with her hands on her hips, berating her husband as much as her two daughters.

'Apologies my dear, we were packing for the journey and lost track of time, but all done now.'

Mrs Morell was not discouraged. 'Well I'm sure the girls are not packed if you have been faffing about with books, when are they to get ready?'

'I packed my things earlier today, mother,' affirmed Ursula, soothingly. Thea had always admired the way her youngest sister managed their family's quirks.

'And so did Miss Thea,' said Mrs Phibbs, appearing from nowhere to serve the meal in Mr Wade's absence and throwing the faintest of winks in Thea's direction. 'Everyone is prepared, my lady.' Thea offered a wry smile to her plate and made a mental note to thank Mrs Phibbs later.

Mrs Morell looked unimpressed but did not pursue the questioning. It was her second daughter Tabitha, and her favourite, who took up the conversation. 'Honestly, Thea, I can't *believe* you missed tea with Georgie and Kitty this afternoon, we had *such* fun at cards and you shan't see Georgie now until the next London season.' Tabitha's tall hair wobbled as she spoke through her meat pudding. Some of the pudding ended up back on the table.

Thea swallowed deliberately in response. 'That's absolutely what I was counting on.'

'Oh, wicked!' professed Tabitha, 'at least *they* were both *devastated* not to see you to say goodbye.'

'Well I'm sure Kitty won't be a stranger, she lives but three miles from Milford and I know how inseparable you are. Did she set her hair alight on the chandelier again?' Thea asked, taking a sip of wine, 'that's always worth attending for.'

Her snipe was ignored as Tabitha's face creased in dramatic grief. 'Oh how I shall miss Kitty, I shall feel quite like I have lost my right arm.'

'You're left-handed,' Thea reminded her coolly. She noticed an amused twitch in the corner of Mrs Phibbs' lips.

'Never mind that. I love her, and I shall miss her,' sniffed Tabitha, 'perhaps I shall waste away with longing.' They were all quite used to ladies having romantic friends – living in each others' pockets, loathe to be apart whilst waiting for the right man – but Kitty was Tabitha's first and she did enjoy a drama. Thea was about to respond when Mrs Morell jumped in to soothe her middle child.

'Do not be despondent my dear, Kitty will be with us in the country in another month. You wouldn't have to be apart at all if Mr Morell did not insist on returning from the season early to see his plants and that infernal library.' She shot her husband a look, which he missed. 'And on Tabitha's first time out too! Oh, I have been so proud of you

my love, you have looked a dream at every ball you have attended!'
She beamed at Tabitha who may have blushed through her powder if
her cheeks were not so heavily rouged with vermillion. Or if she had
enough humility to colour at anything. 'Thank goodness one of my
daughters takes after me and not their father, otherwise I should have
a house full of rubbish and no ribbons at all!' Mr Morell raised an
eyebrow but kept his face aimed at his pudding. His wife was not to be
stopped when she was on a roll and he had long since stopped trying.
She went on. 'What has been *your* favourite diversion of the past three
months in the capital?' Thea and Ursula kept quiet – coming from
their mother they knew it wasn't really a question directed at them.

'Oh the Crowes' ball, without *question!*' proclaimed Tabitha, clasp-
ing her hands under her chin. 'The dresses. *My* dress. The dancing.
The *gentlemen*! Such a night I have never seen, and many of the guests
I spoke to – and I spoke to many – said that they hadn't either. I
danced until my feet were sore, *and* afterwards.' Thea silently cursed
the frivolity of her sister. The Crowes' ball was still a sore point with
their mother, and she braced herself for the return.

'You were a dream my dear and much admired by town society. As
could have been Theodosia Morell, if she had deigned to turn up.'

Their mother threw a glance at Thea, who winced at her full name
and dodged. 'How about you, Ursula, what will the talk be of when
we return to Milford?'

Ursula smoothly matched the distraction. 'The new collections, no
doubt. Mr Blake's was the best I have seen. Not as well labelled as I
would like, but there is always room for improvement.' She smiled.
Mr Morell and Thea nodded and smiled with her. Mrs Morell looked
nonplussed and turned the conversation back to the society she was
hoping for back at Milford for the summer. As she expected no further
input from anyone else into the conversation, apart from an occasional
'hmm', or 'oh', Thea slipped into a consideration of where she would
need to house the new insects in the cabinet back at Milford. The
beetle on the arthropod shelf of course, and the butterfly–.

'–and I won't have any delays from you three.' Thea looked up to find her mother's most determined stare ticking round herself, Ursula and their father. 'We must reach Milford before sundown as you know how my back cannot stand travelling in the dark.' They all nodded sagely, having long since stopped trying to apply reason or logic to Mrs Morell's conversation.

'*And*, as we all know, the Harringtons will be back at Stanbourne. After so many years away on the continent and twenty times richer from the colonies!' Thea closed her eyes and rested her head against the juddering carriage glass, hoping to shut out Tabitha's incessant chatter. They were three hours into the journey from London to Milford and her sister had barely drawn breath. She was too excited about her high hopes for a ball, her wishes to see Kitty again, and how excited she was to be out in country society. 'One must be aware as they are such an esteemed family and if Georgie is to be believed Samuel Harrington, that is *Viscount Stockwood,* is now *quite* the most handsome and charming gentleman there ever was. Not that it will concern you, Thea.'

'It better concern her,' chipped in Mrs Morell, 'she has shown no interest in any of the town gentlemen these last three months, and such pickings to be had!' Ursula peered sympathetically at Thea from across the carriage.

'That's not true,' said Thea, 'I spoke to Mr Daniel Hunter quite at length in January.' She was no stranger to this conversation and she felt a familiar tightness grasp her.

Her mother sighed. 'Daniel Hunter is over twice your age and he could sneeze and mislay his fortune in his handkerchief. You are almost three and twenty and no acceptable suitor will consider a wife who is past it. You barely made an effort this season and it may have been your last chance.'

Before Thea could ask what her mother meant her sister chipped in. 'Don't worry mother, I shall make a good match,' announced Tabitha, 'I have made an excellent impression on all the young gentlemen I have conversed with over the season, and I shall choose well, for the sake of my sisters.'

Mrs Morell smiled at her. 'Thank goodness one of my daughters has a sense of family loyalty.'

The creeping cold anxiety inside Thea had reached her scalp and made her light-headed. While the conversation was nothing new, she knew her mother's fervour on the subject grew with each passing year and there was something about her now that seemed more desperate. Almost five years out and all potential suitors had come to nothing – not for their want of trying, she had to admit, but none of them ever seemed quite right. They were too aloof, too self-serving, too poor, too stupid or just – well – not right. To distract herself, she considered her new acquisitions. She held up the beetle and peered at the way the colours slid effortlessly from chartreuse, to emerald to indigo. It was a thing of beauty. A movement behind the box caught her attention and she saw Mrs Morell's eye's scowling at her from across the carriage.

'For goodness sake, mother, nobody can see here.'

'They can if they look through the windows.' Mrs Morell punctuated her point with a nod towards the glass. Thea's gaze followed it to see the rolling hills of Surrey, a single farmhouse visible in the distance. 'You must make yourself as marriageable as possible this summer,' her mother went on. 'With so many ladies on offer, any such small thing can put them off. And that – ' she nodded at the beetle in Thea's hands – 'is not a small thing.'

'Grandmother was a scholar,' muttered Thea, defiantly willing the anxiety to subside. 'She managed to learn and to keep a husband.'

'Only with his blessing and support,' shot back Mrs Morell. 'And you won't find that now. Learned ladies are out of fashion and I can certainly see why. Being too curious makes you obstinate. There are plenty of acceptable activities you could be spending your time engaging in rather than this fluff.'

'Activities acceptable to whom?'

Mrs Morell ignored her. 'Embroidery, like Tabitha, or painting like Ursula. Apparently the Harrington girl is very good too. Or–'

'Cards like Tabitha?' Thea interjected. She knew it was rude but she was beginning to feel panicked. 'Then another one of us could be asking father to pay off our debts at the table.'

Mrs Morell glared at her. 'As if that's relevant. Tabitha's debts are a drop in the ocean compared to–'

Thea stared at her. 'To what?'

Mrs Morell gathered herself. 'Never mind. My point is that there are a great many acceptable options as to how you may spend your time, and yet you choose – you willingly choose – to be different.'

'Is that so terrible?'

'Anything that reduces your chances of making an advantageous match must be discouraged. We are blessed that Tabitha takes after me in her creative talent but unfortunately she got her money management from your father. And Ursula has no chance of a good match.' Thea looked tenderly across at Ursula. Her mother never considered how her sister might feel, but Ursula simply smiled – she was used to it. Mrs Morell went on, 'You must keep your oddities to yourself and make an effort, Thea.'

Thea knew there was little point arguing. She gave a small sigh, dropped the box containing the beetle to her lap and studied it there. After a while her gaze switched to the butterfly, its wings stretched magnificently against the ivory of the board on which it was pinned. Surely different was not always bad? She put thoughts of marriage to one side and contemplated it closely. An astonishing entity, bold and graceful, arrested by the collectors who roamed the world seeking land, knowledge and riches. Now here it was, thousands of miles away, pinned, static and lifeless. If she were to be pinned as a trophy herself, she vowed she would at least make its journey worthwhile.

As she contemplated the deep azure sheen of the wings, the image of Meg's deep blue eyes flashed before her own and she was lost once more. Her breath caught and she quickly glanced around the carriage to see if the gasp had been audible. Something about the Doctor's assistant had captivated her for the entire season and she had certainly attended, dressed as the footman, a few more times than was strictly proper. Still, she was now well versed in the properties of electricity, and the operation and discharge of the generating machine. Perhaps the kiss had been a bad idea – but she had needed to know. To know what that flash would feel like against her lips, to know what was the force that sent men reeling backwards without so much as a touch. The fusion of light and friction passing from one body into another through the air alone – it defied reason, and yet there it was, an undeniable, unknowable force she couldn't help but experience for herself.

She took a breath. The blue of Meg's eyes appeared once more and she felt breath on her skin, saw that enquiring eyebrow beckoning her forward. While they had not even physically touched, that spark sat in her chest, smouldering, emitting a glow of warmth whenever she breathed life into it with a memory. Kindling it made the guilt glow hot, but she enjoyed the delicious, dangerous flare that existed only for her. She knew she shouldn't have lit it, but she had, and she knew she would make that choice again.

She was, as her mother said, just too curious.

The fire blazed, her chest tightened, her head swam and suddenly there wasn't enough air. She pressed her fingernails into her palms as a distraction and fixed her gaze on the horizon, away from the blue of the butterfly and thoughts that threatened to overwhelm. She knew the signs that it would engulf her if she let it and so at the next coaching inn she took a horse to ride the last leg with her father. The day was bitingly cold, but it kept her from too much thought and her mother's judgement for the whole seven-hour journey.

After some time, familiar Sussex countryside presented itself and Thea felt the tension in her shoulders begin to ease. It was impossible not to be soothed by the rolling hills and dense woodland of the county she called home. As the light of the day dipped low they rounded the corner into the Milford estate and were greeted by the sight of the sun setting on the old house, its yellow stone crenelations and pinnacles glowing against the purple sky beyond, the tall, narrow windows lit by a homely, orange glow. Thea smiled. The house had been purchased by her father's mother after she made some lucky investments. Her grandmother had remodelled the house entirely to her own tastes, not in the modern style, but with personality and gothick quirks. Since then her father had invested in a large library space which had been finished over the winter – she couldn't wait to see it.

As they rounded the last bend and entered through the imposing gates the extensive household staff lined up by the door to meet them. There was Agnes and Mr Wade, but also Scip, her father's gardener and Mr Telford the estate gardener who had both stayed behind over the winter to keep house. Thea and her father greeted the party as they dismounted. She beamed at Scip whose dark face lit with his always-generous smile – it was difficult not to greet him as warmly as she would like, but she couldn't, in front of the household. 'How have you been, Scip?' she asked, instead.

'Very good Miss, thank you, pleased to see the family at home again. And you, Miss?'

'Quite well, thank you, delighted to be back in the country.' Mr Telford took the horses just as the carriage carrying the rest of the party drew up, crunching around the curve of the gravel driveway. Mr Croft the footman jumped down and opened the door while Scip climbed to retrieve Ursula's chair. As he helped her out of the carriage they chatted away happily.

'Thank goodness you're back, Miss Ursula, the winter flowering plants are beautiful this year and there are plenty of samples prepared for you to organise.' Thea smiled at the tenderness between Ursula and Scip and Ursula laughed as she landed in the chair.

'That's excellent news, my sister returns with plenty of artefacts to grace the indoor cabinet too.'

Scip nodded to her. 'A summer of curiosity for you then, Miss.'

'It seems so,' she murmured as she made her way into the house. Too curious. The spark still smouldered insistently, beginning to eat away at everything she knew she should be.

CHAPTER 2

T hea couldn't suppress a grin as Mr Wade and Mr Croft pulled the covers off the glass cases in the cabinet museum. Now that Mr Morell had built a grand library in the space adjacent, the natural history specimens could spread out to where all the books had been crammed in. Morning light lit the south-facing windows, illuminating artefacts and glinting off glass. Some shelves were crammed to bursting with items of the most eclectic nature, many now had plenty of space left over for – who knew what. She had stopped trying to guess what oddities might come off the boats next. She shivered at the potential of it. The assemblage at Milford was so familiar to her, and yet, objectively, very strange. Items of wonder her grandparents had collected for the look of the thing, a few more choice specimens added by her father before his attention had been diverted by plants and books, and then her own additions, limited as they were. She considered the shelves with fondness. Compact but beautiful. The mundane to the wonderful. Collected together in the relentless march towards enlightenment.

A knock on the door interrupted her thoughts and Thea joined her father and Ursula at the large table in the centre of the room. Mr Wade, the Butler, entered. 'Lady Foxmore for you Sir, Miss Thea and Miss Ursula. I brought her straight through, I hope that is acceptable.'

'Of course!' exclaimed Thea.

Martha Smilgrove, Countess of Foxmore entered the room, regally. She couldn't really help it, it was just the way she moved. The Countess was tall and slim with broad shoulders and exquisite posture. Light-chestnut hair was piled on her head underneath a small, grey hat, perfectly toned with her dress. Her deep brown eyes had a serious, severe look and her faintly rouged lips were pressed into a thin line. The perfect picture was only interrupted by a red gash under her left eye, a jarring interruption to her usually flawless, unpowdered skin.

'Mr Morell, Miss Morell, Miss Ursula.' She greeted them formally and nodded to them all in turn, before her face cracked into a broad smile as she bent to meet Thea's embrace. When Thea finally let her go she hugged Ursula tightly and kissed Mr Morell on the cheek.

'I hope you don't mind me calling so early, I was simply too eager to hear what you got up to in your final month in town.'

'Of course not, Martha, it's wonderful to see you,' replied Mr Morell genuinely. The Morells and the Smilgroves were old friends and when the Earl of Foxmore died more than ten years ago Martha had almost become part of the family. 'We were about to head out to the garden, would you care to join us?' They made to leave but as he stood and pushed in his chair, the Countess stepped back towards the table strewn with specimens. Her head tilted to read the handwriting on one of the sheets of paper bearing an arching branch with impeccably pressed, ovate green leaves. She tapped the sample twice with a graceful yet purposeful finger.

'This is butcher's broom, not willow. The petioles are entirely different, Ben.' Martha turned and made her way swiftly out of the room as Mr Morell stared after her, and then down at the sample, his mouth forming an 'o'. Thea and Ursula suppressed another giggle as they trooped after the formidable Countess and through the hall to the garden.

While Mr Morell pushed Ursula on ahead to find Mrs Morell, Thea and Martha took their time on the terrace. Martha sighed audibly and

Thea caught her gaze, noticing the angry-looking wound under her eye.

'What did you do?' she asked, 'it looks sore.' She stopped and raised a hand as if to touch it but Martha flinched away and grasped her hand softly but firmly.

'An *Agave* spike, I was careless while potting on, but also lucky.'

Thea's eyes widened. 'You certainly were, just an inch up and' – she didn't say it – 'here, let me look.' She turned Martha's face to the side with a tender hand and noted the deep puncture wound intruding under the skin. As she ran a gentle finger over it Martha's jaw tightened but she didn't move away. Thea knew she was the only person apart from the doctor that Martha could stand touching her, and she didn't trust Martha to put her own health before that of the plants. 'That could go nasty, have you had calendula on it?'

Martha raised an admonishing eyebrow but a smile gave away her affection. 'I do almost manage to function while you are away you know, Miss Morell,'

Thea was not cowed. 'I have no doubt of it, but I asked if you had put calendula on it.'

Martha's cheeks pinked a little. 'No,' she said, almost belligerently.

Thea tried to hide a smile. 'Wait there,' she said, popping back inside and emerging a few seconds later with a small tin. She deftly slid open the top, scooped out a little of the greenish salve with her middle finger and applied it lightly to the wound. To her credit, Martha did her best not to flinch although Thea could feel her tense. 'You will thank me when it's better, although it does look like it might scar.' She peered at the gash from another angle. 'Although perhaps it will make you look a little rakish.'

She smiled and a cheeky glint entered Martha's eye. 'Perhaps I shall become disreputable and a fresh cause of scandal in Sussex.'

Thea grinned. 'I think it would take more than an Agave to make you anything less than extraordinarily proper and ladylike, Lady Fox-more.' Even though Martha could get away with unconventional hobbies as a widow, Thea knew she would always take great pains to maintain her societal grace.

'As it should,' Martha agreed, tucking a stray wisp of hair behind Thea's ear. 'Anyway, how were the London acquisitions this year? I spied a few new delights in the cabinet, I think?'

Thea took Martha's arm and chatted away as they made for the stove. At least here she could talk about the collections to her heart's content, Martha had been a mentor for years. She had taught Thea almost all she knew about philosophers – about Francis Bacon and John Locke, and how science had the potential to change the world.

When he had found his twelve-year-old daughter poking around in his old cabinet, Mr Morell had engaged a natural history tutor for her immediately. William Fenwick was passionate about his subject and Thea found the subject far more interesting than the art, music and French lessons arranged by their mother. While he provided the knowledge, Martha had brought the subject alive. The scholars spent hours and days in the library, companionably quiet, gathering, identifying and classifying their various, and frequent, additions. As Thea wasn't permitted in the coffee houses of London, vendors often came to Hanover Square or sent items to Milford by post. Now reflecting her interests as well as those of her father, the cabinet was eclectic. The skin of an eel gazing down from the wall, the skulls of birds and dogs peering through the glass, crystals and geodes glittering next to dried fish.

Much to Mrs Morell's consternation Ursula had soon joined the natural history lessons and found it pleased her logical mind to identify, classify and label the items curated by her sister. She had the most astounding capacity for patterns and order and could lay her hands on any collection item at a moment's notice – unlike Thea. Between them they made quite a team and Mr Morell was delighted that at least some of his family shared his joy.

Martha had guessed about Thea's scholarly leanings even before her father caught on and when the Countess had learned how much study helped to calm Thea's anxious mind there had been no holding her back. She had spent time with Thea and quietly supported her, brushing aside Mrs Morell's admonishment about leading her daughter astray and as she got older, encouraging Thea in scholarship when the wrath of his wife meant Mr Morell dare go no further. Her father had given Thea the tools to succeed, but it had always been Martha who leant her study direction and purpose. Their mutual fascination had engendered a closeness that, despite the years between them, was second to no friendship in Thea's life.

The Asian rhinoceros beetle was the topic of conversation as Mrs Morell came bustling towards them.

'Martha how wonderful to see you! We did miss you terribly for the remainder of the season.' Mrs Morell hastened them towards the stove. While she had no time for the indoor collections she did take advantage of her husband's efforts outdoors – the perfect way to impress her friends. She particularly enjoyed having a Countess around the house, or at least being seen out with a Countess, although Martha was not one of the friends she could impress with cursory exotic plant facts. Lady Foxmore's botanical knowledge far exceeded that of anyone at Milford.

The stove house was an expanse of glass, positioned at an angle to a tall wall to form a sort of triangular shaped glasshouse. The wall at the back was heated by fires Mr Telford and Scip kept burning in the cold weather, even through the night, to protect the tender plants which originated from warmer climes. Mr Morell and Martha strode into the musty interior to find Scip tending to seedlings on the planting bed in the centre.

'Good Morning, Scip,' said Mr Morell, cheerfully, 'how have our charges fared over the winter?'

Scip smiled broadly. 'Very well sir, we have had very few losses.' Thea grinned at Scip and he returned it with a bright smile. She would catch up with him properly later – her mother disapproved of the time they spent together but they shared a closeness and she could talk to him like she could to few others. Scip had come to the family when they were both about eight years old and they had grown up in close proximity – geographically speaking, anyway. Mr Morell had originally 'acquired' him as a page for Mrs Morell – she had liked the idea of the exotic in her household, but she had soon got bored and he showed an aptitude for growing. Since then he had built up the plant collections, the productive garden and provided Thea with sensible company of her own age.

It was another thing she had been too curious about. Scipio, they had called him then, the name given to him by the trader with whom he'd started his life in England as a slave. When Thea had found out that Scipio was the name of a Roman general who had triumphed over Africans she was appalled. He couldn't remember his name from Africa and naturally dismissed the one they had given him on the plantations, so had chosen to be called Scip. When Mr Morell had professed that he wanted to free Scip and start paying him when he turned sixteen Mrs Morell had been horrified, but she came round after a number of weeks sulking.

After transforming the plant collections at Milford, Scip was now working on a plant experiment with Martha and Mr Morell and the three of them were quite a team. It hadn't always been that way – Martha had refused to speak to him at first, a fact Thea had found baffling, but as Scip had grown in confidence he had shared more of his knowledge. He understood the medicinal qualities of Jamaican and African plants, had the ability to propagate seeds and plants both Mr Morell and Martha had failed to do, and he had revolutionised Milford's vegetable garden by pairing different plants together. Martha had been unable to resist, and now they engaged with a gracious respect and fondness.

Martha joined them from where she had peeled off to interrogate a juvenile magnolia. 'Good to see you, Scip.'

'And you, Lady Foxmore. How goes the recording of the *Hedysarum*?'

'Slow over the winter of course, but I hope for improvement now the days are lighter. How are the *Mimosa*?' Thea smiled, the plants weren't her passion but she loved listening to discussions between Martha and her family. The experiment was about how, and why, plants moved – a topic that had been exercising Martha for years.

Scip gestured to a small group of plants in pots, small hummocks made up of delicate, pinnate leaves. 'Your sensitive plants are quite well, my lady, they have matured to the point of movement.' In order to prove it he ran a finger down the midrib of one of the tiny leaves. At the contact the two halves of the leaves folded inwards and the whole leaf dropped on its stalk. Scip smiled. 'And they do it at night, just as they're meant to.'

Martha leaned her tall frame to study one more closely while she gave it a stroke with a gentle finger. The leaves duly shrank away from her touch. 'Excellent.' She stood taller and Thea saw her eyes gleam. 'They will give up their secrets in the fullness of time, observation and effort.' She fixed Scip with a purposeful stare. 'You have your record book?'

'I do,' he confirmed, patting the pocket of his work coat, 'and we have enough plants to make a good study.' He cast a furtive glance to Mrs Morell, 'in fact, they did so well that I have pressed some for the herbarium collection. They are waiting in the library closet for Miss Ursula to label them appropriately in her very neat handwriting.' He flashed his bright grin at Ursula who smiled shyly.

Martha beamed at them both. 'I assume you will use the new Linnaean system?' Ursula opened her mouth to respond when Mrs Morell, idly twiddling the fronds of an asparagus fern, snapped her head around.

'Oh no you don't, missy, I've heard all about that from Mrs Denby at the Ladies' Club. Disgusting! All about the – lady and man parts of the plants. Trust a man to come up with *that*. You stay away from that, young lady, I'm not having your mind corrupted by dirty gardeners in the Netherlands.'

Martha took a breath to respond when, without missing a beat, Ursula did so herself. 'Of course mother, would you be happier if I used the binomial system instead?'

Mrs Morell looked pleased that, for once, her intervention had been so effective. 'Why yes I would Ursula, that sounds much more respectable.' Ursula nodded and Thea and Martha shared an amused glance. They both knew the binomial system was simply another name for Mr Linnaeus's new sexual system of classification which had recently set the botanical world alight. It was not without controversy, but still, there was no reason for Mrs Morell to know.

'That does not mean,' started Mrs Morell shrilly, making both Thea and her father jump a little, 'that I am happy with the girls engaging in this kind of inappropriate activity. They are getting too old to be frivolously flirting with such follies. They have always been too interested in learning and you' – she poked at Mr Morell with an accusatory finger – 'have done nothing to stop it.'

'I, um...' said Mr Morell, fiddling with a copper label he had picked from the bench.

'And you, Martha.' Mrs Morell now rounded on the Countess who looked up from studying her pocket watch. Her hastily raised gaze and the flicker of an eyebrow betrayed her surprise. 'How you encourage them, and you know they look up to you. Ladies should make a good wife and be able to run a household. Any other education is a distraction and gives them unnecessary... ideas.'

Martha flicked her pocket watch shut with a snap, pocketed it, and laid a soothing hand on Mrs Morell's arm. 'Oh come now my dear Euphemia, you of course know that it is good for a lady to exercise her mind.' She had plenty of experience of placating her friend and Thea marvelled at the art of it. 'It prevents her from becoming boring in company. Some ladies have no ideas at all and it is so irksome.'

'But these are not ideas that a lady can or should be admitting to in company.' Mrs Morell's voice became shrill as she gestured around the stove house. 'You cannot have failed to notice my eldest's lack of success, and at her age!' They all knew that Mrs Morell was talking about marriage, the delay in this much hoped-for event made Mrs Morell more desperate every year. 'No man wants an educated wife, learned women do too much thinking. And who will have her at all if she ever forgets herself and mentions spiders when she's out in society?'

Thea saw Martha press her tongue to her teeth to battle a grin. 'I do appreciate your concerns, Euphemia, but I am certain that Thea will not have any man who wants a dumb wife and neither should she. Any husband might as well know at the start, otherwise it's only going to be a shock when she turns up at his house with eel skins and butterflies. Women have a place in the new intellectual order and there is no shortage of people who appreciate Thea's virtues, you mark my words.'

Mrs Morell harumphed and muttered something about how nobody must ever know, but knew she would never triumph in this argument with Martha. Thea thanked the Countess with a grateful smile.

As the party took a further tour through the stove house and then into the walled garden beyond, Martha dropped back and motioned for Thea to join her. They walked together through the beds packed with fruit, vegetables and a wide variety of ornamentals until they were sure they were out of earshot.

'It's getting worse then?' asked Martha, keeping her voice in a low register.

'Definitely,' Thea nodded. 'You know she was desperate for an engagement this London season.'

'I do know that,' Martha said, 'she reminds me of it almost as often as she reminds you.'

'Father won't be able to hold her off much longer,' said Thea quietly, 'she is determined. I understand why, of course, and I know I have a responsibility.' It was something she was reminded of often. The entail on the estate, set by her grandmother, was that a daughter could inherit, but only if she married. While the husband would effectively take control of the Milford estate and fortune, he would be duty bound to take care of her and her sisters. If she didn't marry it would fall to Tabitha's husband, or to Ursula's. If none of them married, the estate was entailed to a nephew in the midlands, but goodness knows what would become of spinster sisters then – they had never even met him and heard that he drank.

She ran a hand round the back of her neck as a cold wash of anxiety trickled through her stomach. 'It's only at father's insistence that she hasn't chosen for me yet and even he has to admit that time is pressing on. Something has changed with mother recently – it feels more urgent. I could end up like Harriet before the end of the year.'

As they walked, Martha reached out and plucked Thea's hand from its tense position at the nape of her neck and squeezed it as she dropped it by Thea's side. She knew the signs of an impending attack as well as Thea did by now, and how to help stop it in its tracks. 'That was different. You are not in the same position as Harriet and you do have time,' she said gently, but with concern puckering her brow. 'I take it you haven't heard from her?' She looked at Thea out of the corner of her eye.

'No, I wish I had but I can't write to her as the honeymoon was so hastily arranged and nobody knows where on the continent they are. Anyway, she knows that if she writes mother will intercept her letters, so there's no point.'

'It would be unwise for you to be associated, your mother is correct on this,' said Martha, regarding her with a careful eye. 'And you know my feelings on the matter.'

'I know,' said Thea, staring at the floor. She was still trying to come to terms with Harriet's hasty marriage and departure, and the reasons for it. Harriet had been one of Thea's closest friends and had now been gone a full six months. She didn't know what she thought, in truth. She knew what Martha thought – she had been surprised at how intense and angry her reaction had been and there were rumours about her involvement. Thea hadn't dare ask. As Martha was still considering her carefully, she changed the subject.

'I know I can't hide in the collections forever. Before long mother will choose a suitor for me and you know what her criteria will be.' The words *wealth* and *status* hung unsaid between them as Martha gave one, acknowledging dip of the head.

'You don't think that she'd consider Tabitha..?'

Martha trailed off as Thea met her with a wry smile. 'Whatever she says aloud even mother knows better than to pin her hopes there. Now Tabitha is out it won't be long before she becomes attached – you know how she throws herself in the way of anyone eligible. The way her preference for the cards is going she could lose any fortune in a heartbeat. Maybe that's why mother is as she is?'

'Mmm,' was all Martha said as she retrieved her pocket watch and flipped it open with a thumb. They dipped through the gate leading to the meadow and their feet crunched on the gravel path between emerging wildflowers. Silence hung between them as they rounded the old oak and headed for the river. 'Edgar is looking forward to seeing you,' said Martha eventually, and Thea appreciated the deflection. 'He can't wait to show you his new ventures.'

'Anything of note?' asked Thea, allowing a smile to creep over her face as she thought of their mutual friend. Thea had known Edgar Pickles all her life as an associate of her father's and counted him as one of her dearest friends. For almost seventy years his dearest love had been collecting and experimenting and his exploits seemed to grow more outrageous with every passing year.

'Well that would be telling, wouldn't it,' said Martha, the corner of her mouth twitching as Thea glanced at her. 'I won't spoil his joy in telling you himself, but you should give him a few days – his gout is playing up again.'

Thea nodded her understanding, and the silence settled between them again.

'Thea, you know you can always talk to me, don't you, about anything.' Martha flicked an understanding glance sideways and a nervous chill washed through Thea once more.

She nodded. 'Of course, thank you.' But as the image of Meg's eyes appeared in front of her once more, she knew that was one thing she should never admit to Martha. Not after the things she had said about Harriet's indiscretion.

The following day Thea headed off into the nearby town of Thornbury and called for her old friend Jane Ashby on the way. Jane was the daughter of the local physician and lived only a quarter of a mile from Milford. Thea regaled her with the London gossip as they headed into town across the fields – the Jefferys' ball where Tabitha had been so all over Ralph Jefferys his mother had to intervene, Helena Crowe's wedding where nobody could see in church as the lady's hairdos were too tall, and the dinner at the assembly rooms where Tabitha's friend Georgie had knocked a whole plate of jelly over the floor. Unlike Thea, Jane loved a party and enjoyed experiencing the London season vicariously whenever the Morell family returned to Milford in the spring. The friends laughed easily together, they had been close since they were young despite Mrs Morell's reservations about her offspring socialising with the daughter of a tradesman. Jane pulled a note from her dress pocket.

'Before I forget – this is from father to yours, I think it's his bill.' Thea thanked her and pocketed it, then Jane's face suddenly became serious. 'Anyway, have you heard from her?'

Thea shook her head. 'I don't think we will, for a while.'

'Just as well,' said Jane, 'I shouldn't know what to do or say to her.'

'You could do and say as you always did, Jane,' said Thea softly. 'She's still Harry, and our oldest friend.'

'She's no friend of mine.' Jane's face was still grave. 'I thought we knew her as well as anyone. I wrack my brains to think how she could seem so good and then do something so contemptuous to God and his design. And to think you sometimes slept in the same bed – I do feel for you.' Thea knew there was little chance of bringing Jane round, but she somehow couldn't leave the topic – scared to hear things that made the pit of her stomach drop, while desperately wanting to voice the questions that had niggled at her for the preceding six months.

'Do you think, though, that it is so bad? Tabitha has her romantic friend in Kitty, as plenty of girls do before marriage. I don't see how this is so different.' When she looked up, as she feared, Jane was staring at her with eyes full of incredulity.

'You do know how they were caught, Thea?' Jane's voice was now a whisper, not that there was anyone on the path to hear them. 'Our Harry – the girl we grew up with, *in flagrante delicto* with Emma DeClere. I'd never been sure of Emma but I would never have thought it of Harry. She always seemed so – kind. And nice.'

'It is unusual,' Thea chanced, still not willing to let the subject drop. 'But maybe they were just, curious? It doesn't necessarily make her bad.' Until the thing with Harriet had come out, Thea hadn't even considered that such a thing might be possible. Now it intrigued her more than she dared admit.

'Curious is you and your lizards, Thea.' Jane's voice was now stern. 'Curious is poking about old buildings and reading about the Romans. It is not... well.' She gathered herself. 'Well – I can barely think of it. I keep attempting to convince myself that it must be some artificial corruption of the mind. Something that happened to her, or to Emma, or to both. You know she would be executed for it anywhere else in Europe?'

'I do know,' said Thea, her voice quiet. She knew what Harriet had done was wrong – everybody said such a violent affection for another lady wasn't natural – but she kept thinking of her, being torn from the capital at the start of the season, married to a man she had met but once in a secret ceremony and now bundled off for an extended honeymoon, away from the gossip and the sneers. At least that was a blessing. That Harriet hadn't had to hear the glee with which the tale was recounted all season, in parlours and assembly rooms alike. She couldn't help thinking of her friend – practically alone and confused in a new country. And she missed her. She, Harriet and Jane had been friends since they were small. As they had grown, the more outgoing Harriet had helped Thea to overcome her social anxieties and had been a great source of support at a myriad of social events and the relentless company they presented. This year had been much harder, without Harriet there. Thea had been saddened by the fact that her friend hadn't mentioned anything of her attachment to Emma, but she understood why. The consequences of the information being in the open were just too serious, as they were all finding now. 'I do know, Jane,' she said more firmly, 'but I should like to know of her state of mind nevertheless. The episode must have been extremely difficult to bear.'

'You have always been so kind, Thea,' said Jane, a smile finally curving her lips, 'and so keen to see the best in people. But let's not spoil our meeting with talking of that any longer. What about the Crowes' ball, wasn't that touted as the social event of the season?' She tucked a stray wisp of blonde hair behind her ear. 'I hear they had prawns and a cake three feet tall?' Jane indicated the height with her hands. By now Thea was pleased at a change of subject but sighed on the inside, she'd never understood the appeal of balls.

'Oh, I didn't go. There was a lecture I wanted to attend on combustion, so I had father say I was ill and give my apologies. He didn't tell mother until they were leaving in the carriage – I was already out by that time. She still hasn't forgiven me.'

Jane's eyes widened in genuine surprise. 'I bet she hasn't! You know that she has hopes of your match with George Crowe.'

Thea snorted as she walked and ran her hands through the grass growing at the side of the path. 'My mother needs less than that to despair of my hopes of matrimony, Jane, as you well know.'

Out of the corner of her eye Thea saw Jane shake her head. 'Even I need less than that to despair of your finding a husband, Thea, you will never secure a match while you insist on only hanging around men who like to explode things.'

Thea knew she always became petulant during this conversation, but couldn't help it. 'At least, there are men there.' It was a good job Jane was a patient friend.

'Not ones you should want to marry. Honestly, I fear I shall never begin to understand your taste in men!'

Thea sighed, conscious of that inconvenient spark still glowing within. 'To be honest, Jane, I would like to get a handle on it myself.' The tightness gripped her again. A gentleman who would finally claim her heart seemed a receding hope and she didn't dare give space to the thoughts that needled her as to why.

Jane shot her a sideways glance as they ducked beneath an elm which reached its branches across their path. 'And you must, Thea. In all seriousness, you know that George Crowe would be a very good match. He is an Earl already and the family's wealth is almost legend.'

Thea frowned, she understood George Crowe's wealth as well as his reputation. 'And you think he wants to settle down?'

'I'm sure the family would like him to.'

'That is not the same. The family have wished it for years, but he seems determined to try out most of the ladies in the capital first! When he runs out of society ladies there are always the ones in Covent Garden, as you well know. Oh, Jane, I know I should have gone to the ball, but there is more to life than spending your life twizzing about a room hoping that when you stop you will somehow land on the man of your dreams. And I have nothing to talk about, I can't tell them about the collections and everything else just seems so mundane.'

Jane shrugged. 'You don't have to say anything, you are one of the most eligible ladies in the county and probably the ones surrounding. Let your family's name do the talking for you if you must.'

Thea took her friend's arm. 'Perhaps I just need some of your gregariousness to rub off on me. Teach me, Jane, how should I converse with a man in order that we fall madly in love?'

Jane scowled at her but took the opportunity. 'Well, young men generally like to talk about themselves, so ask them about their shooting or fishing, or about their trips round Europe, they've all been there.'

Thea's eyes involuntarily reached for the heavens. 'Honestly, if I have to hear one more account of the Colosseum I shall scream. I feel like I have been there myself.'

Jane knew that Thea would keep deflecting. 'Be serious, Thea. You aren't getting any younger and marrying for anything other than connection is a luxury for a lady of your status, as you very well know.'

'Perhaps I should lower my standards to tolerance then?'

'It would serve you well to do so. If George Crowe and his roguish ways aren't for you, what about the Harringtons? I hear the family are back from diplomatic service on the continent and apparently young Viscount Stockwood has grown very handsome since they were last at Stanbourne, it must be fifteen years now.' She poked Thea in the arm playfully. 'Do you think you could tolerate him? Louisa has been snooping around and says they've been extending the house for over a year – apparently it is huge and quite modern.'

'Oh don't speak of it Jane, my mother is beside herself. She almost has me married off to Samuel Harrington already but I am sure he would rather have someone like Christiana Jefferys, or you.'

'Don't be a prune, Thea, Christiana Jefferys always looks like she's sucking a lemon, just like her mother, and I am the daughter of a physician! No, I am afraid that it is settled – you must do your duty to Thornbury and marry him before he is spirited away by the ladies of London and the family quit Stanbourne altogether.'

'The town would benefit from a family of their status settling for longer, it is true.'

'I just hope young Viscount Stockwood is as well-meaning as his accounts suggest.' She looked at Thea cheekily. 'For your sake, otherwise your life together *will* be miserable!'

CHAPTER 3

'Blue or orange?' asked Mrs Phibbs, hovering one hat and then another over Thea's head in the hallway.

'Which do you think?' asked Thea.

'Well, the blue will complement the jacket but the orange would pick out the detail on the stomacher and bring out your eyes.' Thea shot the housekeeper's reflection a stricken look in the glass. 'Orange it is,' Mrs Phibbs muttered, discarding the blue and beginning to secure the hat with long pins.

The invitation to the Swanham's had finally arrived and the Morell household had been aflutter for two days. Mrs Morell and Tabitha had spent almost forty-eight hours beside themselves wondering what to wear, how they should arrive, how grand the house at Stanbourne would be, how many staircases it would have and how many it could hold for a party.

A strong smell of cloves heralded the arrival of Tabitha. Like many young ladies she burned the ends and used them to enhance her eyebrows. Today, with the prospect of rich, young gentlemen in attendance the strong, medicinal hit of it almost made Thea's eyes water. Tabitha's face was white with powder, her cheeks and lips a striking vermillion, and two thick, dark clove-scented plumes cloaked her light green eyes. She usually wore a velvet face spot on her cheek but today it was tucked suggestively under her lip.

'Tab, you really should wear less of the powder, it's not good for your skin, and mother will never approve of that patch,' said Thea, noting also that her silken scarf was a little too open at the neck. 'At least move it up a bit so it doesn't suggest you are quite so available.'

Mother suggested it, so that's told you!' declared Tabitha, smugly. 'She said I might as well make my intentions obvious. Perhaps you should try it sometime, at least then people would know if you were trying to flirt.' Thea sighed and Mrs Phibbs, now making some last-minute hair adjustments, tried not to catch her eye in the glass. Thea was sure she saw a twitch in her cheek.

Tabitha skittered around, talking incessantly. 'Goodness I wonder what they will be like, will they be kind do you think? And interesting, I hate boring company. Lady Eleanor is about your age isn't she, Thea? I do hope she will be diverting as the best way to a brother is through a sister and I should hate to be bored. And of course *Viscount Stockwood*! I wish he would bring his friends to stay with him for the summer, what fun we shall have.'

Thea interrupted just to stop the talking for a short time. 'What about Ralph Jefferys, I thought you were soft on him?'

'Oh I was, well I am I suppose, but Lord Stockwood has at least twenty times his fortune, and he does gamble excessively.'

Thea looked up, surprised. 'Who? Lord Stockwood? He's only just arrived.'

'No, silly, Ralph Jefferys – he's never away from the card table.'

'Well neither are you.'

Tabitha held her arms out. 'And imagine that. His tiny fortune would be snuffed out like a candle in a thunderstorm!'

This time Thea caught Mrs Phibbs' eye with a smile and was happy to see Ursula emerge into the hallway, assisted by Agnes. As she opened her mouth to greet her sister, Tabitha was ahead of her. 'Oh she's not coming is she? It's not fair, we can never walk far when she comes.'

Thea furrowed her brow. 'Of course Ursula must come, and anyway, you hate walking.'

'Yes, well, I should like to have the option if I chose, and gentlemen always walk or ride out after tea.'

'We could always leave you here? Ursula and I will go and suss out Samuel Harrington – I am sure the wait will only heighten his anticipation of meeting you.'

Tabitha's face yanked up and her green eyes shone. 'Oh, do you think so?!'

Thea rolled her eyes at her youngest sister. 'No, I don't. Now please help Ursula to the carriage. I will ride alongside with father so you have room and won't crumple your best dress.'

Mrs Morell chose this time to arrive, froze stock still in the hallway and dragged her eyes from Thea's feet to her hat with alarm. 'You're not wearing that?' Thea had thought she'd chosen rather well.

'I thought I would ride alongside father.'

'A riding habit? Today? Thea, I despair – how will I ever marry you off if you always turn up to places looking frumpy and smelling of horses?'

'Mother, I shouldn't like to marry any man who objects to me smelling of horse.'

Mrs Morell threw her hands up in despair. 'There's no time to change now, you'll have to go as you are. Remember you are not to mention anything about the ridiculous ways you spend your time with all those bugs and dead things. All he needs to know is that you can manage a household, just like me.' Thea did remember, she was reminded of it before every social event they attended and her mother had pinned her in the corridor for ten minutes yesterday evening to ensure she hadn't forgotten in the past week. She did admire her mothers' ability to run the household and most of the estate – she had a shrewd business head, unlike her father, but hoped for something a little different to do with her life. She and Ursula shared a conciliatory glance as Ursula was wheeled to the carriage and Thea headed for the mounting block where her horse, Frederick, awaited.

Although she would never have admitted it, Thea did wish she had dressed differently as she wandered after the glamourous party in the long gallery at Stanbourne. She had begun to doubt herself as she rode down the long, lime-lined driveway and glimpsed a view of the house. Jane wasn't wrong when she said it had been extended. The length of the buff-stone structure imposed itself on the landscape, low at either end, rising steadily to peak in the middle, three tall storeys capped by a broad triangular pediment supported by six imposing columns. A grand staircase curved around both sides of the entrance, leading to a doorway higher than two men. Lawns and formal hedges stretched away from the frontage, down to a rectangular canal where two small boats bobbed in a gentle breeze.

The feeling had intensified as the sight of the family, lined up to welcome the party, came into view. John and Sybil Harrington, the Earl and Countess of Swanham, their son Samuel and their daughter Eleanor were all extremely handsome. Lord Swanham was tall and genteel with a short white wig. His wife was equally blessed with height and a graceful air. Her strawberry blonde hair had been passed to her children, both of whom had inherited the noble stature and pale complexion of their parents. Thea's eyes had been drawn immediately to the striking Samuel, an imposing and athletic figure in a light three-piece suit, who wore a broad and open smile in welcome. His sister was no less impressive – the picture of a lady of the nobility, an elegant cream dress topped with a ribbon in her light-copper coloured hair.

Now Thea watched Lady Eleanor and her mother navigate the ladies of the party through the gallery with ease, pointing out the family ancestors who lined the walls, how the wallpaper had been chosen and the pieces of furniture which had been shipped from the continent following the troubles with France and their subsequent return to Stanbourne. Lady Eleanor was more shy than her mother or brother, but elegant almost to a fault and spoke eloquently whenever called upon. Thea began to feel more out of her depth with every item they interrogated. She had little confidence around people she didn't know well and she couldn't dream of discussing her greatest passion in company, of course. She gazed longingly at Martha, her father and Mr Jefferys who were listening to Lord Swanham and Samuel talk about the origins of a turtle shell which was mounted on the wall between portraits. At least she could have listened.

She started when she heard her mother hiss her name, and turned her attention back to the group.

'And here is one of Eleanor's paintings,' Lady Swanham was saying from beside a portrait of a grumpy looking soldier with fine dress but no smile. 'She does have quite a talent.' The ladies nodded, making appreciative noises, and Thea muffled a squeak as Mrs Morell poked her in the ribs from behind.

'A truly excellent painting, Lady Eleanor,' she began without thinking, but then looked more closely at the board with its subtle layers of oils blending to create shape and form. She raised her eyes to Lady Eleanor's which were looking at her with something bordering trepidation. 'You have quite the talent for observation, and the way you have captured the light on the breastplate is exquisite.'

Lady Eleanor's features broke into a relieved smile. 'I thank you I am sure, Miss Morell, but I cannot claim the skill for my own. The work is a copy of a Delray from France.'

Thea was about to argue that replicating a work in such detail required quite enough talent, but Mrs Jefferys was ahead of her. 'Quite right too. Landscapes and copies are quite enough to form a lady's painting expertise without overstretching the mind. Not too taxing. Requires little creative thought.' Her lips settled back into the tight position they usually held.

'That is as Eleanor's tutor has suggested,' said Lady Swanham, with perhaps the tiniest purse of the lips, Thea thought, 'but we had to leave him on the continent of course and I hope to engage another for her while we are resident at Stanbourne. He did say, as Miss Morell observed, that Eleanor has a talent for capturing the light in a room.'

'I am impressed that you have such a discerning eye, Miss Morell.' It was Mrs Jefferys again, and there was something about her tone that Thea didn't care for. 'I don't believe you paint yourself, do you?'

'I do not, no.' Thea dared to fix Mrs Jefferys with what she hoped was a soft enough stare. Her lack of talent for coordinating her eyes and her hands on the page had always irked her, and Mrs Morell joked about it with Mrs Jefferys regularly. Thea had never liked the upright older lady who rarely cracked a smile unless at someone else's expense. The Jefferys family had made its fortune in India two generations ago and Mrs Jefferys met every interaction as if daring her company to mention it. The word 'nabobs' was still mentioned from time to time, but Mr Jefferys' father had bought a seat in Parliament and out of politeness nobody asked what skullduggery it was intended to contain. Mrs Jefferys was keen to have her children married well now that the social stench of their business had mellowed after two generations, and it was no secret that she had her eye on the Morell sisters. Certainly links with the Swanhams wouldn't do them any harm either.

Thea went on. 'But I do enjoy looking at art, and I can certainly tell that Lady Eleanor is more skilled than I with her hands.' She was pleased that she managed to keep the dislike from her voice.

'Why don't you tell us a little about your diversions, Miss Morell?' asked Mrs Jefferys as they moved further down the long gallery. 'We have been neighbours for so long and I know precious little about you.' Thea was sure she saw a gleam in the dark eyes.

'I, er...' Thea faltered and glanced at Mrs Morell who was trying to keep the alarm from her face.

'Well?' asked Mrs Jefferys, in a sugary sweet tone. 'Do you not know what it is you like to do?'

'She likes dead things,' piped up Tabitha from the side. 'Spends a lot of time in the library with father, too.' Thea looked round in panic, a fleeting alarm crossed Lady Swanham's features, schooled quickly into interest by her exquisite breeding, but surprise turned to distaste on Mrs Jefferys' face. Even Mrs Morell shot a warning look at her middle daughter.

The silence went on for so long that Thea was the first to respond. 'Thank you, Tabitha, I do help father with the collections occasionally when he requests it, but only in terms of recording and labelling. I also like pressing plants with my sister.' She indicated Ursula and they both cringed at the mundanity of it. 'And embroidery,' she added. That seemed like an acceptable pastime.

'And you do all these in the huge new library your father has built?' asked Mrs Jefferys sweetly.

'Of course not,' Thea forced a chuckle. 'Mostly in the library, I read books.' This didn't seem to reassure the party. 'Poetry' she clarified. Lady Swanham visibly relaxed.

'Is that so?' asked Mrs Jefferys, not letting the subject drop as the party filed out of the gallery and into the drawing room where tea awaited. 'And what have you enjoyed recently?' When Thea was silent, she went on. 'Have you read any Gray, for example, Miss Morell?'

'Um, no,' said Thea, wondering why she had been reckless enough to choose poetry.

'Or Pope then, perhaps?' By now the party was circled in the drawing room and all eyes were on Thea.

'No, no Pope, either,' she muttered, a cold sweat breaking out on her back and her chest beginning to tighten.

'Then what have–' began Mrs Jefferys, but she was truncated by Lady Eleanor, who cut in over her.

'I feel like Montagu is probably more Miss Morell's style,' she said, her eyes fixed to Thea's. 'Hymn to the Moon is one of my favourites. Anyway, how do you take your tea, Mrs Jefferys?' She finally took her eyes from Thea's to direct Mrs Jefferys and Mrs Morell to where the butler and the footman waited with tea and a tray of macaroons, candied almonds, nutmeg and marshmallow.

'Oh I absolutely shouldn't!' exclaimed Mrs Morell, before taking one of each sweet treat from the outstretched plate and piling them up in her palm. Thea stared at them, tension uncoiling through her spine making her head light.

'Lord Swanham is in sugar,' came Martha's whisper from behind and Thea turned in to her. Martha took one look at her, took a firm hold of her arm and navigated them both towards the open window. 'A few slow breaths,' she said, smoothing Thea's habit down her arm, her brow puckered in concern.

'Thank you.' Thea gave her a weak smile. 'Just Mrs Jefferys.' Martha nodded her understanding.

Thea made a mental note to thank Lady Eleanor later and stayed close to Martha as her heartbeat settled. 'Sugar,' she said, gazing around the room as her sensibility returned. 'You can tell.' She furrowed her brow a little at the ostentation. Terracotta-coloured drapes flanked the windows from where light flooded in from the park and the walls sported bright yet tasteful Chinese wallpaper filled with twining vines, flying birds and butterflies. The furniture was grand and plush, the fabrics sumptuous and the wood gleaming and exotic. More portraits of Harringtons past gazed benevolently down from the walls, approving the elegant family who chatted easily to their guests. Lord Swanham was still deep in conversation with Mr Morell and Samuel was joking with Ralph Jefferys while Tabitha hung on their every word and giggled in a girlish sort of way at seemingly anything they said. Ursula was chatting away to Christiana Jefferys, sharing stories of the London season so when Lady Swanham came to engage Martha, Thea directed her attention out of the window for a little respite.

Work was ongoing on what was presumably to be a flower garden near the house and the park beyond stretched as far as the eye could see. Before too long she was joined by Lady Eleanor, who still looked a little uncomfortable in the company but positioned herself by Thea admiring the view.

With no conversation forthcoming and the silence between them growing louder, Thea thought she should open. 'Thank you for your insight on the poetry. Earlier.' She forced herself to look at her companion. 'It was appreciated.'

Lady Eleanor smiled shyly. She had a kind face and impeccable skin, Thea noticed. 'You are very welcome, I hate poetry too but my English tutor forced it upon me for a morning every week.' She flashed a smile full of perfect teeth. 'I am very glad that is over but I do enjoy some time in father's library – he has an interesting collection of books.'

Thea allowed herself to be charmed despite how frumpy she felt next to such elegance and accomplishment. 'The alterations to Stanbourne are impressive, Lady Eleanor, but I hope that you won't be too bored by country society after the excesses of London and the continent?'

'I am exceedingly happy to be here, Miss Morell, London and Europe were both terribly diverting, but I have always craved the more genial and quiet society of the countryside.' Lady Eleanor stared out at the hills rolling into the distance, a faint smile threatening to break through.

Thea was a little surprised. 'You prefer the country?'

'I do find being out in nature a solace, and to be honest I have never quite taken to the society of London or Paris in the way that others do. I had a friend who always said that living in the country is little better than being buried alive, but I could not agree. You will probably think me very dull.' Her gaze slipped to her fingers and she looked so lost that it was all Thea could do not to reach out and touch her. At least it slackened the awkward tension she usually felt in forced small talk and she relaxed a little.

'Indeed, I do not, Lady Eleanor, the society is something I have always struggled to get along with myself. I enjoy London for a time, but the whole year would exhaust me. There are only so many dances to be danced and so much tea to be taken before it becomes a tedious bore, don't you think?' Even as she concluded the sentence her gaze dropped to her teacup and a small, internal panic tightened her chest. It rose to flush her face and she put up an involuntary hand to her cheek. 'Ah – not that I don't enjoy tea immensely, only it is different in the country.' Her eyes warily searched Lady Eleanor's face for fear of offence, but her words were received with a genuinely joyful laugh. Lady Eleanor turned into the room where the ladies gossiped over their teacups and Tabitha leant on the arm of Ralph Jefferys while she whispered something into his ear.

'I dearly hope you are right, Miss Morell,' she dropped her voice to a low whisper and inclined towards Thea's ear, 'but you have yet to convince me.'

The mischievous tone made Thea grin and breathe easy once more. 'Please, do call me Thea.'

'And you must call me Ella.' Her face broke into a broad smile which shone in her eyes. Thea noticed how unusual they were, one was brilliant blue, the colour of lapis and the other a vibrant jade green flecked with strokes of chestnut.

A pleasant warmth began to seep through her before a commotion in the room brought her back to herself. Tabitha had nearly upset a plant from its stand by trying to lean on it coquettishly. 'Oh lord, I am sorry,' Thea started, she was used to offering deflection from her boisterous sister. She nodded to the piano in the corner. 'Do you play, Ella?'

'Very poorly I am afraid, a particular lament of my brother who loves music in the house. Would you give us a tune?'

Thea hummed avoidance. 'I am afraid that if you are poor, I would almost certainly be worse, but my sister Ursula is very good. Shall we ask her?' Ella agreed enthusiastically and before long Ursula was entertaining them with a lively jig. Samuel Harrington looked delighted and not a little relieved to remove himself from the company of the middle Morell sister, with her face spot set to flirt.

Everyone enjoyed the playing so much that on its conclusion Samuel Harrington announced that Ursula must choose the next mode of entertainment, and so they all prepared for a walk around the grounds of Stanbourne. Thea found herself with both Ella and Samuel and soon decided they were both extremely agreeable. Viscount Stockwood was amiable and generous. Ella relaxed in his company and they teased each other good naturedly about their various hopes and worries about the return to Stanbourne.

'My brother is exceedingly concerned that he will have no occasion to wear his fine Italian outfits he bought during his tour. It is possible, Thea, that he would eclipse the whole of Stanbourne with the feather on one of his particular favourite hats.'

Lord Stockwood laughed freely. 'I must heartily object. Miss Morell, please do not let my sister taint your opinion of me so soon.'

Ella furrowed her brow at him. She was certainly more comfortable outside of the social formalities. 'Do you deny there is a ridiculously large hat in your wardrobe?'

He graciously assented to the accusation. 'I am afraid I cannot, but, Miss Morell, you must not entertain the allegations of my sister who presents me as a macaroni! Step forward the man who has never made a foolish fashion choice on the continent, I say.'

Thea laughed heartily, quickly relaxing in the company of the affable siblings. 'Many of us manage to make them with some regularity, Lord Stockwood, even without the influence of a trip to Italy. I shall not judge you for a large hat so early in our acquaintance if you won't judge me for choosing a riding habit today.'

'I think you look wonderful,' said Ella, genuinely, 'I have been thinking that the orange really brings out your eyes, Miss Morell.'

Before Thea could respond, with she didn't know what, Martha appeared beside the group as they passed into a grand, tree-lined avenue which cast dappled shade onto the gravel underfoot. Lord Stockwood welcomed her confidently. 'Have you visited Stanbourne before, Lady Foxmore?'

'Yes indeed, but not for a number of years. The grounds were much more formal then, your family has done a lot of work.'

He inclined his head in agreement. 'All over the past year in anticipation of our return. Father wanted the major groundworks to be complete by the time we moved in. I understand that we could do worse than engaging your expertise in the plantings, my lady?'

Martha smiled at the flattery. 'I shall be interested to watch its progress, but I cannot claim a particular expertise, I am afraid.'

To Thea's horror a snort escaped her. She tried and failed to cover it with a cough. Her three companions turned to her as she coloured and she felt compelled to support Martha's position. 'You must not listen, Lord Stockwood. Lady Foxmore is quite the most proficient plantswoman in the county.'

Lord Stockwood looked impressed. 'Is that so? Well, I should be delighted to be the beneficiary of her expertise.'

'It would be a pleasure, Lord Stockwood,' said Martha, 'however, I must now beg some time with Lady Eleanor, I had hoped to hear her account of the gardens of Italy.' Martha took Ella and Ursula away and internally Thea's eyes hit the heavens. It wouldn't be the first or last time her mother engineered an opportunity to leave her alone with a young gentleman but today's intervention was particularly rapid.

She cast around for a suitable topic of conversation and her mind slid gloomily back to Jane's advice. 'I would be interested to hear about your travels on the continent, Lord Stockwood.'

His sideways look was accompanied by a knowing smile. 'I doubt that very much.'

Her head spun to him. 'I'm not sure I follow.'

'It is my opinion that gentlemen are never more dull than in the recollections of their tour adventures. I have observed many a lady attempting politely and desperately to remain engaged while secretly wishing for release.'

Perhaps he was different, Thea decided, and chuckled. 'I cannot disagree, although from extensive experience I believe the issue to be in the exhaustive telling of the tale. Small snippets are quite agreeable. Tell me of the most interesting place you visited.' The resulting tale of the ruined Villa D'Este, once the most grand villa and garden in Italy and now its majestic fountains silenced and extravagant statues sold, was not what Thea was expecting.

'It was one of the most melancholic places I visited, but also made me reflect on our own situation. What we have here, however luxurious and admired it is by others, is but ornament, and a fleeting moment in time. I should dearly like my life to have some greater consequence. A legacy, however small, which exists not only in the furnishing of an estate and the parties I hold.' He looked around at Thea and seemed to remember himself. 'But I have only just met you and I expect you think me utterly mad.'

Thea allowed herself a small smile, it was the same question she often grappled with herself. 'Not in the slightest, it makes you far more interesting than I had dared to hope. Kindness and charity are always remembered.'

He nodded slowly and looked carefully at her, as if confirming something in his mind. 'Indeed they are, Miss Morell, and here I have a request of you, if I may?'

'Of course.'

'I wonder, if you feel it appropriate and if your characters allow, if you would consider making a friend of my sister while we reside in Stanbourne? She is truly a good soul, but I have observed her becoming increasingly withdrawn since our aunt passed two years ago. The two of them were particularly close. I worry that the quiet here in the country may not be good for her or for' – he hesitated – 'the state of her mind. I am sure a friend and an occasional change of scenery would help enormously, if it would also be agreeable to you.' He looked at her hopefully, eyes full of concern for his sister and Thea felt her heart soften towards him.

'I would be very happy to oblige, Lord Stockwood, I like her extremely well and I am sure we shall find lots in common. You must care for her very much.'

'That I do, we have always been close as a family and she is of course my closest friend. Do you find the same with your sisters?'

Thea smiled, sure that this perceptive man had already drawn conclusions of his own. 'I do with my youngest, Ursula. She has a brilliant mind and a quick wit.' They both looked over at Ursula, pushed along by Mr Croft and now laughing with Ella and Martha.

'Has she always used the chair, if you don't think it an impertinent question?'

'Not at all. She hasn't always, she had a riding accident when she was young and lost the use of both legs. But her brain is brighter than any of the rest of us, she is an extremely accomplished painter and she is an excellent pianist as you have heard.'

'It must be very difficult for her.'

Thea contemplated the party ahead. 'I often think it must, but she bears it very well. My father is insistent that the whole family engage in all activities and she outdoes us all in company.'

This made Lord Stockwood chuckle as he ducked under a low bough. 'I take it that you are not quite so close with your middle sister?'

Thea chose her words carefully. 'Tabitha and I have a great affection for one another of course, but she and my mother have always understood each other better than I can understand either. She enjoys ribbons and hats and boys, which is of course quite understandable for a young lady. It is I who am the curiosity.'

He looked down at the gravel crunching under his feet. 'A curiosity I am sure myself and my sister will enjoy becoming better acquainted with.' His shy smile returned and Thea felt that she had to agree. There was something genuine and insightful about Lord Stockwood that calmed her.

Her deliberations were cut short by Tabitha who barrelled in between the two of them. 'Is this not an agreeable way to spend an afternoon, Lord Stockwood – won't you take us to that little grotto I can see delightfully nestled by the lake?'

As the party set off down the hill, winding through the trees, Thea found herself once again in the company of Ella Harrington. 'How are you enjoying the walk, Lady Eleanor' – she caught herself – 'I mean, Ella?'

Ella smiled broadly. 'Exceedingly well – your sister Ursula is quite charming. And how did you find the company of my brother?'

'Most highly agreeable,' Thea confirmed, 'certainly more so than many young men.'

Ella sighed. 'He is the best I have ever met. My mother laments the fact that I have not yet found a man to marry, I am afraid I blame his goodness for spoiling me.'

For some, unfathomable reason Thea found herself relieved that Ella didn't have a suitor. 'My mother has the same concern, but I sadly do not have your excuse. I am afraid I disappoint her a little.'

'Even if that is so, you certainly do not disappoint Lady Foxmore, Thea.' Ella was sincere. 'She was full of praise for you and I now feel quite intimidated by your cleverness.' They had fallen behind the group a little and watched Ursula and Martha in deep discussion as they moved towards the grotto.

'Lady Foxmore is too kind,' said Thea, her heart full of fondness for Martha and her unwavering support, whilst hoping that she hadn't said anything incriminating about the collections. 'She is quite the cleverest woman I know and has taught me as much about the world as anyone.'

They watched as the footman struggled with Ursula's chair at the entrance to the grotto. Martha shot him a look of dissatisfaction, took charge of the chair and pushed it smartly over the threshold. Ella's brow creased. 'I am perhaps a little intimidated by her also.' Thea only laughed, took Ella's arm and guided her after the rest of the party.

CHAPTER 4

'What's wrong?' asked Martha, as they rode the lane to Thornbury side-by-side, Frederick's hooves tapping out a reassuring, hollow rhythm on the grass.

'What makes you think anything is wrong?' asked Thea, shifting in her side saddle but not looking at Martha who ignored the question.

'Was it Mrs Jefferys?' Martha stared, and Thea looked away. 'I heard a little of the conversation. She's never been noted for her social skills.'

'No,' said Thea.

Out of the corner of her eye she could see Martha looking at her, concerned. 'Don't let her bother you,' she said gently. 'You know she's always been resentful of anyone with better prospects.'

'I thought mother might explode,' said Thea, finally looking at Martha again. 'Mrs Jefferys might as well have stood me in the cabinet with a microscope. And Tabitha made it worse. Goodness knows what the Swanhams must think now.'

'I wouldn't worry about Lady Swanham,' said Martha, thoughtfully. 'She seemed sensible, I thought, and the children too.'

'I did enjoy Lady Eleanor's company,' said Thea. 'She seemed so proper and perfect at first, but when she relaxed she was extremely personable.'

'Yes,' said Martha, 'and Viscount Stockwood. What did you think to him?'

'Don't you start,' smiled Thea, flicking Martha on the leg with her whip. 'And don't think I didn't notice your well-timed extraction.' She put on an affected accent, mimicking Martha's low tones. 'Oh, Lady Eleanor, please won't you tell me of your visits to Italy.'

The two of them finally laughed together. 'I do have to acquiesce to your mother a little and occasionally, after I've led her daughter astray into the scurrilous world of science.' The light that their banter lit in Thea faded quickly.

'I know I shouldn't,' she said, looking back over the landscape, 'but I do get tired of it sometimes. Never being able to share any of it in public. Do you never find it exhausting, being different?'

'I'm old and widowed, I can get away with it.' Martha's mischievous smile dragged a mirroring one from Thea's lips.

'Stop it, you are not yet in your fifth decade and one of the youngest spirits I know. Once you get past all the haughtiness.'

'I count on it,' grinned Martha. 'One can get away with most things with a commanding enough presence.' Her smile turned tender. 'But I do understand how you feel. It can be difficult, and especially at your age when there is so much at stake.'

'I just feel like I'm always on the back foot.' Frederick's hooves continued their beat towards home. 'Like I've thrown a shoe before the race has even begun, then I have to work extra hard to catch up. It's only you, father, Ursula, Jane and Edgar I can be myself with. Sometimes I wish I could just be normal.'

'Do you?' asked Martha, gently.

'It would be easier.'

'That's not the same.'

'No, it isn't.' She knew that, but it didn't always help. Thea reined Frederick round a blackthorn branch fallen on the path. 'Did you mean what you said to mother about any man being aware before he agreed to marry me?'

'I did,' said Martha, 'perhaps not right at the beginning, but I saw how the collections helped you in your mind before. I would be concerned for you without them, and you have a talent for it that would be a shame to waste. The right, forward-thinking man wouldn't stand in your way.'

'Then I better pick one before my mother chooses a backwards Tory.'

'Probably,' said Martha, utterly serious. 'I joked about it, but Viscount Stockwood did seem affable to me.'

'He did,' said Thea, 'very much so. And kind, and like he would apply a sensible head. I am not sure he quite appreciates the ostentation of their new residence.'

'I did get the impression that he may not be as keen on the sugar trade as his father seems to be,' noted Martha. 'It's a nasty business.'

'I am glad father never invested,' said Thea. 'He's too busy with his plants and his new library. Even with his current collection of books he'll have to invest more to fill it.'

'Mmm,' said Martha, and flicked open her pocket watch. 'It'll be dark soon, we should get on.'

Thea eyed her curiously. 'Why are you being evasive? You couldn't stop talking about it when he built the new glasshouses.'

Martha glanced sideways at her, took a breath to speak and then let it out. She stared between her horse's ears. 'I should know I can conceal nothing from you. Your father does need to be careful, Thea.'

Thea stared at her as their horses moved in rhythm. 'What do you mean?'

Martha couldn't stop her eyes meeting Thea's. 'I just mean that the extensions he's made were pricey, and with him not inclined to invest further in business overseas your grandmother's money won't last forever.'

A chill settled in Thea's stomach. 'Tell me honestly, is he in trouble?'

'Not that I'm aware,' said Martha, reassuringly, 'but there was a little talk in the town of some bills left unpaid.'

'Jane gave me an account for him from Dr Ashby yesterday,' said Thea. 'It was for last year – I just assumed he had forgotten to pay it.'

'Perhaps,' said Martha. A thought suddenly struck Thea and sent unpleasant chills to her feet.

'That's why mother is so worried.' She turned to look at Martha. 'Is that why you are keen Lord Stockwood and I should get to know one another?'

'It wouldn't hurt to keep your options open,' said Martha quietly, and Thea saw her swallow. 'He's a sensible and wealthy man and for now society is under the impression that you are one of the wealthiest families in the country. The Morell name carries centuries of prestige.'

Thea nodded her understanding while the cold set into her veins and they rode in silence until the road split and Martha made for Denbury.

After dinner that night, the talk was of nothing but Stanbourne and its returned inhabitants. The family's grace and grandeur, the furnishings, the money spent on the gardens. Mrs Morell and Tabitha were beside themselves. 'It is indeed a grand setup and I shall be hoping for you girls to spend more time there this summer. If your father had placed his efforts in the West Indian plantations instead of gardens and books the whole setup could have been our own! Lady Swanham was telling me they own above a dozen properties out there. But if you play your cards right, Thea, Stanbourne may still play a part in the future of the Morell family.' Thea met her father's eyes across the table and he quickly looked away. Was it her imagination, or did he look a little sheepish?

'Of course, the Swanhams aren't quite as rich or established as the Crowes and George Crowe will eventually become Duke and presumably have a place at court like his father, so we must consider our options carefully. But yes' – Mrs Morell steepled her fingers in front of her – 'Samuel Harrington would certainly do.'

'He would do for me,' sulked Tabitha, 'if Thea hadn't kept him to herself the whole time.' She threw the embroidery away from her onto the floor of the parlour. 'Why are we having to do this anyway?'

'Because your sister told the Swanhams that she enjoys embroidery,' said Mrs Morell, her sweet tone not reflected in the accusatory gaze she levelled at her eldest daughter, 'and what will they think if they visit and there is none here to be seen? Thea and Ursula can do some but you are much faster and better, whether you like it or not.'

Thea busied herself with threading another green into her needle, cursing that she hadn't had the presence of mind to choose a pastime she didn't loathe.

'She could have George Crowe and I could have Samuel Harrington.' Tabitha poked at the abandoned needlework with a stockinged foot. 'I think he liked me.'

'Don't be ridiculous,' said Mrs Morell, 'Samuel Harrington's position is such that he would only be interested in a wife with similar prospects. The Morell name, at least, carries prestige.' Thea noticed her throw an accusatory glance at her husband, and her heart dropped. Her mother must know about his problems too. 'Thea is the eldest and we cannot overstate her financial value. It would be a good match as long as she doesn't mess it up, but we will still throw her in the way of the Crowes and keep our options open, just in case she does.'

Ursula looked up from her threadwork which was already intricate and beautiful. 'I found Viscount Stockwood quite agreeable. Unfortunately George Crowe is not credited with the finest morals.'

Tabitha let out a shrill peal of laughter. 'That's true, don't they say his only talents are with horses, halieutics and harlots?'

'Tabitha!' their mother interjected.

'Well they don't actually say that, they say whor–'

'That's enough young lady!'

Tabitha was unrepentant as usual. 'Well, I no longer think the Swanhams will disrupt my summer so much as I imagined. Ralph

Jefferys showed quite an interest in my playing and I found Lady Eleanor extremely dull.'

'Tabitha, you mustn't say such things.' Thea found herself jumping more forcibly to Ella's defence than she meant to.

'I found her incredibly charming,' said Ursula, 'I would be delighted to spend more time with her this summer.'

Thea was pleased, perhaps this would be a diverting season in the country after all.

In the morning Thea, Ursula and Mr Morell headed out in the carriage to Pook End – the house of Edgar Pickles. Pook End was three miles to the west of Milford and Thea had missed it and its owner terribly. His enthusiasm was infectious and she couldn't wait to tell him about the sights she had witnessed at Dr Gibson's in London. She was full of excitement when the timber-framed and slightly rickety house with small, leaded windows came into view. Doves perched on the sagging roof and Edgar stood in the old oak porch, rushing out as the carriage drew up. He shook Mr Morell's hand and hugged Thea and Ursula tightly.

Edgar only bothered with a wig for social occasions. His own hair was white and everywhere. He had made an effort in his dress as they were visiting for the first time in a while, but his suit still didn't quite match and there was a burn mark on one sleeve. He beamed with delight at seeing them, his gnarled, expressive face alight with joy. He marched them into the house where Martha waited in the drawing room.

Edgar looked at his pocket watch. 'Mr Grimston also plans to join us this afternoon but is late as usual.' Thea's heart sank a little and glancing at Martha she knew hers did too, although she would never say so. Stanhope Grimston was grumpy, opinionated and full of his own self-importance, but being part of the Thornbury social circle and curating a collection of his own the party tolerated his ways. Edgar was used to Mr Grimston being late and had a back-up plan as usual. 'While we wait let us take a walk to the menagerie and I will show you one of the most exciting things to happen this spring.'

He turned on his heel and made for the garden, leaving the party to follow along behind. The grounds at Pook End had once tried to be neat, but the clipped box hedges were now rough at the edges and the lawn left to a pleasing meadow, bejewelled by wildflowers and buzzing with happy bees. Edgar strode through them out into the landscape, moving surprisingly quickly for a man of his advancing years – the gout must have cleared up, Thea supposed. Mr Morell pushed Ursula along with some difficulty, helped by Thea and Martha when the terrain got particularly troublesome.

Eventually they came upon Edgar's menagerie, a brick-built building overlooking fields and a small lake. It was the one part of his property he made an effort to maintain for the sake of his animals, and where the groundsman spent most of his time. They walked past exotic birds and a couple of small monkeys, and finally reached a pen in front of which Edgar spread his arms wide, and beamed. 'There, look!'

They all looked.

The pen housed four adult chickens and two rabbits, in addition to some chicks which must have been about a week old. They were quite ordinary, compared to the other curiosities in Edgar's collection. Thea tossed a sideways glance to Martha, who gave an almost imperceptible shrug.

Mr Morell was the first to break the silence. 'Are you breeding pies, Edgar?'

Edgar chuckled and gestured to his captives. 'These are not just *any* rabbits and chickens my dear Ben, look more closely. Especially at the little ones.' They all did. Thea even screwed up her face to ensure Edgar knew she was trying, but still just saw rabbits and chickens. Edgar's eager face took in each of them in turn.

Thea pursed her lips and tried next. 'Are they – a lighter colour than normal chicks?'

Edgar looked delighted and strode around the pen to her side. 'Quite possibly, my dear. What we have here is a faithful repetition of the Brussels experiment of crossing rabbits and chickens! As you can see, these chicks have shorter wings than usual, and you may be right, Thea, they *are* a different colour. It may be the prelude to a whole new species. In *my* menagerie!' He nodded, smiling, and proud. They all looked hard. Thea glanced at her father who was staring intently at the chicks and nodding slowly.

Ursula was the first to chip in. 'Do you know, Mr Pickles, I think you are right. Now you have explained, I can clearly see the difference for myself.'

Edgar beamed. 'Indeed, indeed, can't you see how their gait is more bouncy than usual!' Ursula managed to nod, and Thea managed a small 'mmm.' Edgar put his hands on his hips and smiled as the little ones ran around after their mother. 'I shall leave these in with the rabbit and have another brood, and we shall see how different they look then. Now, back to the house.'

He strode off without another word and after a few sideways glances the group followed obediently. Thea caught the arm of Martha who stared at the floor as she walked. She whispered into her ear as they made for the house. 'They are absolutely no different to normal chicks, are they?'

She still didn't look up. 'Absolutely not, no.'

Thea grinned. 'Are you going to tell him?'

Martha stopped and looked straight at her. 'Goodness no, Thea, let us not shatter his illusions, look how happy he is!' Thea smiled and reminded herself to be thankful that she had friends who were so kind. As they crowded back into Pook End after Edgar, the butler announced Mr Grimston.

Stanhope Grimston's portly frame shuffled through the hallway to-wards the happy party. His heavily brocaded jacket did nothing to contain a bulging waistcoat, and his ruddy, crotchety face was framed by a wig worn long and curled, a fashion abandoned by the previous generation. 'You started without me, Pickles,' he barked in a gruff voice.

Edgar was unfazed. 'We started on time, and anyway, we have only been to see the chickens, you haven't missed the cake, although by the look of you it might not be a bad idea. Why don't you have a date?'

'Dates? Is that a fruit? What's wrong with you man, are you going soft?' A pudgy finger stabbed the air between Grimston's own belly and Edgar's competing one. 'George the First died from an excess of strawberries.' He nodded and waggled his unruly eyebrows as if to prove his point. 'You think on.' He turned to the rest of the group. 'I suppose he's been trying to convince you he has bred a rabbit and a chicken. Bloody ridiculous. For your information, Pickles, I am late as I received a very important letter from the President of the Royal So-ciety, which clearly I must prioritise over this gathering.' He gestured to the group in general as he spoke. 'Anyway, you said cake?' Martha's eyebrow twitched. Thea was always impressed at Edgar's kindness and patience towards the grumpy, older man.

They spent a happy hour catching up with Edgar; Mr Grimston had cornered Mr Morell as ladies weren't worth his time. Mr Pickles regaled Thea, Ursula and Martha with tales of his recent experiments, often quite hair raising. The ladies, in their turn, recounted the many lectures they had seen in London, and the array of collections they had visited. Thea left out the bit about the kiss. Edgar listened intently and questioned them thoroughly, wide eyed and fascinated. 'Oh, I would so dearly love to see these spectacles for myself, but I just cannot bear to travel to the noise and bustle of London at my age. I do prefer a quieter life these days!' Thea shared a grin with Ursula – whatever happened at Pook End, it was rarely quiet, and often involved some sort of small explosion.

Mr Grimston's voice occasionally breached their conversation enough for them to register his laments on the current state of the Byam's coffee house, the only one he had always found exclusive enough for his tastes. 'Even they are starting to let anyone in now,' he ranted to Mr Morell, 'the other day a merchant tried to converse with me. Me, of all people! I informed him that I had just that moment come from the cabinet of the Duke of Sunderland and was not yet prepared to converse with people of his station. Even the Royal Society are letting in anyone and everyone. Lawyers, physicians, clergymen, it's ridiculous.'

Thea saw Edgar bristle, but Mr Grimston didn't slow. 'As soon as they start letting women in I'm leaving.' Edgar flicked an eyebrow at the ladies in his circle, who traded amused glances. They knew any one of them could run rings around Mr Grimston in any discussion on natural philosophy.

They watched him tap the side of his nose and lean into his confidant, although he ensured to increase the volume of his speech. 'The society is currently looking for a new president, and I have it on very good authority that yours truly is a strong contender. Naturally. They have been trying to get their hands on my stuffed bird collection for years, but I have important work to do with it yet.' He grinned smugly and cast his gaze around the room to judge the reaction. The ladies and Edgar made sure to look deep in conversation as they stifled their smiles – Mr Grimston did no work at all with his collection, save telling people how amazing it was.

Edgar put a hand on Ursula's shoulder. 'Let us save your poor father,' he whispered to her, and then to the room. 'Natural philosophers of Thornbury, please accompany me to the cabinet, I have summer activities to introduce.'

'At last,' grumbled Mr Grimston, 'all this procrastinating over cake, ridiculous.' He pushed past the group towards Edgar's cabinet room, snatching a biscuit, muttering at Ursula's chair and casting a snide glance at Martha as he passed.

Edgar sighed, offered a knowing smile and gestured to the door. 'You first, ladies,' he announced, over-gallantly, just loudly enough for the retreating figure to hear. They all trooped after Mr Grimston, into the familiar chaos of the cabinet and experiment room. The windows were high on the walls and dust danced in the rays that pierced the gloom of the oak-clad space. Unlike the small cabinet at Milford, with its well-ordered glass cases and carefully labelled specimens, Edgar's assemblage was everywhere. Rocks, fish, medals, animals, corals, dried plants and unidentified jars were crammed on shelves, jutting out of open cases, bursting out of trunks and hanging from the walls and ceilings. Thea was so familiar with the disarray she barely noticed anymore, but today it was even worse than usual.

'My god, Pickles,' announced Mr Grimston, 'you are always lecturing me that my collection should be in some sort of order but look at this!'

'My dear man,' trilled Edgar, soothingly, 'intention is one thing, execution is entirely another. The collections of natural history had taken second place as soon as Edgar had discovered that machines and experiments were more exciting, so the majority of the room was crammed with large and beautiful pieces of equipment, mostly formed of mahogany with brass trimmings. There was a telescope, test tubes, jars and flasks, a concave mirror, a grand orrery with its small models of the planets, and now something new, clear in a space in the centre of the room. Thea felt a prick of excitement within as she identified it as a static generating machine. Just like Dr Gibson's it was a large, transparent sphere with a handle to spin it. They clustered around it. 'I plan to make electricity my new *thing*,' said Edgar, caressing the smooth glass with his calloused hand. Everyone smiled their willingness, but the idea of marrying Edgar's relaxed attitude to safety with the electrical power Thea had seen in London made her anxious.

The idea must have come from one of his contacts, she thought. Edgar was a man of letters. Many letters. She knew his study was no tidier than this room, the desk essentially a pile of paper held up by straining mahogany. He wrote to natural philosophers across the world, sharing his knowledge and receiving more in return. She imagined that must also have been where the idea for the rabbits and chickens came from.

Mr Grimston had been poking at a large pile of natural history specimens on the floor but was clearly listening in. 'Load of bunkum,' he muttered into the dust. 'You'll never gain notoriety with that rubbish, Pickles. What you want, is one, spectacular thing—' he drifted off mid-sentence and held aloft a large, blue-and-white vase from the pile he had been poking through. 'What's this, Pickles?'

Edgar lifted his head from the electrical machine. 'No idea,' he said, 'a vase? Ladies, this is the thing I shall need your assistance with this summer, if you would be so kind.' He ushered Thea and Ursula to the pile while Martha and Mr Morell remained to study the generating machine. 'My old friend Stanley Burrows passed away last month and left his collection to me. Your knowledge in figuring out what everything is would be greatly appreciated.' He gestured to more items spilling out of trunks, some in cabinets and some piled loose. 'I have no idea what most of it is, but there seem to be some items of interest.' He dug around in the pile and drew out a huge, white bone with protrusions at odd angles. 'This, for example. No idea.'

'It's a whale vertebra!' Thea's eyes shone. 'I saw one in Mr Blake's cabinet and asked him – but this one's bigger. Think how big the animal must be.' Edgar held it out and she took it reverently, when she rested it on a hip the tip of it was still at eye level. At times like this, she was almost overwhelmed with the variety of the world, and how little of it she had experienced.

'Let's make a start then. Shall we pop it over there on the fish shelf?' Edgar made to go but Thea passed the bone to Ursula and took him by the elbow.

'I'm not sure – apparently whales share much in common with quadrupeds, there's talk of them being reclassified elsewhere.'

'It's already happened.' Ursula spoke from behind the bone, shifting it sideways on her lap so she could see them past its chalky protuberances. 'In the latest version of *Systema Naturae* Linnaeus has categorised cetacea – which includes whales,' she added kindly, 'in with the mammalia.'

Edgar could only blink at her. 'Volume ten only arrived a fortnight ago,' said Thea, still often incredulous at her sister's capacity for knowledge.

'Which is plenty of time to note the significant changes since volume nine.'

'Of course it is.'

Edgar looked between them. 'And what does that mean?'

'It means that your whale needs to go over here with your elk,' said Thea, shifting a hairy, bony leg along a shelf to their right and placing the whale vertebrae alongside it.

Edgar furrowed his brow. 'You know I trust you both implicitly, but are you telling me that a whale is more akin to this' – he pointed to a stuffed muntjac deer lurking by the door – 'than that?' This time he gestured to a blowfish, dried and tipped at an angle across the room.

'Mmm,' said Thea, 'you mean on account of it not having legs?'

Edgar looked desperate by now. 'Well, exactly!'

'On the surface it does seem that way, but it has been observed that whale suckle their young - a feature exclusive to the mammal class, and so here it goes.' Thea stood back from the shelf, wiping the dust on the back of her gown.

'Oh.' Edgar looked pleasantly defeated. 'Well, I'd believe it from nobody but you. Fish legs it is.' He wrapped a kind arm around each of their shoulders. 'I do wish you would not be so reticent of sharing your knowledge in public, Thea. Your expertise is something to be proud of – celebrate it!' He squeezed her a little to emphasise his point and looked at her with kindly, wrinkled eyes.

'You know why I can't, Edgar,' she said, looking away.

'I know why your mother doesn't want you to,' he said, now letting go of Ursula and taking both Thea's shoulders in his hands, 'but that is not why you don't.'

She smiled weakly. 'Perhaps my mother's insistence avoids me being dismissed and belittled by men who are certain they are the voice of authority.'

'Nonsense,' said Edgar, 'you both just proved me wrong with superior knowledge.'

Thea raised an eyebrow at him. 'Let's talk again when all men are as generous and accepting as you.'

'Don't let them diminish you, Thea,' he said. 'I've seen Ursula speak up!'

'Ursula has more confidence than me,' said Thea, honestly.

'I have less to lose than you do,' retorted Ursula. Thea took a breath to counter but Ursula held up her hand. 'No arguments, you know it is the case eldest sister. Anyway, what is Mr Grimston up to?'

They all looked around to where Mr Grimston had begun to methodically explore the drawers of a cabinet. Edgar gave a chuckle and lowered his voice so only Thea and Ursula could hear. 'He has been desperate to come and have a rummage. As my oldest friend' – he checked himself as he watched the grumpy figure of Grimston – 'well, acquaintance – he is sure I'll leave the collection to him when I pop my clogs. He's only interested in the items he deems wonderful or spectacular of course, he has no interest in true natural philosophy, or experiment.' As they watched, Mr Grimston took a glinting stone out of one of the drawers, considered it for a moment against the dim light, and popped it straight in his pocket.

Thea and Ursula gasped but Edgar only looked amused. 'He thinks I won't notice you see, and of course he is right. He is looking for the next thing with which he can impress his precious Royal Society. Shall we have some fun?' Thea glanced at Ursula and they shared a smile, Edgar teased the pompous Mr Grimston terribly, not that he usually noticed.

Edgar picked up a brown object which looked like a furry brown log, around twelve inches across and slightly hairy in the middle with five sticks poking out of it. It looked to Thea like a dried bit of plant. Edgar raised his voice so everyone could hear.

'Now here is something special, ladies, I remember Burrows being particularly excited about it. Said it might make him famous. What a shame he went and died first.'

He lowered his voice to Thea. 'Is he coming?' Thea cast a quick glance and gave a tiny nod. Mr Grimston had straightened up, alert like a magpie, and was moving towards them in what he presumably thought was a nonchalant manner.

Edgar took his chance. 'What we have here ladies, is an extremely rare example of the Vegetable Lamb of Tartary.'

Ursula played along. 'Golly, it looks extremely unusual.'

Thea sniggered quietly and Edgar suppressed a smile. 'It is an organism which begins life as a plant. This stem here serves as a kind of umbilical cord which sprouts from the leaves, then the vegetable matter on top grows and gradually metamorphoses into a small lamb as it develops. Here we have one which is only partly formed. They are difficult to catch once they detach themselves, you see.' He winked at them both, pleased with his final detail.

Mr Grimston's large face appeared beside Edgar, eyes glistering with greed. 'Couldn't help but catch your conversation there, Pickles – sounds remarkable. If you like, I could take it to the next Royal Society meeting and present it on your behalf?'

Edgar feigned surprise. 'On my behalf? Oh goodness no, I thank you but it is too special to part with and too fragile to travel. But for something almost as spectacular you could take the barnacle goose?' He pointed to a large, stuffed bird from the pile. Mr Grimston looked sideways at Thea and Ursula, loathe to admit that he had never heard of barnacle goose.

For once, Edgar spared his blushes. 'Of course you will know of it, Grimston, given your experience in ornithology, but for the benefit of the ladies I will explain. The barnacle goose is a bird which does not spring from an egg, but instead from a barnacle. The barnacle originates from one particular island in the Pacific Ocean and adheres to driftwood or trees. When these wash up onto foreign shores a goose is generated from the very shell.' By now his speech was low and conspiratorial and Mr Grimston leaned in close to listen. 'It is almost unique, apart from the lamb, in that it crosses boundaries between the different kingdoms of nature.'

Mr Grimston's eyes were wide. 'And you would be willing for me to take this and present on your behalf?'

Edgar clapped him on the back. 'Goodness no, man, you must take it as your own. Burrows collected it and you are *quite* the expert on all things avian. I am sure he would be delighted.' Thea suppressed a guilty smile but thought Stanley Burrows would probably be delighted too, if he knew Mr Grimston at all. Mr Grimston hurried off with the goose and she turned to Edgar with her hands on her hips but a smile on her face.

'Mr Pickles, that is very cruel. You know neither of those stories hold a shred of truth.'

'Indeed,' he said, 'nobody has believed either for over a hundred years and the society will have none of it, but our friend needs to learn to apply his mind and tell fact from fiction. He may one day, but I hope not before that goose reaches the Royal Society. Let's have more tea, shall we?'

As the happy party trooped back to the drawing room and Martha lay an instinctive hand on her back, Thea felt a pang of guilt. Martha would be furious if she knew about Edgar's most recent game – she always sided with propriety even when Mr Grimston was being his egotistical worst. She was sometimes far too kind, Thea thought, underneath the indomitable, scholarly exterior there was a soft heart. She almost made up her mind to give up the whole story to Mr Grimston, until she saw the glint of pyrite in his pocket and resolved to let him make as much of a fool of himself as he deserved.

CHAPTER 5

It was a sparklingly clear April morning, the kind that preludes the best days of spring. Thea was making the most of the crisp sunshine in the walled garden when Tabitha rushed from the house.

'Thea, quick, the Harringtons are come!' She made to return inside but twisted back to her sister. 'Goodness, you look a fright.' Thea looked down at herself. The dress itself wasn't bad – a simple pale green, but the morning dew had crept up from the hem and dirt smears betrayed where she had leant on the walls of the stove beds and slithered down the grass bank. Never mind, it was too late now.

As she entered the drawing room, slightly out of breath, Ella was the first to notice her, an amused smile growing on her lips as her eyes wandered down Thea's person. Lady Swanham's attention came next, with a head-to-toe visual assessment – one Thea was quite used to from society ladies. She waited for the look of distaste to cloud the Countess's features, but only the corners of her mouth twitched upwards. 'A good morning in the garden, Miss Morell?'

Before Thea could politely respond in the affirmative, Mrs Morell's head snapped around and a look of horror animated her features. 'Goodness, Thea, get upstairs and change, that is no way to receive guests!'

'Not on our account, Mrs Morell, please,' said Lady Swanham, extending a pacifying hand to kindly assuage the situation. 'There is no shame in an active lady and I assume you plan more outside enjoyment following our interruption, Miss Morell, you must not dirty two dresses in a day.' Thea grinned and bobbed her thanks. Lady Swanham went on. 'What you *may* need to change for, Miss Morell, is this.' She held out a piece of sturdy paper to Mrs Morell, who took it, read it, and handed it to Tabitha with a gasp.

Tabitha snatched up her hands to her face, the invitation creasing against it. 'A ball! At Stanbourne next month. Oh how exciting, the country is so dull without a ball, don't you think so, Lady Eleanor?'

To Thea's mind Ella didn't look quite so sure, but she smiled as she placed her teacup back on the saucer. 'The local families around Thornbury have been so welcoming, we are very pleased to host everyone for an evening of conversation and dancing,' she said, graciously.

'You may count on the whole of the Morell family's attendance,' affirmed Mrs Morell, now with her own excitement almost under control, 'our girls love dancing and are always delighted to have a chance to do so.' Thea shared an amused glance with Ursula – it was an ideal activity for neither of them.

Ella broke the slightly awkward silence that ensued. 'Miss Ursula, my brother has asked that you should know how very much he enjoyed your excellent playing at tea, and requests that you should play again at Stanbourne if it would be agreeable to you. He would be delighted to send his carriage for you and your sister any time you like, if she would wish to accompany you.' Her eyes rested on Thea with a shy smile as she spoke. The gaze lingered and Thea felt her stomach churn. The feeling persisted as Ella's attention slipped back to Ursula who confirmed she would be very pleased to visit and play.

'Excellent, then it is settled, Miss Ursula, we shall look forward to–' Ella was cut off by Tabitha who flounced out of her seat and to the harpsichord in the corner of the room.

'Please do inform Lord Stockwood that *I* would be very pleased to play for him any time. I flatter myself that I have a greater range than my sister, Lady Eleanor, even though I allowed her to take the instrument at Stanbourne. Let me show you.'

'Oh, of course,' Ella stammered and coloured a little. 'Of course you must, Miss Tabitha, I didn't mean to–' but her sentence was truncated yet again, this time by the harpsichord. What Tabitha may have gained in range on her sister, she certainly did not equal in finesse. Thea offered apologetic glances to both Ella and Lady Swanham who had the grace to adopt an impression of enjoyment.

As soon as Tabitha had finished her first tune and was turning the page for another, Thea stood, quickly. 'A walk in the grounds perhaps? It is such a beautiful day.'

Mrs Morell steered the group to the stove house – this was the perfect opportunity to show off her husband's exotics. She trilled her way through the collection with an admirable impression of knowledge. 'Here is the Indian shot plant from the Americas – it will have huge orange flowers by the end of the summer, and the fuchsia, all the way from the West Indies. Mr Morell is supplied them by a very sensible gentleman who advises him on all the best plants. I do like to encourage him,' she went on, as Thea shot her a disbelieving look, 'there is no progress without knowledge, as they say.' Thea rolled her eyes at her mother's simpering to the Countess.

There was a crash behind them and they turned as one to see Mr Morell struggling through the doors with three terracotta pots. 'Ah, here he comes now.' Mrs Morell's smile faltered only for a second. 'Mr Morell, do come and show Lady Swanham and Lady Eleanor your botanical treasures.'

Mr Morell nodded obediently, placed the pots down and dipped between the beds to the back of the colonnade. Before long he emerged with a small pot holding a plant which looked like numerous green, knobbly fingers with a large, furry, pinkish flower stuck on the side. It wasn't until he held it proudly aloft that the smell hit Thea, and a sideways glance at the wrinkling noses of their guests confirmed that the aroma was a traveller.

'Isn't it spectacular?' asked Mr Morell breathlessly, sporting a smile that threatened to escape off both sides of his face. He held it out so they could get a better look. Thea noticed it was only Ella who leaned in, subtly holding her breath.

Mrs Morell's smile was the same one she'd exhibited when she'd seen the sample of elephant poo in Mr Blake's museum. 'What on earth is it, Ben?' She tried and failed to keep the irritation from her voice.

'It is a *Stapelia,* my dear.' Mr Morell managed to be oblivious. 'This is the first time it has flowered since it came all the way from the Cape of Good Hope.' If Mr Morell had hoped that the provenance, at least, might impress his wife, it didn't.

'And why does it smell like something dead?' asked Ella, now eyeing it with what seemed to be genuine interest.

'An excellent question, my lady.' Mr Morell warmed to his subject. 'It smells because it is pollinated by flies, and so attracts them by simulating rotting flesh. Isn't it beautiful!' He beamed at it like some men might regard a fine vintage port or a silver snuff box.

'That is – extremely interesting.' Lady Swanham was certainly drawing on every bit of her exquisite breeding but had paled somewhat.

Mrs Morell scowled at her husband. 'Let me show you the trained fruit, Lady Swanham,' she said, ushering their guest outdoors and gesturing for Tabitha to follow with Ursula. 'No need to follow, Ben.' Mr Morell looked only a little affronted, but Ella was now bending to peer more closely at the plant in his hands.

'Is that true?' she asked. 'How remarkable, if so.'

'It's also furry, and the colour of rotting meat, if you look closely.' Mr Morell pushed it nearer to her and she did, even daring to take a cautious sniff and reeling back despite herself.

'Amazing. And disgusting.' Thea and her father both smiled at her enthusiasm. 'You must be a very talented grower to make it flower so far away from home, Mr Morell?' He puffed up at her compliment and was about to respond but at that moment Scip entered, carrying a bucket of tan for the hot beds. He grinned a welcome to them all. 'Scip here grew it from seed that came on a boat from Africa,' Thea said, 'he can grow anything.' The bucket in his hand didn't smell any better than the *Stapelia*, but Ella was apparently unfazed.

'It is a pleasure to meet such an expert grower, Scip,' she said smoothly and gestured at his bucket. 'What's that for?'

'It is tanner's bark, miss – left over from when they tan the leather. It goes in the beds, rots, and warms the roots of the plants which come from more exotic places than Sussex.' His natural cheer always put people at ease.

'And why does *that* smell so bad?' The stench from the bucket was already rasping at Thea's throat. Scip shot Thea a look which asked how truthful his answer should be. She gave an almost imperceptible nod – strangely curious to know how Ella would react.

'It's on account of the urine, Miss,' Scip stated cautiously, 'that they use to tan the leather.' Ella barely blinked. 'That and the cow hair, Miss, they keep my babies warm on the chilly nights. That is, Mr Morell's babies,' he clarified, shooting a glance at Mr Morell who only chuckled and waved away the slip.

Ella thanked him warmly as Mr Morell replaced the *Stapelia* and Thea led her out into the walled garden. 'Where did you get your gardener?' asked Ella when they were out of earshot. 'Mother has been wondering whether she should bring one over from the Indies.'

'A gardener?' asked Thea, confused. 'Don't you have enough already?'

'No,' laughed Ella. 'I mean a black. So many households have one now and she does like to keep up.'

Thea's skin prickled at the thought of Scip as a fashionable accessory, like one might talk of a mahogany chair or a nutmeg grater. Still, mindful of the need to remain in favour with the Swanham's she didn't dare voice her thoughts. She chose supporting him personally.

'Scip is here as he is an excellent gardener – he used to tend the plots in the plantations and has set up a more productive rotation system than our old gardener could ever manage. We have better tomatoes and capsicums than any family I know and he is expert at coaxing life out of the seeds and roots father receives from abroad.' She stopped herself outlining more of his virtues. 'Did I hear your family has links in the colonies?'

'Yes.' Ella tugged at a glove to neaten it. 'Father owns plantations, although he doesn't get involved directly.' One of Thea's eyebrows twitched involuntarily. 'It's a nasty business but has meant we can move back to the country,' went on Ella, 'so I can't complain.' Thea took a breath to respond, but Lady Swanham beckoned to them from the house and they switched direction. 'I would love to find out more about the collections, Thea, if you would be willing?'

'Of course,' said Thea. She knew the plantations were a nasty business but there was little she could say. Neither could she help being delighted at the thought of spending time with Ella – who wasn't involved directly, she convinced herself. 'Let me know when and I can arrange some time for you to talk with Scip.' Secretly she thought it would be good for Ella to spend time with him – she might learn about more than just plants. 'He will be delighted to share, while I am no expert.'

'That's not what I have heard,' said Ella, and Thea looked up at her, alarmed. 'I told you Lady Foxmore was singing your praises at Stanbourne and Sam and I heard more when we called to deliver the invitation to the ball. I understand you are perhaps more informed than you are letting on. She told us all about your collection.'

'Did she now?' asked Thea, a smile playing on her lips. She could imagine Martha speaking of Thea's love of scholarship and watching Sam like a hawk to ensure he was amenable. 'Well, it seems my secret is out. I would be delighted, of course, we should arrange a time – before the ball, perhaps?'

'An excellent idea,' agreed Ella, 'and then we shall have more to discuss between dances. Perhaps you and I could find a corner in which to secret ourselves away for the evening?' Ella laughed again, and so did Thea on the outside, but her insides had inexplicably turned to jelly. Her laugh died quickly and a fleeting glance at Ella met suddenly serious eyes.

Ella took a breath, looked away and brushed her hand through the soft fronds of a tall grass as they walked. 'I really shouldn't let on, but my brother was quite taken with you on your visit to Stanbourne.' Thea snapped back to reality. 'He speaks of you often and would dearly love for you to visit with Ursula one day soon.'

Thea filled her lungs with some effort as they approached the rest of the party. 'We would be delighted to, I shall ask father for the carriage.'

'Then it is settled. And thank you, I have found today extremely enlightening.' She touched Thea's arm gently. It sent a stream of warmth through her body and roused a not unfamiliar heat which scorched inside her chest. She found she could only smile her assent as Ella and Lady Swanham made for their carriage.

Enlightening, yes. That's what it had been.

After church on Sunday the crowd stopped to chat in the churchyard. Mrs Morell fawned over Lady Swanham and spoke loudly about how she had taken Thea to Whiston's, the drapers, and bought twelve yards of cloth for new dresses. 'Of course, we usually prefer to fit the girls out in London at the mercer's, however, Whiston's do have a tolerable range and it is charitable to support local businesses.' Thea wilted at the memory of being dragged to Whiston's following her fashion *faux pas*, and at Mrs Morell feeling it necessary to inform Lady Swanham. 'We shall choose Thea's dress for the ball after they have been made up, but I am sure Viscount Stockwood will find it quite to his taste.'

Thea could only offer Lady Swanham an embarrassed smile and excuse herself before she perished entirely.

Tabitha had made a beeline for Samuel Harrington, she noticed, and Samuel had kept his sister with him – presumably for protection. Edgar and Martha were absent as usual and so Thea joined the Ashby party who were chatting happily by the handsome old yew in the churchyard.

Jane nudged her on the arm and grinned. 'I am delighted to find you have taken my advice.'

Lord Stockwood and Ella were starting to extricate themselves from Tabitha, Thea noticed, so she spoke without thinking. 'Yes of course.' She looked back at Jane. 'I mean, have I?'

'Apparently.' There was glee in Jane's eyes. 'Lord Stockwood hasn't taken his eyes off you all morning. I watched him through the whole service.' Thea craned her neck to look again at the handsome siblings. 'Don't look!' mumbled Jane through clenched teeth, but it was too late. Ella's gaze met Thea's and the Harringtons headed over.

'Miss Morell, what a great pleasure to see you this morning.' Lord Stockwood took Thea's hand and kissed it.

She felt herself glow pink as Jane's eyes widened. 'Lord Stockwood, Lady Eleanor, please let me introduce you to Dr and Mrs Ashby and their daughter Jane. Dr Ashby is the physician in the village and our families have had a close acquaintance for as long as I remember.'

The gentlemen tipped their hats and the ladies dipped in greeting. 'A pleasure to make your acquaintance Lord Stockwood and Lady Eleanor,' said Dr Ashby. He was an affable man, with a little too much weight, a loose grey wig and a kind, expressive face. 'I can confirm I have indeed known Miss Morell for as long as she can remember, in fact, I was the first person to greet her in this world.' He beamed and Thea coloured once again. 'I also provided some help for your mother after you arrived with us, my dear,' he said to Ella, 'but your family were gone to London by the time Lord Stockwood joined us so I did not have the pleasure of seeing him into the world. Nevertheless, you seem to be none the worse for it, sir!' The party laughed good naturedly.

'Perhaps we may have the pleasure of your company more often now we are back at Stanbourne,' said Ella. Thea noticed how her striking eyes seemed alive in the spring sunlight. 'But I hope that this time it will be for pleasure, rather than business.'

'Indeed, Dr Ashby,' Samuel added to his sister's generosity, 'do you shoot?'

'I fish mainly, but I have been known to be partial to a grouse or two.'

'Then do join us next Wednesday if you are free, I have made an arrangement with Mr Jefferys and Ralph that they will join me and my father on the estate, although I don't know if they were so happy about it.' They all looked over at the Jefferys family who were standing, stony faced with Stanhope Grimston.

'Worry not, Lord Stockwood,' said Dr Ashby, 'the Jefferys are joyful on the inside I am sure. If they ever crack a smile you will know that you have delighted them beyond measure.' Thea was struck by how effortlessly Ella and Samuel engaged others and put them at their ease.

'Then I really *must* press you to join our jolly party, Dr Ashby,' said Lord Stockwood with a smile, 'it is a beautiful day, shall we walk towards Thornbury?'

After agreeing it with Mrs Morell and Lady Swanham the party set off. Thea hoped to walk with Ella, but her new friend had fallen in with Dr Ashby and Jane feigned an urgent conversation with her mother, leaving Samuel Harrington her companion. He smiled at her fondly. 'How did you enjoy the service today, Miss Morell?'

'Very well thank you.' When it came to her views on the local church service she was only ever honest to Martha, who avoided the event when she could. 'Although the organist was a little off,' she added.

'You certainly have a better ear than he did.' He grinned but peered at his feet. 'Ella and I are looking forward to seeing you and Miss Ursula at Stanbourne this week and hearing your sister play, I am sure with fewer – eccentricities than this morning.'

'Of that I am certain,' she said with a chuckle. 'We are very much looking forward to the visit.'

He smiled that affable smile once more. 'I must thank you for becoming a friend to my sister. I know we spoke about it, but I had not expected it to happen so fast. I was delighted when she suggested you visit us – I have not seen her so animated in many years.'

Thea's head snapped up and she stared at Ella, walking in front of her with Dr Ashby. She wondered if she could have misinterpreted Ella's invitation at Milford but remembered only Ella suggesting that Sam was keen to hear Ursula play. 'Is that so?' she began carefully, before a warmth crept through her and she found an involuntary smile toying with her lips. 'I am delighted, we do seem to enjoy each other's company. I find that there are a limited number of people whose company delights me, and I suspect that you and your sister may be two of them.'

She looked up at his happy face and smiled. His pleasure, already evident, seemed to grow. 'I am delighted to hear it. Please call me Sam, Miss Morell.' He held her gaze and she smiled back, benignly, remembering at least to suggest he also address her informally. She did genuinely enjoy his company, and although she couldn't say she felt compelled by him in the way she perhaps should, she had certainly experienced worse conversations with men and wondered if her feelings might grow. Just as she wondered what to say next, Ella turned to engage him in a query with Dr Ashby.

Thea felt Jane take the opportunity to grab her arm from behind – her friend gave her a hard and meaningful stare. 'What?'

'What do you mean, what?' Jane's voice was an urgent whisper. 'How could you not tell me you were so thick with the Harringtons?'

'I don't know that we are really.' Thea needed more time to consider what she had heard from Sam. 'Lord Stockwood asked me to be kind to his sister as she was lonely.'

'And it seems to be going more than well!'

Jane's conspiratorial glance made Thea's heightened senses start a little. 'Well – uh – she's a pleasant girl and we get on tolerably well–'

Jane shoved her with a shoulder. 'I don't mean her you prune, him! He is made up with you. Don't tell me you didn't notice the way he was looking at you just now?'

Given that Thea had little grip on her own feelings, she wasn't about to share them with anyone else – not even Jane. 'Of course he isn't, he's just pleased for Ella.'

Jane rolled her eyes, 'I despair of you, Thea Morell. If he doesn't beg of you the first two dances at the ball I will dance with Ralph Jefferys himself. Twice.' Thea only smiled, but on reflection she became a little concerned that Jane was right. Samuel Harrington was the perfect gentleman and utterly charming. She could barely choose better, but try as she might she could not bring herself to be enthusiastic about the situation.

Not *that* situation, anyway.

The carriage was arranged for Thea and Ursula to take a trip to Stanbourne and the visit took place the following Thursday. Samuel Harrington and Ella were attentive hosts and the four of them spent a pleasant afternoon walking in the grounds and taking tea and macaroons. Thea thought that barring the complexities of attraction she would be very happy to spend more time with either brother or sister. They were both diverting company and now Ella had relaxed she told them stories of the family's exploits on the continent and made them roar with laughter.

As they walked down by the canal, Ella and Thea chatted happily and watched Samuel and Ursula up ahead, she pointing out the species of tree in the landscape. Thea regarded him with interest. 'I hope you don't think this an impertinent observation, Ella, but your brother is an extremely eligible match. I wonder that he is not yet intended to a young lady, especially after so long on the scene in London.'

'Not impertinent at all,' reassured Ella, 'you are right that he is, and such a good man. He has had a number of opportunities as I am sure you can imagine, but he has always been very clear with our mother and father that he wishes to marry for love.' She glanced sideways at Thea. 'Do you find that hopelessly indulgent?'

'Not at all,' reflected Thea. In odd, whimsically optimistic moments she had occasionally allowed herself to hope for the same. 'Who would not, given the chance, and your brother has the opportunity and the time to make it a reality. If he chooses love and fidelity over fortune and freedom, I can think of few men in the country who would be equal to him.'

'I tell him so regularly, and yet still he doubts himself. I do have high hopes that he will make such a match, before very long.' Ella paused a little, before continuing. 'I am lucky that I know Sam and his fortune will take care of me, but with only two sisters I fear you do not have that luxury, Thea? If you don't mind my impertinence in asking?'

Thea gave a wry smile and a small sigh. 'I absolutely do not mind. You are correct that my match must be for fortune. I should like to marry for love, although I seem not to have the constitution for it in any case. I shall be happy, Ella, if my sisters are so.' Ella nodded and regarded her walking companion briefly as they turned back towards the house.

Back in the drawing room, Samuel listened appreciatively to Ursula's playing and Ella guided Thea to the chaise by the window. Thea enjoyed the increasingly confident Lady Eleanor, her rust-coloured hair alight against the sun streaming through the windows and her ivory dress rucked up as she sat sideways to face her guest. How many people had two different coloured eyes like that? Thea wondered. And why did it happen?

Suddenly she became aware that Ella seemed to be waiting for an answer. 'I am sorry, I was – distracted. By the sun.'

She noticed that Ella's parted lips paused for a beat before her gentle and slightly amused voice repeated its request. 'I was only saying that I believe your invite here was dependent on me hearing a little more about the excellent collections at Milford.'

'Oh. Yes.' Thea recovered herself. 'I could talk to you all day about natural history collections, but I am afraid I may disappoint you on the plant collections – they are mainly my father and Martha's domain. And manuscripts for my father, too.'

Ella sat up a little and looked intrigued. 'There are different types of collections?'

'Oh, absolutely.' At least Thea could lose herself in this subject. 'Really it depends on the interests of the owner. In addition to my father and Martha, Mr Pickles, at Pook End, keeps animals in his menagerie and likes to experiment with machines. And Stanhope Grimston at Wickmarsh has a bit of everything, but mainly birds. Stuffed birds,' she corrected herself at Ella's surprise. It didn't seem to help. 'They're dead first,' she qualified, and Ella finally exhaled. 'But all of the collections have one thing in common – they assist their owner in the pursuit of knowledge and truth.'

'What kind of knowledge?' asked Ella, seemingly in awe of the enormity of it.

'Anything – everything,' said Thea. 'Many collectors, myself included, hope to contribute, in some part, to the wider understanding of the universe.'

She became aware that Ella was staring at her, a little flushed, and suddenly panicked that she was boring her. 'Apart from Mr Grimston's, he just collects what he thinks he can show off,' she added quickly. When Ella failed to respond she deflated. 'I'm so sorry, I can go on for hours, but I mustn't.'

Ella's eyes, that had dropped lower, now refocussed on her face and she sucked in a breath. 'You absolutely must, Thea, I would love to know more.'

Thea shook her head. She found she was suddenly nervous of putting Ella off her company. 'I would hate to bore you.'

The face that stared back at her looked horrified and Ella's hand twitched forwards as if she had been about to offer comfort but thought better of it. 'I am not sure you ever could.' The force of the statement and the earnest gaze that accompanied it sent a gust right through Thea. It kindled that spark in her chest and sent a warmth crackling through her veins.

Highly inconvenient.

Ella was talking again and Thea forced herself to concentrate. 'I would love to hear more about your own collections.'

Whether it was Ella's enthusiasm, her excitement to share the collection or the glow of the pleasant time they had spent together that morning, the warmth inside Thea flooded her and she felt suddenly bold. 'Perhaps it would be best if I showed you sometime?'

CHAPTER 6

S o it was that Ella arrived at Milford a few mornings later. Martha and Ursula worked in the library identifying plant samples from the Burrows collection and broke off to greet Ella warmly before Thea guided her into the cabinet room.

Ella gasped as she stared around at the cabinets and shelves, one after another. When she had completed a full revolution her wide eyes rested back on her host. 'It is magnificent.'

Thea smiled, 'it is small and mostly father's, but I hope to have my own one day.'

'How do you choose what goes in it?' asked Ella.

'There are no particular rules, no two collections are the same,' started Thea, warming to her subject. 'It depends on the availability of goods and which part of the world is being explored at any one time, the collectors' connections and also what they can afford. But mainly it depends on what the owner likes.' She paused to assess her audience but Ella seemed to be listening intently, so she went on. 'Father used to enjoy geology, but he is now mostly concerned with plants and botany. I enjoy natural history – fossils, insects and sea creatures for example. Father helps me to source them from our contacts in London and then Ursula and I classify them – I mean, figure out what we think they are – then put them in an order, and label them. It's called a taxonomy, and it's how all living things in the world, and things that used to be living, are organised.'

'In the hope of better understanding the world? Like you said at Stanbourne?' asked Ella.

'Exactly.'

Ella regarded her carefully and then looked back at the collection. 'Is any of it still alive?'

'No, not in here,' smiled Thea, remembering how grotesque the collection must look to the uninitiated. 'Have a look in this one – it's my favourite.' She gestured to one case which contained various dried items with fins, tails, vacant eye sockets and other unsavoury features.

Ella raised an eyebrow but joined Thea at the case and bent down next to her, their united breath fogging the glass. 'Let me guess. There are two things in here I recognise as fish. One thing which looks like a fish-hedgehog, a saw, a fat star, something dubious in a jar and a large, wobbly ring with' – she leaned closer – 'ugh, is that *teeth*?!' She looked back at Thea, a mixture of wonder and distaste writ on her face.

Thea kept her amusement hidden out of politeness. 'You are almost exactly correct.' She pointed to the items Ella had started with. 'They are trunk fish, the spiky ball is a puffer fish, the saw is the snout of a saw fish, then a starfish, and those are the teeth of a shark.'

Ella blinked at her. 'And what about the thing in the jar?'

'Nobody is quite sure,' admitted Thea, screwing up her eyes to peer at it more closely, 'but it came out of the stomach of a shark, apparently.'

Ella wrinkled her nose but turned to Thea, her blue and green eyes sharp with amazement. 'And these things all live in the sea, or did, somewhere in the world?'

'Yes, thousands of miles from here in places it is almost impossible for us to imagine.'

She had been gazing into the cabinet, but became aware that Ella was staring at her, intently. Thea was suddenly very aware of their proximity – she could smell Ella's perfume, like sweet jasmine and orange blossom. The scent seemed to spread down her body, into her stomach and rendered her knees useless. She didn't dare look at Ella so stared resolutely at the fish while she felt her face colour.

'What will you do with it?' asked Ella.

That was a question that Thea herself didn't really know the answer to, but she knew what she hoped for. 'I would like to make a contribution,' she said quietly. 'To science, I mean. I would like to publish one day, about what I have learned.' Ella looked impressed.

'You played down your interests so feebly the first time you came to Stanbourne,' she said, never taking her eyes from Thea's face. 'I would know none of this if it were not for Lady Foxmore. Why are you so reticent to share?'

'It doesn't do to be a learned lady,' said Thea, still not looking back at Ella, 'my mother may tolerate it in private, but certainly not in company.'

'But you even evaded when talking to me alone.' Clearly Ella was not going to let the subject drop. 'You are dismissive of your own passion and talent.'

'You can never be sure,' said Thea, certain that she had never studied a fish this hard in her life, 'of how people will react.' She finally found the courage to look at Ella. 'Speaking up isn't always the liberating experience it should be. Men have a monopoly on knowledge and ladies are not always accepting. All in all, I have found that it is easier to say nothing, until I am more informed of the character of any particular company.'

Ella's eyes still burned into her. 'And do you now feel like you are informed of mine?'

Thea squirmed internally, but somehow couldn't look away. 'I think I am beginning to be.'

After what felt like an age, Ella looked back at the cabinet and Thea let go of the breath she held. 'Thea, there is something I should probably tell you. As you have shared with me.' Thea nodded, encouraging her to go on and Ella kept her voice low lest Martha or Ursula could hear. 'It isn't something I usually share, and I would appreciate your discretion.'

'Of course.' A nervousness rose in Thea's chest.

'It's not that I'm ashamed, it's just that it isn't usual.' Surely it couldn't be..? Thea held her breath. 'I like classical literature.' Ella's face pinked with the breathy admission and Thea could only stare at her. 'I know it isn't always considered appropriate for a lady, but like I said to you before, I do spend time in father's library and the books are just there and so much more interesting...' She trailed off and Thea was still unable to find words to respond. 'Oh I shouldn't have said anything, Thea, I've never told anyone before but I thought that with the collections you might–'

Ella's panicked ramblings finally brought Thea back to herself and she interrupted. 'I think that's wonderful.'

'–understand me. Oh... what, you do?' Ella looked back at her.

'I would love to hear more about it sometime.' Thea smiled in confirmation, she hoped warmly against the mess of emotion that churned inside her.

'Yes, good, thank you, of course,' said Ella, huffing another clouding breath onto the glass as she peered back in, evidently through with her confession. 'And, hmm. Why is the puffer fish so... round? Surely it can't swim like that?'

Thea refocussed at Ella's attempt to change the subject. 'Usually it is much smaller, and fish-like, but it can blow up into a spiky ball as a defence when threatened or alarmed.'

Ella thought for a minute, her mouth slightly agape. 'Thank goodness people don't do that.' Thea was slightly embarrassed by the bark of laughter that sprang from her.

Thank goodness they don't, she thought, as Ella's kind and amused smile met hers.

Three days later Thea found herself in the Harrington's carriage, traversing the drive into Denbury – Martha's estate. After seeing Ella's enthusiasm at Milford, Martha had invited Ella to visit her own living collection and Ella couldn't accept fast enough. The house at Denbury was all archways, steep, pitched roofs and chimneys, the large leaded windows stark against the yellow-grey stone. The drive to the house showed off the gardens to their fullest, the central canal aligned on a large and impressive greenhouse which Lord Foxmore had built for his wife.

Ella bit her lip. 'Lady Foxmore lives here alone?'

'Yes, since Lord Foxmore died. He doted on her and built everything she could possibly desire, but sadly it was he who she could not keep.' Thea had not been above ten at the time, but she knew the death had hit Martha hard.

Ella's brow furrowed in sympathy. 'It is beautiful, but I have no wonder she spends so much time with you all at Milford. It must be extremely lonely.' Thea had often thought so herself.

'She is busy with her experiments, but yes, I think it must.'

Ella fiddled with her own fingers as she stared at the imposing landscape. 'I have to admit that I still find her a little intimidating.'

'So do most people,' said Thea with a grin.

They drew up through the gates and were welcomed by Mr Fletcher, the butler, who showed them into the grand hall – wood clad, dark and austere. Only plants on the windowsills softened the look. Thea had always found Fletcher a little sullen and Ella didn't look any less unsettled as she looked around them. Thea squeezed her elbow for reassurance. 'She spends most of her time in the garden.'

As if to prove it, Martha strode through the archway which led to the grounds, her footsteps echoing around the high, wainscoted space. The apron she wore over her dress swung at each bold stride and revealed her sturdy, long boots beneath. The healing scar below her eye gave her a slightly rakish air and she cut quite a figure with a leather belt slung over her apron like a sash and snippers and a saw hung at her side in a sheath. Thea gulped at her reaction and quickly averted her eyes – that feeling she had buried was the last complication she needed today.

Martha flashed them a smile as she wiped her hands on a muslin at her waist and flicked open her pocket watch. 'Ladies, apologies for my lateness and for not welcoming you myself.' She waved a hand in the direction of the outdoors. 'Observations in progress. Shall we go straight to the stove?' They followed dutifully behind, through the dusty great hall lined with tapestries, weapons and armour of the Foxmore line, and out into the striking contrast of verdant green springtime. There was barely chance to enjoy it as they trotted along, trying to keep pace.

After crossing the lawns they entered the relative seclusion of Martha's walled garden, its well-ordered beds sown in neat lines, ready to burst forth for the growing season ahead. Ella stopped dead. Thea sometimes forgot how impressive it was. A huge stove stood immediately ahead taking up almost the full length of the west-facing wall. The glass was clear and sharp, reflecting the mid-morning sun whilst betraying the lush greenery within.

'It's quite something isn't it?' whispered Thea. 'Father is quite jealous, although he would never say, but he has Scip, and Martha is jealous of him.' Ella smiled, but Martha had almost reached the stove and they hurried to catch up.

Thea was the last to step into the jungle and close the doors behind her. The heat enveloped them like a velvet shawl and she drew in a lungful of humid air which smelled musky and lush. Martha put out bowls of water on her tan beds and stove pipes as well as damping the floor five times a day, which made the atmosphere more humid than in the stove at Milford. Ella gasped and stared around her at the greenery that thrust up from the floor, emerged from raised planters and trailed from every vertical surface.

Martha watched her with eager eyes and a smile. 'Welcome to the new world, Lady Eleanor. How do you like it?' Her voice dripped smoothly from her, like the *Tillandsia* air plants from the shelves. This was Martha's domain and in it, she was even more formidable.

Ella looked like she couldn't speak for a moment while she stared at the tangle of plants in front of her. 'I – I like it exceedingly well, Lady Foxmore.' She took another gulp of thick air. 'Where do they all come from?'

'There are plants here from every corner of the globe, and there will be more – the world is still offering its treasures. Even then, so many plants cannot be brought to Britain alive as they will not survive the journey. I would dearly love to study them in their native habitat, but sadly most of us cannot travel ourselves and so we cultivate them here.' Thea knew that to see the plants in the wild would be Martha's greatest wish, and yet such opportunities for women were almost non-existent.

Ella looked surprised. 'And then you make them grow into this?' she asked.

Martha smiled generously. 'Well, we figure out what they want and need, and they create this spectacle themselves. The hardest job is to figure out their requirements. Scip is excellent at it, and my gardener McCarthy is learning from him. It takes skill. These plants are often ripped from their native lands with little care and if they come from traders rather than botanists there can be no information on provenance or growing situation at all.'

Ella's voice was small. The enormity of the plant kingdom sometimes did that to people, once they realised, Thea thought. 'It is like being in another world.'

Martha gazed around her own space. 'There are plants here, and plants as yet unknown which could make a new future for mankind; they could cure common diseases, provide timber, or new foods and drinks, they will make people rich, and populate the gardens of the wealthy for them to enjoy, and to enjoy showing off to their friends. People cannot live without plants, Lady Eleanor. By studying them, we can, in our own little way, change the world.' A familiar thrill ran through Thea. Martha's passion for the natural world never failed to excite her, no matter how many times she heard it.

Ella, for her part, looked completely in awe. 'Thea told me you are doing an experiment. Will that change the world?' Thea smiled to see her eyes wide, hanging on Martha's every word.

Martha's lips twitched. 'I wish it were that simple, Lady Eleanor, but I suppose the answer is *perhaps*, if I can get the results to the right places. We are shining new light on the truth of the world one tiny piece at a time. The more lights we shine, the more we come to understand the whole.' As she spoke, Martha gently ran a thumb over the broad leaf of a taro plant. 'We must shatter the glass of magic through which our ancestors saw the world, and build our understanding anew based on firm foundations of experience, knowledge and reason.'

Ella's voice was as small as Thea felt. 'How do you know where to start?'

Martha gestured at her plants. 'This is based on exactly the same principles as the cabinet at Milford. Francis Bacon told us that true knowledge is only possible through a methodical observation of nature, and John Locke that the human mind is a blank sheet which gains knowledge through experience and observation of the world.' She took a notebook out of her apron pocket and flicked back through the pages, revealing sketch after sketch of leaves, stems and buds. 'As we make the observations, the observations make us, Lady Eleanor. Thea is pursuing that through natural history, and I attempt to do so through plants.' She placed a proud and tender hand between Thea's shoulders to emphasise her point and Thea swelled with emotion. She suddenly felt very small under the weight of Martha's ambition. Put like this, it made her efforts pale in comparison.

Ella, for her part, couldn't take her eyes off the notebook. 'There are so many drawings.'

'We are studying plants that move in response to different stimulus,' said Martha. 'In order to understand why they move we must first observe. I methodically record the movements in this book, which means that the results can be compared to and replicated by others.'

Ella's countenance was still full of awe, but she also gained a sharp, thoughtful look. 'What if a plant dies?'

'An excellent question, Lady Eleanor.' Martha smiled and Thea saw Ella relax a little. 'The plants are pressed and mounted in large books called a *hortus siccus* – that means dry garden in Latin. Or they are painted. Then they can be classified and catalogued as can any other dry collection.'

Ella's curiosity seemed satisfied and Thea finally recovered enough to find her voice. 'Lady Foxmore is an excellent artist and paints many of the plants herself – in a different way to most. She splits out all the defining characteristics of the plant and ensures they are represented through the seasons, along with any insects or caterpillars which live upon them. It is remarkable and she will make the experiment a success.'

She looked proudly at Martha who coloured a little, despite herself and gave her an almost-stern glare. 'You must not do your father a disservice, Thea, he and Scip are central to the work.'

Thea saw Ella shrink a little as Martha turned to her. 'Would you like to see, Lady Eleanor?' She set off through the beds, Ella following and Thea bringing up the rear. Suddenly Thea almost crashed into Ella as she came to a sudden halt.

'Are they,' Ella paused, 'Straplutias?'

Thea followed her gaze to a shelf at the back of the stove where numerous, healthy plants showed off an almost embarrassing array of dusky pink flowers. '*Stapelias*,' she whispered to Ella through a smile, pleased she had remembered the one, single flower on her father's plant of which he was so proud.

'*Stapelias*, yes,' said Ella as Martha turned back to see what was the delay.

'Oh yes, they are, well done, Lady Eleanor.'

Ella looked pleased. 'But look at all the flowers.'

'Indeed, can't stop them,' said Martha as she turned and resumed striding down the narrow path, 'they've been going at it for months.'

Thea and Ella shared an amused glance. 'Don't tell my father,' whispered Thea.

They followed further into the stove to a clear area between the raised beds where an unassuming plant stood in a large pot. It was about the same height as Thea with dark green, oval leaves. Some were large, but at the base of each one were two other, much smaller leaves. 'I said the experiment was about plants that move,' went on Martha, circling the plant and stroking a leaf gently between thumb and forefinger. 'This is *Hedysarum,* or the telegraph plant, so named as its leaves move like a telegraph given from a distance. Watch closely.' As Thea and Ella watched, the small leaves shifted almost imperceptibly.

'Why?' asked Ella, pursing her lips.

'That, Lady Eleanor, is what we are trying to find out,' said Martha with relish. 'I have been tracking the leaves over some weeks with sketches and timings and I am still unsure. Last summer Thea and I tried to record it over a full twenty-four hours but we fell asleep and had to start all over again.' Thea smiled, remembering Martha waking up from her shoulder with a start and horribly frustrated.

Ella laughed at the thought. 'The movement is so delicate – your recordings must have to be very detailed.'

'They do,' Martha agreed, 'with sketches every thirty minutes on particular days and it is now the half hour and I must complete the next recording. Thea, would you please show Lady Eleanor the *Dionea*?'

Thea led Ella further into the stove as Martha took out her notebook by the telegraph plant. They proceeded down two bays of beds past arrays of plants in beds and climbing up the frame of the house.

Eventually they came upon some tiny plants in pots, which looked like open, toothy mouths on short, red-green stems. Ella screwed up her nose. 'They look like tiny versions of your shark jaw.'

Thea laughed. 'You are closer than you think – look here.' She picked up a small stick and lightly touched inside the jaws of one of the open mouths. It closed around the stick, holding it tight. Although plants weren't her area of expertise, she had picked up enough from Martha and her family over the years.

Ella goggled. 'Wow! Why does it do that?'

Thea's skin tingled a little. The joy of imparting such wonders of the world to those new to the sphere was something she never tired of. 'It eats flies.'

Ella stood back and eyed her suspiciously, one brow raised. 'It does not – plants don't eat.'

Thea gestured to the other plants around them, with long tubes and pitchers. 'All of these ones do – they capture flies or other insects, and then, it seems, digest them.'

Ella screwed up her face again but peered towards the tiny plants, no doubt noting the few pairs of jaws which grasped winged insects in various states of decay. One recent victim buzzed feebly. She took a breath to speak, but then let it out and simply looked at Thea with an intense stare. 'How?'

Thea shrugged. 'That's what Martha and the others are trying to find out. Here – you have a go.' She passed the stick to Ella, who tentatively approached a fly trap. Thea giggled. 'Don't worry, it won't eat *you*.'

Ella gently poked the stick into one of the pairs of jaws. Nothing happened. She cast a glance over her shoulder. 'Am I not a good fly?'

'Here, let me help.' Thea moved behind Ella, reaching around her and taking a yielding hand in her own to assist in the direction of the stick. Immediately she realised her mistake as her quickening pulse informed her of their proximity. What had seemed like a natural gesture suddenly felt inadvisable and far too intimate, but it was too late to back out now. Ella's body didn't flinch. Thea sucked in a quiet breath and convinced herself this was entirely normal and that Ella would absolutely not be able to feel her heart beating through her stays. Unsteadily, she manoeuvred their hands to one of the open mouths and gently brushed the stick inside the fragile leaves. The jaws closed and the stick was held tight once again.

As she relinquished the stick to the jaws Ella let out a small 'Oh' and gently, almost imperceptibly, pressed backwards until their bodies touched. It could have been surprise at the plant's rapid movement, Thea told herself. They stood looking at the trap for what felt like an age. Thea stared round Ella at the buzzing fly, struggling helplessly against the jaws of the plant which seemed so passively unrelenting. Her head fogged with a mixture of exhilaration and panic as her mind and body vied over whether she should let go. All her senses seemed heightened, she could smell the scent of jasmine and orange blossom rising from Ella's warm skin, and the sounds of the rapid clicking of McCarthy bringing water from the well set her on edge. She was wound so tight that her whole body jumped when she heard Martha's footsteps approach.

'Sorry about that. Have you been successfully captured, Lady Eleanor?'

The girls sprung apart and Thea saw Martha round the corner with a purposeful stride, slipping the notebook into her apron pocket. 'Um...' said Ella, her eyes newly focussed on the advancing figure. 'Yes, but...' She looked at Thea, seemingly finding it difficult to meet her eyes. 'How does that happen?'

'Nobody knows,' said Martha, with a small smile, 'there are still many things we can't explain, Lady Eleanor, but all will become clear, in time.'

Before long Ella and Thea found themselves back in the carriage. They had barely said a word to each other since the stove house. Thea was mostly embarrassed, by now she probably had to admit that she had an inappropriate crush on Lady Eleanor. It was inconvenient, but not terrible, she thought. If she was honest with herself, this wasn't the first time she had developed an inappropriate attachment. Everyone had them, after all? Look at Tabitha and Kitty. She had never credited that with being more than a slightly obsessive friendship, an emotional support and preparation for marriage as polite society deemed appropriate. But if this was how it made Tabitha feel perhaps she should be kinder to her on the subject. She didn't allow herself to think of Harriet.

That lean into her. The feel of Ella's warmth and delicate form against her, just for that second. The thought made her eyes involuntarily close with both embarrassment and exhilaration. If Thea was a blank sheet of paper, Ella was certainly scribbling all over her. That spark in her chest glowed, raw, menacing and threatening to ignite. Despite her fear, something about Ella made her curious to breathe on the budding flame.

But Ella was friendly with everyone. She was engaging and interested and the risks of overstepping the mark were great. Their friendship was no different to any other and if she carried on like she had today she would lose it entirely. Thea determined that she would not slip again.

Ella gazed out of the window peering up at the trees by the road as they passed. 'Oh, horse chestnuts, my favourite!' It followed after such a long period of rumination that it took Thea by surprise. 'I love collecting oblionkers in the autumn.'

'Oblionkers?' blinked Thea. 'What are they?'

'You know, that come from horse chestnuts. They're brown and you can put them on a string...' Ella's gaze, now directed inside the carriage, seemed a little less carefree.

'Oh!' exclaimed Thea, as brightly as she could manage, 'you mean conkers?'

She laughed, and Ella looked a little stung. 'Sorry, my family have always called them oblionkers – are they really conkers?'

Thea suddenly realised her forced enthusiasm may have sounded mocking and she softened her voice. 'I don't think there's anything *really* about it. Only different names.'

Ella nodded, but fiddled with her hands and stared at her feet. 'Thea, I wanted to thank you for being a friend to me over these past few weeks. I know that my brother probably asked you but there would be nothing more disagreeable to me than being in your way. You and your sister and Lady Foxmore have been so kind, but I hadn't realised how busy you are with your endeavours nor how accomplished. I am sure you have better things to do with your time than teach a simpleton about the basics.'

Thea watched as self-doubt seemed to seep through Ella, and she understood what Sam had meant. 'Is that what you really think?' She leaned towards Ella and kept her voice gentle. 'It is a pleasure to have you around, Ella.'

'But I don't want to be here because you feel obligated. Because my brother asked–'

Ella looked so downcast that Thea reached out and took up her hands, this time thinking only of providing comfort. 'Ella, your brother did ask me to be a friend to you, he is very kind and cares for you a great deal.' She took a breath. 'But that isn't why I like to spend time with you – I do it because I want to. Because I enjoy it.'

Ella managed a half smile. 'Only if you are sure. I would hate for you to have to entertain me if you would rather not.'

Confusion flitted through Thea's mind, closely followed by concern. Was Ella trying to find excuses to stay away? Suddenly, she worried that she had noticed Thea's diversion in the stove and found her abhorrent. 'If it is my company that is worrying you, and you would rather not meet so much, you only have to say.' She ignored the cold sweat and bit back the searing disappointment as she spoke.

But Ella grasped at Thea's hands. 'Oh, Thea, I love your company, please do not think that.' Tears threatened at her eyes and Thea was lost in a curious mixture of anguish and exhilaration. 'You have made me consider what else life could be, you have made me – curious.' Ella's striking eyes searched her new friend's face which was unfortunate, because Thea could feel the colour flooding into it. What on earth did Ella mean by that? Probably nothing, she decided.

Thea forced a smile against her conflicting emotions, desperate to reassure Ella without raising questions she could not yet answer. 'Then, Lady Eleanor, I insist that we spend more time together,' she ventured. 'I realise we have not known each other long, but you must know how much I appreciate your friendship. We just seem to – get along, don't you think?'

She looked down at her feet. Suddenly she felt unsteady and it wasn't the carriage's motion. Why had she had to ask a question? But in no time the welcome words slid into her ears. 'Yes, I do.'

Ella still held her hands tight. Thea looked back up into the blue and green eyes, moist and filled with worry. So much for her resolution, the next sentence was already on its way out. 'Ella, you should know that I value the time we spend together–' she faltered. *So much*, said her heart. *Too much*, said her head. '–Very much,' she settled on, out loud.

Against the tumultuous mass of her emotion it sounded utterly vapid but Ella seemed satisfied. She smiled and squeezed Thea's hands. 'As do I.' For a second their eyes held and Thea felt like her heart stopped, then Ella smiled. 'Who would have thought I would become so entranced by a puffer fish!'

CHAPTER 7

Ella's education continued the next week in the form of a visit to the cabinet of Stanhope Grimston. Mr Grimston had decided upon impressing the Earl and Countess of Swanham and had invited a party to his house at Wickmarsh for afternoon tea. 'Tea, because he is too tight to offer everyone dinner,' whispered Edgar Pickles as he and Thea squeezed through the door. 'You and I wouldn't be here if he thought he could get away with only inviting the Swanhams.' They filed through the vestibule and into the cabinet with the Morells, Martha, the whole Harrington family and the Jefferys.

The room was dark and wood panelled. Small, high windows peppered the north wall but captured none of the mid-day sun. A coat of arms loomed ahead of them as they emerged into the dusty gloom; the musty smell of old fur and feathers, tinged with something more chemical hit them immediately. Rows of stuffed birds lined the walls, perched on uniform shelves which spread from floor to ceiling. As Thea scanned the cabinet she also took in eggs, fancy shells, jars containing unidentifiable pickled objects, a random selection of animals and their component parts, medals and intaglios, rocks and fossils, an assortment of weapons, clothing and jewellery, items from the new world, statues, decorative porcelain, paintings, glassware and silver. The variety had grown since her last visit she was sure.

She turned to judge Ella's reaction, smiling at the briefest wrinkling of her nose and flash of alarm in her eyes before polite approval was restored. 'Quite something isn't it,' Thea mumbled through her teeth, and Ella shot her a wary smile. This was the first time they had met since the day with Martha at Denbury. Thea was both desperate to speak to Ella and terrified of doing so. Her lengthy musings over the past week had brought her no further to a conclusion in her mind but seeing Ella at Wickmarsh confirmed her insides hadn't changed their enthusiastic opinion on the situation.

The party spread out around the room, politely peering at the curiosities on display. Mr Grimston fawned over Lord and Lady Swanham, pointing out his largest and most spectacular items and ensuring the scale of his investment was well understood. Martha, Ursula, Mrs Morell, Tabitha and the Jeffereys milled around, peering at the dusty displays.

Samuel Harrington beckoned Thea over to a shelf at the opposite side of the room. He was inspecting what used to be a sandpiper, inexpertly stuffed and mounted on a board with some dried grass, sand, and a messy nest with an egg in it. 'Look at this one's eyes,' he whispered, turning towards the shelf so Mr Grimston couldn't hear, 'they're pointing in different directions and look like they're about to explode out of its head.'

'I'm not surprised,' said Thea, eyeing it with amusement. 'That egg must be from a bird four times its size – your eyes would be doing the same.' They both hid their giggles in the shelving until Thea remembered herself. 'Not that I would suggest you set much authority on my opinion, Sam,' she said, 'I am sure Mr Grimston knows what he is doing.'

'And I am quite sure he does not,' said Sam, brushing a small cobweb from the bird. 'You have no need to pretend with me, Thea. I can assure you my sister has informed me of your extensive knowledge and about the collection at Milford. In fact, she hasn't shut up about it this past week.'

Thea stifled a smile as she looked over at Ella. 'It doesn't bother you?'

'Indeed, it does not,' he said, now brushing the dust from the shelf with a cautious hand, 'in fact, it has long been my opinion that women's minds are quite as good, if not better than men's, and I heartily approve of scholarship for all.' He rested his arm on the now clean shelf and looked at her intently.

'Well that is good to know,' said Thea, thinking what a pleasant man he was and mentally building a picture of the collection she may be permitted to build as his wife. 'Now, have you seen how the sandpiper's beak is perfectly created for pushing into the sand and probing for food?'

Before Sam could respond their host's booming voice carried across the room as he moved his favourites on to a new section. 'And here you can see my conchology collection.' Ella cast a glance across the room to Thea in panic. Thea mouthed '*shells*' to her, as Mr Grimston's back was turned. He went on, a pudgy hand resting on his round belly and flicking a finger at each of the items he noted in turn. 'I receive all my shells from the very agent who supplies the cabinet of the King himself. There are sometimes specimens which nature has not made perfect and so I improve those with paint, to make them more agreeable to the prestigious nature of my cabinet. Here you can also see some of my other handiwork.' He indicated a section where shells had been glued together to make little faces. 'And of course, the masks and spears.' Mr Grimston pointed to a cabinet packed with artefacts of wood, leather and hair, and painted in all colours. 'Taken from a tribe in South America, came through the Portuguese of course, but I have a man who knows. I understand the tribe were handy for trading at first but had to be destroyed when they became too demanding. Still, I am certain my man will find another.' Mr Grimston shot Lord Swanham a laboured wink and Thea's insides turned, but she kept quiet, mindful of the company. After polite questions from Lady Swanham Mr Grimston moved the party on and reached Lord Stockwood and Thea by the bird collection. He ensured that Sam had a space in his selected circle and placed his back to Thea, sandwiching her uncomfortably between his bulk and the shelf so she had to extricate herself sideways.

'Now for something particularly special, my lord.' He even managed to simper pompously towards Lord Swanham, thought Thea. 'My bird collection, I am told, is one of the finest in the country – if not *the* finest! The Royal Society repeatedly press me to sell it to them for their Repository, but I say to them, "Gentlemen, you may either have me for President, or you may have my birds," and that soon ends the enquiries.' He guffawed loudly, his eyes interrogating the group's appreciation. Lord and Lady Swanham tittered politely.

'They are, indeed, quite something Mr Grimston,' ventured Lord Swanham, seemingly aware that he was yet to speak. 'How are they… created?'

'An excellent and worthy question, my lord.' Mr Grimston dipped his head slightly and ushered Lord Swanham closer to the shelves. 'The birds are despatched when they are in their prime, and then the skins scraped, mounted on wire and stuffed with straw. I used to have a man to do it but we lost him in a routine fumigation a few years back. Since then I have taken on the job as I could find nobody expert enough, and flatter myself that I am rather good at it.' Thea followed Ella's gaze to where a wonky parrot bulged threateningly. Lord Swanham managed an appreciative, 'mhmm.'

It was Ursula's voice that broke the silence that followed, from across the room where she was being helped around by Martha. 'How do you remember what everything is, Mr Grimston?' She peered along one of the shelves containing dusty animal limbs. 'Nothing is labelled.' She held up a carved piece of ivory to support her point. 'And having your books in another room must be highly inconvenient.'

Mr Grimston's face turned immediately to thunder. He sputtered and then drew himself up to his full, if not impressive, height. 'When you are a proper collector, Miss Ursula, you do not need labels or books, you can simply *remember*.' He placed a rolling emphasis on the last word. 'You will perhaps find it difficult to understand, Miss

Ursula,' he went on, calming his demeanour as he glanced at Lord and Lady Swanham, 'what with you being of the female persuasion. It is good for you to see better examples than the cabinet at Milford. Here you will find items of wonder in which we may marvel at the unique and discreet design of the creator.'

Ursula drew in a breath to counter, but Mr Grimston was quicker. 'Anyway, gentlemen and ladies, I believe it is time for the *pièce de resistance.'* He stepped to the side and gestured to a thin pole which looked like twisted rope but was rigid and tapered at the end to a point. It was almost as tall as Mr Grimston himself and was mounted on the wall by a metal bracket. He puffed out his chest proudly and rested both hands on his stomach. 'Now, can anyone guess what it is?'

An awkward hush ensued as everyone realised that he was actually expecting them to contribute. Thea shared a smile with Ursula and Martha as she edged next to them. The three of them were very aware of the identity of the object thanks to their museum visits but they wouldn't spoil the fun for the others.

'Is it some sort of finial from atop a large tower?' It was Christiana Jefferys, who always enjoyed having an opinion.

'Nope!' asserted Mr Grimston, acknowledging the effort with a small raise of a finger.

'How about a decorative lance from the Tudor period?' That was Sam, gleefully catching his sister's eye.

'A good guess, but you are not correct, Lord Stockwood.' The awkward silence stretched out as Mr Grimston's priggish smirk met each of them in turn.

'I bet my sister has an opinion.' Thea's heart jolted at the sound of Tabitha's voice, loud from across the circle. Something in her eyes challenged Thea who vowed to interrogate her later, but for now, her mind searched for a response appropriate for the company.

'I am afraid I have no opinion worth offering,' she stated carefully, warning Tabitha with her eyes. The thought of being ridiculed, dismissed or devalued kept her silent, but then gentler tones came from the right.

'I find that difficult to believe, Miss Morell.' It was Ella, and Thea was drawn to her sparkling eyes. 'I should very much like to hear your opinion. Knowledge should be shared, after all.'

All eyes were now on Thea as she stared at Ella who gave the smallest of smiles and gestured hopefully in the direction of the object. Buoyed by Ella's encouragement and Sam's acceptance she felt suddenly bold. If a potential suitor could accept that she was learned, then why should she not show it in public? She forced herself to turn and focus on their host despite the turmoil in her stomach. 'It is a narwhal tusk, Mr Grimston.' She knew he wouldn't be happy that the joy of imparting the knowledge had been taken from him by a woman, so she accompanied it with what she hoped was a modest and slightly apologetic smile. A muffled expression of surprise scurried around the room.

Mr Grimston's eyebrows drew together until they almost touched. Coupled with the way his face reddened and the buttons on his waistcoat bulged, the effect was rather startling. 'What nonsense,' he finally sputtered, bits of flying spittle testament to his vehemence. He glanced up at Lady Swanham and composed himself a little. 'Of course we couldn't expect you to present an informed opinion, Miss Morell. It was unkind of me to allow you to contribute.' His penetrating stare was full of venom. Despite herself, Thea retreated a little until Martha placed a reassuring hand on her back.

As quickly as it arrived the anger was gone and Mr Grimston once again became a showman for his guests. 'As nobody has correctly guessed, I will tell you myself. This, ladies and gentlemen, is one of the only examples in this country of' – he swept a glance around the room as he paused for effect – 'the horn of a unicorn.'

There was silence for a few long seconds as he stood with his arm outstretched towards the elevated item, guiding their silent gazes towards it. A horse whinnied in the distance. Lady Swanham, exquisitely practiced, was the first to recover. 'The horn of an actual unicorn, Mr

Grimston? Goodness.' Her face was perfectly serene and Thea was utterly impressed.

'Indeed, my lady.' Mr Grimston retracted his hand and almost bowed. 'My agent has contacts in the furthest reaches of the globe and selected this for me as he knew there were few collections in which it could find its equal. As he values propriety over profit and understood that such an exclusive item would be at odds in lesser cabinets, he sold it to me for the greatly reduced price of one hundred pounds.' Martha's fingers squeezed into the small of Thea's back as they shared a brief but knowing glance.

Ella, who had barely taken her eyes off Thea, was the next to speak. 'How on earth did it fit on the head of a unicorn, Mr Grimston? It is very long.'

'That it is, Lady Eleanor, longer than even I was expecting.' He held up a finger and waggled it from side to side as if she had hit on a pertinent question. 'It apparently came from a mature unicorn, and as every natural historian knows, the horns continue to grow throughout their life.' He nodded, assuredly.

Even the Swanhams now seemed to have run out of questions. Across the circle Thea could see tears of repressed mirth threatening in Edgar's eyes as he coughed to express a little of the tension. Ursula pressed her lips together and Mr Morell suddenly found his feet extremely interesting. Thea's attention was once more taken by Tabitha, who stepped into the circle beside Mr Grimston and fixed him with a sombre stare.

'Do you think it might have magical powers, Mr Grimston? They do say that about unicorns.' She gazed up reverently at the tusk. 'It is marvellous.'

Mr Grimston gave a small exhalation of surprise and looked suddenly unsure. 'Now, Miss Tabitha, nobody could be certain of that. Yes, it is marvellous and the unicorn as a beast is assuredly magical, however, we cannot be positive about its component–'

'Can I touch it?' Tabitha interrupted, the earnest stare directed abruptly back towards Mr Grimston.

'Well, I suppose... I suppose it can't hurt if you really must,' he stuttered. They all watched as Tabitha extended a single, reverent finger towards the tusk. Thea felt Martha's fingers twitch on her back, Edgar looked at the ceiling, fighting to keep his glee internal and her father shot her a brief look of resignation. Mr Grimston's face was trained intensely on Tabitha and the finger almost at its target, the look on his face alert, as if he half hoped for fireworks on contact. As the digit advanced Tabitha closed her eyes expectantly as it met the firm resistance of the cold surface.

'Tea is served, sir.' The butler's booming announcement came from the doorway.

'Look at that, it *is* magic!' announced Lady Swanham smoothly, gently pressing her hands together with an amused smile on her face. 'Shall we, Mr Grimston?' She extended her arm towards him and deftly manoeuvred him out of the room, sharing a perfectly serene glance with Thea on the way.

As Thea traipsed down the passageway towards tea she felt a hand on her arm. It pulled her sideways into an alcove and she ended up following Ella through a doorway into what turned out to be a tiny, dusty library. Ella shut the door behind them and collapsed in laughter against it. 'Oh, Thea,' she wheezed grasping Thea's hands in her own, 'you were wonderful.'

'I was?' asked Thea, not sure about that, but taken up in Ella's jollity regardless.

'Oh, you were,' gasped Ella, 'even I can tell he's talking bunkum. I couldn't go straight to tea or I should have burst out laughing right there.'

Thea smiled. 'Well I suppose everyone knows now.' She was beginning to regret being reckless with her knowledge and couldn't even think about facing her mother.

'And why shouldn't they?' Ella's laughter abated and she looked into Thea's eyes. 'Surely if you show your knowledge society will have to see how brilliant you are? I certainly do.' She squeezed Thea's hands between her own and Thea gulped. Their eyes held for too long and just like in Martha's stove Thea knew she should move away, but she couldn't. Actually, she didn't want to. Their breath mingled as their mirth began to give way to something else.

'Honestly, as if a girl would know.' Thea jumped back and their contact broke as Mrs Jefferys' monotone filtered in from outside the door. 'She's been getting above herself for a long time, that one, and there have been rumours.'

'What kind of rumours?' Thea flicked Ella a wary glance. The other voice was Lady Swanham.

'You can always tell, you know. There's always been something different about her, she's never been able to *settle*.' Mrs Jefferys inflected the last word, as if they were both aware of what it meant. Thea's heart hammered in her chest, she didn't dare move in case they were heard, but Ella was so close in between her and the voices. Neither of them looked at one another.

'I'm not sure what you mean?' asked Lady Swanham, dispassionately. But Mrs Jefferys wasn't put off.

'Her mother always hoped it was just a phase,' said the voice filled with distaste, 'but I think she will now have to intervene.' The voice lowered as if she were sharing a confidence. 'It isn't easy, of course, when it is one's eldest who exhibits unnatural tendencies. And despite everything that has been done for her.'

'What is it about Miss Morell, that is unnatural?' Lady Swanham's voice asked, clearly losing patience with Mrs Jefferys' blithesome gossip. Thea closed her eyes, she couldn't bear to look at Ella – to see the trust drain from her eyes and be replaced by disgust.

'It's the learning,' said Mrs Jefferys' voice, knowingly. 'They say she only takes her nose out of a book to visit that cabinet of theirs and all those artefacts are not the domain of her father, they are really for *her*. You could see the jealousy in her eyes in Mr Grimston's museum room and she practically confirmed it herself. They say she is quite frantic in her mania for knowledge. It isn't right.' Thea's mouth was open now, and she forced her eyes to do the same, glancing at Ella where she saw some of the same relief she felt.

'I really am not sure that I see knowledge or any interest in scholarship as such a dreadful thing for a lady,' said Lady Swanham's voice, and Thea's spirits lifted once more. 'Don't you dislike boring women, Mrs Jefferys? I do, I find it makes them vindictive.' Thea could almost hear Mrs Jefferys falter and allowed herself a moment's pleasure.

'But women's minds aren't built for it, you see.' Mrs Jefferys was not easily put off. 'They are not as robust as those of men and interfering in a man's world.' There was the unpleasant sound of teeth being sucked. 'It makes them unnatural in other ways, so I hear.' A protracted silence as Thea's eyes widened a little. 'Romantically.' Mrs Jefferys dared to clarify. The voice lowered further, suggesting that the woman was leaning in. 'I am not sure if you are aware, but she was good *friends* with Harriet Nichol, and we know how monstrously she turned out.' All the moisture disappeared from Thea's mouth.

'I see,' said Lady Swanham, not sounding like she saw at all, 'then I am sure we will all keep an eye on Miss Morell and steer her down the right path if the knowledge seems to be getting to her. Now, I am parched, aren't you?'

The sound of two pairs of footsteps receded into the distance as Thea fought to control her breathing. Had Mrs Jeffery's just insinuated that her scholarship was causing a romantic attraction to girls? How could she even look at Ella? She scrabbled for the doorknob, her chest pounding and her throat becoming thicker by the second. A hand grasped her wrist.

'Thea, it's just prejudice,' said Ella's voice, but it barely registered. 'My mother won't believe a word of it.' This time Thea found the doorknob but then felt Ella's hands on her face, compelling her to look. Finally, with hot, red cheeks and her lungs snatching at air her eyes met Ella's. They were so close, in the tiny room. Ella's breath mingled with hers and her eyes held only concern. Those captivating eyes in blue and green wrenched her back immediately to the lecture hall, to Meg's languid eyebrow drawing her in. 'She's wrong,' she heard again, muffled against the thudding in her ears, but as she imagined the sting of that kiss and the spark that still burned inside her chest, all she could think was, *what if she was right?*

The conversation washed over Thea as she stood in a small circle with Edgar and Mr Grimston. She had eventually pulled herself together enough to pretend to laugh off the overheard conversation with Ella, still, she was glad Ella seemed to be taken up with Ursula and Christiana Jefferys and she could begin to gather her thoughts.

'So, Pickles.' Thea tried to focus on what Mr Grimston was saying. 'What do you think, eh?' He poked Edgar in the shoulder with a haughty finger. 'Pretty impressive, even for someone only interested in explosions, I think?'

'The unicorn horn?' Edgar attempted to look unfazed. 'Indeed, Grimston, it fits seamlessly into your inimitable style of collection. What do you intend to do with it? Aside from making Miss Tabitha's dreams come true?'

Mr Grimston lifted an unimpressed, but hirsute eyebrow. 'I will present it at the Royal Society of course, it is my duty to share such a piece with the other learned minds of our country.' He waved his teacup in an exaggerated manner as he spoke.

If Thea had been in a better state of mind she would have chuckled at Mr Grimston's ego and chided Edgar for not trying to dissuade him, but in her fuzzy-minded state she just stared at them and swayed slightly on the spot. 'Quite right, my man,' she heard Edgar saying, 'get it out there for everyone to see, that President's medal will be yours before you can say "mythical beast". What do you think, Thea?' He jogged her with an elbow, evidently noticing she wasn't quite with them.

'Absolutely,' she said, absentmindedly. One thing polite society did prepare you for was engaging with conversations when you were only half concentrating. 'I'm sure they'd be fascinated, Mr Grimston.'

Mrs Morell barrelled into their group, tea and cake in hand. She scowled at Thea to let her know there would be recriminations later, but then simpered at their host. 'A top afternoon, Mr Grimston,' she announced, crumbs liberally provided to prove her point. 'The cake is divine, and you choose your company well.'

He inclined his head towards her. 'You know I have no truck with tradespeople mingling too much. I hear that the Ashbys are invited to the ball with the Earl and Countess! I mean I would be the last to criticise their choice, but a physician and his family! Who will stand up with the children?' He made a play of looking sympathetic. 'It would be kinder to them if they stayed at home.'

'Quite, quite,' agreed Mrs Morell as Thea finally locked eyes with Edgar. She took another bite of cake. 'I say, did you see *Tête-a-Tête* this week? An excellent sensation if I do say so myself.' One of her greatest joys in life was gossiping with Stanhope Grimston. The *Town and Country* magazine ran a weekly column on the story of the day, implicating some poor noble, celebrity or member of a prominent family. The column never mentioned names, providing only descriptions and portrait miniatures of the perpetrators of the scandal alongside dialogue speaking of intrigue and forbidden amours. Between the two of them, Mr Grimston and Mrs Morell could spend hours picking apart the riddles and matching the portraits to people they recognised.

'I did!' Mr Grimston cackled. 'What a ruse!'

Mrs Morell waved her cake about in mirth. 'To organise a dinner party for the wife, and then slip out of the back dressed as a sailor to run off with a merchant girl. The poor woman must have been distraught!' Mrs Morell's glee didn't suggest much sympathy for the wife and Mr Grimston looked delighted at the story. Before they could say another word he had whisked Mrs Morell off to the corner of the room to analyse the piece in more detail.

At their departure, Edgar and Thea joined Mr Morell and Martha. Martha raised an eyebrow as they approached. 'I don't suppose that horn is anything to do with you is it, Mr Pickles? I know how you like to toy with him.'

Edgar chuckled at the thought but held up his hands in surrender. 'Alas I can claim no credit for this particular deception. Aside from a lack of emendation of his understanding of course, of which I observe we are all guilty.' He peered at each of them in turn drawing guilty smiles. 'Anyway,' Edgar went on, 'he will soon find out his error. His precious Royal Society will tell him very plainly, I have no doubt. They are touchy about such tall tales as they are so keen to be taken seriously. I do wonder that they bother with him at all.'

'He doesn't plan to take it to the society?' Martha was aghast. 'We must stop him!'

'And why must we, my dear? The man needs very little encouragement to disgrace himself, and no assistance at all.'

Martha put her hands on her hips. 'You are his oldest friend, Edgar. What about his position for the presidency?'

Edgar softened and placed a hand on Martha's arm. 'You know as well as I do that the story is as sound as the unicorn, Martha. It is kinder to leave him to his own decisions. Or, at least if not kinder, more amusing.' The cheeky glint in his eye returned.

Martha looked exasperated and checked her pocket watch. 'Well if you won't tell him, I suppose I will have to.' She stalked off towards Mr Grimston and Mrs Morell who now had *Town and Country* open on the card table and were openly discussing their theories on the latest intrigue. Even Thea managed to muster enough interest to look on as Martha inserted herself between the two gossips and watched as Mr Grimston progressed through shades of pink and red as she spoke. By the time she had finished he was a concerning purple. There was a lot of bluster and his arms waved around in the air. They all watched him go as he took Mrs Morell's arm, snatched up the paper and stalked off to the opposite corner of the room.

Edgar jostled Thea on the arm again. 'Are you alright, my dear? Are you not diverted?'

'Quite,' she said, managing a smile, 'but I'm surprised she even bothered. I suppose she has too much goodness to just let him go.'

When Edgar's face turned to hers his eyes were fleetingly serious. 'Indeed.' He considered for a moment, before placing a hand on her shoulder. 'Although I would avoid pulling on that particular thread if I were you, as much as she loves you.'

By the time Thea had taken in his words to her fuzzy head and thought to respond, Martha was stalking back to their group. 'He took it well, then?' asked Edgar, after a slight pause.

Martha raised an eyebrow and shrugged. 'He can't say I didn't try.'

'You can't protect him from himself, Martha,' said Edgar, squeezing her arm tenderly.

She smiled at him. 'It seems not.' She took a breath in. 'Anyway, I must catch Lady Swanham before she goes.'

Mr Morell also took his leave, and Edgar took Thea's arms. 'Now, what is wrong with you, young lady? You have not been yourself since the collection. Was it Tabitha?'

She knew she couldn't lie to him, and with his kind eyes on her was suddenly overcome with a desire to share. 'Not really. I should never have spoken out.'

'What? Why not?' he asked, looking utterly confused by the desperation she knew must show on her face.

'This is what happens, when it comes out in public. People think things. And I must keep my thinking to myself.'

'Why on earth would you say that?' he started, and then his gaze was taken by something over Thea's shoulder. 'Now, here's someone who I think would be displeased to hear you say so. She was quite your champion in that cabinet and with good reason.'

Thea whirled round at his words, chills spreading through her veins even as she saw Ella approach. But the girl just smiled at her and placed a reassuring hand on her arm. Thea felt like she was about to implode. 'You have told me so much about Mr Pickles, Thea,' said Ella, easily. 'I do believe it is time we were properly introduced.'

Thea mumbled her way through the pleasantries and Ella smiled politely as Edgar swept up her hand, kissed it and pressed it between his palms. 'Lady Eleanor, it is a true pleasure. Thea has told me so much about you. I understand that she is introducing you to new and exciting experiences, eh?' Ella's eyes snapped to Thea's. As Thea felt heat vie with the chills inside her, he went on. 'You can do no better than starting with the cabinet at Milford and the plant collection at Denbury.'

Some of the tension dissipated from Ella's shoulders. 'I have no doubt of it, Mr Pickles, Miss Morell has indeed been very generous with her time.'

'Oh phooey, please do call me Edgar. Anyway, now you have seen the cabinet of Stanhope Grimston I must insist that you visit mine. We can't have you missing out on the most exciting collection in the county now, can we?' He winked at Ella dramatically, making her smile, but then her face dropped and became serious. Thea marvelled at how she didn't seem phased by what they had overheard, and how she could still bear to be in the proximity of someone she would now be well within her rights to consider 'unnatural'.

She noticed Ella was speaking again. 'It is a generous offer, Edgar, but are you sure I won't be disappointed?' Edgar's face fell at the thought, but Ella went on. 'It's just that today's cabinet has a unicorn horn. I assume you have little that could compare to it'? Even Thea had to suppress a smile as Edgar stared at Ella, uncharacteristically lost for words. The silence stretched on until Ella was able to hold her composure no longer and a mischievous grin cracked her face.

Edgar audibly exhaled and guffawed with laughter. 'Lady Eleanor, I like you already. You are smart – and there are a great many opportunities for the curious in Thornbury.'

'So I hear,' said Ella smoothly, 'but I could never manage the magnificent knowledge Thea demonstrated today.' She looked Thea directly in the eye, and Thea couldn't look away, despite the tightening nerves in her chest. 'Nobody there with a sensible mind could deny the rational knowledge she demonstrated, and her good intentions.'

Thea knew Ella was trying to reassure her and was grateful for it, but the raw confusion and embarrassment now made rational thought challenging. 'I do wish I hadn't,' was all she managed to mumble to her two companions.

Edgar laid a hand on her arm. 'I don't suppose this has anything to do with the fact that we are in the cabinet of Stanhope Grimston, who makes shells into little faces and nevertheless is big in the Royal Society, and that while your knowledge is infinitely greater, the chances of it being recognised are, shall we say, slimmer?'

Thea tried to produce a smile but was pleased to let him believe that for now, at least with Ella here. Edgar gave her a small squeeze as Mr Grimston beckoned him away. 'Keep at it, Thea, talent and passion will out.' And he left her with a meaningful stare.

Thea's head was light and her head swam. Wherever she wanted to be right now, it wasn't alone with Ella, not until there had been time to reflect on the possibilities now clouding her thoughts. 'He believes in you,' said Ella gently, placing her cup carefully on the saucer and placing three fingers on Thea's arm in the lightest of touches. It did nothing to calm Thea's nerves and sent that inconvenient heat through her once again making her shift. Tea slopped over the side of her cup and into her saucer.

'I should have kept it to myself,' said Thea, running a hand round the back of her neck and squeezing to calm herself. 'What must your mother think? This is why nobody can know.'

Ella gave a small shake of her head. 'My mother is no fool – she had the measure of Mrs Jefferys early on. She will think no more on it, and neither should you.'

'Perhaps,' said Thea, knowing she would think on little else but that conversation for at least the coming week.

'And both Edgar and Martha are right, you should believe in yourself,' Ella whispered, closer to Thea's ear than she could cope with, breath hot on her cheek. 'Mr Grimston thinks he has a unicorn horn in the house. You are observant, and rational, and you are in control of what you want to write on your own blank page.' She walked away towards the house and Thea felt the loss keenly as those fingers slipped gently off her arm.

There was no longer any way to deny it. Thea Morell was absolutely not in control of the script being scrawled across her mind. She wanted Ella in an entirely unnatural way, and she had no idea what she was going to do about it.

CHAPTER 8

Thea watched Ella as she sipped her tea and dropped a burnt almond onto her tongue. Through the windows of the Stanbourne drawing room the sun lit the curves of her elegant figure – the smooth line of her shoulders and the cinch at her waist – encompassed in that simple ivory silk dress. It was over a week since the incident at Mr Grimston's cabinet. Thea had applied her mind to the problem as rigorously as she could. She had looked inside herself and out for rational proof, something that could provide a more solid anchor than just that feeling, but there was none. Still, the feeling was incontestable and she knew she had to find a way to stop it. If not that, then to hide it, at least.

Ella was the perfect young lady, with the perfect manners and the world at her feet. But her brother was the perfect gentleman, and so why was he not exercising the same feelings in Thea? It wasn't the first time she'd felt this way. Last time it was George Crowe's sister, but it had only been a brief crush before she was married to the Earl of Tonley. Then there was Meg of course, but that was different somehow. This felt dangerous and daunting. She could actually talk to Ella, she felt she could be forever in her company, happy and satisfied.

One unfortunate symptom of being a lady in the country was that there was a lot of time to think. Not just at night when she couldn't sleep for the thoughts in her head, but at tea, after breakfast, and while they were visiting dull acquaintances. Most prominent in her mind were confusion, shame and fear. She couldn't stop thinking of Harriet – the disgrace and disgust her dalliance had caused, and now she was having the same, deviant feelings. She wondered if it was catching, or if there had been something that happened that caused it in them both. Despite her growing loathing of Mrs Jefferys, she had even begun to consider that she may have a point. Perhaps she had spent much time in a man's world of scholarship, one's self shaped by experiences marking its pages. The thought was almost better than the notion that her mind had betrayed her of its own accord.

On the day of the visit to Mr Grimston's cabinet Thea had called Mrs Phibbs to her room in the evening. She had thought of sharing everything, of shedding the weight of the heavy, filthy thoughts that filled her head, but in the end she couldn't do it. Couldn't bring herself to give them life through language, couldn't bear to burden Mrs Phibbs with a dirty secret she would have to swear to keep. In the end she had wrapped her arms around the housekeeper and cried hot, desperate tears until there were simply none left. Mrs Phibbs was used to Thea's occasional melancholy, but even she had looked concerned at the voracity of this most recent outburst. She had simply held her, listened to her attempted, weak explanations with a patient, concerned disbelief, and stayed until Thea finally slept.

It was unfair to even be around Ella, Thea had decided. Not if she couldn't control her thoughts. Someone so good should not be on the receiving end of the inappropriate musings of Thea's mind. In occasional reflections late at night she had considered that Ella might feel the same, but in the pragmatic light of morning she knew that she couldn't. She had avoided Ella all week and even tried to decline this latest invitation to tea at Stanbourne but with the whole family in attendance and the prospect of developments with Samuel Harrington her mother wouldn't hear of it.

Now, mid-visit and watching Ella as she engaged Ursula in lively conversation the need within her was almost unbearable. Thea felt exposed and her nerves raw every time Ella raised the cup to her lips or retrieved a crumb from the crease of her mouth with an elegant finger. Any rationalisation she had achieved in the week fled, and with Ella in the room and society persisting around them it felt stark and wrong. She resolved to keep her distance, to protect Ella as far as possible from the feelings so sharp and dangerous. How astonishing, she thought, that sensations so threatening could be contained within her and weren't somehow visible on the outside for everyone to see.

As she watched, Samuel Harrington apologised as he interrupted and asked Ursula if she would play for them. Her sister agreed happily and Thea's reflections came to an end as Ella began to make her way over. Thea's heart fell and she shuffled uncomfortably as the object of her thoughts joined her on the chaise. She looked around, but there was no polite way to leave. Ella took Thea's hand and the leap of her pulse sent a guilty tingle right to her toes. She managed only a small, awkward smile as Ella's eyes searched her face. 'Forgive my intrusion, Thea, but you don't seem quite yourself today.' She paused, perhaps expecting a reaction, but none came. 'You surely aren't still thinking on Mrs Jefferys?' Ella's beautiful eyes were soft and full of concern, Thea noticed painfully.

She painted a smile and forced her words against the knot in her throat. 'My apologies, I am absolutely myself, I was simply deep in thought.'

Ella furrowed her brow and pursed her lips. 'I would like to believe you, but as I don't, I have something to show you that will cheer you up.' She stood, keeping hold of Thea's hand and led her out of the drawing room into the garden, through the wide glass doors which reached almost from floor to ceiling. Thea followed pathetically and anxiously, trying not to dwell on where they connected, desperately certain that this was a bad idea.

'Ella, I shouldn't,' she said, trying to pull away, but Ella held tight.

'You should,' was all she said, as she led them through the flower garden and to the service area where a small glasshouse leant up against a wall.

Ella turned with a hand on the door. 'Close your eyes.' Thea silently obeyed, cursing the thoughts in her own head and hearing the door squeak before she was led into the musty warmth. The air was dry and smelled of warm soil and cedar. She was aware of little but Ella's breathing next to her and a soft hand grasping her own. 'Now, open them.'

As Thea's eyes adjusted, the sight that greeted her momentarily eclipsed her misery and she let out a cry of delight. 'For you?'

Ella looked proud as their eyes settled together. 'All mine, I asked father to send for them for me. It isn't much, but one must start somewhere.'

Thea looked away to the three plants in front of her. A wallflower, a fig tree and a buddleja. A strange selection on its own, but a good start. 'I had no idea you enjoyed it this much.' She allowed a smile to seep through as she regarded Ella's pleasure at her green investments.

'A month ago I had no idea that I ever would, but I do.' Ella paused and her eyes settled on Thea's. The wide smile fell a little. 'At least, I do when I'm with you, Thea.' Ella's gaze was suddenly intense and nervous, her eyes a little wide and her chest rising and falling quickly. Despite her musings all week, this was something Thea had absolutely not prepared for.

The breath left her body almost completely and her heartbeat seemed to leap into her ears. A more reckless version of herself swept Ella into her arms and kissed her tenderly. The actual Thea knew she mustn't, went pink and cast her eyes desperately around the glasshouse for something – anything to divert them. She turned back to the structure of the hot house and picked up the buddleja. 'Um... This should flower later in the summer. September maybe. A nice purple.'

Ella said nothing but sharply moved towards her and she felt the brush of breath on her neck. It seemed to linger, seeping into her skin and making it taut and tender. She felt her name being whispered and carefully placed the plant on the staging, in danger of letting it fall, and turned slowly towards the girl who had occupied her thoughts all week. Quickly she became lost in those expressive eyes and a thrill flowed through her. Ella's breath came as quickly as hers as she felt a hand placed softly on her waist. Her gaze dropped as she saw Ella's lips part just slightly.

'Here they are, you were right, clever Lord Stockwood!' The harsh words brought them both back to their senses and they quickly stepped away from one another, Thea's heart thudding in her chest as Tabitha appeared at the door. Ursula and Sam were visible on the path a little way behind her, he pushing the chair towards them. Tabitha hesitated a moment, considering the scene, and then continued. 'Come on you two, Lord Stockwood has suggested a walk in the grounds. He said we'd find you here in the glasshouse. Honestly you and your plants.' Thea didn't dare look at Ella as they exited the structure and headed to the wilderness. She also couldn't help noticing that Ella maintained her attention in the other direction.

As if by mutual agreement the two split. Thea joined Sam and Ursula while Tabitha grabbed Ella's arm and chatted away, their mothers following on behind. The warm, spring air and the rustling of fresh, green oak leaves calmed Thea's senses to a degree. She had been so close to doing something inappropriate, how was it that she seemed unable to control herself?

Ursula's chair crunched on the fresh gravel and her voice brought Thea back to the conversation. 'How are the works to the gardens progressing, Lord Stockwood?'

'Tolerably well, thank you, Miss Ursula, the walking route is almost finished and we shall have the carriage ride complete before the winter, I think. Then just to populate with all the features my father desires, which I fear may take longer.'

As they entered the dappled shade of the wilderness a shriek of laughter drew their attention to Tabitha, who looked delighted, as Ella nodded at her, a cautious smile on her face. 'Look at her, Thea,' said Sam, leaning towards Thea as he pushed the chair. 'I know I have said it before, but the change in my sister is remarkable. Your friendship has awakened something within her – she suddenly seems – more alive.'

The words did nothing for the nagging pain in her chest. 'Nothing could give me more pleasure than seeing her happy, Sam, I have become extremely fond of her myself,' she dared to admit.

As they watched, a giggling Tabitha dragged a protesting Ella over to their group. Ella effected a smile, but there was something of concern in her face. 'What do you think, Urs?' laughed Tabitha to Ursula. 'Lady Eleanor has had a letter and you wouldn't guess from who?'

Ursula raised an eyebrow. 'From who?'

'It turns out they were friends all this time – from being little. And we had no idea. Small world.'

'From who?' asked Ursula again.

'Emma DeClere, of course.' A chill ran through Thea from her head to her toes. 'It's so delightful to hear that she is well after that terrible scandal, don't you think so, Thea?' At this she looked straight at Thea, and the chill deepened. Tabitha rarely thought of anyone enough to be delighted they were well.

Ella spoke loudly. 'Shall we walk down to the hermitage, do you think, Sam?' she asked. 'It is exceedingly pretty today.'

Despite the deflection Tabitha was unswerving in her pursuit and stared straight at her sister. 'I am exceedingly pleased to hear that she does well,' said Thea, tightly. 'I hope she is enjoying the continent.' While she hadn't known Emma as well as she had known Harriet, they all moved in the same circles and she was very aware that Emma, too, had been hastily married and waved off on an extended honeymoon to Europe.

Tabitha fixed Thea with a gleeful, but slightly hard-edged stare. 'Given that we have yet to hear from Harriet, it is pleasing, is it not, to know that there can be a future once one has engaged in – unconventional activity. They should be back in society within the year.'

The pool of Thea's consciousness froze. Did Tabitha know? She couldn't know. Unless she had seen them so close in the greenhouse. But nothing had happened. Now the silence was stretching on and Tabitha's eyes were still glued to her. Think – she had to say something. 'It isn't nice to gossip, Tabitha. We must not speculate, certainly not here.' She shot Tabitha a warning look, but to no avail.

'Pah!' exclaimed Tabitha, 'you know what happened quite as well as I do. Mr Fairclough saw what he saw and there are not many reasons to have your back against a wall, your leg flung over Harriet's shoulder and her face–'

'Tabitha!' exclaimed Thea, forcefully, stopping her sister in her tracks. 'That is enough.'

Tabitha shrugged. 'As you wish, sister,' she said coolly. Her countenance switched in a heartbeat and she turned to Ella. 'Did you say we should walk to the hermitage, Lady Eleanor?' She called across to Mrs Morell. 'Mother, shall we have to walk all the way to the hermitage? I am not sure my legs will take me.'

Mrs Morell looked at the sky which threatened a tinge of purple to the west. 'It does look a little like rain.'

Sam, who had been listening indifferently to the girls' gossip, interjected. 'I think my sister is keen for a visit, why don't you accompany her, Miss Morell, and the rest of us will walk back towards the house?' He looked to Lady Swanham who nodded her approval. She looked as pleased as her son that Ella had found a friend.

Thea was once again full of confusion as she stared after the group meandering back to the house. What had Tabitha meant by that? Had she meant anything? Goodness knows she was always gossiping and was silly enough to bring scandal into polite conversation. It was just – that topic, and right then. But she couldn't stand there forever and Ella's presence behind her scorched trails of uncomfortable heat into the cold sweat of her back. She made herself turn. Ella, she noted, looked as awkward as she felt. The darkening sky had robbed the woodland floor of its lively dappled sun and the path ahead now seemed airless and claustrophobic. 'So, the hermitage?' They were the only words she could think to force out even though she wanted nothing more than to escape Stanbourne altogether. Ella nodded sanguinely and they proceeded awkwardly along the path beside one another.

The silence became worse with every step. Thea turned over questions in her head but they all seemed hopelessly banal. In the end there seemed to be no other option but to address the predicament head on, so she stared at her dragging feet and took a breath. 'I am sorry about my sister. She doesn't think. I hope she didn't make you uncomfortable.' Quite the understatement.

Ella didn't raise her gaze from the path but was politeness itself. 'Not at all, your sister is extremely diverting.' More silence. But when Ella spoke next it sounded loud and strained in the soft acoustics of the wilderness. 'Thea, what do you think? About Emma and Harriet, I mean? Tabitha says you were close with Harriet.'

Thea's throat turned as dry as ash. 'I do, I mean, I was – but I knew nothing of the thing, I swear.'

'That's not what I mean,' said Ella, still staring at the floor. 'What happened between them was obviously real enough. I'm asking – how you feel about it.' She glanced sideways, her face betraying her nerves.

The pause stretched out. Thea's heart pounded both in her ears and her toes at once, rendering it impossible for her to think. The clouds darkened and a breeze rustled through the fresh foliage. She tried to swallow the dry lump in her throat but Ella looked again, expectantly, almost pleadingly with those earnest eyes. Suddenly it was clear. She had to leave. Every instinct seemed to pull her physically closer to Ella and she was losing the battle to fight it. Her mind really had betrayed her utterly and completely, and now her body was following suit. She knew what would happen next, if she stayed.

'I'm sorry, I have to go.' She turned and began to make her way back up the wooded path, the arching branches overhead making her feel claustrophobic, raindrops beginning to penetrate the canopy. She heard her name shouted from behind but didn't dare turn. At a fork in the path she hesitated, unsure which way they had come.

'Thea.'

The voice was right by her now and she tensed, but a hand encircled her wrist in a surprisingly firm grip bringing her to a sudden halt. She kept her eyes focussed down on the path in front of her. 'Ella, I can't, I have to go, you don't understand.'

The grip only became firmer. 'What if I do?'

Thea tried to pull away, had to leave, had to make Ella understand. 'Mrs Jefferys was right, something has happened to me.' She dared to turn slightly and glance up at Ella's concerned face. 'I can no longer trust myself around you. I'm so sorry.'

The grip slackened for a second and Thea turned once more and made to move away, but her forward momentum was suddenly arrested as Ella moved, grasped Thea once again and jerked her back around so they were face to face. Before she could protest once more Ella had closed the gap between them and pressed her mouth to Thea's. Their teeth clashed and Thea tasted sweet macaroons and a hint of coffee. As the pressure lessened, her mind was dimly aware of the softness of lips releasing themselves from hers before Ella stepped away.

Thea felt like she was rooted to the spot, unable to comprehend and unable to move. Their eyes flicked quickly between each other's and then they both jumped as a cracking boom of thunder rolled overhead. Fat drops of rain peppered the ground around them but Thea felt entirely incapacitated. By pleasure or fear she wasn't sure.

'Come on,' shouted Ella, against the din, adjusting her grip on Thea's arm to pull her into motion and propel them back towards the hermitage. Somehow Thea's legs carried her and they kept pace with one another, bursting through the door into the small but dry log-built hut as a second peal of thunder echoed through the trees.

Dripping wet and panting from exertion they never took their eyes from one another as their vision adjusted to the gloom. Thea was dimly aware that she should say something but verbalising any of the swirling emotions within her seemed unlikely and probably inadvisable. What would she say? What *should* she say? Was it possible that Ella felt the same as she did? She had kissed her, after all. What if it had been an accident? The silence stretched. Ella's eyes pinned her to the spot, a hand laid over her own throat as her chest rose and fell with quick breaths – Thea felt the motion mirrored in her own and then her pulse leapt chokingly as Ella took a step towards her.

'Thea. Should I be sorr–'

She stopped as Thea managed to break her inertia and move forward. She could only shake her head. Now distinctly within Ella's space she reached out and slowly removed Ella's fingers from her throat, holding them firm between shaking hands. She couldn't do this, could she? But it felt inevitable. She should check, at least.

'Are you sure?' she whispered, searching Ella's eyes for any sign of doubt, but there was none.

'I am.' They were so close she could feel Ella's breath on her skin. Despite the certainty in Ella's voice Thea noticed with a pang of tender affinity that Ella's hands trembled as much as hers. The world felt utterly still as she moved haltingly forward, drawn by some invisible thread until she paused, her face an inch from Ella's. It felt like a moment suspended in time – she closed her eyes and felt warm breath on her lips until she could bear it no longer.

This time the kiss was soft and gentle. Such tenderness seemed at odds with the searing current arcing through her, awakening every nerve. They broke away as Thea's lungs snatched a sudden breath, but as she pulled Ella to her by the waist, Ella's lips captured hers once more. Thea felt Ella's hand slip behind her neck, pulling her into a deep and soft caress. The spark that had threatened for so long now burst into flame, engulfing Thea's doubts, her fears, and searing a longed-for certainty into her anxious heart.

And just like that, as easy as a breath and as quietly as a whisper, everything changed.

CHAPTER 9

Four weeks later, Thea walked back from church with Jane Ashby, the two of them picking and chewing on hawthorn buds as they went. The fields and trees were abundant with the verdant vitality of spring, lush greens, not yet afflicted by sun or drought, glowed in the new season's sunshine. Thea was full of joy, she and Ella had taken every opportunity to see one another since their kiss, and there had been plenty of opportunity. Each time she felt a fierce exhilaration that threatened to consume every part of her, and the two of them were becoming more confident around one another – especially in their quiet moments together. It seemed inconceivable that anything that felt so right, could be anything but.

Even the worries about Tabitha also seemed assuaged – her sister had been exactly her usual self and had said or insinuated nothing more about Emma DeClere. It was no shock that Tabitha was capable of gossip with people she knew so little and Thea began to resolve that it had perhaps been nothing more than an unfortunate coincidence.

As if reflecting Thea's private joy, Jane had attracted the attention of Thomas Harker, the village attorney's son, and nothing could quell her happiness. Thea laughed along with her as she heard tales of their meeting as he was bled in her father's surgery following a bad flu.

'Goodness, he looked awful, Thea. I must have been under some sort of spell as no woman would fall for a man in that state. But as he made repeat visits we got to talking and he is an extremely pleasant young man.' Jane grinned shyly, but widely.

'And what of when he is better? I assume he cannot be bled too regularly, so you must contrive another way of meeting?'

'Well, I do fear he continued the visits a little longer than necessary, although I like to think of him enduring those leeches for our love.' Jane pressed her hands to her chest dramatically as she spoke, drawing an involuntary laugh from Thea. 'We have met in Thornbury with his sister, and – oh, Thea, I can barely contain myself – he is to attend the ball at Stanbourne later this month!'

Jane's happiness was always infectious. 'Then I can see that it is all but settled. You will dance with him, he will be smitten, and you will be married before the year is out. Wait.' She stopped. 'Isn't Thomas a Quaker?'

Jane buried her face in the haw blossom, drinking in the heady scent. 'He is, and if we got married we would have to discuss it with the friends.' She stopped as Thea smirked at her. 'Oh I know I must not get carried away, but Thea, as my dearest friend, you must know that I desire it with all my heart. It makes me go all... fluttery when I think of him.' The hands were pressed to her chest again, this time a little trembly.

'Well then,' Thea smiled, 'You must secure him at the ball, or I will tell him what a ridiculous man he is. Has he assured the first dance with you?'

Jane's eyes sparkled and she took Thea's hands. 'He has! He said that nothing would give him greater pleasure than standing up with me and– Oh! But that reminds me, Thea, I have been so taken up with myself that I forgot to ask. You must think me a dreadful friend. What about your first dance with Samuel Harrington? Has he asked?'

Thea focussed on their entwined hands; it had been inevitable that the topic would arise. 'Indeed, he has Jane. I shall take the first two dances with him.'

Jane looked at her expectantly and blinked. 'Well?'

'Well, what?'

Jane rolled her eyes, dropped Thea's hands and they carried on walking. '*Well*, how did he ask you, and did you faint with delight, or did you treat him with your usual haughty civility?'

Jane's commitment to romance couldn't help but draw a smile. 'He asked me at Stanbourne when we went for dinner a fortnight ago. I confess that my heart was a little exercised at the time and I told him that I would be delighted.' It wasn't a lie, but she could never tell Jane that the heightened emotions were due to Lord Stockwood's sister, sitting opposite, twining her feet around Thea's and engaging her with those expressive eyes.

Jane sighed. 'I hope you were a little more eloquent than you let on, but no matter, I am sure he will turn you to him over the course of the evening. Isn't it wonderful to have one's feelings enticed so, Thea?' Thea heartily agreed that it was and wished with all her heart that she could share her own excitement with her best friend.

Two mornings later there was little excitement as they both found themselves bored and being talked over by Stanhope Grimston in Edgar's drawing room. He wasn't speaking to them of course, but they had been excitedly swapping tales with Edgar when Mr Grimston had barged between them. Martha and Mr Morell had strategically removed themselves to the garden, away from Mr Grimston's monologue. The room was still, except for his rambunctious tones and the loud ticking of the clock. '...and what do you know, Pickles, another letter from the society, accepting my presentation of that goose. Not the horn yet.' He circled a finger in front of him. 'But I have a feeling they are saving that for something special. That presidency will be mine before you know it, I was writing to Ephraim Herbert only the other day and said to him that I was not sure if I had the time, but–'

'Wonderful, Grimston.' Edgar rolled his eyes at Thea and Ella. 'I am sure you will be in post by the autumn with all the wonders at your disposal. Now, shall we all get down to business?'

They eagerly followed him through to the cabinet and while Mr Grimston busied himself with the Burrows collection, Ella gaped around her and Thea placed a gentle hand on her arm. 'Edgar collects machines and scientific equipment. It sounds like we're about to see an experiment today.'

'What kind of experiment?' Ella looked a little worried.

Thea shrugged. 'Could be anything. The last time we were here he was into electricity, but you never know.'

Ella stared at her blankly. 'Electricity?'

Thea chided herself once again. 'Electricity is a force which can be created by friction and then passed through objects to create some sort of attraction or spark.' Ella flicked her eyebrows, making Thea smile. She looked up at Edgar who was affixing a glass vessel, a little bigger than his head, to the top of a tall mahogany stand.

'Mr Pickles, can I show Ella the generating machine?'

He looked over. 'Of course, my dear, you know how it operates better than I do. It's connected up to the beam and chain so get her to stand on the stool at the other end.' Once they had moved the mountain of journals, pamphlets, letters and auction catalogues off the table, the sphere's lustred surface glinted into view. A chain hung against it, running up and along a horizontal wooden beam, suspended from the ceiling. After about five feet, the chain hung down at the other end.

Ella looked slightly nervous as Thea helped her on to the stool. 'Is it safe?'

Thea kept hold of her hands. 'Would I suggest it if it wasn't?'

Edgar appeared next to them, having finished with the vessel. 'Excellent, now take hold of the chain, Lady Eleanor, and Thea will wind the machine. Ready, Thea?' She nodded, and wound the handle of the glass sphere quickly, so that the chain clacked rhythmically against it.

Her heart beat faster at the sound, unconsciously rekindling the tension of the lecture theatre months before. She thrilled at the thought that unlike Meg, the girl at the end of the chain was now one she was allowed to kiss. In private, anyway.

After a little while, Edgar held out a tray filled with small pieces of paper. 'Don't touch the tray, Lady Eleanor, but just hold your hand over it lightly.'

Ella did, and the pieces of paper jumped to her right hand. She exclaimed and tried it with the left. 'I know it can't be magic.' There was a look of delight on her face as she regarded Thea and Edgar. 'But what is it?'

Edgar chuckled. 'It is the force of electrical fire, Lady Eleanor, isn't it something? It is also why your hair is standing on end.' Ella put up a papery hand to her head and goggled. 'Now, Thea,' said Edgar, an impish glint in his eye, 'would you like to help your friend down from the stool?'

Thea understood, stopped winding, and approached. Ella held out her hand but Thea pulled back before they made contact. 'You will feel something quite startling when I touch you, but don't be alarmed.' Ella's face was a picture of both mischief and trepidation, but she kept her hand outstretched, trusting and eager. As their eyes locked Thea was transported once again to the lecture room in London and the crackling anticipation built. Looking into the blue and green of Ella's eyes was different. It was exciting, but there was also comfort there, a feeling of belonging she had so rarely felt. She reached out a hand and their fingers met. They both jumped and Ella exclaimed out loud as a spark crackled between them and earthed itself through Thea's body. On the way it set her insides alight, the spark from Meg combusting into flames at Ella's touch.

Ella stepped down laughing, holding on to Thea's arms and looking with delight into her eyes. 'I have never felt anything like it.' Her eyes scorched Thea's for a second before she came back to herself. 'Thank you, Edgar, that was – quite something!'

He smiled and tipped his eyebrows ever so slightly at Thea. 'I'm delighted you found it so pleasurable. Lady Eleanor. Now, shall we proceed?'

He gestured them over to the mahogany stand and the vessel. Now Thea regarded it more closely she saw the dome-shaped vessel was mounted on a thick seal and a pipe from its base led down to an odd contraption which looked to be made up of a brass frame enclosing two cylinders and a lever. 'Whatever is it, Edgar?' asked Martha. Having returned from their solace in the garden she stood with Ursula and Mr Morell, peering expectantly but keeping a sensibly safe distance.

'It's an air pump, my dear,' announced Edgar with glee. 'Also known as a pneumatic engine. It arrived two days ago from Benjamin Cole in London – I think I've put it together right.'

Thea wasn't sure whether to be amused or concerned. 'And what does it do? Not too dangerous I hope?'

'Hmm, that depends,' he mumbled, his voice muffled from where his face pressed against the glass, fiddling with the pipe. He placed a small, dubious looking bag inside the glass and affixed it to the stand. 'Apparently things can go wrong but I don't anticipate any problems.' Martha shot Thea a look of mostly mock alarm, although Thea saw some of her own concern reflected in her eyes. 'Now,' said Edgar, straightening up, 'to test it!' He began to pump the lever that emerged from the brass cylinders, slowly at first, but then gaining in speed. The party kept a safe distance but craned their necks to look.

'Aha!' exclaimed Edgar, still pumping, 'it's working!' As they watched, the small bag inside the vessel began to inflate, slowly but surely getting larger until its outer skin was stretched tight, almost translucent and veined with pinkish threads. He stopped pumping and beamed around at them all.

Thea chuckled. 'What just happened?'

Edgar raised an acknowledging finger. 'I am very glad you asked. The pump is removing all of the air from the vessel, but not from the sealed bladder, and therefore the air inside the bladder is able to take up more space. Isn't it fascinating?'

'That's – a bladder?' Thea looked round just in time to see Ella's face pale as she spoke.

'Indeed it is, Lady Eleanor,' said Edgar, unperturbed. 'Shall we deflate it?' He took her cautious nod as affirmation and pressed a second lever on the pump. There was a whooshing sound, and the bladder shrank back to its original size. Edgar beamed around as the party clapped politely.

'So, what are we achieving here, Edgar?' asked Martha. Thea always admired her drive for purpose and made a mental note to stop being taken up with the excitement of the performance.

'An excellent question,' Edgar stated matter-of-factly, 'natural philosophers are using this machine to figure out the air around us. What happens when there is less or more of it in a space? Do flames burn in it? Can sound travel through it, and so forth.' Martha looked impressed. 'I, however,' said Edgar, gleefully, 'simply plan to have a little fun.' He picked up an old apple and held it in front of him, pinched between three fingers. 'Shall we try this first?'

A few minutes later the apple was in the vessel, its skin becoming noticeably taut as Edgar was pumping away. Soon its delicate skin began to rupture and juice burst from the inside, bubbling and spitting.

'Excellent, Edgar!' Thea grinned, she had enjoyed this experiment and nobody had got hurt.

But Edgar didn't stop pumping. 'Just a little more,' he said, as the apple became less and less apple shaped, 'I wonder what happens next?' By now juice was spattering the inside of the glass making it difficult to see.

'Perhaps you should stop now, given that it's the first time?' suggested Thea, stepping back and noting that the others surreptitiously did too.

'Almost!' exclaimed Edgar, his voice raised in excitement. At that moment there was a creaking sound, just before the glass vessel imploded sending shards of itself ripping across the room. Edgar cried out and staggered backwards into a pile of the burrows collection – glass jars, papers and dusty animal parts rained down on him from the shelves which shook at the impact. Ella's hands were at her face and Mr Morell and Ursula were wide eyed. Both Martha and Thea ran to him.

'Edgar?!' Thea shouted, as they threw aside antelope legs and turtle shells to find him motionless and bleeding from the temple.

'You really needn't bother, you know. I am fine,' stated Edgar flatly as he and Thea trudged to the menagerie. It was a few hours later and he was patched up and had stopped swaying.

'We just need to be sure you're steady enough to be out and about.' She nudged him tenderly. 'You took quite a blow.' He harumphed grumpily, making her smile. 'And you really must be more careful. Did you read the instruction pamphlet it came with?'

'Of course I did,' he mumbled as they reached the pen containing the rabbits and chickens. Thea dropped her head and gave him a stern, upwards glare. 'No, I didn't.' His bushy eyebrows were almost knotted together in consternation and Thea had to suppress a giggle.

'Perhaps it would be wise to be more careful next time?'

'Rubbish.' He drew himself up, defiantly. 'Sacrifice is sometimes necessary for progress. Natural philosophy will shape the future of all of us and I plan to be amongst the change. It is the root of everything

Thea, and the more we understand it, the more we can control it.' His eyes shone again with that worrying fervour.

'And control is key to understanding.' She gave him a last stern look but knew he would risk it all again the next time. 'Anyway, speaking of growth, how are the rabbit-chickens?' She peered into the pen to watch the now adolescent creatures pecking happily around the food.

If anything, Edgar's pout became even greater as he waved a dismissive hand at them. 'Can you see any difference in them?'

She pretended to consider them carefully as one squawked and scurried away from Edgar's gesticulation. 'Not really, no.'

'That's because there isn't any. They're just chickens. Blasted rabbit not turning up for duty.' But Edgar could never stay grumpy for long and he immediately brightened. 'They do say that failure makes a natural philosopher, and by that score I am bloody excellent.'

This time Thea gave him a squeeze. 'Perhaps it will work next time?'

He shook his head. 'I think I shall leave the breeding to Belgium. Perhaps it is folly of us to try to sport with the natural' – he paused slightly – 'romantic, inclinations of conscious beings.' He regarded her carefully from beneath his eyebrows and she blanched.

'Romantic?' she asked, quietly.

'I think you know what I mean, Thea,' he said gently. 'You have no need to pretend.' The breath seemed to leave her. After all these years she could read him like a book, and apparently he could read her too.

'How did you–?' Despite their unwavering friendship her heartbeat had jumped into her throat. Nobody was supposed to know of her irregular arrangement with Ella and she couldn't know how he would react.

To her relief Edgar's eyes showed tender amusement rather than alarm. 'Don't worry yourself about being indiscreet, Thea, you are very subtle about it – but to an old romantic like me it was clear that you hardly needed the static generating machine to cause that spark between you.'

Thea knew that her face was fully pink and she gawped at Edgar as he spoke, but the relief that flooded through her at being able to share her secret with another person was palpable. 'Oh, Edgar, I do have to admit, we have become – close. I know plenty of ladies have romantic friends but this feels – different. Do you think that is terrible?'

He chuckled. 'Certainly not, I think it is splendid. Finding someone who sets off the electrical fire within you is one of the most wonderful things about life, don't you think?'

Thea smiled and stared at the chickens, but a wrinkle still puckered her brow and a weight dragged at her conscience. 'I do. But that electrical fire isn't – usual is it? Not caused by another lady anyway. We haven't talked about it, but I know Ella feels it too.'

Edgar tutted loudly. 'Never mind unusual, you wouldn't be the first of my acquaintance to choose – unconventionally.'

Mrs Jeffery's assertions about scholarship and unnatural tendencies flicked back into her brain. 'I did wonder,' she said, 'if the collections might have something to do with it?'

'How so?'

'They say it can change you, and I have seen it turn good men to thievery and deception in the conquest of items of natural history. What if it changes women in a different way?'

Now Edgar placed his hands on his hips. 'Mr John Locke got many things right, Thea, but his blank sheet did not include our animal instincts. Our mind may be written on by experience, but since when did love bow to logic? We are all individual, in our way.'

'But that's quite a difference, isn't it,' asked Thea, keen for is insight. 'And everyone says it is wrong.'

Edgar squeezed her elbow. 'My dear, we would understand love more fully if we were able to observe, discuss, and explore without prejudice. However, there must always be a human limit to our endeavours and so, like science, our public explorations must focus on those which society deems acceptable. You are quite at liberty to observe and understand yourself and others like you, but you are right that it is not usual and the set that call themselves polite are anything but. They will set upon any difference they can and use it for their own amusement and personal gain. You must think carefully about your future and the path you wish to take.'

Thea's heart dipped. 'I am afraid I may not have much choice. You know I am the most likely of my sisters to make a good match, and I believe father might be in financial trouble. A prudent match with a secure family would be sensible.'

Edgar gave one, understanding nod. 'Then enjoy it while you can. There is little need to make your present miserable because your future is uncertain. But there are some observations which must only be made within a trusted circle and you should know that when it comes to the terribly thrilling situation you are in with young Lady Eleanor, that you are amongst friends here.'

Thea blinked and felt a warm tear slip down her cheek – she had no idea how much she had craved another's recognition. She enveloped Edgar in a warm embrace, surprising herself at the gratitude she felt. As she let him go, he wiped an eye with the back of his finger and gave a small cough. 'Apart from Grimston. He's a biggoted bastard, obviously.'

Tabitha's chatter was worse than usual at dinner, the anticipation of tomorrow's ball getting the better of her. She had a letter from her friend Georgie in London and news that she was to marry Mr Davies from the militia had sent Tabitha into a whirl of self-pity. 'I must work on Ralph more ardently,' she said, wistfully, clattering her cutlery onto her plate. 'Or indeed I have not yet given up on Samuel Harrington. He may have the first two dances with you, Thea, but if you persist in being as disinterested as you are inclined to, I may marry him after the third and fourth.'

'She better be interested,' cut in Mrs Morell, leaning over her plate towards Thea and placing a purposeful hand flat on the table. 'Thea, in all seriousness tomorrow is your chance to secure a member of the Harrington family and the future of this estate. You must exhibit a dignified ease and graceful control.' She straightened up and dragged a hand across the front of her chest to illustrate the point. 'I have bought you a dress but only you can account for your behaviour and I beg that you would be agreeable.'

'I will be agreeable,' muttered Thea, dipping a mouthful of chicken in her celery sauce, 'but I can't make Samuel Harrington want me.'

'Of course you can,' stated Mrs Morell, waving away her concern with a dismissive hand, 'although that may not be the best outcome. Rumour has it that George Crowe is looking to settle. He ranks higher than the Harrington boy and I think perhaps now, I would rather have him.'

Thea saw their father blanch a little across the table. He had looked pale throughout the whole exchange. 'Let's not forget the boy does have something of a reputation, my dear,' he offered to Mrs Morell, but she only waved away his concerns in the same manner as those of her daughter.

'And that is exactly why there is a chance for him to become my son in law,' she announced, 'Thea has a great standing but has shown herself to be something of an oddity. If others think twice on him due to his reputation she may stand a chance.' Thea stabbed another forkful and pressed her lips together – her mother was not to be deterred. 'Yes, you must make them both want you, Thea. Flirt, for goodness sake, I will not have you throwing away this opportunity for the family. Use your womanly wiles'

'My womanly wiles?' Thea looked down at herself. 'That shouldn't take long.'

CHAPTER 10

T he revelries at Stanbourne could be heard before the majestic building appeared in view. As the Morell carriage drew to a halt a footman opened the door with a deep bow. Around them local families exited their own carriages and swept up the grand staircase beneath towering stone columns. Even Thea couldn't help but be impressed as she glided through the entrance with her family and Lady Foxmore. Everyone was done up without exception in fine clothes, lace and gilt. She always felt nervous around large groups of people and she slid a nervous hand around the back of her neck between skin and silk. She immediately felt Martha's steadying hand on her back and relaxed at the reassurance.

Inside, foliage, spring flowers and ribbons adorned the generous Stanbourne vestibule and music floated in from the depths of the house. The Harrington family were lined up to receive their guests, ensuring they reached everyone in the bustle of bodies, hats and ruffles. Thea was greeted warmly by Lord and Lady Swanham, and then by Samuel.

'Good evening, Miss Morell. It is my duty to inform all of the guests that I am delighted to see them, but at least to you I can confirm that it is absolutely true.'

He kissed her hand and she offered a genuine smile. 'The delight is all mine, Lord Stockwood. I shall look forward to our dance.' She curtseyed her exit and moved left to Ella, their eyes scribbling their own story on the neat face of formality. Reaching for Ella's hand she lifted it to her lips. 'Good evening, my lady,' she said in a low tone, as smooth as she could make it.

Ella smiled with soft eyes and leaned in, the whisper dancing on Thea's ear. 'And a good evening to mine.' As she straightened up her gaze was dragged to Thea's feet and back up to her face. She caught her breath. 'My goodness, you are dazzling.'

Their gaze was wrenched apart by the next guests in line and Thea was whisked away. The Morells and Martha entered the great hall, a huge room with fine tapestries and richly adorned portraits, now done up finely and ready for dancing. A band of musicians in the corner enlivened the atmosphere with a spirited air and guests mingled noisily, their voices carrying around the cavernous space. The Morells and Martha wandered around the circuit, Thea pushing Ursula ahead of her. There were cards in the drawing room, the dining room was set for tea, and a harpist in the saloon prepared for those who preferred quiet conversation to dancing a jig. Families bustled around them and talked over each other and staff circulated with trays of wine. Thea took two and handed one to Ursula.

'Well, I am not sure what to think,' announced Mrs Morell as they completed the circuit and returned to the hall. 'In my day you kept to one room and everyone partook of the festivities whether they liked it or not.' As she spoke her hair wobbled. Feathers and leaves framed a large and bug-eyed artificial bird that threatened to set the whole thing off balance. She had laughed with glee at the diversion it would cause Mr Grimston when he saw. Thea would rather she had dressed to please their father, but she supposed manuscripts or fly-attracting plants weren't quite as desirable in one's hairpiece.

'Oh mother, that was the old way!' Tabitha tutted at the judgement of the evening's entertainment. 'These days you may pick and choose as you wish and I like it. I am likely to spend much of the evening at cards, after I have had my fill of dancing. Whenever will we start, do you think?'

Tiring of her sister already, Thea took Martha's arm and steered her away. Usually she hated large, social events, out of place due to her oddities. Tonight, however, she had Martha, Edgar, Jane, her father and Ursula, not to mention their thrilling hostess, and was determined to keep the anxiety at bay.

Together, Martha and Thea surveyed the room. There were some significantly wide dresses – not as wide as in the forties, noted Martha, but still wide enough to cause a problem in doorways. As usual Thea had chosen as alternatively as her mother would allow – a twilight-blue gown with pineapple broom, daisy and another flower Thea didn't recognise embroidered around the bodice in silver detail. The line cut a slender silhouette which gained her a few pitying looks from the modish crowd, but she couldn't bear to be hindered. Martha, as always, was dressed impeccably in a sleek, claret gown with elegant gilt detail picked out in the shoulder and sleeves. She would effortlessly set the fashion in any room, Thea thought.

The two of them were comfortable company. As Thea felt a reassuring hand on her once more she felt the imposing Lady Foxmore next to her like an anchor point, a brace against which the melee of society could be endured. For a moment she was full of gratitude for the Countess who had taken her under her wing and helped her navigate the recent, difficult years. Martha understood her more than anyone, of that she was sure. For a second she considered confiding everything. The two of them had shared so much and Martha had always been clear she could tell her anything. It was she, after all, who crusaded so ardently for women's independence and free choice. But perhaps a large social occasion was not the time for revelations. She only squeezed Martha's arm to her more tightly in a gesture of appreciation, receiving a warm smile in response.

'Will you dance tonight, Lady Foxmore?' she asked, gentle mischief lightening her mood as her eyes slipped from Martha's and back to the room. 'There must be a gentleman or two here who would dare ask for your hand? Or, at least, who wouldn't dare refuse if you wished him to offer?'

Martha raised an admonishing eyebrow as Thea flashed her a smile. 'You know very well I am past all that. But I will take pleasure in watching you all dance.'

'Past it?' Thea chided Martha in mock-horror. 'That is absurd, you are one of the most beautiful ladies in the room and certainly the most impressive. We both know you could debate the stockings off any of the guests, male or female, professional or gentleman. It won't be easy to find a beau worthy of you, but perhaps we have as much chance in this crowd as any?' She teased and knew she made light of it, but happiness for someone she cared so much about was one of her dearest wishes.

The look that met her was imperious but amused. 'Thea, I have well more than forty years behind me. I do not need anyone else to complete my happiness and I shall be delighted to retire with my plants,' said Martha, returning her gaze to the ballroom and her smile fading. 'However, you must go and secure yourself a husband or your mother will bend my ear for the next three months. And for goodness sake choose one worthy of you, I will not see you bored and diminished by a man.' She flipped open her pocket watch just as the announcement for dancing was made. Before Thea could excuse herself Martha turned to her, grasped her gently by the shoulders and dipped a little until their eyes were level. She dropped her voice to a low timbre so the words would remain between the two of them. 'I mean it, Thea, only take a man who will allow you to thrive.' The intent took Thea a little by surprise, but she was required on the floor to do her duty. She kissed Martha gently on the cheek, hoping it communicated the depth of love and gratitude she felt, before she was taken up in the mass of bodies eager for merriment.

At the head of the room, Samuel Harrington bowed theatrically to Thea and the festivities began. They conversed but as their shoes clattered on the wooden floor Thea's mind kept switching back to Martha's words. *A man who will allow you to thrive.* That's what she had said, not *one you love*. Did Martha understand? Or did she simply recognise Thea's innate inability to endure life without purpose? The familiar fear slipped in at the thought of it, its sharp, mocking rush burning her nerves and prickling her scalp. But this time it wouldn't win. Her future was no more assured and Ella's place within it was inescapably uncertain, but the past month had brought an understanding about herself that offered some comfort. Of course, the crushing doubts about right and wrong had to be kept at bay but knowing that she wasn't alone elicited a welcome respite. It was a strange mixture of feelings, but Martha's words reminded her that marriage was still her family's route to security and the thought made her stomach turn.

Despite her confusion she found she could quite enjoy dancing with Samuel Harrington. He was a true gentleman, elegant and refined in a buff-coloured three-piece and shoe buckles so shiny they glowed in the reflected candle light. None of his grace or interest had faded since their first meeting and she found him pleasant company – not a feeling Ella shared about her own dance partner, she noted with a small grin.

Ella had stood up with George Crowe – his invite for the first two dances had arrived by letter to her father and Ella was compelled to accept. She had sought Thea's thoughts on the matter, but once Earl Axbury had designs on a lady he was almost unstoppable and Ella was the most eligible lady in the room. Thea's stomach twisted at the thought of it but slackened with every one of Ella's bored glances in her direction.

Thea made a play of watching the other couples on the floor. Thomas Harker looked as delighted as Jane that they were dancing together, and it made Thea glow inside to see them so happy. Tabitha had taken Ralph Jefferys who, Thea supposed, must have been enjoying himself deep down, although Tabitha had gaiety enough for them both. In reality, though, Thea's eyes were only for Ella. Thea watched her glide around the room, perfect, in a cream dress and a deep blue shawl that matched Thea's dress almost exactly. How her heart leapt every time Ella glanced in her direction, and how she would give anything to be the one partnering her.

The music stopped, jolting her out of her musings. Samuel kissed Thea's hand. 'Miss Morell, I am afraid I have a duty to entertain some of the other ladies in the room, but I hope that we shall converse again before the night is out?' Thea readily agreed, but then turned to find George Crowe in wait of her hand for the next. She agreed with caution, they lined up, and the music began. Ella looked happier dancing with Matthew Ashby, more radiant, and her smile lit up her whole face. Thea fell helplessly into her contemplation once again and was so distracted she almost tripped over George's feet as their bodies came together. She shrank away from his woody scent, mixed with sweat and wine.

'What do you think, Miss Morell?' she came back to herself in a panic as she realised he had asked a question.

'I'm sorry, I couldn't quite hear you over the music.'

He looked a little abashed. 'I was saying that I felt that the musicians could play louder, give us more atmosphere.'

'Oh yes,' she faltered, 'I mean I'm sure they could but I don't mind it–'

'They play much more loudly on the continent.' He cut her off. 'I have lately returned from a tour of Europe you know, my second actually, the French really know how to throw a party.'

Thea sighed and settled into her role. Dull as it was, it was some-how comforting after so many years. 'I don't suppose you visited the Colosseum on your tour?' she asked. 'I hear it is beautiful.'

'Indeed I did, Miss Morell, it was bigger than I had imagined. We visited on a dull morning in autumn–' Lord Axbury went on, but

Thea didn't mind, her thoughts were not engaged with her current dance partner and it saved her the trouble of contributing.

In the break between dances as she tipped back a little wine, she felt a pressure on her waist and turned to see blue and green eyes smiling down at her. A grin lit her face and the words bubbled up her throat and fell out of her mouth. 'My goodness, you are beautiful.'

Ella giggled, cast her eyes over Thea's whole form and leant in with a whisper. 'You are everything I could ever desire.'

Thea groaned quietly through her teeth. 'Am I to get the pleasure of dancing with the most beautiful lady in the room?' She squeezed Ella's hand through her silken gloves, desperate to feel the warmth of her skin.

'With Lady Foxmore?' Ella mischievously glanced over to the side of the room where Martha debated with Mr Morell and Edgar. Martha caught their gaze and gave Thea a kind but reticent smile, no doubt recalling their earlier conversation and Thea's various dance partners. 'I think you would have to ask her.' Thea scowled at Ella's cheekiness and squeezed her harder. Ella's smile became genuine. 'Soon, I hope. I am bound to dance with a few more of our guests but I will stand up with you before the night is out.' And so she did. The lovers managed one, joyful reel before Ella was once again swept away to be the perfect hostess.

Thea decided to sit out a few dances and headed to the quiet by the terrace. The night air refreshed like a tonic as she stepped through the parlour doors into dusk settling over the Stanbourne estate. Light glinted off the lake and the air smelled clean and pure after the stuffiness of the great hall. She made her way down the steps towards the garden, sliding off her gloves as she reached the balustrade to feel the reassuring texture of the cool stone. As she gazed over the formal lawn she heard footsteps behind her.

'I thought I saw you head out here.' She turned, it was George Crowe, his steps purposeful on the stone.

'Ah, Lord Axbury, not tired of dancing with the ladies I am sure?' She flashed him a smile that only required the lower half of her face, but her nerves tightened at the thought of being alone with him – and at the thought of what it may do to her reputation if anyone knew.

'Not at all, Miss Morell, there is little I like better, but I confess to having enjoyed one partner tonight more than most.' He leant on the rail, one leg cocked, arms folded and eyeing her carefully.

'Is that right?' she asked, jealousy flooding her at the thought of his designs on Ella. He had every right to the woman she wanted, in a way that she never could. She bit it back. 'Lady Eleanor is an extremely accomplished lady.'

Before she knew it he had swept her hand into his and kissed it, his lips coarse against her skin. 'Not Lady Eleanor. My attentions are only for you, Miss Morell. I have scarcely found any other lady I can converse with on equal terms.' This was certainly not what she had been expecting and supposed Ella's complete indifference had dashed his hopes early on.

Anxiety washed through her once more. 'Lord Axbury, I have to say this is very unexpected.' She bought herself some time to think.

He smiled the assured smile of one accustomed to success and slid closer, now taking both of her hands in his. 'Miss Morell, please call me George, I would dearly love to become better acquainted with you. Perhaps we could start now?' He reached forward and grasped her waist, pulling her roughly towards him. He was flushed with exertion from dancing and his breath smelled of rank wine.

Shocked, she dashed his hand off her, stepping out of his reach. 'I would say that your politeness is more conspicuous than your sincerity,' she managed, sounding calmer than she felt, 'but neither are particularly evident. I must return to my family.' She made to leave, but anger suddenly welled inside her making her bold. She turned back. 'Actually, I think it is you who should return inside following your entirely inappropriate proposal.' It was risky but Martha was right, why should she always make way?

He kept her eyes uncomfortably for a few seconds, a smug smile playing on his lips. She almost didn't dare breathe, but then he shrugged, unconcerned. 'Suit yourself.' He turned and stalked back inside, his boots harsh and rapid on the stone steps.

Thea leaned on the railing to steady her mind. Anger and anxiety combined to make her a little unsteady. 'Are you quite alright, Miss Morell?'

Samuel Harrington gazed at her, concern in his eyes. She took a breath to gather herself. 'Yes, thank you, Sam. I just had a – slightly unexpected conversation with Lord Axbury.'

Samuel's eyes narrowed. 'I suspected as much. I am aware of his reputation, so I confess to observing the situation from the window. I thought you handled it admirably, if it is any consolation.'

She managed a weak smile. 'Thank you. I think Lord Axbury is in no doubt about my opinion.'

Sam looked a little uneasy himself. 'I hope you are not too distressed?'

'Not at all, I am quite myself,' she lied, and decided on a change of subject to settle both their nerves. 'Do you enjoy the ball, Sam?'

'Exceedingly so, although I feel my feet may not last out too many more reels.' She laughed, and he paused, fiddling with the cuffs on his shirt. 'Miss Morell – Thea – I must tell you how delighted I am at your conduct with George Crowe. I had hoped that your affections–' He checked himself as her eyes implored him not to continue. This was certainly not as unwelcome as the previous exchange, but now it came to it she couldn't bear this either. At least she had an excuse and reached out to steady herself on the railings once more to remind him of her recent predicament.

He cast his eyes to the floor and back to her. 'Of course. I apologise, this is not for now. You have had a difficult night.'

She nodded and moved in to take hold of his arm. Despite everything she couldn't afford to burn all her bridges tonight. 'Perhaps – perhaps another time, Sam?' With every word she felt she betrayed his sister, but her family relied on her and she needed more time.

He nodded and gulped. 'Of course.' Thea could see him force himself to be brighter. 'Now I know what will cheer you up. I will bring my sister to you, she has been dying to see you all evening.' He kissed her hand gently and left.

Thea leaned back on the rail, holding her face to the stars as she took a gulp of air and considered the night's events. It was not even ten of the clock! Two suitors in one evening. It was one thing to know she must marry, but the reality of being approached brought the picture into all too sharp relief. She certainly had no intention of encouraging George Crowe, if, indeed, he had considered that their acquaintance would extend beyond the conclusion of the night. But what of Samuel Harrington? Common sense and duty said that there was no better match and he was undeniably an excellent man. Could she endure the limit to her own happiness? And could she deceive someone so good in order to enter a union of convenience? Ella had told her he wished to marry for love. The situation seemed hopeless.

'Thea, is anything the matter, my brother said you wished to see me?' Ella was running softly down the steps towards her, a hand outstretched and eyes full of concern.

Relief chased away tension Thea hadn't realised she held in her body. She held out her hands and Ella drew her into a comforting embrace. 'I am so glad to see you, it has been quite the evening. Or at least, quite the quarter hour.' She nestled into Ella's neck and breathed in her scent, instantly reassured.

'What happened?' Ella pulled back and beautiful, worried eyes searched her face.

'You may never believe it, but I was propositioned by George Crowe, and then–' she wasn't sure if she could even utter the words to Ella.

'And then what?' Ella breathed. Thea was in too deep to deceive.

'And then, I think – your brother.'

She stared resolutely at the floor unable to reconcile the propositions with her emotions, but Ella cupped her cheek and raised her head so their eyes met. 'I thought he may. What did you say?'

The question wrenched at Thea's insides and she shook her head. 'I couldn't let him finish. Ella, it is too much.' The tears came now, the shock of it punching through her and the turmoil inside winning out. There was no doubt left that her heart lay with Ella. She had watched Tabitha and Kitty through the evening and there was undeniably an affectionate connection between the friends, but nothing like this intensity, this passion she felt so keenly. Pressing her head against Ella's neck once more the words slipped out in a breath. 'Oh Ella, I wish I could marry you.' She pulled back, startled at herself. 'Do you think it is terrible of me to say so?'

Ella shook her head gently. 'Of course I don't.'

Another wave of fear brought fresh tears. 'I don't understand. I am supposed to be delighted in their attention. What happened to me? To us? Why are we not–' She sought for a word. 'Normal? Why are we so different?'

'We're not different to Emma and Harriet,' said Ella, softly.

'And look what happened to them!' Thea's voice raised a pitch in desperation. She looked around to ensure they were still alone on the terrace and lowered her voice. 'Mrs Jefferys said that knowledge could corrupt a lady's mind. Harriet studied astronomy and we encouraged one another. What if we did it to ourselves?'

She could have sworn she saw a twitch in Ella's eyebrow before she took her hand. 'Come with me,' she whispered after a pause. 'There's something I want to show you.' Ella took her hand and led her across the moonlit terrace to a side door to the house. She lit a candle before leading Thea down corridors lain with plush carpet until the sound of the ball faded into the distance. Ella retrieved a key from an urn and unlocked a heavy wooden door flanked by two family busts. She guided Thea through it, smiling, and locked it behind them.

Thea squinted around the large room before her, the candlelight glinting off the gilded spines of hundreds of books. 'Now this I am familiar with,' she said, comforted, 'but if it is the knowledge that's to blame, surely this can only make it worse?'

'Perhaps,' said Ella, and the candlelight lit her perfect smile.

She pulled Thea over to the opposite side of the room and slid a large green book to the side. Inserting a key behind it, she clicked a lock and a whole bookshelf hinged inwards like a door. Astounded, Thea realised it was an entirely fake section of the library, mocked up books concealing a secret room. She followed Ella through the gap, who then closed the fake shelf and locked it behind them.

This room was much smaller, but still crammed with shelves and had a square table at its centre. Thea stared around it, trying to make out the wording on the spines. Moonlight lit their edges from a small window high on the wall. Ella's breath was suddenly hot on her ear. 'Books my father would prefer were concealed from others.'

'Why?' asked Thea, confused as to why anyone would feel the need to hide literature. Ella didn't answer but used the candle to light the works low on a shelf. She selected a book and a pamphlet and placed them both on the table. 'Memoirs of a woman of pleasure,' muttered Thea as she read the font of the book. Then the words struck her. 'Oh, it isn't?'

Ella only peered upwards at her briefly, her eyes shining but slightly wary as she flicked through the pages of the book. Here and there an etching revealed itself to Thea, confirming that the protagonist of the book was, indeed, experiencing a significant amount of pleasure. 'Oh,' she said again, feeling like she should look away, but couldn't quite convince her eyes to let go. 'Are you sure we should be here? What if we get caught?'

A more certain smile lit Ella's face. 'Thea, few people other than us would rather be in a library than at a ball. Also,' she said as she nodded to the key on the shelf, 'that is the only key. Nobody can get into the library or into this room. We are quite safe.'

Thea relaxed a little but was still both fascinated and disturbed by the book. It had rested open on a page showing a hand-coloured etching and Thea knew instantly the image would be seared into her brain for some time to come. A lady reclined on a chaise, her skirts rucked up around her waist and hand at her temple. A bewigged man with a large ruff straddled her legs, his breeches round his ankles and... 'Oh my goodness.'

Thea wanted to look away but couldn't – just like the lady in the picture, it seemed. She put a hand to her eyes but still looked through her fingers, 'Ella is this supposed to improve my feelings towards men, because – well – it isn't likely.'

'Worry not,' said Ella, 'that is not what I brought you here to show you. 'She began to flick through pages of text once more and Thea dared to take her hand from her eyes. She swallowed involuntarily. 'Are they all that... pink? And...'

'Bulbous?' asked Ella, distractedly as she hunted for a page. 'In this volume they are, yes.'

Thea blanched. 'You mean there are more?'

'Goodness, yes,' said Ella, 'most of that lower shelf there. She gestured to where she had retrieved the book.

'And you read it?' asked Thea, beginning to think she may not understand Ella as well as she thought.

'A little,' said Ella, 'I am fascinated by it as I am about literature in general. Father doesn't know I am aware of this room but I found it years ago. Its contents are certainly interesting and I can't deny I have enjoyed many of its contents.' She looked a little bashful. 'Most of that shelf is pictures and poems, this is one of the only novels of the type my father owns. There is clearly a good market as it is well produced and it is written for male eyes only of course – notwithstanding that no woman could read this with any thought to reality or credibility – and it is relatively well-written.' Thea stared down at the book and then up at Ella, astonished at how anyone could consider this so pragmatically. Especially with all the protuberances present on the pages swiftly flicking past her vision. 'Ah, here we are,' said Ella at last, and motioned Thea to look at the engraving displayed on the pages now spread wide on the table.

Thea gasped. And then leaned in for a closer look. 'Is that–?'

'It is,' said Ella, a smile warming her tone. Two women, this time, presented themselves to Thea. One lay in the centre of a four poster, reclined on her side and facing the reader with all on show that could possibly be. Her arm thrust above her head in evident pleasure, pre-sumably elicited by the hand between her open legs. The hand be-longing to the woman who lay half naked behind her. Thea stared at it for what seemed like minutes before Ella broke the silence. 'Not just you and I,' she said softly, 'or just Emma and Harriet. It is known, if not encouraged. Our heroine, here, looks to me like she is having an exceedingly good day.'

Thea had to clear her throat before she spoke. 'But then why? Emma and Harriet.' More words wouldn't present themselves. She was feeling at once confused, slightly disgusted and pleasantly warm somewhere below her stomach.

A small chuckle escaped Ella. 'Thea, most of the men in this world cannot cope with the fact that you may have a mind to rival theirs. The thought that two women may manage to exist together without a man and experience pleasures possibly even greater than even they can provide is too much for them to bear. And so we speak not of it, ridiculing and controlling those who engage in anything other than the standard order. But passion will always find expression.'

Thea looked up into Ella's eyes, dark from the candlelight, and something else, Thea suspected. 'And I thought my curiosity would get me into trouble. Your taste in literature turns out to be far more questionable.'

Ella stepped in towards her and she looked up at the moon shining through the window. Thea felt hands slip around her middle. 'Thou silver deity of secret night, direct my footsteps through the woodland shade, thou conscious witness of unknown delight.' Her eyes locked back to Thea's at the last two words and Thea looked questioningly. 'Montagu,' Ella whispered, and something registered in Thea's mind.

'The day we met at Stanbourne, the poems and Mrs Jefferys.'

'Well remembered.'

'You were not flirting with me on that first day?'

Ella giggled. 'Not consciously, but you captivated me from the start. You were like nobody I had ever met. It wasn't long before I revisited this engraving. Wondering.'

Thea's heart skipped, registering Ella's meaning as their eyes held. She couldn't deny that she had thought about doing more with Ella than just kissing her. 'You really want...?' She broke off and swallowed, her eyes flicking to the book. 'Are you sure?'

'I am,' said Ella. 'Beyond sure. But only if, and when you are also.'

Thea thought for a moment, the idea warming her through. She gave a single nod. 'I am, but I'm not sure–' She faltered again as Ella shifted her backwards against the table.

She looked directly into Thea's eyes and her lips curved into a smile. 'Neither am I, but I'm looking forward to finding out, with you.'

Thea slid a hand to Ella's waist, pulled her close and kissed her gently. Ella bent her head and returned the kiss like she had a hundred times before, but then something between them shifted. The heat intensified inside Thea, curling like smoke through every part of her. Ella licked along Thea's lower lip, eliciting a tremble, then the kiss deepened as Ella slipped a hand around Thea's waist, pressing their bodies together. Thea felt Ella's thigh hard against her and gasped against her mouth. The spark ignited in the lecture hall touched the dry kindling of her soul and burned hot, searing away any reserve that remained. She broke away, alarmed at her own response, but only saw her desire reflected back in Ella's darkened eyes.

They sank back into a deep and delving kiss, exploring further with their hands, each responding to and encouraging the other in turn. Thea's hands wandered over the firm lacing of the stays at Ella's back, and then round to her front, pressing against Ella's breast which rose and fell with increasing fervour. She trailed a hand down Ella's gown, feeling the rough embroidery of the stomacher give way to the silk of the skirt. Suddenly she felt like the skin was stretched too thinly over her body, not uncomfortably, but so she felt raw and transparent, like Ella's hand could reach out and touch the very being of her – a core that she hadn't known existed, until this moment.

As her hand slid lower she hesitated. Ella broke from the kiss with parted lips and inhaled a faltering breath. The words that came on the shallow outbreath contained barely any volume, but they slipped through Thea's tightly drawn skin and she felt them deep at her core. 'Thea, please.'

Thea gently guided Ella down onto the floor behind the table and began to explore with hungry fingers. She kissed Ella's lips, her cheeks, and down her neck, drawing in every scent of her and marvelling at the sweet musk she found by her collar bone. Everything inside her was aflame. She felt enveloped by desire, and yet, desperately anxious.

Ella seemed to sense it and rolled Thea who groaned on an exhalation as Ella settled over her, a thigh slipping suddenly between hers. Instinctively she shifted to meet it and heat surged within her, mocking the cool of the evening.

She grasped at the ivory of Ella's gown, pulling lengths of silky material until she found her way to the hem. Her hand grazed stockings and then she sighed into Ella's kiss as she traced the soft skin of her thigh. Ella gasped and encouraged her with gentle murmurs as her hand moved higher. Thea's heart beat fast as her fingers met their mark, sliding against Ella and eliciting a gasp against her lips. Suddenly, the contact broke as Ella shifted and began frantically pulling at Thea's skirts, hungrily seeking her skin. Thea muffled a cry as Ella touched her for the first time, light searing through her body, her consciousness wild. They moved together until Ella's muted cries intensified and she slid harder and faster against trembling fingers. Ella arched backwards, pushing herself to her lover, convulsions ripping through her body. As Thea observed with elation she was taken by surprise as fire exploded and engulfed every inch of her, making her whole body shudder and a growl emanate desperately into the nape of Ella's neck.

They clung to each other as their breathing settled, weak and unsteady. Eventually Ella loosened her grip and pulled away to look into Thea's eyes. Thea could think of no words which would do, and so she traced a hand over Ella's cheek and kissed her tenderly. They lay together, looking at the moon, Ella propped in the crook of Thea's shoulder and arms entwined around each other.

'This might be my favourite library so far,' whispered Thea.

Ella smiled and raised one of Thea's hands to her lips. 'I am delighted to hear it. You make me happier than I have ever been, Miss Morell.'

CHAPTER 11

Milford, June 1758

Thea and Ella padded up the grand staircase at Milford, Mrs Phibbs leading the way and Mr Croft following with the trunk. Thea felt sure that the glow of her excitement must somehow show through to the outside, it was almost a week since the ball, and Ella was to stay with her for two whole weeks. As the two of them had crept back to the festivities after their trip to the library, their mothers had collared them in the drawing room. Panic had given way to elation as Lady Swanham had explained that Lord Swanham had been called back to London to advise on the continuing tensions with the French. She would go with him and had arranged with Mrs Morell that Ella could stay at Milford if she wished. Mrs Morell had been only too delighted at the strengthening of relations between the families and Thea and Ella had been almost overcome with joy.

Ella was to have the room next to hers and before long all of the luggage was brought up and dresses hung by Mrs Phibbs. 'Will there be anything else, Miss Thea?'

'No thank you, Mrs Phibbs, we'll call if needed.'

Ella practically launched herself at Thea as the door clicked shut. She kissed her tenderly and hungrily before pulling back and fixing her with a soft gaze. 'Happy birthday. Also, I missed you.'

Thea couldn't think of a better birthday present and grinned against the kisses. 'And I you.'

'Can you believe that we have two whole weeks together?'

Thea laughed with delight. 'I barely can, but it is true.' She pursed her lips and tapped a finger on her chin in mock thought. 'Now, however am I going to entertain you for that length of time?'

She leaned in for another kiss, but almost fell forwards as Ella straightened up. 'I wondered if perhaps Scip, or you of course, would be able to teach me some things about plants? I have mine now, and I would love to know how to care for them properly.'

Thea raised an eyebrow.

'Although I can think of some other things'

Thea met her mark this time, and kissed Ella deeply until there was a knock at the door. They sprung apart and brushed themselves down. It was Mrs Phibbs, come to inform them that Lady Foxmore had arrived and it was time for the birthday tea.

As she opened a third parcel full of ribbons and lace, Thea drew on a smile for Tabitha. 'Thank you, sister, as every year you have remembered that pink is my favourite colour.'

'What? Oh, yes, never mind that, I hope you like it.' Tabitha was staring out of the window. 'They're Ralph's favourite you know, he complimented me on them no less than four times at the ball, did I tell you?' She had told them. She had told them every day during the week following the ball, usually more than once. After dancing with Ralph Jefferys four times and spending the rest of the night with him at cribbage, he was her new obsession. She was entirely unconcerned at the debts Mr Morell had needed to settle for her at the close of the evening, but it was beginning to trouble Thea more deeply.

Mrs Morell looked at Tabitha adoringly. 'It is so exciting my dear, we must get you more ribbons just like it for when you see Ralph in Thornbury.' Thea was mostly pleased that her mother had been in a relatively good humour after observing her daughters' partnering at the ball. If only she knew, thought Thea, of the real romance that occupied her mind and the two propositions that had been deflected.

Thea pushed the open parcel of ribbons towards her sister. 'You can borrow these if you like? I mean, until you get more of your own?'

Tabitha squealed and gathered them up while Ella grinned at Thea across the drawing room where they sat in a circle, taking tea.

'Happy birthday, Thea,' she said softly, as she rose and offered her own parcel. It was small, but heavy.

Thea weighed it in her hands. 'Is it a rock?' she asked, laughing. Ella gave her another sly smile as Thea undid the string and the paper fluttered to the floor.

'Oh my!' she exclaimed, gently cupping a small, cylindrically shaped, pinkish-grey lump with small dots all over one side.

Tabitha leaned closer despite herself and wrinkled her nose. 'It *is* a rock.'

'It's a stigmaria!' announced Thea, the delight evident on her face. She had wanted one for the collection and remembered mentioning it, in passing, the first day that Ella had visited Milford. Ella nodded at her and Thea's heart swelled. Tabitha lost interest and wandered back to the ribbons, and Ursula, peering studiously from her chair, asked Thea to spell it.

When she had, and stopped laughing, she passed it to Martha. 'It's the fossilised root of a coal forest lycopsid tree from the secondary period. Isn't it wonderful?' She exchanged a look of thanks with Ella, and Martha nodded.

'How amazing to witness parts of plants which no longer live. An excellent gift, Lady Eleanor.' Ella smiled shyly, and Mrs Morell, bored by now, suggested the present opening should continue.

The next was a large, rectangular-shaped package. 'Aha,' said Thea, grinning at Martha, 'I wonder what this could be?' She carefully peeled back the paper and ran her hands over the firm leather of the book she found inside, before flicking through the many pages, her eyes shining with delight. Martha was sitting next to her so Thea leaned over and placed a hand on her arm. 'Thank you.' She meant it.

Martha smiled. 'You are very welcome. I hope it will come in useful.'

'What is it?' asked Ella craning forward.

'It is volume six of Diderot's *Encyclopédie* – it is the only ency-clopaedia in the world which tells us how we know information, not just what we know.' She looked warily towards her mother but found her deep in conversation with Tabitha. 'Lady Foxmore began to buy the series for me when I turned eighteen and she knew my interest wasn't just a phase.'

She grinned at Martha, who squeezed her arm. 'I know of nobody else who would make more use of it I am sure, it is a pleasure to add to your library and your development as a scholar, Thea.' Thea was full of gratitude that she had two excellent women in her life who bothered to understand the woman she was, rather than the lady they thought she ought to be.

Ella took in the pages Thea was craning through. 'Are there many volumes? How old will you be when you have collected the whole set?'

Thea counted on her hands. 'Six and forty!' she exclaimed, looking horrified. Ella and Ursula burst out laughing.

'Oh my goodness,' laughed Martha. 'It will be a miracle if I live to see you past *'Refraction.'*

After a walk around the grounds and a little instruction on wildflower identification from Martha, it was time for dinner. They discussed the activities of the upcoming two weeks and how Ella was keen to learn about plants. Martha and Ursula were keen to help – Mr Morell was a little quiet, Thea thought. She made a note to ask Martha about his finances later.

Eventually Tabitha's voice cut across the table. 'I did think George Crowe looked tolerably well at the ball, didn't you, Lady Foxmore and Ella? I have been saying it to my family for the past week but none of them except Mama will have it. He was asking after Thea and I am sure had thoughts of her for a short while. She did look less frightful than

SUZANNE MOSS

usual that night and goodness knows he's gone through most other eligible women in the county.'

'I thought we'd agreed to talk no more of it, Tab?' pleaded Thea, looking uncomfortable. She had no desire to dredge up the subject in front of Ella, and Martha certainly wouldn't approve.

'Between ourselves, yes,' admitted her sister, 'but I am keen to know what Ella and Lady Foxmore think. Don't you think he would make a good suitor for my sister?' She propped an elbow on the table and rested her chin on her hand, her intense, questioning gaze never faltering. Ella became increasingly interested in her pigeon and rice and Thea was pleased when Martha came to her rescue.

'If Thea is concerned with fortune over fidelity, then I think she can do no better than George Crowe. As a match for anything else, however,' she said, returning an enquiring stare to Thea, 'it seems – unlikely.'

'I suppose you mean love?' questioned Mrs Morell, 'You may have achieved it in your own marriage, Martha, but not everyone can have that luxury.' Thea's stomach clenched at her mother's indelicacy, but thankfully with the sister of another potential suitor in the room, Mrs Morell checked herself and glared at Tabitha, who desisted from her questioning.

With their appetites sated, tea taken and Martha seen off to Denbury, Thea and Ella made their way upstairs. 'Lady Eleanor and I will do for each other tonight, Agnes,' said Thea to the maid as she set the water jug on the dresser, 'just until Lady Eleanor gets settled.' She tried to sound calmer than she felt. Agnes nodded, bobbed and clicked the latch shut behind her. Ella, who had hovered near the door, leaned back against it.

'Finally,' smiled Thea, sauntering over to her lover and gently but firmly pressing her against the door with the heel of her hand. She kissed Ella gently, any reticence she felt fleeing in the instant.

Ella frowned and held Thea away with two hands at her waist. 'I feel bad.'

Thea's heart sank. 'What's wrong?' Worry suddenly lodged in her chest and Ella's eyes were solemn.

'It's just – I only got you a rock for your birthday, so I wondered if I might be able to make it up to you tonight?' The tension eased from Thea's shoulders as Ella smiled and giggled, and then kissed Thea deep, and long, tracing her silken tongue across Thea's eager lips.

'Mmm, good start,' Thea mumbled. 'But first things first.' She undid the pins on Ella's dress, quickly and carefully, and worked until the gown was strewn over a chair. Turning Ella round and planting a gentle kiss on the base of her neck, she undid the laces on the stays until they and the petticoats smothered the gown. She pulled the pins out of Ella's hair and marvelled as it flowed loose and lustrous around her graceful shoulders. Ella turned her around and repeated the ritual, until the final garment between them slid to the floor.

As Thea drank in the exquisite curves and pale, silken skin she felt nerves tighten her chest. Ella stepped forward and slid her hands around Thea's waist, pulling her near. Thea gasped as she felt Ella's soft, warm skin on her own and gently slipped a hand to the small of Ella's back, drawing in closer. The nerves dissipated as she drank in the dusky scent and nestled in the nape of the taller woman's neck, lost to the world for a few, precious moments in which she could convince herself that what they had could last.

'This is perfect,' whispered Ella into her ear. She led Thea to the bed and laid her down, hair cascading over both their bodies as she settled on top of her lover. Her hands caressed Thea's body and hot kisses followed as she made her way lower. She made delicious yet purposeful progress until each of Thea's thighs nestled over a shoulder. Thea's breath came quickly and anticipation flooded her veins as Ella looked up with an uncharacteristically wicked grin. 'Happy birthday,' she breathed.

As usual, Thea awoke to the sound of sliding curtains and light streaming through the bed posts. This morning, however, it was accompanied by a sudden panic as her eyes snapped left to Ella beside her. They must have fallen asleep before they could clear the clothing and get Ella back to her own room. This was a disaster; being found out on the first day could be an end to the whole thing. She noted with relief that Ella was close and had gently shifted beneath the covers, so if you didn't look too closely you might not notice the two bodies in the bed. Only a pair of eyes was visible, and a glance from them betrayed as much alarm as Thea felt. When her vision adjusted to the light she noticed with added horror that it was Mrs Phibbs and not Agnes opening up this morning.

She cleared her throat and sat up a little, clutching the covers around her bare chest and trying to sound nonchalant. 'Good morning, Mrs Phibbs.'

Mrs Phibbs looked around from where she was tying back the second set of curtains. 'Ah, there you are, I thought you were still asleep.' She sounded cheery. That was good. 'Good morning, Miss Thea' – there was a tiny pause – 'and Lady Eleanor. I trust you both slept well?'

The girls shared an urgent glance as Mrs Phibbs moved on to the next window. The silence was more than Thea could bear as she struggled to fabricate a justification. 'Yes, thank you. Lady Eleanor came to sleep here, in the night, as she had a nightmare.' The weak excuse was all she could think of in the moment, and she saw Ella's eyes roll.

Mrs Phibbs turned and cast her eyes over the gowns, petticoats and stays strewn over the furniture 'Well, it is lucky that she managed to dress in full dinner gown before she made her way in here. Or did Lady Eleanor have a nightmare whilst preparing for bed?' Mrs Phibbs arched her brows, but Thea was sure she saw a slight twitch in the corner of her mouth.

Thea looked back at Ella, resigned, and sat up as far as she dare whilst preserving her modesty. She wasn't sure why – Mrs Phibbs had seen it all before while Thea was dressing and bathing, but after obvious intimacy it seemed different, somehow. Now she had no choice but to try and talk Mrs Phibbs round, and to plead with her to keep the secret. Mrs Phibbs had done so for her many times over the years, although this was a different matter entirely.

Thea's voice was smaller and softer this time. 'I am terribly sorry, Mrs Phibbs, I do hope that we haven't offended you. I – I really don't know what to say–'

Mrs Phibbs snapped her head around from where she had just finished the last curtain. 'Offended me? Goodness no, Miss Thea, your business is your business and I will say nothing about it.' She turned back and began to tidy the muddle of clothing.

Thea and Ella shared a puzzled glance. 'Are you certain? I mean, it must have been a little – unexpected?'

'Unexpected?' Mrs Phibbs turned the word over on her tongue as she retrieved and folded the shifts. Thea was twisted with awkwardness as she remembered the moment they had slipped out of them the night before. 'I don't know if I'd quite say that, Miss, I have known you all your life after all, and I've been waiting for it ever since you kissed that electrical venus. I do have to admit it's a good job it wasn't Agnes as she does have something of a mouth on her, which is why I came up myself this morning.'

Thea was non-plussed. She hadn't thought it was that obvious. 'So you're not – angry? Or disgusted?'

Mrs Phibbs sighed and turned to the bed, hands on her hips. 'Miss Thea, I have worked for many more families than yours over the years and I have seen a good many things more interesting than this I can assure you. My previous mistress of the house – when I worked in London this was with my sister – would throw notorious sapphic parties that ladies would attend from miles around.' She smiled nostalgically and Thea's eyes widened. 'We would find more young ladies than this in her bed come morning for certain, and everywhere else in the house for that matter.' She sucked her teeth and sounded thoughtful. 'A lot of sheets to wash too. No, you will have to try harder than this to shock me, Miss Thea, although I am sure you will have a good go over this coming fortnight.'

By now Ella had emerged from the covers and both she and Thea stared at Mrs Phibbs, open mouthed. Not receiving any response, the housekeeper carried on. 'Anyway, I will do for you both whilst Lady Eleanor is here, I'll do her room as well as yours and will make certain you're not disturbed by anyone in the evenings or morning. I'll leave you here a bit to enjoy the, er, morning sun, before I come up for dressing, if that's acceptable to you?'

They both nodded convulsively, and Thea managed a small 'Thank you.'

Mrs Phibbs smiled and held up a cup and saucer. 'Now, tea?'

Tea in hand, and mouth still agape, Thea watched Mrs Phibbs exit the room and then slumped down in the bed. She dropped her head left to Ella who she expected to be similarly wrought, but who was, in fact, staring at her furiously.

'What?' she asked, alarmed.

Ella sat up and crossed her arms. 'Who on earth is the electrical venus?'

Later that afternoon they lay on the lush bank by the lake, swans gliding across gentle ripples and the long grass whispering around them. Thea sighed contentedly. 'That was a lovely day.'

Ella made a face. 'It was, if you didn't show yourself up in front of your lover's sister, an expert gardener and a Countess.'

Thea laughed. 'You didn't.'

Ella's mouth twisted. 'Thea, I potted on thirty plants directly into tan. I had to do them all again, *and* my hands smell of urine.'

She held them out to Thea who pulled away, laughing. 'I'd rather not experience it again thank you. It made Scip chuckle though.'

Ella groaned. 'And Ursula couldn't contain herself. *And* Lady Fox-more.'

Thea tried to stifle her giggles, she had seen Ursula and Scip hiding their smiles together. 'Who doesn't need a little extra joy in their lives? Anyway, it's an easy mistake to make.'

'If you have no sense of smell.'

Thea smiled warmly. She was only impressed that the neat and proper Lady Eleanor had got stuck into any kind of dirt and knew their companions had been too. 'At least you didn't spend all the day being instructed by Ursula and Martha – their herbarium collections will be overflowing by autumn. *And* we have to do more at Denbury next week.'

This seemed to cheer Ella. 'I'm looking forward to it, I like Lady Foxmore very much, and I can't wait to see her greenhouse again. I mean the one here is wonderful, but hers is fabulous.'

Thea propped herself up on an elbow and fixed Ella with a crooked grin. 'I am beginning to think you might have a bit of a crush on Lady Foxmore.' Ella sputtered a laugh and Thea feigned horror. 'Do you?!'

'Thea, she is an accomplished, attractive and accommodating lady, and although she still terrifies me of course I have a crush on her.' She prodded Thea in the ribs making her body twitch. 'Come on, tell me you don't.'

Thea laughed, but the sound stuck in her throat and a wave of shame rushed in. Mostly she could smile about it now, but sometimes it took her by surprise. 'Perhaps once,' she said, quietly, 'but I squeezed it out like all the rest.' At the time it had taken her completely off guard, the sudden realisation one night in the cabinet as they studied a cinnamon coral, that she desired something from Martha other than friendship. She had never allowed herself to journey too far in her mind, nowhere near as far as she had actually journeyed with Ella, but now she was clearer in her own mind the want was unmistakeable.

'And it's a blessing I did. When it all came out about Emma and Harriet I have never seen her in such disquiet. She made it quite clear what she thought of,' she hesitated, 'that sort of activity.' She said it quietly, almost wishing it weren't true. Her stomach twisted as it had then, remembering Martha's disquiet. She even suspected Martha had played a part in the subsequent marriages of Emma and Harriet but hadn't dare ask. Before that point she hadn't been able to put language to her thoughts, but knew she was very glad she had buried her feelings before they betrayed Martha's tutoring, time and trust. They were hidden so deeply that she barely ever thought of it now.

Ella's voice was gentle and understanding. 'It is a shame you couldn't confide in her – I know how close the two of you are.'

'We are,' said Thea, a twinge of guilt making itself known, 'and I have thought about it, but we have been too lucky with Edgar and Mrs Phibbs. Others would not be so understanding and I can't risk it with Martha. She is very particular over what she deems wrong and right.'

'Then it shall just be us,' said Ella, using a finger to investigate a dandelion clock emerging from the long grass.

'What about you?' asked Thea, recalling something Ella had said earlier. 'Have there been – others?'

Ella looked sideways at her. 'Perhaps a few crushes. At a distance of course. There was Lucy Adams, then Heather Steele, then the stern dress fitter at Whistons and my music tutor.'

Thea's eyes widened as Ella went through the list. 'Anyone else?' she asked, incredulously.

Ella cocked an eyebrow. 'A few,' she said, 'but nothing like this. And then there was you.' The smile faded, Thea suspected she knew why. She didn't want to ask, but felt she had to.

'So, what happens now?'

Ella shrugged and picked the dandelion, twirling the stalk in her fingers. 'For now the world thinks we are only romantic friends, we have nothing to concern us as long as we are careful.' She blew on the globe, causing the seeds to take to the wind on their tiny parachutes.

Thea sighed and pressed her temple to Ella's shoulder, watching them dissipate. 'Of course.'

Over the next two weeks the new lovers enjoyed themselves to the full with estate visits, days out with Jane and plenty of time with Martha and Edgar. When he made artificial thunder and lightning with an assortment of chemicals it choked them all so much they had to throw open the windows and decamp to the garden until it settled. At night they enjoyed each other. Thankfully Mrs Phibbs was as good as her word and there were no interruptions. The two of them grew in confidence together, exploring and enjoying, and finding new ways to delight one another.

The Monday evening saw a dinner party at Milford, but not the kind Mrs Morell enjoyed. Mr Morell had invited Martha, Edgar and Stanhope Grimston, to return the favour of all the tea and dinner they had partaken of at Pook End. After the obligatory visit to the cabinet and the stove during which Mrs Morell and Mr Grimston hung back and discussed the latest in the *Tête-a-Tête* gossip column, they all sat down for dinner. Mrs Morell and Tabitha ensured to sit themselves down one end of the table in order to avoid the monotony of natural philosophy discourse.

As usual, Mr Grimston pontificated at length. 'I don't know if you were aware that I had dinner with Elias Thompson last time I was in town, were you? I only mention it as he supplies the cabinet of the Prince of Wales, and he may be able to make suggestions for improvements to the collections at Milford if you wish me to speak to him on your behalf, Morell? I understand that your collection is not as you would wish it to be, but with some considerable work I am sure that it could almost reach the standard of parts of my collection at

Wickmarsh.' He paused to shove in another mouthful of beef pudding and Edgar took the opportunity to change the subject.

'Ben, Martha, would you do us the honour of an update on your plant experiment? It sounds fascinating!'

Mr Morell nodded but hesitated and Martha took up the question. 'It is coming on excellently well, Edgar. We have successfully observed and recorded the movements of various plants in response to a variety of different stimulus.' Edgar clapped his hands in appreciation and Martha went on. 'We now need to replicate the experiment a number of times through and attempt to disseminate the research somehow. Wouldn't you agree, Ben?'

Mr Morell was about to respond when Mr Grimston addressed him directly. 'What's that you say, Morell? You're measuring plants?'

'Well.' Mr Morell shifted uncomfortably. '*I* didn't actually say anything, but plants' movement in response to stimulus, yes.'

He glanced at Martha by way of apology but she shook her head, understanding. He went on. 'Stimulus like light, dark, and touch. We are observing how *Hedysarum,* the telegraph plant, responds to light, and how the sensitive plant – that is *Mimosa*, and *Dionea*, the venus fly trap, respond to touch.'

Mr Grimston stopped dead with the next lump of meat halfway to his mouth and addressed Mr Morell once more. 'Sounds dull as hell, Morell, I hope you have a boy doing the work?' Mr Morell greyed a little at the impertinence but responded in his usual, generous manner.

'Lady Foxmore, Scip and I are conducting the experiment together. In fact, the concept is Martha's own and Scip has done most of the work here at Milford.'

The fork hovering near Mr Grimston's mouth maintained its inertia but his face turned aghast. 'The negro? And a woman? God man, give it up now and stop wasting your time. Or get a proper man to help you.' The mouthful was finally engulfed.

Thea's fist tensed around her knife and she saw Ursula's eyes harden. She flicked her eyes to Martha for the reaction, but she simply raised her eyes to the ceiling and clenched her jaw. Mr Morell's voice was tight in response. 'I beg your pardon?'

Mr Grimston waved his recently cleared fork. 'Neither women nor savages' brains are capable of the same level of thought as men. You want to read some Rousseau. Sensible man. He'll have none of this ridiculous notion of women engaging in scholarship. "Women's entire education should be planned in relation to men. To please men, to be useful to them, to win their love and respect". That is his good advice. Morell, your daughters must know that their place is in serving a man and if they see you treating a black as an equal then, well' – his eyes bulged then receded – 'then we're on a path to God knows where. They have no manners or sense of civility.' He speared another hunk of beef and shoved it between his teeth.

Thea's eyes had flicked from her father to Martha through the whole diatribe. Mr Morell's face had lost whatever colour it had and Martha had simply set her jaw and not taken a breath. Surprised at Martha's silence Thea suddenly remembered Edgar's strange reaction at Grimston's cabinet when Martha had tried to warn him against showing the unicorn horn. What was the issue between Martha and Mr Grimston?

Despite her reticence at speaking up Thea would not hear either Martha or Scip spoken about in this way. She caught her fathers' eye just before he spoke and he gave an almost imperceptible nod. 'What do you say to the further writings of Rousseau, Mr Grimston?' Thea asked, more steadily than she felt. 'I refer particularly the passage which asserts that "people who know little are usually great talkers, while men who know much say little"? And when speaking of manners and civility I see more in our stove house than I do in much of polite society.' She held his gaze across the table while he gawped back at her. She rather enjoyed his discomfort until Ursula broke the tension.

'And what about the teachings of Francis Bacon, Mr Grimston? He advocates observation. Surely women and blacks are just as able to observe and record the natural world as any white man? In fact, some may say that women are more attentive and so must excel in the new science.' Thea watched Edgar duck his head to hide a smile. Martha's face was still stony.

Mr Grimston pointed his fork again, this time at Ursula. At least here he was clearer on the point being levelled at him. 'Ha! Poppycock! I have no time for these newfangled ideas, all this faffing about with peering in microscopes and doing experiments others have already completed! Observation, experience! Rubbish! Where's the glory anymore? And as for women excelling in scholarship – it is a proven fact that their natural tendency to emotion renders them incapable of objective reasoning. And for those so taken with science it must be observed that their brains are significantly smaller than men's. That is the danger of female curiosity. It began at the fall and nothing more positive has come of it since.'

Mr Morell smiled weakly into his barely touched pudding as Thea took up once again. 'I wouldn't say Bacon's ideas were so new-fangled, Mr Grimston,' she posited, 'didn't he publish them over two hundred years ago? And I do believe progress is being made based on his methodology.'

Grimston glowered. 'Progress?! Morell has a tiny cabinet of insects and rocks.' He pointed at Martha. 'She has twelve books of dead plants and Pickles almost blows himself up on a weekly basis. Myself, I own only the finest curiosities – objects of wonder which all have a story to tell. I have said it before and I will say it again, they should never have let the lower classes engage in this kind of vital activity – physicians and suchlike just do not have the capacity to tell quality when they see it, neither can they afford it and so you end with this ridiculous focus on the ordinary. It takes breeding to recognise class and to create a true cabinet of wonders.'

Thea caught her father's anxious demeanour as Ursula cocked her head to the side and eyeballed Mr Grimston. 'I find it interesting that you use the word "wonder" about your collection, Mr Grimston. Wasn't it Robert Hooke who told us that the use of such a collection is not for "divertisement, and wonder, and gazing, as 'tis for the most part thought and esteemed... but for the most serious and diligent study of the most able proficient in Natural Philosophy"?'

Mr Grimston's mouth opened and closed like a stranded cod. There was a little cough, and Thea realised with a slight thrill that Ella was about to weigh in. 'I am sorry to interject, and I have to say I have visited all of your cabinets and find them all fascinating in their own different ways, but I was just wondering. Surely if Mr Locke is correct, and the human mind is a blank sheet which is only filled by experience, then it stands to reason that observations and experiment are essential to progress? It is surely impossible to conceive of advancement in the world of natural philosophy without stable collections founded on a sound taxonomic basis?' There was a hush as everyone stared at her in astonishment.

Ursula dropped a glance to Thea, who was staring at Ella, impressed and a little bit aroused.

Mr Morell and Martha nodded in agreement.

Mr Grimston sputtered. 'Enough of this ridiculous notion! If I ever consent to becoming President of the Royal Society I shall banish all of this nonsense. I have said time and time again that–'

Edgar, who had enjoyed the evening's sport but had short patience with his old friend on matters such as these, cut across him. 'Oh, Grimston, do stop being such a bore. The young ladies in the room have shown you up as the dusty virtuoso you are, with collections based firmly in the realms of whimsy. You can quote Rousseau and spout rubbish about tiny brains and savages all you want – but Lady Foxmore, these two young ladies and young Scip have made more progress in natural philosophy in the course of this dinner than you have in a full two score years. You need to get up to speed and in touch with the times old boy, nobody wants your sparkles and gumph. Get to proper scholarship, my man!'

Mr Grimston's eyes goggled and he drew breath to counter, but was interrupted by a commotion and a scream from the end of the table. As they all spun and stood in reaction Thea saw Mrs Morell and Tabitha standing over Mr Morell, who had slid from his chair and now lay motionless on the floor.

Chapter 12

Thea took her father's hand. 'How long has it been coming on?'

'I barely know,' he said with a slight wheeze, shifting himself in the bed. 'I suppose a couple of months if I track it to the first time I felt unwell, but it has been so gradual and comes and goes.' He patted her hand and gave her a weak smile. She kissed his head and reassured him that the very best would be done, hoping with every fibre of herself that the doctor would bring good news.

While she ensured he was comfortable and cooled him with a damp muslin he seemed to improve a little in spirits, but was still clammy, short of breath and light-headed. As she sat with him Thea noticed that his legs were swelled and tight. Mrs Morell fussed around her husband and ordered the servants but generally gave the air of it being a terrible inconvenience. Edgar and Mr Grimston had returned home and Martha had arranged tea for Ella, Ursula and Tabitha to calm their nerves. Thea felt sick with worry – her father was the steadying influence in the household and was always so constant. Seeing him vulnerable and unwell shook her to the bone as she knew only something serious would permit him to show it.

Doctor Ashby arrived within the hour and after a thorough examination and questioning he announced that Mr Morell had dropsy. Treatment was to be powder of jalap, cream of tartar and Florentine iris every two days, and an electuary of chamomile flowers, ginger and orange peel on the other. Thea left her mother with the patient and caught Dr Ashby on his way down the stairs. 'Is it serious, Doctor?'

The Doctor tipped his head to the side. 'It could be, Miss Morell. Dropsy can be erratic to treat and if I had seen your father when the symptoms first occurred things would be simpler. Nevertheless, we will monitor in the upcoming days and revise treatment accordingly.' Although Doctor Ashby was his usual, jovial self and made a valiant attempt to reassure, the look on his face made Thea's stomach churn.

The next day was tense. Mrs Morell was in high drama and had bestowed her agitation on Tabitha. The two of them seemed not so worried for Mr Morell, but rather for themselves in the event of the unspeakable. Mrs Morell reminded them again and again that as none of her daughters were yet married the estate would be entailed away to her cousin in Oxfordshire. Tabitha bemoaned Thea's lack of interest in finding a husband which would have saved them all. By the evening they were all in debtors' prison and it was Thea's fault – neither she, Ursula or Ella could wait to leave the dinner table. They all trooped miserably to Mr Morell's room where Mrs Phibbs had sat with him over dinner. He seemed no better and they shuffled to bed utterly despondent.

Thea sat on the bed, hugging her knees with worry, feeling generally wretched. It certainly wasn't how she had planned Ella's last night at Milford. When Ella had changed she climbed in next to Thea, wrapped her arms around her and placed a gentle kiss on her temple. 'I hate to leave you like this.'

Thea closed her eyes and leaned into the reassuring pressure. 'It will be unbearable without you, but it would be miserable for you to stay. If mother and Tabitha keep up the histrionics I think Ursula and I might take to father's room with him.'

'Whatever way,' soothed Ella, holding her tight, 'you only have to send a note and I will be here.' Thea smiled gratefully. Ella's presence was pleasantly solid after the vaporous fluttering of her mother and sister but she still felt helpless.

'I just feel so – responsible. For them all. The reality of their futures without him...' She tailed off and felt her throat tighten with anxiety.

Ella felt her distress and squeezed her. 'Any one of your sisters could make a good match. That would support all of you.'

Thea gave a wry, breathy laugh. 'Technically yes, but Tabitha is not to be trusted with money or responsibility and Ursula – she is the most sensible of us all but sadly it is a rare gentleman who would look past her chair.'

Her hand reached out to Ella. Talking of this further felt jarring. Thea's marriage must mean an end to everything they had, but Ella simply kissed her and held her, facing headlong into what seemed an impossible predicament. Thea sank into the warmth of Ella's arms but nothing could ease the uncomfortable reality.

After some minutes of quiet reflection, Thea suddenly remembered something forgotten in the drama of the day. From her bedside table she drew out a piece of abalone shell, about an inch across and pleasingly polished. It wasn't as complete as some of her other shells, but it was truly spectacular – turned one way it looked as green as an emerald, the other as blue as a lagoon.

She held it to Ella who was watching curiously. 'I wanted you to have this. Ever since I met you I see your eyes reflected in it every time I see it.' Ella held out her hand and Thea dropped it into her palm. 'Would you keep it as a reminder of this time we spent together?'

Thea's smile was touched with sadness and Ella's eyes pooled as she ran a thumb across the shimmering surface. 'It is beautiful, Thea, I will treasure it. It will remind me of you' – she paused – 'whenever you are not there.'

Their eyes held for long moments, bearing emotion impossible to verbalise. Words rose and fell in Thea's throat but none seemed like they would do. Ella suddenly gathered Thea in her arms and held her tight. Thea clung to Ella's shoulders, she had never felt this way about anyone. Had never found anyone who set her aflame, or with whom she wanted to spend every hour of her life. She felt vulnerable and didn't mind. Her life had started to make sense for the first time since she could remember. Whatever happened, she had that.

Two days later Doctor Ashby visited again. Mr Morell had insisted he try to get up, but dizziness had caused him to fall almost immediately. The Doctor spoke to Mr and Mrs Morell together while Thea and Ursula waited in the drawing room with Martha. They were wound so tight they started as one when Mrs Morell entered. 'How is he, Euphemia?' asked Martha, standing stiffly and intense with worry.

'Not good at all I'm afraid.' Mrs Morell lowered herself into the high-back by the window, shaking her head. 'His pulse is weakening and his body is retaining water.' She was quieter than usual and had ceased the drama. Thea had never seen her so grave and knew it must be serious. 'Doctor Ashby has given him more medicine but has little hope of its working. He says there is nothing more he can do.'

She drew a ragged breath and Thea squeezed Ursula around the shoulders, as much for herself as for her sister. 'There must be something else?'

Mrs Morell nodded weakly. 'He has sent for his friend Doctor Withering of Birmingham, who will arrive tomorrow. He is our last hope – apparently he has some pioneering new treatment for the dropsy.'

Martha moved to the window. 'I have read about this in the *Transactions*.' She turned to Thea and Ursula. 'He uses *Digitalis* – the foxglove. The treatment is very new, but he seems to be having success.' This brightened them a little and Thea was thankful for Martha's attention to plant-based literature. She couldn't help thinking, however, that it would be a miracle if the plants that grew wild in the woodlands of Milford would work as Dr Ashby's cocktail of exotic remedies had failed to do.

The day passed feebly. Tabitha tripped off to play cards with Christiana and Ralph Jefferys, Mrs Morell took to her room and Martha, Ursula and Thea spent time trying to keep each other from dwelling on possibilities. One of them was in constant attendance with Mr Morell although he was now so weak that he spent little time awake. After dinner, when it was her turn, Thea's eyes skimmed the words of the book in her lap but nothing entered her head. It was too full of worry for her father, for her family and the responsibility which had never felt more pressing.

As the light slipped from the day and she lit her first candle, the door creaked and Martha's form appeared. 'Everyone has turned in. Do you mind if I stay? I worry about you all.'

Thea's heart warmed at her friend's kindness. 'Of course.' She cleared blankets off a second chair. Martha dropped a kiss onto her forehead before nestling into the seat.

'Still no change?' The candlelight flickered across Mr Morell's pale face and Thea shook her head sadly.

'I feel so awful I didn't notice how ill he was. When I look back he'd been looking peaky, on and off, for weeks. He was clearly struggling at the dinner – I was too wrapped up in Mr Grimston's drivel to pay attention.'

Martha fixed her with a sympathetic gaze. 'It is always easy to reach a conclusion in hindsight. We were all taken up by Grimston, it is unfortunate when he dominates an occasion.' She looked back at Mr Morell and as Thea regarded her she saw Martha's knuckles whiten on the chair arm. Perhaps now wasn't the best time, but Edgar's comment and the way Martha was obviously affected by Mr Grimston played on her mind.

'His views on women are abhorrent. All the drivel about brains and emotions. At least others have the grace to be polite, even if it is what they think.' She tested the waters, keeping her voice steady.

Martha's chest rose and fell a couple of times before she responded. 'You all seemed to have it well in hand at dinner. I was proud of you for speaking up.' A soft glance landed on Thea making her warm through, although she could see Martha was still tense.

'I know I can lack courage at times, but I couldn't see him disparage people I love in such a way.' Martha's eyes flicked to her, and away again. 'I admit to being a little surprised you didn't join the defence.' Thea watched Martha carefully. Now she considered it, Martha didn't ever speak up when Mr Grimston did down the abilities of women. Was she nervous of the response? Not likely, thought Thea – but was it a worry about confirming her fears? That women would never be permitted a voice?

Martha didn't take her eyes from Mr Morell. 'Sometimes I worry about Edgar's frankness to Grimston. It can border on hurtful.'

Thea couldn't repress a snort. 'Well, Mr Grimston seems to have no concern about the feelings of others. He and Edgar have been friends for long enough to know how to handle one another, Martha.' Martha remained silent so Thea went on. 'Anyway, Edgar does him a service. What he says is true – Mr Grimston is behind the times and he will be found out by his precious society.'

Martha's gaze landed on her and she smiled weakly. 'You are right, of course, but debate is lost on men like him. He will not listen to reason or logic and so it is difficult to argue against him.'

That much was certainly true and Mr Grimston was by no means a solitary voice. It irritated Thea and she was struck by how severely it seemed to affect Martha. She reached out a hand and plucked Martha's from the chair arm. 'I understand, but you said yourself we must fight for it if we want to make a change.'

Martha's gaze rested thoughtfully on the hand grasping hers until she took it and traced Thea's fingers with her own. Her voice was darker when she spoke. 'You are so very right. And like I said, I am so proud of you, Thea, for speaking out. Usually I would do the same, it is only that in the past... In the past I have not always conducted myself well with regard to Mr Grimston.' She jutted her chin forward and clenched her jaw, staring at their entwined hands. 'I try to avoid any further unpleasantness, for the sake of both of us.'

Thea was intrigued and took a breath to speak, but Martha righted herself, reached for her pocket watch and flicked open the cover. 'It is after nine, we should cool your father – do you have a muslin?'

Thea's gaze switched to the bed and the peacefully sleeping figure. 'Agnes did it not a quarter hour ago–' she started, but Martha cut her off.

'Ah, here it is.' She reached for the cloth and water at the side of the bed and gently mopped Mr Morell's forehead, still refusing to meet her companion's gaze. Thea knew better than to persist.

Doctor Withering had made haste and arrived by noon the next day. Thea, Martha and Mrs Morell stood nervously while he entered – after a night in the chair Thea felt tired and dishevelled against his boundless energy. The new physician greeted them warmly and lost no time in examining his patient, seeming satisfied after fewer than five minutes.

'I am in agreement with Doctor Ashby's diagnosis of dropsy – anasarca to be exact – fluid retention in the subcutaneous tissue of the body. I will prescribe two ounces of digitalis three times a day. You must continue the dose until the stomach or bowels become affected. If the stomach, it means that the digitalis is working, if the bowels, you must give him opium to stop the purging and increase the dose of digitalis until it affects the stomach or an improvement is evident.' Thea tried to digest the instructions and hoped that between her,

Martha, her mother and Doctor Ashby they would remember. Doctor Withering worked fast.

With a few further directions he seemed satisfied and all pleasantries discharged the physicians took their leave. Thea hurried down the stairs after them and shuffled nervously as Doctor Withering was being helped into his travel coat. 'Do we have reason to be hopeful, Doctor?'

He turned to her kindly, clearly accustomed to anxious family members. 'Most certainly, Miss Morell. The medicine has proved itself extremely effective on many occasions. I should warn you that there seem to be some cases in which it has little or no effect, or indeed quite a severe adverse effect, up to and including death.' Thea blanched and he caught himself. 'But do try not to worry.'

CHAPTER 13

Ella sent a note every day. To Thea it felt like a chink of light shone from the paper every time she broke the seal. On paper Ella was discreet, of course, but there was no doubt of her tenderness and concern. On the day of Doctor Withering's visit there had been no note – although Thea had been preoccupied at the thought that either the disease or the remedy could kill her father within hours.

On the following day, Mrs Phibbs entered Mr Morell's room while Thea and Martha read to him. Mrs Phibbs bobbed her head as she entered. 'If you please, Lady Foxmore and Miss Thea, Mrs Morell is asking after you downstairs. Lady Swanham and Lady Eleanor are with her.' They rose to go and asked the housekeeper to wait with Mr Morell.

Mrs Phibbs stood aside to allow Martha to exit the room, but as Thea passed her she felt a tentative but purposeful hand on her arm. Looking up she saw worry in Mrs Phibbs' eyes. 'You should know, Miss Thea, before you go down.' She whispered close to Thea so not even the retreating Martha could hear. 'I overheard them in the hall, there has been a letter.'

Thea couldn't begin to think what she meant. 'A letter? Are the Earl and Viscount quite well?'

'Not that.' The concern on Mrs Phibbs' face chilled Thea. 'The letter is about you and Lady Eleanor.' She dropped her voice further. 'About your closeness.'

Thea's blood ran cold and she raced down the grand staircase after Martha. Her haste was in direct opposition to the inertia which met her in the hallway. Lady Swanham and Ella stood inside the door, their faces grave. Ella glanced at Thea but then quickly averted her eyes. Mrs Morell stood, rigid and ashen faced, clutching a letter in a shaking hand.

The letter was brandished at her before she reached the bottom step. 'What is the meaning of this?' Mrs Morell hissed as she stepped towards her, her voice taut and quiet, like the still in the air before a storm.

Thea tried to maintain a cautious calm, despite the tattoo beating against her chest. 'What is it, mother?'

Mrs Morell closed her eyes before she spoke as if to shield herself from her own words. 'It is a letter, sent to Lady Swanham yesterday, to inform her that you' – she gritted her teeth and took a deep and noisy breath through her nose – 'to inform her that you have been engaging in inappropriate – relations – with Lady Eleanor.' The words were halting and when they came she almost spat them. They seemed to fill the cavernous space.

Thea felt like the room was suddenly devoid of air. If she had been able to draw a breath, she certainly couldn't speak through her thick throat. Gripping the banister to steady herself as an icy rush reached her head and made her sway, she became aware that she was still staring at her mother.

Mrs Morell's glare bore into her. 'Well?' she hissed. Thea somehow found the strength to look at Ella, who kept her gaze steadfastly fixed to the floor. Struggling to extract words from her own daughter in the face of Lady Swanham, Mrs Morell lost her patience. 'Am I to beat it out of you, child? What is wrong with you?' Her shrill voice now reverberated around the vast stairway. Thea knew her mother would deplore the idea of the act itself, but that it exposed her family in front of the Swanhams would be the worst outcome she could imagine.

Thea's panicked gaze ticked around the always-cool Lady Swanham, a grey Martha and her livid mother. The fear coursing through her dashed all possibility of rational thought and she clutched at the memory of the conversation by the river. 'Ella and I are simply friends. We have become close, but that is not unusual. Like Tabitha and Kitty.' She knew her voice shook and her eyes dropped to the floor as she spoke.

'Miss Morell, if I may enlighten you a little further.' In contrast to Mrs Morell, Lady Swanham was calm and measured. She clicked two steps forwards on the marble floor. 'The letter is anonymously written and mercifully short. It alleges that relations between you and my daughter have progressed further than you suggest to the point that they are habitually and unnaturally physical.' The matter-of-fact delivery felt almost like a physical blow. Lady Swanham went on. 'Ella and I spoke at length yesterday and she has confirmed its validity. Please could I beg your courtesy to do the same?' In the face of such determined pragmatism Thea's hope withered and her throat constricted further. A convulsive nod turned out to be all she could manage while a wave of nausea hit her. Out of the corner of her eye she saw her mother start and Martha stare at her with barely disguised astonishment.

Lady Swanham gave one brief nod of the head by way of acknowledgement. 'Thankfully the news seems to be contained within our families and I suggest we do all we can to keep it that way. I would like to confer with you, Mrs Morell, if I may, about what is to be done.' Mrs Morell nodded, no doubt pleased to be involved in the reckoning, and gestured to the drawing room.

Before following, Lady Swanham looked between both Thea and Ella. 'Lady Foxmore, could I prevail on you to supervise my daughter and Miss Morell in the interim?' Martha agreed and Lady Swanham and Mrs Morell retired.

With the immediate threat passed Thea's senses returned to her in part and she contemplated both of her companions. Martha stood rigid, her face ashen. She glanced over as Thea's gaze settled on her, her face now unreadable but her breathing shallow. Martha quickly averted her eyes. Thea's attention turned to Ella who still studied the floor in front of her. She knew if she stared long enough Ella would have no choice but to look and before long she was proved right. Thea's heart broke to see Ella's features overwhelmed with sadness – it was agony not to be able to reach out and comfort her. Thea tried to convey some sort of question with her eyes but Ella simply gave an almost imperceptible shake of her head and dropped her gaze once more. One letter to change their world completely. As Thea's pulse began to slow the implications dripped into her head one by one. Nothing could ever be the same between them. They would never be left alone, they may not even be allowed to see each other. The thought knocked the breath out of her for the second time that morning.

After long, silent minutes Lady Swanham and Mrs Morell returned. Thea looked to them both with reticence. 'Thank you for your patience. We have decided that you will both go away from the county for a time.' It was Lady Swanham who delivered the news. 'You will go first, Miss Morell, and Ella will go a month later so as not to arouse suspicion. The distance will ensure that there is no further temptation and any rumours which may be circulating within society will be quelled. Ella will travel to Germany to stay with her cousins for a year or so. Miss Morell, your mother will discuss your destination with Lady Foxmore, as your father is currently indisposed.' She nodded to Mrs Morell. 'Thank you for a swift resolution, we will now take our leave. Girls, we will wait outside while you say your goodbyes. Be hasty.' The Countess stepped aside to allow Mrs Morell and Martha ahead of her. Discomfort was writ on both of their faces but neither dare protest. Thea was grateful for the tiniest sliver of charity from Lady Swanham.

Finally alone, Thea ran to Ella and took her hands. 'Do you know who sent the letter?' Ella squeezed her eyes shut and shook her head.

Thea's hands gripped trembling fingers and her heart clutched at hope. 'Perhaps we can still remedy it.'

'Remedy it?' Ella's voice was barely a whisper. 'Thea, of course we can't.'

This was all too new, too fresh, and there was no time to think. 'We can fix it, I am sure. We can find a way.' Despite her words any glimmer of hope was extinguished as soon as Ella's eyes met hers. Anguish, fear, and something else. Anger?

'For goodness sake, Thea, what did we think was going to happen?' Ella tried to keep her voice low, but tension raised the pitch. 'That we would set up home together, take in three unfortunate children and live happily ever after?' Thea blanched. In her indulgences that was exactly what she had imagined and hearing Ella mock it was like a blade through every wish. She stepped back, releasing Ella's hands but unable to find words. Ella went on. 'We both knew it could never be for the long term. I will accept my penance in Germany, and you should too, whatever is decided.'

'Perhaps we can write?' Thea's panicked mind clutched at a final hope. 'A year will pass and–'

'No, Thea.' The voice that cut through hers was firm and resolute. 'We cannot do this anymore. Don't you see? It has been fun, but this is not a way of life that can endure. You knew that as well as I did. I had hoped we would have longer – to enjoy more of one another, but it was not to be.'

Thea shook her head, still at an impasse. 'But – what we feel, what we said–'

'It doesn't matter, none of it matters, do you not see?' Ella's voice shook a little but contained a hint of ice. 'I have a place in the world I must inhabit and you have responsibilities. It was always impossible for this to be more than what we have had.'

The coldness in Ella's tone was as much of a shock as the letter. Suddenly the nuance in the words hit. Ella had never planned to commit. 'What was I to you?' she asked. Ella said nothing and fear and disgust rose inside Thea. 'Only a plaything to ride out the fantasies you built from those filthy books?' She tried and failed to keep tears of anger and hurt from her eyes.

Ella stood up straighter, her teeth clenched and fists balled at her sides. Her eyes flicked between Thea's who dared to hope, but then Ella's shoulders sagged. 'Perhaps,' was all she said, quietly.

Tears finally overflowed in Thea's eyes, she was ashamed of letting Ella know how much she had hurt her, but she was powerless to stop them. 'Then go,' she said with a throat so tight it hurt. 'I have nothing left to say.'

Ella nodded once. 'I wish you all the happiness you deserve,' she said in her ladylike way, turned on her heel and marched through the door.

Thea's breath became shallow and her hands shook as she heard the carriage carry Ella out of her life. Time seemed to pause, as though her mind were delaying the inevitable scene with her mother which she felt so emotionally helpless to endure. As her world turned slowly, Mrs Morell burst back into it, launching herself through the front door and into the space of her eldest daughter. Beside herself with anger, she threw her hands in the air as she spoke. 'What on *earth* were you thinking, Theodosia Morell?' She was so close Thea could feel the fury radiating from her. 'Obviously you were *not* thinking, as you never do! What is wrong with you? That kind of unnatural behaviour is something that happens in the madhouses of London, not in respectable society.' She paused as Martha re-entered the hallway, tucking her pocket watch back into her belt. If Thea had hoped for support from that quarter there was none forthcoming. Martha seemed disinclined to contribute, only gesturing to suggest they retired to the drawing room. There was no let up from Mrs Morell as they made their way through the door. 'And while your father is so ill! You have besmirched the name of the Morell family and taken the daughter of a noble down with you.'

As the door clicked shut Thea defended herself from the tirade before she considered if it were wise. 'I'm sure you heard it wasn't just me, mother, there were two of us.'

Martha leant on the sill, focussing her attention out of the window and Mrs Morell became frenzied. 'As if the daughter of an Earl would stoop to giving her virtue without encouragement! I have spent my life building the reputation of this family and you go and dash it to smithereens in one reckless, disgusting act!'

Any contrition Thea felt was shrouded by resentment to her mother's outburst. 'I am sure it will be forgotten in a month.' She hoped, rather than believed it was true.

'Forgotten! It will never be forgotten by us or by Lord and Lady Swanham! We only have to hope that we can contain it. At least we now have proof that this' – she waved a hand in the air – 'philosoph folly is bad for your mind. Lady Swanham has confirmed it.' She nodded, as if the conclusion were absolute.

'What?' asked Thea, another wave of cold anxiety settling in her stomach.

'Lady Swanham has heard that engaging in scientific activity can cause unnaturalness in ladies.'

It was as Thea had feared. 'That's just what she heard from Mrs Jefferys and you know what she's–'

'You mean you knew?' Mrs Morell's eyes were ablaze.

'It isn't a matter of knowing.' Thea tried to play it down, even though she still harboured doubts herself. 'I have heard Mrs Jefferys say the same thing, but there's no proof.'

'Proof?' screeched her mother, now pacing the room and gesticulating every which way with her arms. 'My daughter is standing before me, having debauched the daughter of an Earl. What greater proof do we need? It seems that for all your pretended study that I am the one to be the most rational.' She managed to look proud of herself, and Thea bit back a response on the potential variety of causal factors.

'Euphemia.' Martha's strained voice from beside the window made Thea jump, and she looked across in hope. 'I really don't think–' but Mrs Morell's eyes settled on her with venom, no doubt blaming her in part. As Thea's eyes met Martha's the words stopped in their tracks. Thea tried desperately to communicate something with that look – apology, a plea for forgiveness, a request for help. She thought she may have seen Martha's eyes soften for a moment, but then she straightened and looked away. 'Maybe you're right, Euphemia,' she said coolly, and the fight left Thea's body entirely.

Mrs Morell paused in her triumph as another thought occurred to her and her voice dropped. 'Who sent the letter?'

Thea shrugged. 'I don't know.'

Her mother's eyes raged again. 'Well, you must have some idea who could have known, I assume you didn't flaunt your... your... relations around Thornbury so blatantly that it could have been anyone in the town?' Disappointment flared in Martha's gaze.

'No,' was all Thea could manage, but Mrs Morell kept staring. 'I suppose it is possible that Tabitha might have seen something in the greenhouse.' She offered, quietly.

'*In the greenhouse*?!' Mrs Morell was incandescent. 'What were you–?!' She closed her eyes and spoke through her teeth. 'Never mind. Anyway, your own sister wouldn't disgrace the name of Morell as you have, what a ridiculous notion. At least we have one daughter who behaves with propriety.' She shot Thea a revolted look. 'And who values the continuation of the Morell line and fortune.' Thea had no further argument, and simply dropped her head, now impatient to bring a close to proceedings as soon as possible. The light-headedness had returned and emotion was beginning to seep up through her stomach – she knew it wouldn't be long before it found its way out.

Mrs Morell straightened up. 'Very well. I will consult with Lady Foxmore and we will see you back here in an hour.' She came close and poked a finger in Thea's chest. 'And you are *not* to see your father until I have spoken to him. He is not strong enough to deal with this and goodness knows it may kill him.'

Thea walked from the room as steadily as she could manage. She attempted one more glance at Martha but her mother's friend only looked away. Once out of the room, Thea ran. Past the prying eyes of Tabitha, out of the house and past the walled garden. She leant against a tree at the edge of the copse, swayed, and lost her breakfast in the long grass. Any joy she had felt, any comfort in herself or hope for the future had been obliterated in an instant.

CHAPTER 14

'Enter,' came her mother's voice one hour later. Thea tentatively pushed open the heavy oak door and her mother and Martha stood. She knew she must look a fright with red eyes from the tears and a stained dress from sitting in the wet grass. Her head felt fuzzy – from the shock of being exposed, but also from the revelation that Ella had not cared for her as she thought.

Martha flicked her the briefest of glances. Thea searched for any hope within it, but her features were perfectly schooled. The look of detachment was almost startling. The distance brought a painful pang of sadness, but also guilt. She knew Martha well enough to know that she would feel her trust had been betrayed and it made her nauseous to think she was the cause. The truth was, she had engaged in an activity she knew Martha had found abhorrent. The blank look hurt so much more than the anger of her mother who then broke her reverie.

'I have consulted with Lady Foxmore and we have reached a resolution that we are certain your father would condone. You will go away from this house for two months at least, possibly longer. You will consider your behaviour, attitude and responsibilities for the future. And restore your – health.'

Thea nodded curtly as her mother went on. 'You will of course be chaperoned. Lady Foxmore has been kindness itself in agreeing to accompany you, despite the distasteful situation.'

Thea's spirits lifted a little. Once Martha got over her surprise – as she must do, surely – time away with her wouldn't be so bad. 'Thank you. And where shall we go?'

'Scarborough.'

She stared at her mother. 'Scarborough?!'

Mrs Morell stared back. 'Yes, Scarborough. It is in the north. There is an iron spring and not so much festive society as you might find elsewhere. You will be able to take the waters in relative solitude and the sea air will revive you. And you are not, ever, to engage in collecting, or philosophy, or anything remotely resembling learning and we shall just have to hope that it is possible to reverse whatever it has done to you.'

It made sense, Thea mused. To send her out of reach of her current circle and possibly even of polite society. Scarborough, though. While she had never been to the north, she understood it was barren, and rained a lot. 'It'll take us days to get there.' It was more for something to say, than for the fact she thought it would do any good.

'Five, in fact.' Martha's voice startled her, it was harsh and cold. 'For some time I have wished to visit Mr William Constable of Burton Constable Hall. We will visit on the return journey. The time prior to the visit will be spent in Scarborough where you will reflect. We set out a week tomorrow at ten o'clock, so do be ready.' She turned back to Mrs Morell. 'I will check on Ben before I go, Euphemia.'

With that Martha was gone and Mrs Morell shouted at Thea for a full hour. She had brought shame on the family, would never make a good match and had jeopardised the futures of not just herself but all of her sisters. Mrs Morell even brought in Tabitha and Ursula so Thea could apologise directly for their loss of prospects and undoubted future destitution. By the end of the tirade Thea was exhausted and thoroughly disconsolate. She slunk to her room, didn't go down for dinner, and nobody sent for her.

Day slipped into night and back into day. Thea slept only briefly and fitfully, dreaming she fled from Thornbury residents and the *beau monde*, being pursued into the wilderness until she became tangled in monstrous briars. The following day she kept to her room and nobody visited. Not even Ursula – whether by choice or because nobody would bring her Thea didn't know. She would have remained the whole day in bed if not implored to dress by Mrs Phibbs who wordlessly held her as she cried hot tears for what seemed like the hundredth time. What was wrong with her? First science and now girls, why couldn't she just be normal? Why couldn't she control herself? As night fell once more a gale howled and rain battered the windows in unseasonably dismal weather.

Her thoughts were in turmoil but kept returning to her family. Her father's devotion, if questionable money-management. Ursula's goodness and generosity. Her grandmother's cleverness and invest-ments. The estate was built on it and the duty of securing the future of people and place fell to her. Was there a way of reconciling what she knew about herself with her responsibility to keep her family from destitution? As she lay on the bed, lit only by a single candle, she decided she could keep from her father's room no longer. She crept across the black gulf of the staircase, observed by portraits of Morells past, looming in the darkness to accuse her anew. At her father's door she peered gingerly inside, hoping her mother had taken to her own room. Her heart thudded when she realised it was Martha who sat with him – she looked up at the sound of the door, then her jaw twitched, and hardened at the sight of Thea.

'You shouldn't be here.'

'I know, but I had to see him. I – I hoped you wouldn't mind.' Thea searched Martha's face for some sign of reassurance or comfort, but still Martha remained impassive. At least the clench of her jaw and the tightness in her shoulders told Thea this was hard for Martha too. She truly had taken the news worse than Thea had imagined. Still, she thought, surely she would come round, when the shock wore off.

Martha stood and walked to the door without laying an eye on her. 'Let me know when you're done.' Thea watched her go, her heart sinking with every step Martha took. She turned her attention to her father while he slept, oblivious to the drama unfolding around him. He would have known what to do, would have dealt with it calmly, and rationally. He had spent his life building this family, caring for them, educating them, running the estate and ensuring his daughters had the best start in life, and she had ruined it, in one, fell swoop. She really had betrayed him, and while he was ill. Would he be as cross as the rest of the family, when he awoke?

The silent tears finally slid down her cheeks as the weight of the day lay heavy. Tears for her own loss, but also tears for Ella, for Ursula, and even Tabitha. Tears for her father – and how guilty she felt about her own misery when here he was, clinging to life. She laid her forehead on his sturdy arm and let the moisture pool in her eyes, daring to make no noise in case she was overheard by Martha.

When the sobs abated and her father's sleeve was thoroughly wet, she ensured his hair was properly arranged, covered him with an extra blanket and squeezed his hand. 'I'm sorry, father,' she whispered. It was a wrench to leave him as she softly slipped out of the door, dashing traces of tears from her red face.

'Thank you,' she mumbled to Martha who waited in the corridor. Martha only nodded and made to move past her into the room. This was too much. Thea could manage her mother's rage and her sister's gloating, but she couldn't cope with Martha's anger, or contempt, or whatever this was.

She reached out and caught her arm as she walked past. 'Martha, please don't be like this. I'm sorry. Truly I am, I never meant to offend you.'

Martha stared at her, eyes boring into her own. 'Offend me,' she said. It was more of a statement than a question. This close, Thea noticed the lines around her tired eyes and the quick of her breath. Her heart skittered in hope when Martha moved back towards her. 'I am not offended, I am disappointed.' That was worse than Thea had imagined. 'After Harriet I had wondered about you, and if there had been anything between you–'

Thea quickly cut her off. 'Martha, there wasn't, I swear it. Ella was the first.'

She saw Martha's throat work as she swallowed. 'But how will I ever know? We trusted one another, and now this.' Her voice faltered a little on the final word and she gathered herself again. 'Whatever your feelings for either of them I had hoped you would be more sensible.' She snatched her arm away from Thea and stalked back into Mr Morell's room, as haughty and aloof as Thea had ever seen.

Mrs Phibbs was waiting for her once more when she returned to her room, she had made sure to replace Agnes in attending to Thea's duties after the letter's arrival. Thea practically threw herself onto the housekeeper and buried her face from the world.

If she had thought her tears were exhausted on her father, she was wrong. Martha's rational assessment of the situation was more devastating than the blind fury of her mother. She sobbed again into the shoulder that had comforted her as a child and felt the familiar embrace calm and sooth her. After some time, words finally found their way to the surface. 'I think I have done a terrible thing.' Her voice was muffled against muslin.

Soothing hands stroked her back. 'Not terrible, Miss Thea. You have done what is right for you, but the fact being known is certainly

– unfortunate.' She pushed Thea to arms length to look at her and wiped her tears with a rough thumb.

Thea screwed up her eyes in the hope that it might banish a little of the raw emotion. 'We were too bold. Who could it have been? Who sent the letter, I mean?'

Mrs Phibbs turned her around and began to unpin her dress. 'Mmm,' she said, through the pins in her mouth. She mumbled something which Thea took to be, 'who knew?'

'Just you. And Mr Pickles. And Tabitha did almost walk in on us in the glasshouse at Stanbourne. And Lady Foxmore nearly found us in the library. And maybe Scip.' She turned to the housekeeper, who by now had her hands on her hips. 'Oh weren't we so reckless! We have nobody to blame but ourselves.' Anger began to seep in, forcing out tears and making her back prickle unpleasantly.

Mrs Phibbs removed the gown and turned to loosen the stays, allowing Thea time to unravel the situation. 'Mr Pickles was so accommodating and you were so understanding – oh we were so foolish and complacent.' She placed both hands on her toilette table and leaned forward to take a deep breath to her stomach as the stays came loose. On top of her family's reaction she still smarted from Ella's revelations in the hallway. 'I am also not sure she was what I thought.'

'They rarely are, Miss,' said Mrs Phibbs as she unlaced.

'A rude awakening, and hardly one I don't deserve. Everyone is furious – even Ursula can barely look at me and she's delightful to everyone. And Martha...' She couldn't talk about Martha, it hurt too much.

Mrs Phibbs brought her nightgown. 'They will come round Miss Thea, it's a shock, is all.' Thea slid into the silken garment, featherlight against Mrs Phibbs' rough hands.

'I would have expected such emotion from mother, but Ursula and Martha are rational. They understand the variety of the world. But of course there are limits.' She turned back to the housekeeper. 'I have been so foolish and naïve, haven't I?'

Mrs Phibbs smiled at her kindly and brushed the hair from her face. 'What was it I always used to say to you when you were little and you had vexed your mother?'

Thea's brow crumpled as she thought. 'You told me it was only a lesson in how to become more discreet and resilient.'

The sad eyes opposite her softened with the flicker of a grin. 'Exactly. You won't change how people think, Miss, not in the profound way that would benefit you at any rate, but you may change how you live around them.'

'You don't think I should stop it? It – well – it isn't normal.'

'I wouldn't say that,' said Mrs Phibbs, a melancholy smile lightening her face. 'It isn't ordinary, but then, when have you ever been that?'

The next day Thea ventured out of her room but was mostly ignored. Mrs Morell would have nothing to do with her, Tabitha only smirked in her direction, and even Ursula avoided her, though tried to make it less than obvious. Martha returned to Denbury to her own commitments but at least it spared Thea the discomfort of her disdain. The one positive was that Mr Morell started to vomit mid-morning. Doctor Ashby was sent for immediately, the dose of digitalis reduced, and by the evening Mr Morell was awake for longer periods than he had been for over a week.

There was one person in the house who Thea couldn't bear to be distant from. In the evening she popped her head around Ursula's door. Her beloved sister, who had kept her distance for days, was already in bed. 'Could I come in?'

Ursula looked reticent but good as her nature she couldn't refuse. 'Of course.'

Thea shut the door behind her and sat down on the bed. 'Father seems to be strengthening a little, he took some broth just now.'

'That's great news.' The silence stretched on.

'We'll get past this, won't we?' Thea's eyes searched her sister's desperately and Ursula put a hand on her arm. It felt good.

'Thea, of course we will, I suppose it just shook me a little.'

The knot in Thea's chest began to loosen. 'Yes, me too.' She tried a smile and almost succeeded.

Ursula looked at her steadily. Usually Thea was in awe of her analytical abilities, but today she felt scoured by them. 'I don't think I understand what made you do it?'

The direct nature of the query took Thea by surprise but she knew she should expect nothing less. 'Oh, Urs, I wish I could explain, but I'm not sure I understand it myself.' Thea groped around for reassurance for her sister, but her strength had been sapped and Ursula both demanded and deserved the truth. She settled on honesty, however painful. 'I liked Ella. A lot. And now I miss her.' God how she missed her, or at least, missed what she had thought she knew about her.

Ursula thought for a few moments. 'But not as much as you could like a man?'

Thea thought back over every false start with every suitor her mother had picked out for her or that she had tried, in vain, to pick out for herself. She confirmed it to herself at the same time she confirmed it to her sister. 'More than I have ever liked a man – more than I think I ever could.' She kept her countenance steady but she knew her eyes betrayed her unease. 'Although I have liked some wonderful men, very much – I mean you know I am incredibly fond of Mr Pickles.'

As she had hoped it made Ursula laugh and the tension between them was broken. Ursula gave her a shove on the arm. 'But you wouldn't want to marry Mr Pickles. What about Matthew Ashby, or Samuel Harrington? They both like you very much, Thea.'

'Yes.' Thea was thoughtful and resigned to Ursula's gentle interrogation. 'And I like them and dearly love their company. Samuel Harrington is one of the kindest, most generous and most handsome men I have ever met. But all I can tell you, Ursula, is that when I was with Ella, something lit up inside my soul in a way that it never had before. Something raw, that I couldn't control, and it scared me as much as it delighted me. With good reason it seems.'

Ursula's lips curved upwards as she understood, then earnestness descended on her face once more. 'I had no idea you felt like that, I thought you were just – messing about. Do you think–' She paused and fiddled with the blankets around her. Her next words came out in a rush. 'Do you think that maybe you were in love with Ella?'

Thea's teeth pressed together, but she squeezed Ursula's hand gently. 'I am certain of it, but it is of no consequence now. Mother has seen to that. And Ella made it clear at our parting that she wasn't in love with me.'

'She wasn't?' Ursula looked concerned.

'No, as it turned out.' Thea wasn't sure how far she wanted to pursue this line of conversation.

'Then what did she want?' Thea only looked at Ursula. 'Oh,' said her sister, furrowing her brow as her cheeks flushed. 'They do say it is always the quiet ones.'

Thea couldn't help the guffaw that forced its way out. 'Thank you,' she said gently. You have no idea what it means, that you are speaking to me again.'

'Oh, Thea, I am sorry,' said Ursula, genuinely contrite. 'I just didn't know what to say. I have never felt like anything could come between us but this seemed so unlike you. Now I realise it was just like you to throw yourself head-first into something you cared about.' Thea swallowed a smile.

'I suppose I did, but I fear I shall have to find another diversion to entertain me.'

'Might you engage yourself with the collection?' Ursula asked. 'Take your mind off things?'

Thea shook her head. 'Mother blames my unnatural behaviour on too much study.'

A snort escaped form Ursula. 'That's ridiculous.'

'Is it?' Thea smoothed the bed sheets. 'I have even wondered myself. It's impossible to prove, but it seems like quite a coincidence–' A terrible thought suddenly struck her. 'Wait, you haven't had any, have you? Feelings, I mean. You know…' She ran an awkward hand through her limp hair. '…Different ones?'

'Are you asking me if I fancy ladies?' Ursula's face was expressionless.

'Um. Yes.'

'Well no I don't, as a matter of fact.'

Thea breathed a sigh of relief. 'Wait, is there someone that you…'

'No,' said Ursula, quickly.

'Are you sure?'

Yes, I'm sure.' Ursula shoved her playfully with both hands. 'Now can we get back to your abject disgrace? It's less uncomfortable.' Thea smiled, despite herself. 'You don't really think it might have been the collection, do you? Where's the proof?'

'There's none on any side, that's the problem.' Thea shared the thought that had been bothering her for weeks. 'It's just a feeling, Urs, I have no idea whether it's real, or how I can stop it if it is.'

'If you feel it, it is real.' Ursula took Thea's hands, solemnly. 'And why would you want to stop it?' Thea only looked at her. 'Well?' Her sister pressed on. 'Wasn't it joyful?'

'It was. Until it wasn't.'

'Yes, I suppose so.' They were silent for a while. 'So what now?'

'Now, I must recover myself and reflect in Scarborough, perhaps it will be useful time to make sense of myself. Goodness knows I will probably only have myself to talk to with Martha in the mood she's in.'

'I'm sure she'll have something to say when she learns you plan to give up collecting.'

Thea felt her eyes begin to fill with tears. 'I'm not so sure about that anymore.'

Ursula dropped her gaze. 'I am sorry, Thea.'

'You have nothing to be sorry about, I am only glad you are talking to me again.' Thea kissed her sister on the head and left her for the night, desperately thankful that here at least, there was a light of hope.

As Thea made to head back to her room a now familiar nagging feeling rose within her. She made a detour to the east wing and knocked on a second door before inviting herself in and slumping into a chair.

Tabitha regarded her from where she reclined on the bed, robe open to her waist, slowly spinning a glass of wine between her fingers. 'You really messed up, didn't you.'

It wasn't a question and the smirk on her sister's face made the bile inside Thea rise, but she kept her countenance steady. 'Mmm, and it seems that someone spilled beans that weren't theirs to spill.'

Neither the smirk nor the assured gaze wavered. 'You assume it was me, the same as mother.' Another statement.

Thea was surprised. 'She spoke to you?'

Tabitha inclined her head, the wine glass mid-way to her lips. 'Enquired whether I sent the letter to discredit you. Obviously.' Her laugh was shrill and in Thea's tender state seemed to bore right to the bone.

'And did you? I have noticed that Mrs Jefferys has seemed rather keen to make people aware of my scholarly activities over the past few weeks. That wouldn't have anything to do with you either, would it?' Their gazes matched each other during the pause while Tabitha drank. She wiped a glistening slick of red from her lips.

'I don't know what you could mean.'

'So you didn't see us. In the glasshouse at Stanbourne?'

That piercing laugh again. 'Oh I saw you. In fact, I have been aware of your liaison with Lady Eleanor for some time. If you are going to conduct an illicit romance with your own sex you could at least be discreet about it, sister. I'm sure half the town knew – the letter could have been from anyone.'

Thea raised an enquiring eyebrow. 'If I do not marry, then the rest of the town are not set to inherit our family's fortune. You are, if you marry and I do not.'

Tabitha's eyebrows lurched in return. 'Naturally the thought did occur to me. I am not a simpleton, despite what you think. I knew you had never been one for romantic friendships with girls and there was always something suspect about your inclinations – especially after the business with Harriet. I watched you carefully with Lady Eleanor and decided there was a greater chance of my securing the estate through the two of you holing up in a cottage in the country and living out your sinful days as companions.' Thea blanched at the truth of it as Tabitha went on. 'You took so long about it I had to broach the subject of lady's relations myself – the time we were at Stanbourne walking to the hermitage. Then, as I had hoped, you became close and after I found out at the ball that Lord and Lady Swanham planned to take Ella away to London I suggested that she stay here. I knew it would only push you closer together and I was right. You are stubborn once you set your mind to something, Thea, but unfortunately, someone had other ideas. As it has turned out, everyone will have forgotten before these two months are passed, mother will insist you marry, and I am no better off.'

She tipped her glass to Thea whose insides were seething. 'I cannot condone what you have become, but I am not your mystery author, sister. As for Mrs Jefferys, you would have to ask her.'

Two warm, early-summer days passed during which Mr Morell began to make more water and spent more time awake. Ursula was almost back to her usual self, but as expected, Mrs Morell's fury had yet to abate. She kept coming down with attacks of the vapours and, whenever there was anyone interesting around, so did Tabitha. Thea had reflected long and hard on her sister's admission and thought, for once, that she might believe her. As she wasn't allowed out there was no way she could press Mrs Jefferys on her part in the affair, and so she had to determine to be ignorant on the point of the letter, for now.

The thing that hurt Thea the most was that she was becoming resigned to exclusion by Martha. Her former friend came to visit Mr Morell and ignored her outright as they passed on the stairs. As she wasn't permitted to visit Mr Pickles or Jane, Thea's circle diminished to Ursula, Mrs Phibbs and Scip, but there was one person she was desperate to speak to.

On the fourth day Doctor Ashby visited and confirmed that her father was quite improved. Thea's spirits soared. 'May I visit him, Doctor?'

Dr Ashby smiled kindly. 'Absolutely, Miss Morell, some stimulation will do him good. I do believe he is quite bored.'

Thea ran to her father; Mrs Morell could hardly argue with the doctor. As she entered the room she felt a momentary rush of anxiety. He must know by now, and what if he was just as cross as the rest of the family? She checked herself as she rounded the door and froze as he turned to look at her.

A gentle hand extended from the luxurious quilt. 'My Thea – how I have missed you.' Relief washed through her. She couldn't suppress a laugh as she witnessed him sitting up in bed, colour in his cheeks and happiness on his face. His voice was still a little weak, but she blessed the digitalis which had effected such a miraculous recovery.

Taking the proffered hand, she sat down on the bed. 'Father, you look so much better, how do you feel?'

He smiled the reassuring smile which always brought comfort to her heart. 'Quite fantastic, I feel that I could jump up and dance around the room, although I am afraid your mother forbids it.'

She fixed him with what she hoped was a firm glare. 'As do I. You must rest and get yourself well.'

'Well if *you* insist, I will leave the dancing a couple more days.' They shared a smile and his eyes became a little worried as he peered over his spectacles. 'I am only thankful of Dr Withering.' His tone was a little more wistful. 'All I could think was that if I went–'

'Please do not speak of it,' she said, tears at the thought welling once more in her eyes.

'I mortgaged the house,' he said, quietly.

Thea looked at him, stunned. 'For the library?'

'Yes, he said, only temporarily,' he waved a hand in an attempt to be dismissive. 'Despite her eccentricities your mother does have a better business mind than me and has seen to it that we do enjoy income from the land – we will make up the difference soon enough but it would have been bad timing for...'

'Yes,' said Thea, as he trailed off. 'Another reason why mother has been so on edge, I suppose.'

'I fear so,' he said. 'How has she been?'

'Terrible,' said Thea.

He nodded knowingly, and then peered at Thea softly. 'And how are you, my dear? I believe you have had an eventful few weeks.'

She cast her eyes down to the bed. 'Mother has told you everything?'

He tipped his head to the side. 'Your mother told me her version and then I ensured to gather more objective intelligence from Ursula. I understand that I am to lose you to the north for the remainder of the summer.'

'Mmm. With Lady Foxmore.'

'And how is – that?'

Thea slowly shook her head. 'She's hardly uttered a word to me in the past week and looks at me as if I had plucked the blooms from her day lily and stamped on them myself. I fear she found the situation particularly disagreeable.' She looked down at her father's hands and then back up to his kind face, tinged with worry. 'As must you, father. I am truly sorry.'

His strong, familiar hands enveloped hers and held them firmly. 'Thea, I have no quarrel with a little... experimentation. It is even encouraged in young men before they marry. I have always supported you in your interests which have not been distinctly feminine and I doubt I will change your mind on either natural philosophy or this. You are your own woman and must forge your own path, however, at least conduct yourself with decorum.'

The relief she felt at hearing his pragmatism could not assuage her guilt. 'But the effect it could have on our family and friendships. That it already has–'

He waved a dismissive hand. 'Do not worry yourself unduly, your family are none the worse. Despite your mother's protestations there will be no lasting damage. You know scandal happens all the time amongst the debauched gentlefolk of the country.' He tapped her hand gently. 'And I do believe that Martha will come round, just give her time.'

PART TWO

CHAPTER 15

Milford, July 1758

Thea stood nervously on the driveway, her trunk and bags beside her as the carriage carrying the Foxmore livery crunched to a halt. By now she was prepared to be overlooked, so it hurt less as Martha exited the carriage and greeted Mr and Mrs Morell, bypassing her completely. Mr Morell had insisted on seeing them off and Thea was delighted to see him up. He steadied himself on Ursula's chair but his bright manner and the way he joked with her sister lifted a weight off her mind as she prepared for a long separation. As Mr Sanders, Martha's footman, loaded her luggage, she said her farewells. Her mother managed a stiff embrace, as did Tabitha, but both Ursula and Mr Morell's moist eyes echoed hers. She had left strict instructions for them to look after each other and knew that Mrs Phibbs and Scip would be there for them too.

Goodbyes complete, she turned to the carriage. Martha gave her the briefest nod of acknowledgement before swiftly ascending the steps and taking her seat. Thea followed taking the backwards facing bench, and the journey began.

She was lucky that the rocking of a carriage didn't upset her stomach as it did for some, but she certainly wouldn't be able to read like Martha who buried herself in a book in the seat opposite. Thea was sure they couldn't spend the whole journey in silence and bided her time, but by the time they reached the first coaching inn a word had yet to be exchanged. Martha spoke with the proprietor and informed him that they would take dinner separately. Before she knew it Thea was in her room with her travel bag and realised that the journey really would provide her with ample time for reflection.

Clinging to her father's words Thea hoped Martha would come round, but every moment they spent together etched another speck of doubt into her mind. How completely matters of emotion and morality could divide people. This friendship was one of the most greatly valued in her life and she lamented its loss desperately. To think she had considered confessing the whole thing at the ball! If Martha with her fiercely analytical brain could not forgive her, she knew that few people would be able to come to terms with her oddity.

The following day they breakfasted together in silence then resumed their journey with fresh horses. The problem with a long, silent carriage ride was that it provided too much time to think. Reality started to slip back in, feelings that had been quelled by having Ella so close. Anxiety filled her and she sank deeper into a gloom from which she could see little way out. She had lost her lover and her mentor, two of the most important people in the world to her. What was left? The reality of her future prospects loomed large. Marriage, being seen to work with charities without actually helping, endless tea. She shut her eyes to banish the panic but it only threatened more closely in the darkness, taking the breath from her, sending chills under her skin and settling uncomfortable nausea in her stomach. Perhaps the trip would have the effect her mother desired after all.

As the carriage raced along the road on the third day Martha buried herself in literature once more. More than once Thea filled her lungs to speak and then emptied them when she lost the courage. When they resumed after lunch she knew it was now or never. Surely their friendship was worth more than one indiscretion?

She took a breath and tried a light-hearted tack. 'This will feel a very long two months if we have no conversation, Martha. What say you to a truce?' It sounded ridiculously trite against the tension between them, but Martha simply looked up at her and right back to her book. Thea had expected a challenge and gritted her teeth. 'Where shall we stop tonight do you think?' This time Martha didn't even raise her head. Thea felt desperate. She leant forward, her voice now lower and serious. 'Martha, please, let's not be like this. I can't stand it. You are one of my closest friends and have been for as long as I can remember.'

Martha's head raised and her jaw set. She only looked out of the window but it lit a spark of encouragement which Thea determined to kindle gently, in case it might be extinguished by too much breath. 'Remember when I accidentally spilled ink on father's copy of John Hill's *Herbal* and you helped me clean it up? He still hasn't noticed. And when we spent four days waiting for the bud on the frangipani in your conservatory to open and then the mouse ate it?'

Her eyes roamed Martha's face and her pulse thudded urgently. There was definitely a twitch in the corner of the mouth and a slight softening of the eyes before Martha caught herself and pursed her lips. Thea pressed on. 'I will reflect on what I have done and try to make amends, I swear it. You have taught me everything I know about who I should be. And also' – emotion rose inside and her eyes filled with tears – 'it has only been a week and I miss you, Martha.'

Martha's eyes now met hers and her chest leapt. Thea thought she saw the eyes moisten for a few seconds before Martha drew a breath and hardened. 'I have clearly failed at teaching you anything about who you should be, Miss Morell.' She pointedly addressed Thea formally. 'You should have thought of how it would affect your wider relations before you took up with Lady Eleanor. You have severely damaged her reputation, and your own.'

'It wasn't all me.' Thea spoke quietly. She hadn't expected Martha to take her mother's line. 'There were two of us involved and she came along very willingly.' She sat back in her seat, knowing the spark was well and truly smothered.

Martha closed her eyes for a second and took a composing breath as if to banish the repugnant image. 'Whoever is responsible, you conducted an entirely inappropriate affair. It is not to be tolerated. I do hope that as you say, you can reflect on that in Scarborough. Perhaps then we will be able to resume some sort of – acquaintance.' With that Martha returned to her book and Thea, defeated, stared resolutely out of the carriage window, seeing none of the view.

Thea didn't awake until Mrs Jenkins returned to draw the curtains. The first night in a proper bed after the lumpy offerings of coaching inns was a welcome relief. The boom of waves was audible from the window and she could smell the salt in the air. She realised she felt nervous. This was the furthest she had ever ventured from home and with Martha so distant she felt quite alone. They hadn't arrived until a late hour the night before and Scarborough was as yet, unknown. She stretched and yawned, sitting up in what she now realised was a very pleasant four poster. 'What time is it please, Mrs Jenkins?'

'Just after nine, Miss.'

'Nine? I must have slept for as many hours!'

The housekeeper smiled. 'That you did, Miss, I put my head round to you earlier but you were fast on so I left you to rest a while.'

Thea had always liked Mrs Jenkins, Martha's housekeeper, who would also lend her hand to cooking on this trip. She was a kindly, portly lady older even than Mrs Phibbs, and so far she was proving the most agreeable company available. 'I assume Lady Foxmore didn't sleep as long?'

'She was up and out early, Miss. She's certainly been waking early this couple of weeks past. Must be the summer air.'

Thea sighed. 'I am afraid Lady Foxmore is not in the best humour with me, Mrs Jenkins. I am sure you have noticed.'

The housekeeper clucked her tongue. 'I couldn't say it had escaped my attention, Miss, but I wouldn't take it to heart. She has been out of sorts as a rule for as long as she hasn't slept. I think your father's illness hit her hard.' Thea lay back on the bed as she chewed her roll and marmalade miserably. At least her indiscretions hadn't been shared with Mrs Jenkins.

After breakfast and dressing, she headed out, unwilling to wait around the house until Martha returned from wherever she had gone. Their lodgings were modern – a tall, brick-built terrace with high windows and grand, columned doorways, directly atop a steep slope down to the sea. Thea now understood why Martha had taken the second-floor room rather than the first; the view of the natural bay was exquisite. Beaches stretched away in both directions and curved back towards the horizon in golden slivers. The sun hung high above the blue sea, casting a river of white light across the gentle waves. To the right, the looming bulk of the castle dominated the view, well sited on a promontory thrust out into the sea. As she stood atop the scene the slightest wave of enthusiasm washed through her for the first time in a fortnight. She had only ever seen the sea on the southern coast where beaches were pebble and the sea seemed gentle and well-mannered. The landscape here was rugged and the dramatic cliffs at odds with the elegant houses on the front. The sea breeze stung at her face and she felt a curl of hair come loose from its pins and whip around her shoulders. She wondered if she might learn to enjoy the north, if the rain held off.

She returned to the lodgings at noon and found Martha in the ground-floor room they were to use as a parlour. Her companion looked her up and down with alarm. 'I see you have found the beach, Miss Morell.'

Thea was aware she looked a little wild. She had carried her shoes and stockings up the hill after being too keen to feel the sand between her toes and being well aware that stockings and sandy feet were not a good match. The wind had whipped her silk scarf from her dress and more wisps of hair had come loose at the air's constant insistence.

She was too invigorated to be surly with Martha. 'I took a walk down the bay. It was – bracing.' The small selection of pebbles she had collected on the beach came out of her pocket and she began to arrange them on the fireplace. 'Did you have a nice walk, Lady Foxmore?'

Martha looked uncomfortable with being drawn into conversation but looked resigned. 'I visited the south bay to locate the spa. It is about a half hour walk. I suggest you wash and change before tea and then we will set off.'

The bay to the south of the castle was busier than their bay to the north. A whole town nestled in the valley between two towering cliffs, spilling down to the sea front with shops almost reaching the beach itself. From where they stood atop the hill they could see a church nestled slightly inland and a pier stretching out into the sea. The curved harbour provided a sheltered bay at the base of the castle cliff, two large ships and various smaller vessels were moored along its banks and bobbing gently in the waves. Long, stone paths wound down the hill to the sea front, all bustling with people. On the sandy beach groups promenaded on foot, rode on horses and even drove in carriages, while small huts on wheels stood both on the sand and in the water. 'What are those?' asked Thea.

'Bathing machines,' said Martha. 'To protect your – modesty – if a swim is to your liking.'

'I should like a swim.'

Martha set off down the hill. 'So you shall, it is recommended for the constitution.' Thea trotted after her. Soon they entered the town, its old timber framed houses and new brick and stone buildings jostling for position on the crammed streets.

Thea was surprised at the bustle. 'It is so busy, why are we not staying on this side?'

'Quieter,' offered Martha as she strode through the crowds not bothering to turn around. Thea understood with a sigh that not only would they get a better night's sleep but that her interaction with Scarborough society would be more carefully monitored.

After a long descent they reached the buildings on the front and Thea followed Martha down steps on to the beach, slightly breathless at the pace. 'Aren't we going to the spa?' Martha wordlessly pointed ahead of her. Nestled at the base of the cliffs to the south of the town was a small, stone building of two storeys, with a flat façade and terracing jutting from its front. People milled around in groups and sat on benches on the terrace. As they drew closer Thea could see that most of the people were sipping small glasses of murky liquid. She had heard stories about the taste of spa water, but everyone looked happy enough so presumably it wasn't too bad.

In front of them a girl in a light, salmon-coloured dress took a sip and spat it out all over a gentleman next to her. 'Eeuck!' She stared at the glass in her hand and then back at a lady Thea presumed to be her mother. Neither seemed particularly concerned about the gentleman brushing droplets of spittle off his suit. Maybe it would be bad. And Thea would have to do it regularly.

They approached the desk inside the door of the building where a spritely-looking woman stood surrounded by oak shelves, bottles of brownish liquid and numerous items of porcelain with variously successful views of the town painted on the front. Thea wasn't sure how the lady managed to stand enthusiastically; it was just an energy that seemed to radiate from her.

'Good afternoon, ladies, have you visited the Scarborough spa before? I don't remember seeing your faces and I have an excellent memory for that kind of thing.' She grinned brightly while they confirmed they were first-time visitors. 'Well aren't you in for a treat! The waters at the spa are proven to be effectual against a wide variety of illnesses and ailments that may affect an individual in a diversity of ways at any given time.'

By the time Thea had unravelled the statement the lady was leaning into them, conspiratorially. 'May I ask if there is a specific malady you are hoping to achieve relief from by the present taking of the spa waters, or is it a more general vigour and vitality of health that you seek with us today.' Thea felt the corner of her mouth twitch involuntarily, and she thought it best to let Martha respond.

'General – thank you.' Martha maintained her poise as always.

'Of course it is, ladies,' the proprietor soothed, 'I only ask because we do have some customers who have very specific requirements of our waters.' She leaned in again, face solemn and eyebrows raised. 'Some are particularly personal and unsavoury.' She straightened up. 'We have two wells here you see, the second uncovered during a rockfall about twenty years ago and they both provide quite specific health benefits. A mixture of the two can be offered for particular ailments, or, in fact, just a draught of one will sometimes suffice.'

Thea flicked a glance sideways at Martha, who she knew would be diverted if she wasn't in such a bad humour. She was standing ramrod straight with a thumb tucked into the pocket where she kept her pocket watch. 'We are simply here for our general health. Thank you.'

'Right you are then. I will recommend a mixture of water from both our wells which will have you pepped up in no time. You should take the waters once a day whilst you are here in Scarborough and then they are available in readily convenient bottles for when you must take your leave and journey back home to...' She let the question hang in the air.

'Sussex,' offered Martha, curtly.

'Sussex is it, in the south?' The lady's eyes widened momentarily, and her lips pursed. 'I'll tell you what I'm going to do then in that case, I'll pop an extra bottle in for free for the both of you. You can partake of it this evening and it'll give you a little bit more of a head start as you get going.'

Martha opened her mouth to respond and shut it again. They were both relieved when the glasses were placed on the counter and paid for, and they could return to the fresh Scarborough air with the remaining holiday makers. Thea looked at the brownish liquid through the glass, it didn't look like something that would either do her good or sort out the fact that she wanted to kiss girls, but what did she have to lose?

She swilled it round and took a swig. Her face crinkled involuntarily. 'Ew.' It tasted like she had bitten her lip and eaten dirt – both at the same time. Martha took a gulp and Thea saw her contain a shudder in her stomach and shoulders.

Thea heard a chuckle to her left and turned to see a young lady in a pale green dress, drinking down a glass in one. 'Don't worry,' she said in a soft voice, 'you get used to it. In about a week you'll barely notice.' Thea hardly had time to register her before she was gone, running after her family on the beach, but she had noticed some pretty grey eyes and a warm, engaging smile. Maybe more than one sip was required before she would feel the benefit.

The sun woke Thea early the next day, so she rose and took herself for a walk on the beach before breakfast. The sea air was supposed to be healing, and she needed that, she thought. Now the anxiety of the journey and unknown places was behind her, she needed to consider the future. Yesterday hadn't been terrible, if you didn't mind silence. When they had drunk their quota of spa water and returned their glasses they had spent the remainder of the afternoon exploring. They found the assembly rooms which held gatherings almost every night and a small theatre which offered productions throughout the season. There was a church and as wide a variety of shops as you would find in any reasonably sized town. With that, the beach and the coastal walks, Thea thought she could be quite content in Scarborough under different circumstances, but having too much time to think, the hurt of Ella's betrayal and not having the distraction of the collections or even scholarly books which her mother had also forbidden, she worried she may struggle to stay above water.

Collecting pebbles must be fine, she thought. Nobody could suggest she would learn too much or be corrupted by that. They were so intriguing, glistening in the sand in a multitude of colours and shapes. As she stooped to collect a round, black nugget and clean it off in the waves, a shadow loomed above her.

'What are you going to do with them?' asked Martha's voice, making Thea jump a little at the harshness of the tone.

She turned the pebble over in her fingers, avoiding Martha's eyes. 'I like them,' she said, watching the way the sun glinted off the surface. 'Don't worry, I won't attempt to classify them geologically.'

Martha only sighed at her impertinence and looked out to sea.

'You couldn't sleep either?' asked Thea, as the silence stretched on. 'I hate to waste the day.'

'Considering everything that we have to achieve while we're here?' Thea asked, wryly. Martha's structured formality was starting to irritate.

'I thought we might take a walk on the cliffs today.' Thea only nodded her assent. 'I believe there may be some plant samples that I don't yet have in the *hortus siccus*.'

'I shall keep my distance, to avoid any negative effect.' Thea tried to keep the sarcasm from her voice but she couldn't seem to help being obstinate about it. It was difficult to equate this Martha with the person who had encouraged her learning so ardently. Martha now looked at her for the first time, and stared, displeased. 'I suppose I shall paint?' asked Thea, when their locked eyes became too uncomfortable. She gave in and broke the stare, refocussing on the cliffs. Her mother had decreed that painting would be a suitable pastime, mostly out of spite, she assumed.

'I suppose you shall,' said Martha, and stalked off towards the house.

'This is ridiculous,' said Thea, as she threw her paintbrush on the floor a few hours later.

Martha looked up from the portable eyeglass she was using to examine a toadflax. 'I am certain you will improve if you keep trying.'

'I have lugged the easel up here and tried for two hours. I am dreadful.'

'It can't be that bad.'

Thea stood back and with a wave of the arm invited Martha to come and look. Martha sighed, stared at the horizon for a few seconds and then rose, wiping sap off her hands on a rag as she came. 'Painting takes time,' she said as she approached, 'you just have to... oh.' Her eyes widened despite herself as she rounded the back of the easel and took in the painting in front of her.

'See,' said Thea, sullenly.

'Well, it's...' said Martha, seemingly lost for any word to describe the scene Thea had taken such pains to depict. 'Why is that boat in the air?'

'It's a seagull,' said Thea, through gritted teeth.

'Oh,' said Martha, again. 'And is that..?'

'You, yes.'

'Oh.'

They both stared at the painting for a while, a resigned hopelessness settling through Thea. Was this what life was to be? She reached up to rub the back of her neck, but then felt Martha's hand pluck it away, as she always had when she knew Thea was sinking into distress. She turned gently, afraid to shatter what must have been an accidental moment of affection, but a welcome one nonetheless. Not being able to help the hope in her eyes she felt pathetic, yearning for Martha's acceptance, and for a second her blood raced as they shared a look of such knowing tenderness before Martha dropped her hand by her side and cleared her throat. 'I believe your mother also suggested that embroidery would be acceptable?'

Thea could only nod as Martha walked away.

The following day Thea found herself atop the promontory in between Scarborough's bays, being buffeted by the wind from every angle. It had been calm by their lodgings but the castle jutted out into the sea enough for the air to take on a distinctly different character. She could feel the salt spray on her face and her blood rushed in response as she gazed up at the castle ruins. A wall stood tall on the rock, punctuated with towers and turrets which stretched around the solid stone keep and its ancillary buildings. She was so lost in her thoughts that she started when she heard a rustling to her right. When she turned, she was met by a pair of soft grey eyes.

'Sorry, I didn't mean to startle you.' It was the girl from the spa, meeting her gaze with the same engaging smile. Her light brown hair was held in soft curls and her blue-grey muslin dress echoed the sea at her back. Thea's breath caught, despite herself.

'Not at all, I was simply wondering about the history of the place.' She noticed an enthusiasm flash across the grey eyes – one she usually associated with natural philosophers in the possession of information and given the opportunity to share it.

'They say there has been a castle on the site for many hundreds of years. A lady in the town told me it was blasted half to pieces in the civil war, before the Royalists were starved out.'

Thea was surprised. 'It was such a key base? Here?' Her companion nodded.

'Apparently so, and for Richard the Third before that.'

Thea was impressed. 'And how about now, there are still guards on that gate over there.'

'It is still used as a barracks so we can't view the outer bailey, but the inner bailey and keep are open for visitors.' Those eyes shone. 'Would you care to accompany me?'

Thea thought she would care to do so very enthusiastically. Especially if there would be the opportunity to engage in some – or actually any – conversation. She produced what she hoped was a warm and not too needy smile, and extended her hand.

'Indeed I would. I'm Thea Morell.'

Her companion's hand was soft with a firm grip. 'I am very pleased to meet you, Miss Morell, I am Olivia Calvert. What brings you to Scarborough?' Thea explained as they made their way to the keep, but left out the bit about Ella, social disgrace and banishment etcetera. It was quite a short story. Miss Calvert was on holiday with her family from York and had already spent a week and a half exploring the town and enjoying the beach. They explored the ruins of the tall tower together, the blast marks still evident a hundred years on. From high up Thea could see Martha walking the walls of the inner bailey and looking out to the sea, alone. She felt a pang of sadness at seeing the familiar gait, considering the fun they could be having in such a thriving town if the situation allowed.

As they descended the steps a young man in a middling brown suit strode towards them. Thea thought his approach a little bold until he spoke to Miss Calvert with ease. 'We wondered where you'd got to, Liv.'

That engaging smile again. 'Nat, this is Miss Morell. We have been exploring the ruins together. Miss Morell, please meet my brother Nathaniel.'

Thea grinned and extended her hand which he took up and kissed. He had the same broad smile as his sister which made his face inviting and honest. 'A pleasure to meet you, Mr Calvert.'

'The pleasure is all mine I am sure. It is not often my sister finds someone willing to accompany her on her explorations, or listen to her throughout, for that matter.'

Olivia kicked him gently and Thea laughed. 'It has been a delight, Mr Calvert, it has been welcome to blow away the cobwebs for a change.' She would have enjoyed talking to Olivia and Nathaniel more but Martha was approaching, along with another lady and gentleman who had been walking the promontory. The groups met, and Thea and Martha were duly introduced to Mr and Mrs Calvert, completing the family. They all set off down the hill towards the town in happy conversation.

As they reached the beach they split with an agreement in place to join for dinner in two days' time. Thea and Martha made their way to the spa for today's waters. Enjoying the novelty of recent conversation, Thea carried the momentum through. 'I think I shall enjoy dinner with the Calverts, they seem like a diverting family.'

Martha didn't look at her, but did speak, at least. 'Indeed. Mr Calvert has a plant collection.'

Thea smiled to herself. If there was anything that would encourage conversation, it was that. 'You found that out already?'

'Of course.' Martha checked but couldn't help herself. 'It is a dry house only but sounds like he has numerous specimens of interest and an herbarium which we shall discuss.'

That was the end of the exchange. It wasn't much, but Thea was pleased with their progress and that Martha would at least have an enjoyable conversation over dinner.

Chapter 16

'More wine, Miss Morell?'

Mrs Calvert was indeed an attentive hostess, Thea thought, as her glass was filled again. She was beginning to feel quite mellow as she finished her mutton and mashed swede. It was a pleasant relief, she thought, from the gloom that she had failed to shake. The extent to which she missed exercising her mind on natural philosophy had surprised even her, and it wasn't helped by having so much time to think while she churned out terrible painting after terrible painting.

'Tell me more about York, Miss Calvert,' she said, placing her knife and fork neatly on the plate and twisting to her left to get a better view of Olivia. 'Can you really see the Roman wall underneath the Minster?' The truth was that while she was interested in the history of the city, she was taking greater delight in her companion's telling of the tale. Neither abstinence from the collections nor the spa waters seemed to have quelled her unnatural desires, and the wine was helping her to ignore the reasons that was a problem. Olivia chatted easily about history, with Nathaniel chipping in from time to time. While Mr Calvert engaged Martha in talk of his garden, Thea enjoyed watching his daughter's eyes light up as she imparted an interesting fact, and the way her throat worked as she swallowed sips of wine between anecdotes.

Before the suet pudding was served and while Olivia excused herself, Thea sat back and considered the situation. It seemed that her awakening in Thornbury had only made her feelings more vibrant, if anything. A new town with new company had helped to lessen the pain of losing Ella and she was beginning to look forward. Now that Thea understood, if not accepted how she felt, she observed with interest the things that excited her a little, even though she knew they shouldn't. In moments of guilt she chided herself, remembering the purpose of her stay and what was at risk, but the distance had the effect of lightening her sense of responsibility, even though temporarily.

Deciding to avert her attention she tucked into the pudding and focussed her attention on Mr Calvert. He outlined his growing facilities which seemed modest but well-tended, extolled the virtues of the nurseries in York and detailed his pressed plant samples. Thea watched Martha listen politely. She would never laud her own skill or success and was content to listen to the achievements of others, yet she could have taught Mr Calvert everything he knew about growing. Thea was still proud of her friend, even after everything that had passed between them.

A sweet wine was served and a gap in conversation presented itself. Thea was suddenly intent that the evening would not pass without the Calverts knowing of her companion's accomplishments. 'Lady Foxmore is too modest to tell you, Mr Calvert, but she has a rather impressive stove of her own and cultivates a wide variety of plants from around the world.'

Martha looked at her plate and pressed her spoon through her pudding meaningfully, but Mr Calvert looked pleased. 'Is that so?'

Further emboldened by the wine, Thea wasn't finished. 'She is currently mid-way through an investigation into plant movement.' Martha coloured and looked to Thea – for a fleeting moment she softened, but then turned back to Mr Calvert who was a little thrown, having spent the past ten minutes explaining how to take an offset from a pineapple. Martha was as generous as ever and shared her knowledge and aspirations, whilst taking care to avoid illustrating the total grandeur of her collection in a sparing of the gentleman's feelings.

Thea enjoyed listening; she hadn't heard Martha speak so passionately for what seemed like weeks. She missed it. Missed the matter-of-fact way Martha reported facts which were obvious to her and yet beyond the comprehension of most. Missed her ambition to share her findings with the world through whatever means she was able. Martha had been one of the first who had roused the inappropriate feelings with which she was now so familiar. She had put it down to admiration and respect and had packed the feelings away where they couldn't cause trouble. Listening to her companion now, aware of her own feelings the admiration and – dare she even admit it to herself – desire, emerged from the corner of her mind and crept into view, mocking her in her own head.

She batted it away. This was ridiculous. She couldn't be attracted to two of the only three women in the room. If she wasn't careful she would turn into a flirt as dreadful as Tabitha and realised with a start that she probably would be, if social convention allowed. What if this journey of self-discovery revealed depths she didn't even want to admit to herself?

A mention of her name jolted her back to the room. 'Miss Morell is also an aspiring natural philosopher, along with her sister. Her collection of natural curiosities is growing and her approach is quite ambitious.' Martha spoke easily and it was Thea's turn to colour as the whole Calvert family rounded their gazes on her. She didn't know what to think, given the abrupt halt to her collecting activities and the reason for it which seemed to exercise Martha so greatly. Her slightly fogged head, coupled with her recent musings and the unexpected praise made Thea too flustered to respond.

Mr Calvert was delighted. 'Upon my word, you two must be the most accomplished scholars in Scarborough – how lucky that we shall have more conversation this summer than business and politics.'

Thea became aware that the whole family were staring at her, awaiting a response.

'I am afraid I may disappoint you,' she began tentatively, before looking straight at Martha, 'but the collection is my father's and I have given up any of my own interest in the subject. I am attempting to find more appropriate pursuits for my time.' There were murmurs around the table which indicated that this was a shame. Thea watched Martha for a reaction, uncertain what had compelled her to bring up the subject.

'I do wish you would reconsider,' said Martha, taking another mouthful before resting her spoon on the edge of her plate and meeting Thea's eyes. Thea could only continue to stare, still confounded but unable to mount a challenge in company. She had thought that giving up the collections would mean fewer awkward exchanges over dinner, but apparently that wasn't the case.

'I don't follow?' she managed.

'I mean you are too good to give it up.' Their eyes never left one another's, the most connection they had managed in over two weeks. The intensity of it made Thea's voice a little unsteady.

'I'm not sure my mother would agree with that sentiment, Lady Foxmore.'

'I am sure she wouldn't, but neither does she understand the issue objectively and rationally.' Martha took another sip of wine as their gazes held fast, and Thea wondered if she had also taken a little too much in the novelty of company. Surely that could be the only reason for this inexplicable conversation.

'Well I'm sure it is difficult for her to do so when those with an objective and rational perspective keep quiet,' Thea shot back, thinking back to the painful day of the letter and Martha's silence, mindful of the eyes on them but equally unwilling to submit. 'If they do not agree perhaps it would be prudent to say so. If not to my mother, then certainly to me.'

Martha shrugged, seemingly sloughing off the past two weeks of awful paintings and scholarly abstinence. Thea began to suspect it was the wine that had now loosened her tongue. 'Be that as it may.' Martha finally dropped her gaze and took up her spoon once more. 'Your skills should not be lost to the discipline. I do wish you were not so set on this path.'

The silence stretched on. Thea's mind, now working quickly, could only conclude that while Martha found her actions abominable, she did not agree that they may be caused by a corruption of the mind through application to science. She couldn't think of anything to say, apart from voicing the rebellious thought that suddenly arrived in her head – that she would give it up wholesale, if it would stop her feeling like she wanted to leap across the table and kiss the imperious look right off Martha's face. Instead she and Martha stared at one another until more than one of the Calverts started shifting in their seats. Emotion rose in Thea, feelings she knew she had to despise but with Martha's familiar, dark eyes boring into her she seemed utterly helpless to banish them.

'I think I have to be,' she said, quietly.

She saw Martha start at the same time she did, the connection broken as Mr Calvert cleared his throat and held out a plate. 'Can I tempt either of you two ladies with a fig?'

They didn't talk about the exchange the following day, or the next. Thea desperately wanted to ask, but Martha had retreated further into herself, embarrassed, presumably, Thea thought. Between them they chatted to several families around the spa, as polite as ever to one another when required. They made few lasting acquaintances but continued to enjoy the company of the Calverts. Thea outwardly favoured Nathaniel whilst secretly assessing her continued and pleasant reaction to the company of his sister. It was difficult, with Martha around, however. She rarely left Thea's side and more than once Thea noticed interrogative eyes assessing her interactions. It wasn't so bad when they were at general conversation, but when they went boating and Thea shared a vessel with both Olivia and Nathaniel Martha's boat was rarely out of earshot.

Thea knew it would be the same today with the promise of horseracing on the beach. They made their way to the north bay and viewed the horses in a makeshift collecting ring, their jockeys and handlers struggling to hold the frothing enthusiasm of their mounts. 'Look, the Calverts,' Thea said as she spied their friends descending the terrace to the beach, but Martha took her arm.

'Before we see the Calverts I would like to introduce you to an acquaintance I made yesterday.' She nodded down the beach. 'Here they come now.'

She led Thea away from the terrace and towards the sea where a lady and a girl of around seventeen that Thea assumed to be her daughter made towards the horses. They both wore salmon-coloured silk dresses and neat hats atop tall towers of hair. 'Euck', said the girl, 'Mother, why is the horse frothing at the mouth so?' Thea immediately recognised her as the girl who had spat out her spa water on the first day they arrived. The older lady turned to them and smiled as they approached.

Martha extended a hand warmly. 'Mrs Simmons and Cecily, it is a delight to see you again. I should like to introduce my companion, Miss Thea Morell.'

Mrs Simmons shook her hand, but Cecily simply looked her up and down. 'I wonder that you enjoy grey on a lady, Miss Morell. I have always thought it the most unflattering colour, don't you think?' She spoke with a slight lisp and her dark eyes bored into Thea.

'It is a pleasure to meet you both, I am sure. Are you looking forward to the day's racing?' Mrs Simmons was about to respond, but Cecily turned to the horses and cut across her.

'I don't care so much about the racing, but I had hoped to meet some interesting society in the crowd. Everyone we have met so far has been quite boring and no gentlemen of note at all.'

Martha spoke next. 'The Simmons arrived in Scarborough on the same days as us, Miss Morell, I thought you may enjoy getting to know Cecily a little.' Thea stared at her and tried to make her displeasure known with her eyes, but she knew Martha couldn't really think they would have anything in common.

For the next hour Thea tried to make her way over to where she had last seen the Calverts but almost gave up hope. They may be down at the finish line by now, where the majority of the crowd gathered. Their own progression up the beach was slowed by Mrs Simmons wanting to study all the horses in detail and place bets on those she found promising. Martha seemed to be content engaging with the older lady and so Thea was left with Cecily who eventually took her arm and set off up the beach. She talked incessantly, and nothing was right. In addition to the horses being too frothy, the beach was too soft and made it difficult for her to walk, there were too many people in her way and the air was both too warm and too wet. Thea fought the temptation to ask why she had chosen the seaside as a summer destination and simply placated Cecily with the occasional 'hmm'. It was a little like talking to her mother but without the feeling of familial obligation. One thing Cecily was into was gentlemen. They had to parade around any group of young men while Cecily assessed their breeding and taste in clothing until she decided they were not up to scratch, or until the gentlemen moved away. Eventually one trio proved worthy and Cecily boldly introduced herself and then flirted shamelessly – all the time hanging on to Thea's arm so she couldn't even politely extricate herself from the situation.

Eventually the gentlemen took their leave and Thea spied the Calverts fifty yards down the racecourse. She made for them, dragging Cecily along with her, and took comfort in the sensibility and kindness of her new friends. She gave them each an apologetic look as she introduced her new acquaintance – thankfully they understood and shared amused glances as Miss Simmons insulted their hair and clothing, complained about her lack of winnings and generally lamented the dreadful time they were having.

The remainder of the day passed in much the same manner, the excitement of the races just surpassing the irritation of Cecily. Thea felt her spirits raising and started to feel the despondency and heartache begin to slide away. Olivia won the most out of any of them and glowed with her success. Thea couldn't help but be diverted. At the way she hollered her encouragement at the horses and riders, her patience with Cecily and the way she squeezed Thea's arms as she craned over her shoulder to see the next section of the programme. Thea looked up just in time to see Martha staring at them, stony faced across the track. Perhaps her attraction to Olivia was too obvious, she thought. She put in a well-timed whisper in Nathaniel's ear and was rewarded with his broad grin and eye contact which lasted a little too long. She didn't dare look up at Martha but was quietly confident it would have the desired effect.

A day with Cecily was scouring. Despite her best efforts, at dinner that night Thea couldn't keep from challenging Martha on the new introduction. 'Did you have a nice time with Mrs Simmons today?' she asked blandly, straining to keep her voice light.

Martha met her gaze, unwavering. 'I did. She is an interesting lady.'

'I am surprised she interests you, you seem to have little in common?'

'It is diverting to hear about the north – they come from Skipton. There is more society here than I expected.'

Thea pressed her fork purposefully into an artichoke and rested it on the side of her plate, tired of the charade. 'Not a subject which usually diverts you, Lady Foxmore. I wonder that you found her any more interesting than I did her daughter. And I would like to know why you seem to have undergone such a sudden change of heart on my collecting endeavours.' This, at least, seemed to give Martha pause.

'I never said I agreed with your mother on the subject,' she said, her eyes flicking to her plate, 'but I will not be pressed on it,'

Thea felt her brows raise involuntarily but knew there was little point pursuing Martha's reasoning. She chose instead to return to the subject of their companions. 'And yet you felt the need to replace our only intellectual company with that of Miss Simmonds?'

They fixed each other with a steady stare. It continued too long to be comfortable and didn't break as Martha spoke again. 'You didn't find Cecily diverting?'

'I think you know that I could not.' After another uncomfortably long silence, Martha simply shrugged and speared a piece of curried chicken. Thea was not satisfied. 'I do, however, find the Calverts extremely interesting. As, I think, do you?' Martha shrugged again and didn't respond, so Thea went on. 'I shall be glad to have their company at the assembly tomorrow, at least we shall have some established conversation with reasonable people.' She had been delighted when the Calverts had pressed them to attend the assembly, and Martha had struggled to find a reason to decline.

She watched closely as Martha slowly chewed the next mouthful, and then the next. Finally she spoke, without raising her head. 'I wonder that you bother to cultivate the acquaintance so ardently, they are not the most well-bred family here.'

Martha never worried about breeding. 'What objection could you possibly have? All the family are perfectly charming.'

Martha acknowledged only with the flick of an eyebrow. 'However charming they are the point is moot; their house is north of here, it is not as if you will be able to keep up the society after we return to Thornbury.'

'There are always letters, and we have plenty of time left in Scarborough.'

'I am afraid not,' said Martha, rising from the table as she wiped her mouth on a napkin. 'I have had word from Mr Constable that he is now at home, we are to journey there sooner than expected.'

'How soon?' asked Thea, stunned.

'Saturday.'

'That's the day after tomorrow.'

'Do ensure that you are prepared.' Martha placed her napkin on the table and stalked out of the room, leaving half her plate untouched.

Thea sat back from the table, confused once again and considering their exchange and the events of the previous few days. She was sure she had been careful to limit her interaction with Olivia and so surely it could only be Nathaniel that Martha objected to. But surely male acquaintance was favourable? Had she misjudged her mother's motives for the trip? As the light dimmed and the solitary apple tart arrived, she turned over the possibilities. It seemed like Martha was ensuring that she made no lasting acquaintance. It was unlikely that she would be excluded from society in favour of Tabitha, her father would never agree to it. That meant that a trip to Scarborough only made sense if her mother had a suitor in mind; if finding a husband was an objective of her exile surely they would be in Bath? In Scarborough, the options were fewer and Martha could easily keep her from close acquaintance with anyone to whom she may form an attachment. She had suspected that Martha had played a part in Harriet's marriage to a man she had only met but once. Why hadn't she seen it before?

She let her spoon linger on the side of her plate, her appetite fled. The thought of Martha and her mother in the drawing room planning out her future made her feel utterly helpless. She expected it from her mother, but not from Martha. Her feelings on the subject were clearly stronger than Thea could ever have imagined. But who was the suitor her mother had identified? Not Samuel Harrington after recent events, she was sure. And not Ralph Jefferys, Tabitha would be devastated. More probably, she realised, George Crowe.

Her heart sank as the realisation settled. The match would be good for the family and infinitely preferable to further rumours about her and other girls. But to marry her off to someone so promiscuous and objectionable, simply for his fortune and title. She felt betrayed, and yet the evidence seemed irrefutable. Abandoning dessert and retiring to her room she became progressively angry. Angry at her mother for casting her out, angry at Martha for stooping to her part in such a plot, and anger at herself for being drawn into the thin ruse. As Mrs Jenkins helped her to undress she felt full of bitterness and resolved to draw the plan out of Martha in its entirety.

Thea surveyed the hall over the top of her glass. The assembly in the Long Rooms, atop the hill on the south bay and looking out to sea, was pleasant enough. As soon as they arrived Martha had tried to lumber her with Cecily Simmons, but the other girl wanted to do nothing but dance and Thea had escaped to the sanctuary of the Calverts. Her attention, however, never left Martha. She was determined to watch her chaperone, watching her, and to test the waters of how carefully she would be controlled. To this point she had danced with a number of gentlemen and ensured to flirt with them all. Martha looked uncomfortable, checked her pocket watch regularly and kept a sharp eye on Thea as she chatted to Mrs Simmons. She betrayed little to her companions, but Thea recognised the tell-tale signs of agitation, particularly while she danced with Olivia and Nathaniel.

The evening was only serving to strengthen Thea's suspicions. She and Martha were now well into their third hour of mutual observation and in the state of heightened tension they had both, once again, taken more wine than was perhaps advisable. As a result Thea was feeling a little reckless. Ensuring Martha was watching she slipped a hand around Nathaniel's shoulders and pulled his ear down to her lips.

'I need a little air, Mr Calvert, could I ask you to accompany me?' To him it was an innocent suggestion and they made their way to the terrace overlooking the sea. She knew that Martha would follow and so slipped her arm through his. As they descended the steps she leant on him heavily. 'My apologies, Mr Calvert, I feel slightly lightheaded.' She hoped he wouldn't consider her completely mad whilst she pretended to flirt outrageously. By now he was supporting her in a very gentlemanlike manner while she lolled all over him by the railings that stretched down to the sea. As she suspected, it wasn't long before the footsteps appeared behind them. 'Time to go home, Miss Morell.'

She turned and met Martha's gaze, defiantly. 'At so early an hour, Lady Foxmore? It is not yet ten. Mr Calvert and I were just getting some air.'

Martha almost snarled. 'Mr Calvert is quite at liberty to stay as long as he wishes and take as much air as he likes but for you, as I said, it is time to go home. I shall meet you in the carriage.' Martha turned on her heel and left. Thea may have been feeling a little rebellious but defying her chaperone's wishes would help nobody. She apologised to Nathaniel claiming Martha had felt unwell earlier that day and excused herself.

It was by no means a defeat. As she had planned, the evening's events would now command a frank conversation.

CHAPTER 17

Neither Thea nor Martha spoke as they rode back to the lodgings in the carriage. Thea had hoped that Martha might reprimand her and give her an excuse to question, but she said nothing. Instead, her companion stared resolutely out of the window even though the dark of the night was almost completely formed and the only view was the reflection on the juddering glass. Thea stared at the floor, or the seat opposite, or the dull lamps in the corners of the cabin. She was furious and struggling to keep it contained. Lost in indignation she was abruptly shaken to her senses as the carriage drew to a halt. Before Thea emerged from her self-pity, Martha had thrown open the door and stormed out. Thea watched her stalk up the steps to the pillared entrance, consumed with rage. She propelled herself after her old friend, intent on nothing but receiving answers to questions which were still fresh and ill-formed, even in her own mind.

Martha had gained such a start that she was almost at the first floor by the time Thea thundered into the house and saw the hem of a dress disappearing up the stairs. 'Lady Foxmore,' she shouted.

Martha stopped but didn't turn. 'Please do not detain me, Miss Morell, I must get some rest.'

'I would like you to explain,' said Thea, proceeding up the stairs purposefully, 'what happened tonight.' It was a statement, not a question.

Martha raised her eyebrows condescendingly. 'We socialised with some relatively dull acquaintances and then returned to our lodgings, now please will you now allow me to retire for the evening?'

Thea would not be put off. 'And the reason for the sudden exit?'

'Sudden?' Those irritating eyebrows again. 'We left as the evening was over.'

'Over?!' spat back Thea. 'The food had yet to arrive!' She had planned a rational conversation, but wine and anger had fused in her stomach. Her frustration bubbled over, and she almost shouted. 'I am no fool, Martha, I demand that you tell me what is going on.' Her knuckles were white where she gripped the banister and her voice had reached such a pitch that Mrs Jenkins arrived in the hallway to check on the commotion.

Martha grabbed Thea's arm and bundled her through the closest door to hand, which happened to lead into Thea's own room. 'Will you please refrain from compromising yourself in front of the servants.' Her face betrayed both frustration and alarm at the violence of the onslaught.

Thea rounded on her again now they were alone, her eyes sparkling with accusation. 'As you wish, but I still demand to understand your scheme. It might as well be out in the open so we can avoid its excruciating progression over the coming months. It will be easier, if not pleasant, if I can simply acquiesce to whatever you and mother have agreed.'

Martha's face darkened once more, she clenched her teeth and walked away towards the toilette table, her back turned pointedly. 'I have no idea what you are talking about, Thea, and I have taken too much wine this evening to have a sensible conversation, I must go and get some rest.' Thea could see Martha trying her utmost to stay calm, but her voice was tight and raised.

Martha moved back towards the door but Thea blocked her path and wrenched her hand away from the handle. Her voice came out louder and more high-pitched than she intended, part fury, part panic at her potentially devastating future. 'You are not leaving here until you tell me what is going on. I must know, Martha. Is my fate to be the same as Harriet's? I know you had a part in her marriage. What is to become of me?'

Martha blanched at that. 'Plan? What plan? You are making no sense.' She tried again for an exit. 'It must be the excitement of the evening. Let us talk tomorrow.'

Thea was determined she would have answers and leant on the door with one hand. 'Who am I to be married to? You have been sent to prevent me from making any close acquaintance, haven't you?' She stared at Martha who neither confirmed nor denied it. 'So I can be married off to George Crowe, my entire future dictated after one indiscretion! Was it your design, or mother's? You, who I once trusted and admired above all others, have betrayed me over and over again these two weeks past. You owe me at least the courtesy of making me aware of my fate if it is to be so.'

Martha's usually cool and collected demeanour was now strained, her breath came fast, her jaw was set and anger flared in her eyes. She looked at Thea as if she barely recognised her. When she spoke she spat the syllables but her voice was shaky. 'I cannot deny I have betrayed you, Thea, a hundred times over during the past month. But it is in no way related to your mother or any kind of fanciful plan to marry you off.' She faltered as Thea stared. The next sentence was harder. 'If you must know, Thea, the situation we find ourselves in tonight is the result of my selfish wishes and mine only – not those of your mother or father.'

This was worse than Thea had imagined – Martha's own prejudice, not even that of her mother. 'Wonderful,' sneered Thea, 'why would I ever assume that I should have control over my own life? Pray, tell me what demands *you* have of me!'

This hit a nerve. Martha no longer seemed to be fully in command of her countenance and her voice rose with every word. 'This has nothing to do with demands, Thea.' Turning away she pressed a hand down on the wood of the dresser. She stared at it as if it might save her, but the words seemed to drag themselves slowly from her body. 'It has everything to do with the fact that I am weak when I am with you.' She pulled her eyes from her hand with some difficulty and looked Thea full in the face. 'And. I. *Hate* it. I cannot stand to sit by and watch as you frolic and flirt with as many young suitors as you can lay your eyes on.'

By now Thea was utterly confused – she had no idea what Martha meant but it didn't seem to relate to the scheme she thought she had uncovered. As she hesitated, unsure of her next move, she jumped as Martha slammed a hand down hard on the wood and turned her face away. 'For God's sake, Thea, I cannot bear the fact that you could want them and not me.'

Martha's gaze snapped up to meet Thea's and both women froze. She was breathing hard. A long moment passed and Thea's eyes widened as she processed the words. Martha put a trembling hand to her mouth and let out a quiet, breathy, exclamation. 'Forgive me, Thea. Forgive me. I said I had too much wine to converse further tonight.' She took in a difficult and ragged breath through her gloved fingers. 'I must go.'

She made to leave and Thea caught her once again, but gentler this time. She stared, stunned, whilst Martha tried to avoid her gaze, but eventually acquiesced. Thea's eyes flitted between Martha's and saw only panic. 'You mean–?' She let the question hang in the feverish atmosphere. Martha nodded once then looked away and Thea simply stared. Disbelief mixed with anger and shock as her mind grasped for a response. She still held on to a trembling wrist within which she felt a frenetic pulse. 'You owe me an explanation before you go, at least.'

After a few long seconds Martha's taut muscles slackened. She pulled away looking unsteady but eventually she nodded weakly. 'I suppose I do.'

She tried to calm herself with a few breaths. 'Thea, when you were growing up we were so close. Even from a young age you understood

me better than most – and I you, I think. When you turned into a
woman you quickly became one of the most interesting and engaging
people I had ever met.' She gave a small, hollow laugh. 'Honestly, you
weren't the first of the fairer sex who had stirred my emotion, it was
usual. It was manageable. If it is impossible to translate feelings into
anything more it is easy to keep them at bay. I had done so often
enough and I was ashamed of how I felt for you. You were twenty and
mature for your age, but I had more than forty years behind me for
goodness sake.' She shook her head at herself. 'I was delighted to count
myself as a friend and confidant and please believe me when I say that
I did so with no agenda.' She paused and tentatively raised her eyes to
meet Thea's. Sorrow and pain sparkled within them and it took away
Thea's breath to see her so exposed.

Then Martha's face hardened once more. When she spoke, her voice
was hollow. 'But after I had pushed it aside for so many years, a few
weeks ago it became possible. It became possible that you could love
another like yourself.' There was a pause and when Martha's voice
returned it was so quiet as to be almost a whisper. 'But it was not me.'

Thea's mind raced, this new truth was so irreconcilable with what
she thought she knew, her sense of betrayal hung on. 'So you – you
had feelings for me, but just like that you cut me out of your life?
The person I most trusted and respected. You were disgusted with
me.' Martha shook her head and looked away, but Thea was not done.
'How could you do that to someone you claim to have such affection
for? If there was one thing I was sure of it was that I could rely on *you*,
but you hurt me so much more than the rest.' She knew it wasn't fair.
Not after Martha had laid herself bare but the hurt was still raw. Now
the tears spilled down her own cheeks, as hot as her anger on her skin.

'What was I to say?' started Martha, 'to tell your mother not to
worry? That I would make an honest woman of you?' A shaking hand
raised towards Thea but Martha quickly pulled it back to herself. 'I
desperately wanted you – needed you, close to me, Thea. That was not
possible. So I couldn't have you near me at all.'

Shock filtered in, slowly displacing the anger curling through her chest. If this was the truth, there were too many questions. She tried to keep her voice calm, but it wavered. 'So why bring me to Scarborough?'

Martha shrugged. 'Your mother wanted you to come and could not leave your father. She did not want me to bring you, conscious that I had encouraged your scholarship, and therefore what she construed as the reason for your – situation. I had to reassure her, in no uncertain terms, that I agreed that your interest in natural philosophy was a contributing factor and that I would do everything I could to discourage you – before she would allow me to accompany you.'

'Before she would allow – you mean you wanted to come?'

'Of course I did – how else could I protect you? I knew in my heart that it could not turn out well, but I could not bear to think of where else you would be sent or with who. I didn't dare allow myself to comfort you for fear of what I might say, but I could keep you safe, at least.'

Thea hesitated, disbelief still clouding her thoughts. She stared at Martha's reflection and then her own in the glass – they both looked pale despite the yellow candlelight flickering across their faces. 'This can't be true. I would have known. If it was as you said, it would have been obvious.' Her own ears told her how ridiculous it sounded, and Martha gave a hollow laugh.

'Can you honestly tell me you have never hidden your feelings, Thea? When you have felt like this for so long with no outlet, you get very good at burying it – at pushing it to a corner of your mind where it can't cause trouble. But then it became real when the letter arrived and I was unprepared for how utterly unbearable I found it.' Her face betrayed the pain she felt and Thea wished she could look away, but her eyes were glued to her companion. She thought back to her own feelings and how she had buried them in exactly the same way.

Martha's words dragged her out of it. 'To be reminded constantly that you can never have the love you so desperately yearn for–' There was more but she stopped herself and put quivering fingers to her lips. Fear eclipsed her face once more and she drew herself up. 'I am so sorry, Thea. We must return home. You will go to Milford and I will find alternative occupation. I will tell your mother that I had urgent business in London and send a letter to let Mr Constable know not to expect us.' By now Thea was rooted to the spot and Martha finally made her way to the door. As she opened it she turned back, her eyes cast low. 'I beg of you, do not repeat any part of this conversation, Thea, I am not myself.'

Thea was still awake, staring up at the canopy of her four poster, as the sunrise began to glow through the curtains. She had slept a little here and there, but only short bursts snatched among a confusion of thoughts. After she had let Martha go, she had paced about her room attempting to make sense of their exchange. When Mrs Jenkins had come to undress her, having presumably heard the voices settle, Thea had begged that she check Martha was alright. When she had finally got to bed she had spent hours wondering if she really could have been so wrong and remembering scenes from their lives that now took on a different perspective. The two of them pouring over a newly germinated *Aloe*, the days out collecting geological specimens on the beach, Martha's reaction when the letter arrived and how she had taken it as disgust. She now saw a different inflection in those eyes and replayed every interaction between them. She saw hurt, rather than disgust.

She had thought of going to Martha. Several times she had swung her legs over the side of the bed, and then swung them back. But what would she be going for? To talk to Martha? To shout at her? To kiss her? Thea didn't know what she wanted herself. Well – she did know what she wanted. Those feelings had made themselves well known as the shock dissipated. But she also knew that she couldn't want it. Her situation meant anything between them had too many limitations, and she wasn't sure she could bear the pain of parting a second time.

She sat up sharply as she heard a creak on the stairs and leapt out of bed. Opening the door, she saw the back of Martha disappearing into the hall in her stocking feet and followed her, grabbing her own robe on the way out. Tying it round herself as she padded down the stairs, her heart beat painfully as she caught sight of Martha, on the hall bench, fastening up her own shoes. She must have left them off so as not to wake Thea. A stair creaked under Thea's weight, and Martha stood.

'Oh,' was all she said, as they stared at one another.

Suddenly there was a flurry of humming and clattering as Mrs Jenkins emerged from the kitchen door carrying a tray of breakfast crockery. She froze as she saw the two of them, whose eyes were now trained on her, both in alarm. 'I'll just be downstairs,' she said, rounding a perfect circle and disappearing as quickly as she had arrived.

Thea looked back at Martha who was assessing her warily, and stepped carefully down the remaining few stairs until they were both in the hall, now staring at one another from a different angle. Martha checked her pocket watch, even though the time could have no bearing on any conversation.

'Did you sleep well?' asked Thea. Martha cast her eyes to the dresser on the opposite wall, and Thea noticed how drawn she looked. 'No, I suppose not,' she said.

'I meant what I said, Thea,' said Martha, after another long silence. 'I am truly sorry to have burdened you with this. We will return home and it need not affect you. I will make myself scarce.'

'No,' said Thea quickly, and Martha looked back at her. Thea saw her swallow nervously. 'Martha, we both need time to consider this and – and what it might mean.' She was hesitant, she had no idea what it might mean, but she knew she needed the space to think what it meant for her and suspected Martha did too. It would be easier when it wasn't so uncomfortable and raw. 'I don't know what that is, but I know it will not be best achieved cooped up in a carriage together for five days, or with my mother breathing down our necks.'

'We could travel separately, I wouldn't come back to Thornbury.' Martha tried desperately, but Thea could see that her heart wasn't quite in it. Emboldened she took another step forward and went on.

'We need one another, Martha.' Martha shut her eyes, her jaw clenched and fists balled at her sides. 'I need you. As a friend if nothing more. We can't run from this.' Martha shook her head, in agreement or denial Thea couldn't tell – she wasn't sure if Martha knew either. 'Let's go to Burton Constable,' she said, 'we can take time to think, together or apart, but we also need to talk. On the way there maybe, to begin with. I need to understand and I think you do too.'

In one movement Martha turned to face her, nodded once, and disappeared out of the door.

Despite Thea's assertion that they should talk, once in the carriage she found she had no idea what to say. She wanted to tell Martha how she felt, about her own feelings but how confused she was. She wanted to ask Martha when it had started for her, how wrong she felt it was despite how right it felt, if anything could be done about it, if anything *should* be done about it. But instead, she said nothing. She stared at the moving landscape as the carriage rumbled over the moors, through the villages of Reighton and Fraisthorpe, occasionally noticing Martha staring out of the opposite window. A few times Martha looked over at the same time she did. Mostly she looked away again quickly, but twice she took a breath to speak, let it out again and resumed her analysis of the landscape. After four torturous hours over rough terrain, Martha looked over and gave a small cough which made Thea start.

'Mr Constable has recently built a new stove house. They say it is the largest in the country. He also has a geology and natural history collection.' Thea deflated, but was intrigued, nonetheless.

'We are here to see collections?' she asked. Martha only nodded. 'But you knew that when we left Thornbury, even though... the effect.' She trailed off, and Martha nodded again. Thea was now utterly confused about whether Martha thought study had nothing to do with their unnatural feelings, or whether she thought it did and didn't care. 'Oh,' was all she said, her mind churning. 'That'll be nice.'

'And he lives with his sister, Winifred,' said Martha, 'just so there are no awkward questions.'

'Right,' said Thea, and they sunk back into a silence, the rest going unsaid.

Another hour and a half later thoughts were bursting to get out of Thea, but she couldn't think of a way to vocalise them without being so embarrassed she wanted to sink into the ground for days. She shuffled in her seat as she saw a tall lime slide past the window, followed by another, and another.

'We're here?' she asked, mortified despite her inertia that the opportunity for some sort of reconciliation had passed. When they might get chance to speak alone at Burton Constable was anyone's guess. As the wheels crunched on the drive the house slid into view. The red and yellow brick façade had maintained its Elizabethan style and was pleasingly symmetrical, showcasing large windows, turrets and a prominent family crest above the main entrance. The hall rose dominantly from the flat landscape, two wings thrusting into the pastureland, itself peppered abundantly with trees and avenues.

The carriage swooped left to carry them around the courtyard and to present them by the butler, footman and the finely dressed lady and gentleman who were waiting by the door.

'Martha, I feel the same,' blurted Thea in desperation. 'About you. I mean, you mean more to me than anyone and this is all so new and I'm so confused but I can't seem to ignore it.' The words were coming fast, before she had time to think, and Martha's head had snapped around in shock. 'I know it's all so soon after Ella but we both know how much we mean to one another and I think I always have felt things for you, and I know I shouldn't, and I have tried not to, and I am keeping trying but you're just so' – she sagged in her seat – 'you.'

The carriage stuttered to a halt and the door swung open. Martha stared at her, mouth slightly agape, her face a mixture of astonishment and frustration. She said nothing, rose from her seat and alighted down the steps.

CHAPTER 18

She tapped on the door gently, almost hoping it wouldn't open. 'Martha?'

It didn't open. She tried again, a little louder. Their rooms were in the north wing of the house away from Mr Constable and his sister so she was sure they wouldn't be disturbed, but she was still wary of this conversation. Martha had taken to her room as soon as they had arrived and dinner had been a polite affair. Mr and Miss Constable were jolly and affable so conversation hadn't been an issue but Martha had only interacted with Thea when strictly necessary and had disappeared, feigning a headache at the earliest point she wouldn't cause offence. Thea knew she would have no luck sleeping for a second night running if she didn't talk to Martha, and so here she was, against her better judgement, outside her room.

'Martha, I know you must be in there.' She paused and listened, ear to the door. Still nothing. 'I hope you're decent, because I'm coming in.' The thought of walking into Martha's room unbidden sent a cold wave of fear through her but she knew she couldn't leave without at least a word. Tentatively she turned the doorhandle and heard the latch click. Part of her had hoped it might be locked, she realised now, but the door swung away from her into the room.

'You shouldn't be here,' said Martha's voice, cool and level. Thea's eyes, accustomed to the dark of the corridor, found her sitting in a chair by the curtained window, a candle on a table by her side. She

241

held a book open, but it already had a ribbon marker slid between the pages. Martha stood, closed the book and placed it on the table. Thea suspected she hadn't been reading at all.

'We need to talk,' she said gently, closing the door behind her.

'We don't. We can't,' said Martha, still cool. 'There is nothing to say. You should return to your room.'

'Nothing to say?' asked Thea, incredulous. 'Martha, there is everything to say.'

'And what is that?' snapped back Martha, a little less composed now but there was a hint of pleading in her words. 'Following your revelation earlier I have thought of every possible way this conversation could conclude and none of them are acceptable. None.' She remained still by the table, stiff and upright, her voice tense.

Standing awkwardly by the door Thea raised her arms a little and dropped them back by her sides. 'Then what now? Do we spend the remainder of our time in the north in silence?'

'It would be best, on the whole. We will conclude our visit with the Constables and return home. Once I know you are there safely I will travel.'

'Where will you go?'

Martha paused. 'I have yet to settle on a destination.'

Thea took a step towards her. 'Martha, you can't run away from this.'

Martha looked away. 'I can. And I must. You will return and progress with the life destined for you and I must not be in it.'

'You can't mean that?' asked Thea, appalled. The thought of losing Martha was too much. In a way she felt closer to her than ever, knowing they shared the same affliction, but at the same time their old closeness seemed too out of reach.

'I must mean it.' Martha turned away, her gaze leaving Thea for the first time since she had entered.

'Why must you?' Thea searched her face but Martha remained silent. 'Please don't shut me out,' said Thea quietly.

Martha placed a hand on the cover of the book on the table, still facing away. 'I have to. I have to, Thea.'

'I won't let you.' The fear rising up in Thea propelled her further into the room and Martha turned at approaching footsteps.

'That is not your decision to make.' Martha's voice was harsh and wary.

'And neither is it yours.'

'It is. I am resolved. I will not see you after we return to Thornbury.' Martha was cold again and Thea felt her own tears sting as she saw Martha struggle to retain the distance – physical and otherwise – between them.

'No,' she said, starting forwards and grasping Martha's arms without thinking, only desperate to keep her near. 'I can't do any of this without you.'

'You can and you must,' asserted Martha again, twisting to get away but hampered by the table.

'I don't want to,' said Thea, the desperation now clear in her voice and Martha's efforts to get away almost becoming a tussle. The words fell out of her like the tears. 'I want you.'

Martha froze momentarily and their eyes met. Thea was aware of nothing but Martha's scent and the shock, desire and fear between them. Still clinging to the silken handfuls of Martha's gown she closed the distance between them and pressed their lips together. She felt Martha's breath hitch, and then felt those soft lips move against hers – just once, only momentarily, and then they were gone, Martha holding her away with firm hands on her elbows.

She saw her own raw emotions reflected in Martha's eyes. 'And that is why we must,' she said softly. 'Thea, I don't know what I might do or say if we get close again. I could hide it, I did for so long, but knowing what I do now...' The sentence petered out and Thea stepped back.

'I am so sorry.' She knew that she had likely spoilt everything. How could she convince Martha that they could be friends after this?

'You know this can't happen, don't you?' Martha's voice wasn't unkind, but it was definite. Thea only nodded. She did know. She knew it was too much to risk, understood the potential impacts on her family and the threat to the future of the estate, and yet look what she had just done.

'What if I am weak?' asked Martha. 'What if you are?' Thea wanted to deny that she could be, to say that she could be strong and keep them both safe, but the evidence suggested otherwise. She could only put more distance between them and avert her eyes from Martha's. She wanted to say something, but the lump in her throat seemed to preclude any words.

'You should go,' said Martha, firmly. And Thea knew she must.

The next morning she picked at her kippers and eggs, trying to muster an appetite to be polite while also trying not to look at Martha across the table. She was pleased that Martha seemed to be compensating for the awkwardness between them by throwing herself heartily into conversation with the Constables. Thea wasn't sure she could have managed it, after another night of no sleep and considering the shame she felt.

There was also her decision. She knew she couldn't lose Martha – the connection they had and the affection they shared. But to keep it she knew she must control her feelings in any way she could. As she had told Ursula before she left, she had searched in vain for any reason or cause for her deviance – for something solid that she could observe or act upon, and yet there was none. Another night of delving deep into her thoughts and her past had presented nothing of substance. There was only one thing that had been mentioned as a potential cause for her deviance and in the absence of any other course of action she could begin by controlling that. She would distance herself from scholarship and the collections. It wouldn't be easy while they were here, but she had to try. Maybe then she and Martha would be able to resume their old friendship.

At least there would be little time to dwell on their issue in the daytime. Judging by the fact that Mr Constable had provided them with a visitor guide to the house as soon as they stepped through the door, she assumed today would be rather busy. She wasn't disappointed. The morning began in the great hall – a commanding, double-height room tastefully decorated with paintings, sculptures, animal horns and fine furniture. Above the grand fireplace hung an armorial shield, framed by an intricate garland of laurel leaves carved from oak. Both Martha and Thea consulted their visitor pamphlet at Mr Constable's suggestion. It displayed various coats of arms with a little writing alongside each.

'You may find the guide useful as you peruse the house, my ladies. The arms of the ancestral family adorn the walls of the great hall and there is a full family tree displayed in the chapel passage.' Everything about Mr Constable radiated warmth and a neatness which reflected his pamphlet. He was relatively tall and smartly dressed with a neat white wig and sapphire blue suit. He was quite a portly man in his middle years, his waistcoat stretched a little at the buttons and his round, fresh face always formed into a smile. His sister who fussed around him was a little more slender than her brother but her outline also suggested the generous breakfasts were not unusual. The two of them were so welcoming it was as if they were all long-lost friends. Thea and Martha followed them dutifully although Thea could tell Martha was as distracted as she. They kept their distance from one another and made polite and appropriate comments.

When they had toured the dining room, the long gallery and the library they arrived in the staircase hall for the second time.

'And now, for the museum!' trilled Mr Constable as he threw open a huge double-width door with a flourish, revealing one of the most impressive rooms Thea had ever seen. Proceeding through the doorway both Thea and Martha wandered with their heads tilted upward, peering about the space in awe. The square museum was huge – perhaps fifty feet along each wall – with an octagon of marble columns surrounding a circular table at the centre. The walls, floor to ceiling, hosted cabinets crammed full of curiosities of all shapes and sizes. There were animals, birds, insects, models of machines, actual working machines, astrolabes and much, much more. On the central table sat numerous volumes of Mr Constable's *hortus siccus*, two of the huge books open and showing off their vibrant pressed plant samples.

Mr Constable smiled shyly, his sister joining him by the window. 'I am sure it is less than you are used to, but it serves my purpose and interest well.'

Thea spun on her heel to look at him, her worries momentarily eclipsed. 'It is magnificent, Mr Constable.' At her words Martha turned to look at her for the first time that day, and Thea knew neither the quiet, intense delight she radiated, nor the multiplicity of artefacts in Mr Constable's collection was going to help her endeavour.

His pleasure at their enjoyment was evident, and it gave him confidence. While he showed them his experiment room where he carried out his work on chemistry and physics, Thea thought he would get on very well with Mr Pickles. Indeed, she thought, he was so affable that he would probably get along with anyone. He talked of astronomy, chemistry, physics, electricity, natural history, numismatics and even the most recent developments in agriculture. But mostly he talked of botany and his plant collection which Thea knew Martha was itching to be among.

As Martha reached one of the tall windows, Thea heard her gasp and looked over to see her staring out, wide eyed. At least the collection could distract her from her troubles, Thea thought.

Mr Constable chuckled. 'I see you have spied the other part of my natural philosophy collection.' Thea joined Martha at the window, being careful to keep a respectful distance. The parkland stretched to the horizon but outside the museum, separated only by a driveway, lay Mr Constable's plant collections. They were contained in a walled garden which was set lower than the house, affording an excellent view and a protected microclimate. A stove range extended at length down the southern-facing wall and the remainder of the extensive area was populated by row upon row of plants.

When they finally stood outside in it, the garden collection was as spectacular as it looked from the house. Try as she might to distance herself, Thea could feel Martha's excitement as she moved from one plant group to the next, from familiar plants to the exotic, growing alongside each other in regimented beds. Mr Constable had them all labelled precisely so there could be no question as to their identification and provenance. The stove itself was no less impressive, plants in beds tan beds and in pots housed in a range longer than Thea had ever seen.

'Many of the samples in my *hortus siccus* come from the garden here,' explained Mr Constable, 'but equally many come in already pressed off the boats. As I am sure you do also, I have things dried that we have never seen in cultivation in Britain. The labelling is often completed on landing and can be incorrect. Equally, my identification can sometimes be off the mark, but Thomas, my gardener, has a sharp eye and reviews the collection to ensure all is accurate and in its place.'

Martha turned to him with a look of almost reverence. 'You have arranged them botanically? Outside?'

Mr Constable grinned and nodded, evidently delighted with his learned guest. 'Indeed. It enables me to study them more accurately and to understand similarities and differences between the classes. They are arranged as per Mr Linnaeus's new method. Which do you use, Lady Foxmore?'

'I have recently switched to the new method also, I find it offers much more taxonomic clarity – don't you?' Thea looked between them, her resolution already crumbling.

CHAPTER 19

As predicted, it was not easy for Thea to distance herself from scholarship. Burton Constable was alive with it, but Thea was determined. On the second day of the visit Mr and Miss Constable took delight in performing demonstrations in the experiment room but Thea excused herself and went for a walk instead, earning a confused glance from Martha.

She was pleased that Martha seemed to have become more of her old self in the familiar surroundings of the collection and garden. There was an easiness about her that Thea hadn't seen in weeks, however, it was notable how ardently she avoided being alone with Thea. On the few occasions when the two of them were not with the Constables or Thomas Kyle, Martha kept disappearing, or suddenly found a great need to speak to the gardener.

Dinner that night brought new company and more distraction. Mr Constable's friend Captain Morrison was to visit them from Whitby which excited their hosts greatly. The Captain, Mr Constable said, journeyed around the globe collecting curiosities, and he expected some new items for his collection this evening. Thea knew Martha would be fascinated by Captain Morrison and his accounts of his travels. On his arrival she found that she liked Captain Morrison immensely. He was a wiry, affable gentleman in middle age whose refined wardrobe also betrayed a little of the rakish sailor. The conversation at dinner flowed through voyages and collections – they drank in accounts of the things he had seen and the adventures he had been on, intentionally or not. Thea smiled at Martha's eyes, wide with excitement and interrogating every detail of the New World and the plants she studied from someone who had experienced it first-hand. When she found out that her *Platycerum* – the stag's horn fern – grew on tree branches and not in the ground, Thea could see Martha planning how she would amend its cultivation on her return to Denbury.

After dinner they retired to the museum room and sat round the table in the centre, a glass of port in front of each of them. Captain Morrison's recent expedition to the south of America had been a bountiful one and he produced a variety of items with a flourish. He passed Mr Constable pressed plants, dried fish and insects pinned to boards. Thea looked up and caught Martha's eyes on her, presumably for her reaction, she thought. Thea looked away, this was too akin to the many pleasurable times they had spent together and was not helping her to gain a sensible perspective. Despite her resolution to exercise her mind in less strenuous ways, here she was again, surrounded by knowledge. Maybe that was the problem, she thought, but politeness precluded her from leaving the party and the collections. She wondered if it was possible that she could be amongst it, but just not think too hard about anything?

'But now, Mr Constable,' said Captain Morrison, snapping her out of her thoughts. 'I have something I think you will find particularly fascinating.' He opened a large book and pulled out a ream of loose sheets within which plant material was just visible. Both Mr Constable and Martha craned to look. Captain Morrison laid them on the table. They were frondy, frothy and all colours of pink, yellow and orange, without any sign of flowers.

Mr Constable and Martha looked at him, flummoxed. 'Any ideas?' he asked, flicking his sharp eyes between them mischievously.

'Is it some sort of giant moss?' asked Martha, her tone betraying her own doubt.

'Almost,' said the Captain, 'but think a little more – damp.' They all stared at him blankly. 'And salty,' he said, raising one bushy, expectant brow.

'Oh,' said Martha, 'seaweed!'

'Exactly, Lady Foxmore!' he cried, clapping his hands with glee. 'So much grows off the coast of America and it is in all shapes and sizes. I thought Mr Constable has so many of the land plants already in his garden and his *hortus siccus*, why not start on the sea plants?!'

Mr Constable looked almost beside himself. 'Amazing! You are quite the visionary, Morrison.' He traced the line of one of the seaweeds with his finger. It would require a little more pressing and was still quite springy, giving a reasonable impression of what it must look like in life. Thea recognised in him the awe that beset both Martha and her father when presented with an entity from a different world, that had crossed so many miles and would expand their knowledge that little bit further.

Thea turned to Captain Morrison as Martha, Winifred and Mr Constable spread the samples over the table. 'An inspired choice, Captain,' she said through a chuckle. 'Is this your entire business? It must be nice to spread such joy amongst the scholars of Britain?'

'Indeed it is.' Captain Morrison smiled back. 'It is rewarding to finally trade in joy.' He went on at her enquiring look. 'As Mr and Miss Constable are aware, my previous business was in the triangular trade. British exports to Africa, human cargo to the West Indies, sugar, cotton and tobacco on the return.'

She eyed him carefully. 'But not anymore?'

He shook his head. 'The middle passage was always the worst. At sea one becomes accustomed to the smell of disease and death, but the extent of the devastation on that stretch was shocking even to me.' He placed his glass back on the table. 'I was the captain, not the owner. Ship owners insure their cargo heavily. On my last voyage severe disease spread through the ship. The insurance would not cover cargo lost to disease but would cover drowning.'

He watched her carefully as she stared at him. Martha had placed the samples back on the table and had focussed on the conversation. 'By cargo, you mean...' started Thea.

'Africans, yes.'

'And so..?' Thea's stomach turned at the implication. She hoped she was wrong.

'Over fifty chained and overboard within a few days. So many of the crew see them as nothing but animals but I can assure you that they are not.'

A silence settled around the table at the horror of the admission. 'You couldn't stop it?' asked Thea, unable to keep quiet.

'The crew were a scurrilous set and would not have been paid if orders were not carried out. Had I opposed the ruling they would simply have sent me down with the rest.' He pressed a fist into the table before remembering himself. 'The owner received the insurance payout, and I made it my last voyage.' He tapped a finger on the table and cast them both a weak smile as Thea's stomach turned. 'And that's why I now make curiosities my cargo. When I returned to London I sought some of the country's finest collectors. The ship now runs on a syndicate basis – they fund it, and I search for curiosities I think they will be interested in. I am lucky that the virtuosi are so hungry for specimens and many of them have influence with the East India Trading Company so permissions are not difficult to come by.'

'And an excellent job you do too,' said Mr Constable, 'best to be out of that nasty business. It'll be outlawed before long, you mark my words.'

'With any luck,' agreed the Captain. 'I hear murmurs of disquiet in London but it will be some time before action is taken.'

'Why so, if it is as bad as you say?' asked Miss Constable.

The Captain shrugged. 'Largely as they are not seen as people, but mostly because ownership provides many parliamentarians with their wealth and therefore their land and position. How to convince those in power to vote against commercial self-interest?'

'Then the situation is hopeless? Because of greed?' Thea asked, the horror of the story of the ship still playing in her mind.

'Never hopeless,' said Captain Morrison. 'As long as disquiet with the trade continues to rise then change is possible. We must also remember that there is more to trade and expansion than slavery. It is quite possible to take lands and manage by more reasonable means.'

Martha's brow furrowed. 'But it is not as profitable?'

'Almost, if managed well, Lady Foxmore,' the Captain confirmed. 'For both us and for the populations. We owe it to the indigenous peoples to do God's work in the empire – they have no agriculture, no proclivity to work unless forced, no sense of politeness or civility. There is no enlightened progression to speak of. Our presence there is a kindness.' Thea peered around the table for a reaction. She was certain she didn't approve of enslavement, and although spreading gentility to new lands didn't sound so awful she found it hard to reconcile her experience of Scip with claims of savagery. But no rejection of the position was forthcoming. 'And they, of course, are pleased to trade with us,' said the Captain, interrupting her thoughts.

'And, I assume, to sustain you and your crew, to guide you and to have the grace to show you the best specimens, eh, Captain? Thea was sure she saw an upwards tick in the corner of Miss Constable's mouth. 'How terribly uncivilised'.

There was a slight pause and quiet in the proceedings, before Miss Constable clearly decided she had made the Captain feel awkward enough. 'I am certain you are doing your best, Captain, and I know my brother is grateful to you.'

Mr Constable grasped at the chance to move the conversation on. 'Indeed I am,' he said quickly, beaming at the Captain. 'And I am sure Lady Foxmore would be also if you were to bring some for her. I enjoy a little competition.' He winked at Martha good naturedly, before lifting an orange-coloured seaweed sample to his face and sniffing it.

The conversation deftly turned away from moral complexities the Captain smiled. 'Had I known you had such a keen eye I would have brought more with me today, Lady Foxmore. As it is, I will send on samples to you if you are interested?' Martha beamed happily at him, then dropped her gaze to Thea and back.

'I would be very grateful for any plant samples you come across, Captain Morrison,' she said, 'although it is Miss Morell who would benefit most from your broader natural history specimens like the fish and insects.'

Thea's eyes snapped back to Martha. She wished she wouldn't keep doing this in public.

'I knew it!' cried Mr Constable. 'You have been too modest, young lady, but I have observed your aptitude in the museum room. Knowledge seeps out, it is easy to recognise one's own passions reflected in another.'

Thea held up her hands to calm him. 'I admit I have dabbled, Mr Constable, but no more. Lady Foxmore is too generous in her estimation of my abilities.' She saw Martha frown from across the table.

'Well that is a shame.' Winifred eyed her kindly. 'I am afraid you must be extremely tired of us all if your interest is not collections.'

'Not a bit of it,' said Thea quickly, 'I cannot deny that I find the conversation extremely diverting Miss Constable, almost too diverting.' Her eyes darted involuntarily to Martha. 'It is only that a lady of my age has responsibilities. I am the eldest, you see, with no brothers, and should no longer occupy myself with diversions which may prove detrimental.' She took a sip of port to moisten her dry mouth. 'I have found that I struggle to maintain the two simultaneously.'

'How terribly depressing,' said Miss Constable, 'unless of course there is a certain someone who has taken your heart hard enough for you to cast off your interests with no regret?' Her eyes twinkled mischievously. If only she knew, thought Thea. She kept her gaze steadily at Winifred, desperate not to let it stray to Martha.

'I am afraid not, Miss Constable.' She placed her port back on the table and a silence ensued. She felt the need to fill it. 'At least, not one who offers an acceptable future for my father's estate.' She wished she hadn't filled it.

'Ho ho, I see!' exclaimed Winifred, clearly oblivious of the tension. 'But your parents do not approve?' Thea's stomach dropped and she cast around for a change of subject.

'My choice of suitor has not always pleased my mother, it is true,' she said, bending her head further from Martha to avoid even catching her in her peripheral vision. She saw Miss Constable take a breath to question her further and braced for the continuingly awkward questions when Martha's voice came quickly and loudly from across the table.

'Captain Morrison, won't you tell us more about how you transport the samples from the new world?'

The Captain smiled, unaware of the deflection. 'An astute question, Lady Foxmore, if I had better solutions there would be far more samples for us to peruse today.' As he went on Thea risked a glance at Martha and was unprepared for the grief she saw there. She allowed herself an almost imperceptible nod of thanks before she turned her attention back to Captain Morrison, for politeness as well as to stem the ache that settled in her chest. 'So much perishes on the voyage when taken out of its natural environment,' he was saying. 'The fleshy samples of animals and plants have a tendency to rot. It is possible to preserve them in alcohol but what Captain has room for so many bottles on a ship?' He grinned around at the group. 'And what crew would leave it untouched?!'

'You need Lady Foxmore on your ship, Captain,' offered Thea, forcing jollity but needing him to know of Martha's skills.

The Captain looked at her, bemused. 'I am sure Lady Foxmore could only enhance any trip Miss Morell, but will she help with the alcohol?'

Thea laughed. 'I cannot vouch for that, but she is an excellent artist with a knack for capturing the essential botanical details, so my father tells me.'

She dared to look across at Martha once more and watched the colour rise in her cheeks. Insistent cajoling from the table eventually persuaded Martha to retrieve her sketchbooks and she sat modestly while the party enthused over the detail. Thea couldn't help glowing with pride. After some thorough perusal Mr Constable fixed Martha with a serious look.

'These are truly excellent, Lady Foxmore. Work of this quality requires a learned eye and a talent for accurate depiction which few possess.'

Martha blushed but recovered. 'I simply try to depict those details I would want to know as a plantswoman.'

Captain Morrison smiled. 'And that, of course, is what makes them so useful. My subscribers would be delighted with these. Have you ever considered a life at sea, Lady Foxmore?' Martha only laughed, but by the time he left for his lodgings they had arranged to meet in London for her to speak to his own travelling artists.

Before Thea could make her excuses and head to her bed, Miss Constable had poured them all another glass of port. 'My brother will not say so,' she said, standing and retrieving two large books from the shelves, 'but he is quite desperate to request your assistance with one or two samples in the *hortus siccus* if you would be so kind, Lady Foxmore?' Martha gestured her pleasure at this and Winifred flipped open both of the huge, leather-bound books.

Mr Constable gestured to them and the books stacked on the shelves. 'I am redoing them in the Linnaean system,' he said. 'Although it is taking longer than I expected, even with Winifred's help.'

'May I?' asked Martha, pulling one of the volumes to her and beginning to flick through the pages. 'You have a great many samples here, I am not surprised it takes you the time.'

'It does,' said Winifred, moving closer. 'But the new method is quicker and the relationships between plants are clearer. Within the new *hortus siccus* they are grouped according to the number of husbands and wives each flower possesses.'

Martha began to leaf carefully through the pages and Thea looked at the Constables. 'Husbands and wives relate to the male and female parts of the flower as Linnaeus directs?'

Winifred smiled, but Mr Constable looked a little flustered, and then fiddled with his glass. 'The Linnaean system is perhaps a little indelicate for ladies' ears, Lady Foxmore.'

'Don't worry, Mr Constable,' Martha looked up from the pages smiling kindly. 'You are free to speak plainly with us. We will never attain the truth if we are limited by societal mores, shall we?'

Winifred grinned widely and Mr Constable pulled another book towards him, opening it in an attempt to avoid anyone's gaze. 'Anyway.' He cleared his throat. 'Some of the herbarium samples come from the garden and stove but some come from overseas. I have a particularly tricky sample that looks like...'

His voice petered out as he turned towards Martha and his eyes flitted from the page she studied carefully, up to her face and back again. Thea watched the colour drain from his cheeks. 'That's... um... that's a, a... a *Juglans*, Lady Foxmore,' he stammered.

'So I see,' Martha said, barely managing to keep the smile out of a voice that dripped with mischief as she studied the sample. 'You like to give them their common name too, it seems.'

'Yes, sometimes,' said Mr Constable with another little cough, by now visibly sweating. 'The Walnut. It aids my memory.'

'Mm hmm,' said Martha, 'I bet it does.' She looked straight at Mr Constable with a devilish grin on her face and Thea's heart swelled to see some joy returned. 'I never knew the walnut had more than one common name, but I suppose *Juglans regia* does often grow its fruit in pairs.'

'It, it, it is very hot in here, don't you think?' Mr Constable wheezed, fingering his collar. 'I must go and find Rodgers to bring us more port.' He fled out of the room, leaving a smiling Martha and Winifred looking after him.

Thea, who had been watching the strange exchange with interest kept her distance. 'Why?' she asked, but couldn't add any more as Martha's eyes met hers. Some of the cheer was replaced by concern, but they remained soft.

She stood and slid the book towards Thea across the table, gesturing to the open pages. 'Have a look for yourself,' she said tenderly.

Thea stood from her chair and reached to bring the book closer. 'Shagbag nut?' she asked, reading aloud and looking up at Martha and Winifred. 'What does...' They both lifted their eyebrows at her as one. 'Oh!' Thea felt colour flood her cheeks as she looked up into their faces, tears of suppressed laughter streaking Winifred's and a gentle smile on Martha's.

'Well done,' said Martha, something like pride in her voice. 'It took me a little longer than that. I'd never considered the resemblance.' Her eyes played over Thea's but then she looked away sharply as Winifred rocked back on her chair, barely suppressing a guffaw.

'I admit it's why I avoid walnuts at Christmas,' she spluttered. Despite themselves both Thea and Martha descended into laughter.

The walnut incident brought Thea hope that the breaking of tension might lead to better relations between them, but Martha fled the table after breakfast the next morning. The past two days had, however, confirmed in Thea's mind that she couldn't give Martha up, and she was determined to tell her so. She hunted high and low for the Countess who wasn't in the museum, the library or the garden and so Thea took up watch at a window in the long gallery from which she had a commanding view of the estate. It was almost noon when she saw the figure stride through the long grass past the menagerie, across the footbridge, into the walled garden and disappear into the stove.

Thea moved as quickly as propriety would allow. Even if a conversation only made their interactions slightly less awkward and she could know that Martha would give their friendship a chance, it would be worth it. Rain started to fall as she made her way through the garden and slipped quietly into the stove. Martha stood mid-way down the range, hands on the raised planting beds, looking over Mr Constable's small collection of venus fly traps. Of course.

Martha looked up at the sound of Thea's footsteps and made to leave.

'Don't,' said Thea, firmly, and Martha halted her progress towards the door.

'Thea, this is not a good idea.' Martha spoke as she turned back around. 'It isn't appropriate.'

'We can talk,' said Thea, 'Only that. What happened the other day won't happen again.'

Martha relaxed a little but her eyes darted around them as rain started to patter on the glass. 'If anyone overhears.'

'Nobody is here.' For a second Martha's eyes flicked to the door and Thea worried she might flee, but then she squared her shoulders and risked a glance at Thea.

'Alright,' she said softly. 'What did you want to say?' It was only then that Thea realised that she didn't know.

She swallowed, all her resolutions and practiced openers having fled her mind. 'I can't lose you, Martha. I just can't.'

Martha's face betrayed feelings bordering on desperation. 'Thea, we've been through this.'

'Not together, not properly,' she said. 'Not when it hasn't been new or raw or surprising. I've been thinking.'

There was a pause before Martha spoke. 'I can't stop thinking about it,' she said softly before looking away, focussing through the glass. 'I am so sorry I said anything, then it wouldn't have to be like this.'

'Then we could go back to you not speaking to me and me being miserable because I think you hate me?'

Martha blanched. 'I am sorry about that too.'

Thea dared to take a step closer to her. 'It changes, when you know.' Martha looked back at her and when their eyes met Thea saw her own sorrow and frustration reflected back.

'Yes,' said Martha quietly, 'it does. Knowledge marks us in a way that is irreversible.' She absentmindedly touched a fingertip to the scar beneath her eye. Silence again.

'I am trying.' Thea turned and leant against the brick of the planting bed, brushing a little soil off the top for somewhere else to look. 'Just to make it a little less, insistent.'

Martha's brow puckered. 'That's why you are distancing yourself from the collections.'

'Yes.'

'What if it has nothing to do with it?'

Thea shrugged. 'It is the only thing I have heard as a potential cause for this.' She gestured between them hopelessly. 'If only I could gain a little more control. Then I can be strong when we are together, and I know that if I am, you can be too. Then we can still be around one another. I can't think of anything else it could be and I am trying, but in the meantime...' She trailed off.

'In the meantime, it is desperate,' Martha supplied for her, staring at Thea. Her face had softened and she allowed the pain to show uncensored.'

'Yes, it is,' admitted Thea.

'We should have gone home.' Martha looked away from Thea, fixing her gaze on the fly traps while her fingers played over the pocket watch chain. Her voice was quiet and strained. 'Every time I see you it makes it harder.'

'What is the alternative?' asked Thea, watching Martha for her reaction. 'Look me in the eye and tell me you could give up what we have.'

She saw Martha's throat work and her knuckles whiten as she gripped the rough surface of the bricks. 'I would if it would keep you and your family safe.'

'Safe from what?' Her quiet voice felt loud in the enclosed space. The familiar cold crept up her spine, unbalancing her when it reached her head. 'I know about the estate and fortunes and reputation and all of that, but this' – she gestured to all of herself at once – 'does not feel safe, Martha. Not at the prospect of losing you.'

Martha blinked and took a steadying breath. 'And is it working? The abstinence from study?'

Thea paused, and then shook her head. 'But I have to try, I don't know of any other way. We have to try to be–' The word *friends* stuck in her throat and she gulped it down. That wasn't enough. She squeezed her eyes together and felt the tears overflow, then warm arms were around her and Martha's scent of cedar and sandalwood filled her senses. She held on, shaking while Martha held her, trembling a little herself. Thea vocalised the fear that had eaten away at her for months. 'I need you to help me to understand, Martha. I can't do it myself and it scares me.'

'We'll find a way,' Martha muttered into her ear, stroking soothing hands over her dress, cautiously calming Thea's frayed nerves despite the echoing keenness of her own. 'We will find a way, Thea. I won't leave you alone.' Thea could only sigh with relief and nestle further into Martha, clinging to her with relief and anxiety together.

As the tears abated Thea opened her eyes and watched the raindrops stutter down the outside of the stove glass. She heard the plink, plink, of drops that made their way inside, falling into slowly forming puddles. It happened around them, both of them still, loathe to let go.

Suddenly she felt Martha tense against her.

'Holy Hemlock, that's it.' She heard the mutter right next to her ear.

'What is?'

'That's it, that's the reason.' Martha's hands grasped the material at the back of her dress.

'You know?' asked Thea. 'You've figured it out?' She pushed Martha away from her by the shoulders and looked into her eyes.

'I have,' said Martha, sounding awed, her eyes glazed, 'I think I have.' But then her eyes refocussed on Thea. 'Oh not that, Thea, I am so sorry.' She took Thea's face in her palms and stroked her cheeks. Thea felt the loss keenly when they left, Martha stepping past her to the planting bed.

'The fly traps, Thea.'

'I would never have believed it had I not seen it with my own eyes.' Mr Constable sat back at the dinner table while Martha looked stunned and Thea grinned. While so many feelings were still raw, there was no denying the significance of the afternoon's revelation and the excitement in the house was infectious. Her heart soared each time she looked at Martha, who still wouldn't quite believe it. She had apologised solemnly to Thea for the joy that she felt undermined their distress, but Thea would have none of it. Success for someone she had loved for years was something to celebrate, heartache or not.

'Imagine it, a plant that can count,' muttered Mr Constable for the third time that evening. He sipped his wine and then placed the glass back heavily on the table, leaning over his dinner plate, wide eyes focussed on Martha. 'Astonishing, ingenious!' As Martha had apologetically relinquished her grip on Thea in the stove, she had taken up a stick and carefully brushed it inside the jaw of a fly trap. Nothing happened. Then she had done it again with a double brush. The trap closed. Thea had watched in awe as Martha went through the traps, examining and discovering. After numerous attempts she had deduced that the traps needed two or more stimulations of the hairs on the inside of the jaws, not just one. By counting the movements they ensured that they would close on living creatures like flies, and not on isolated falling objects like rain droplets, Martha deducted.

The thought had occurred to her as she watched a rain droplet fall into a trap over Thea's shoulder. 'I knew I would contribute to a discovery one day,' Thea had joked to her, as they investigated the plants together before they dare call Mr Constable and Winifred for fear of being mistaken. Martha had looked at her ravenously, like it was all she could do not to take her in her arms at once. But she had simply reached out and taken Thea's hands, holding them at a distance as if that was the only contact she dare risk.

'You do more than you know,' she had said gently, and some invisible barrier had dissolved between them. It was easier now. How it would be tomorrow Thea couldn't tell, but right now that didn't matter. The problem was that with every touch or appreciative glance, her affection for Martha seemed to grow. It happened in the stove, and in the drawing room while discussing and making notes, and now at dinner. When Martha laughed with pleasure she felt like her heart may explode, and was too happy to feel any guilt. For now she let it wash over her, appreciated the happy wrinkles that formed at the corner of Martha's eyes and enjoyed the moment, wondering if Martha was doing the same.

Martha opened her mouth to speak but Mr Constable went on. Thea wasn't sure who was more excited. 'You are quite the genius, Lady Foxmore, and to think you discovered it here in my little stove!' Thea looked out of the window at the vast stove range beneath them – in honour of the exciting revelation Mr Constable had cleared the museum table and insisted that they take dinner amongst the collection.

'It will require testing and repeating of course,' said Martha, but her wide smile belied her caution.

'To think I wrote to the philosopher Rousseau only the other day on this subject.' Mr Constable was not deterred. 'I will share the results with him after you publish.'

Martha's face lost a bit of its colour. 'I think publication seems unlikely, Mr Constable.'

'Whyever should it?' asked their host, dabbing at the corner of his mouth with a napkin. 'This must be shared!'

Martha's index finger trailed the edge of her knife, back and forth. 'It would not be received well, coming from a woman.' Thea's heart dipped in sympathy.

'There must be a way,' said Winifred from across the table. 'William is a member of the Royal Society, perhaps you can help, Will?'

'I am certain of it.' Mr Constable clapped his hands together. 'Did you not say you were collaborating with others on the plant movement Lady Foxmore? I am sure that if Thea's father is interested in joining the society that something could be arranged.'

Thea could barely control her excitement. 'Martha,' she breathed, 'just think – to be published.'

'You could make the introduction between us, could you not?' Mr Constable looked between them. 'And then I could propose Mr Morell as a member. It may not be able to be you presenting the paper I am afraid, Lady Foxmore, but the work would be yours.'

'I don't know,' said Martha, uncharacteristically cautious. 'This is all so sudden.'

'What would be the point in delaying?' asked Thea softly, watching Martha's changing countenance with interest.

'Quite right, Miss Morell!' Mr Constable gestured towards her with a wine glass, evidently delighted that one of them shared his enthusiasm. 'I can write to the society today to trail the idea for a paper, I don't need to add any specifics at this stage and–'

'No,' said Martha sharply, cutting him off. They all turned to stare at her, and she softened. With effort, Thea felt. 'It is a kind thought, Mr Constable, but I beg that you wouldn't. If we are to enquire with the society we have a contact at home who is a member and I feel it would be right and proper to do the necessary through him.

Thea was aghast. 'You can't mean–'

'Mr Grimston,' said Martha, 'yes. He has been aware of the research for some time and I am sure would be delighted to be able to play his part.

'But Grimston is–'

Thea was cut off again by Martha's hard stare. 'An upstanding member of the local community and' – she inclined her head almost imperceptibly at Mr Constable – 'a prominent member of the Royal Society.' Thea got the message and pressed her lips together.

'Grimston.' Mr Constable's round face scrunched together a little as he stared, unseeing, at the far corner of the room. 'That name does ring a bell.'

Martha shifted in her chair. 'He lives at Wickmarsh, not so far from Thea and I, and has been part of the Thornbury scholarly set for longer than either of us. He is an... eclectic collector, but favours birds.'

'Aha!' Comprehension dawned on Mr Constable's face. 'The stuffed birds and terrible eyes? The birds' eyes I mean, not his.' A smirk started at the corner of his mouth before it was chased away by propriety. 'I apologise, I didn't mean to offend. I am sure I have seen a very small part of what I am sure is a remarkable collection.'

'Sadly, I am sure you have only seen the best of it, Mr Constable,' said Thea, not trying to keep the smirk from her face. 'All of the birds look like they have seen something surprising in the undergrowth.' She was pleased that this, at least, drew a guilty smile from Martha.

Mr Constable looked between them. 'I am guessing Mr Grimston is not a particular friend of yours?'

'Not exactly,' Martha spoke quickly, 'but I suppose the society must see something in him if they are considering him for high office?'

Mr Constable chuckled. 'I would be surprised if they were, Lady Foxmore, he brought a stuffed goose to a recent meeting, as he called it, a barnacle goose. That is' – he placed a hand on his chest and extended the other away, raising his head in the manner of an affected orator – 'a goose which does not spring from an egg, but instead generates from a barnacle shell which adheres to driftwood or trees.'

Thea grinned to herself, remembering the conversation with Edgar and Mr Grimston in the spring. Mr Grimston had clearly presented the goose as his own discovery.

Martha looked incredulous. 'That is surely impossible.'

Mr Constable clapped his hands together in joy. 'Of course it is. Unfortunately Grimston accepted the story wholesale from whatever crook sold it to him. I believe I last saw him pursuing the goose out of the room after one of the membership was unable to stifle a guffaw.

'Perhaps you can enlighten us then, Mr Constable,' said Thea, meeting Martha's eyes. She had been intrigued about her relationship with Mr Grimston ever since the odd exchange with Edgar. 'I did think that the Royal Society was more discerning and keen to be taken seriously, do they not vet submissions before readings?'

'They do,' Mr Constable admitted, 'however, Grimston is a significant financial supporter of the society and, I suspect something of a supporter of the secretary, Valtrevers. It is amazing how the piece brought often differs in substance from that submitted.'

'And yet he persists because he thinks he knows better?'

'It seems that way.' Mr Constable grinned. 'They at least managed to block his most recent offering – a narwhal tusk apparently that he thought was a unicorn horn. Imagine believing that in this day and age, this is the seventeen fifties, for goodness sake.'

Neither Thea nor Martha could hide their mirth. It was a pleasant relief after the reminder of Mr Grimston's petulance. 'Oh,' exclaimed Martha, looking frustrated and amused all at once, 'I did try to tell him.'

Mr Constable shared their glee. 'Frankly I cringe for him even to think of it. I believe Grimston would be rather hopeful in his nomination for any office of the Royal Society, whatever his connections.' His gaze softened to concern. 'Are you sure you wish to have him propose your paper, Lady Foxmore? You must wish it to be taken seriously and I would be very happy to correspond on your behalf.'

Martha gave a genuine smile. 'You are very kind, Mr Constable, but I do think that, despite all this I must ask him in the first instance. He would expect it.'

Mr Constable nodded in acquiescence, but Thea was left wondering, not for the first time, why Mr Grimston would expect it, and even more so, why Martha felt she should offer.

'Miss Morell, I wonder if you could assist me?' Mr Constable's voice boomed from the stairwell. Thea sat by a window in the long gallery trying to sketch the view. Martha had barely emerged from her interrogation of the flytraps for two days now, and she was pleased of the diversion. She hitched up her dress and descended the stairs, heading to the museum where she found him examining a glass jar full of liquid and something else.

'I was hoping for some assistance with an identification,' he said, sliding the jar across the table.

Thea faltered. She was, after all, trying not to engage and whilst they were in comfortable company the nerves still rose at the thought of sharing her knowledge outside her immediate circle. What if she got it wrong? 'I think you may have more luck with Lady Foxmore, Mr Constable,' she said quietly, both intrigued about the jar and not wanting to look at it too hard.

'She was my first port of call,' said Mr Constable, 'but Lady Foxmore confirmed to me that you are far too modest in your own knowledge and suggested I consult you.' He peered at her from over a pair of round spectacles.

'Did she,' said Thea, not phrasing it as a question. Clearly Martha wasn't as convinced of her hypothesis on deviance as she was. She gave up, retrieved the jar and lifted it to eye level. The thing inside was around six inches long, scaly and lizard-like, with what seemed to be tiny wings attached. 'Interesting,' she mused, shifting closer to the window to catch the light. 'Not something I am well acquainted with but I seem to remember seeing something in the latest Linnaeus, do you have it?'

He retrieved a volume from the other side of the table and hefted it open to a bookmark. 'Might this be it do you think?' The pages clearly illustrated a small flying lizard with wings.

'That's the one!' she said, placing the glass on the table next to it. Looking between the preserved specimen and the page Thea compared the characteristics of the two, the bulbous head with a protruding eye, the reptilian legs and the ribbed wings which splayed at either side. 'I'd say it was a good match. *Draco volans*, the small flying dragon from Asia.'

He sighed. 'I feared as much.'

She raised her brows in question. 'Not what you were hoping for? I may be wrong, but it is an excellent specimen and quite the addition.'

'Mmm.' He took the jar from her and peered at it. 'Ordinarily I would be delighted, but it was sold to me as the skeleton of a dragon.' He looked up. 'A baby one, of course. I paid a significant price for it as although we all know dragons don't exist, this looks exactly like one, does it not?'

'I can see how one might be fooled,' she said, kindly.

'But then' – he patted the open leaves of the book – 'I was flicking through Linnaeus here, and came upon *Draco volans*. I was rather hoping you may have another interpretation for me but no matter, I will update my labels.'

'Whoever you bought it from must have known it wasn't a dragon.' Thea felt her indignation rise, despite the fact that Mr Constable seemed immediately sanguine.

'He must,' agreed Mr Constable, placing the jar back on the shelf, 'and I will speak to him the next time I see him, but it is what it is and there is no use wishing things were other than they are.'

'A charitable view, Mr Constable,' she said, 'who was it, if you don't mind me asking?'

'Valtrevers,' said Mr Constable. 'The same one who smooths Grimston's way into the society. One does have to be wary, he'll pop a sneaky one in every now and again and it looks like I got caught out.'

'I trade with him too,' said Thea, 'Will you find someone else, after this?'

'Goodness no.' Mr Constable gestured to the room at large. 'Valtrevers has supplied at least ten percent of what you see in this room. I'll not make the same mistake again, but a lifetime's pleasure is not worth forfeiting for an hour's pain. I allowed myself to hope against my better judgement and for that I can blame nobody but myself.'

'That's very pragmatic of you, Mr Constable.'

'Not especially,' he said. 'We deal in fact and facts must not be ignored. I seek only the truth whether or not it is the one I expected or, indeed, hoped for.'

Thea pressed her fingertips into the hard surface of the table, allowing the tension it built in her arm to distract her from that in her mind. 'Whether or not that truth is inconvenient.'

'Exactly, Miss Morell.' Mr Constable's eyes shone. He looked up at her from where he studied the jar. 'Deluding myself about the fact of this identification would not mean that I had a dragon in my collection. Is not our curiosity a wonderful way to honour the genius of the creator?'

Thea eyed him carefully, she had been wanting to ask. 'Reason, rather than revelation, Mr Constable?'

Mr Constable stared at the jar. 'If it doesn't offend you?'

'It does not,' she said, interested to hear how, as a catholic, he reconciled study with his faith. 'So, the chapel?'

The flicker of a rueful smile crossed his face. 'It is easier to be a catholic, believe it or not. More time with the collections, you see.' Thea nodded, understanding that being barred from public office meant he would have time on his hands. 'Whilst ever there is a spirit of amicability amongst our neighbours it suits me well. I have yet to be accused of deism but I assume it is only a matter of time.'

Thea hesitated, but decided to risk it. 'I have wondered. I mean, it would seem to make sense...' This conversation was a risky one, but Mr Constable was now looking at her with a hopeful understanding.

'That God creates and does not meddle?'

'Exactly,' said Thea. 'He created everything, but then we were left as custodians, and are able to find out the secrets.'

'The job of a natural philosopher,' said Mr Constable, relaxing and enjoying himself now he knew he was free to talk. 'To unpick the intricacies, order and structure in his creation. There are no mistakes by Him, only different ways of seeing by man.'

'Which may not be as you expect?' Thea said thoughtfully, as she thought of the dragon, and a realisation started to creep into her brain.

'Indeed,' said Mr Constable, picking up the dragon once more. 'Life is full of surprises which we must accept in order to understand. And would it not make life boring if things always went off as we expected?'

Wouldn't it, she thought, as she lay in bed that night. What if that was it? There were no mistakes. What if this was it, and she couldn't make herself any other than what she was? What if she was simply denying the inevitable truth by shunning the collections? What if denying it wasn't *right* as this was how she was made? Mr Constable's words had not left her head, and she thought back to her conversation with Mrs Phibbs. She had never been ordinary. Not since she was a child. She had always been different to the rest even before she took up collecting. The problem was, she had been scared of the truth and had tried to make it different. She almost scoffed aloud at herself – any natural philosopher knew that the truth was finite and unchangeable, and there was no reason that that should not be as true for the heart, as for the mind.

That was when she realised. That moment with the warmth of the sheets enveloping her, staring up into the darkness of the high ceiling. There was nothing wrong with her. This was how she was. As soon as the revelation hit it was a small step to then wanting to know the truth about herself. Not just the best or most convenient parts, but all of it.

She wanted to understand it from its most beautiful expressions down to the most grotesque and painful details.

She wanted to experience everything life was trying to offer.

She wanted to live it.

CHAPTER 20

I t is one thing to make a philosophical decision about one's life. It is entirely another to enact it. While Thea and Martha were speaking again they still orbited one another cautiously. Thea knew she couldn't take her thoughts directly to Martha, not after the speech about her commitment to exist together chastely, and anyway, getting Martha alone was almost impossible. But they couldn't stay at Burton Constable forever. Martha had acquiesced her resolution to return home and had agreed they should journey on to Whitby, not dissuaded by the opportunity to view Captain Morrison's wares in person, Thea suspected. When Thea discovered that Martha had asked the Constables to join them on the trip she felt a curious mixture of frustration and relief.

She was still musing on her approach two days later as she took a hammer and chisel to a rock on Whitby's bracing east beach. It was black, a piece of jagged shale around ten inches across. 'On the seam,' said Mr Constable, 'place the chisel and hit it sharply.' As she did the rock promptly split and there, in one of its two halves, sat a perfect ammonite, as dark as night with lustrous gold veining rippling across its surface. She gasped.

When she raised her head, Martha was standing close. 'Quite stunning,' she said, staring straight at Thea.

'Plenty more where that came from!' announced Mr Constable, waddling off among the rocks in search of more treasures.

Curiosity won out over caution and Thea rose to her feet, brushing chips of shale from the curled form nestled in the rock. She held it out to Martha who took it and traced the spiral with a long finger. 'How wonderfully the world gives up its secrets, if one only knows where to look,' she muttered, almost to herself.

'And how we must be brave enough to see and learn.' Thea leaned in to peer at the ammonite more closely and Martha pressed the rock back into her hands, stepping back a little but sharing a tender smile.

'Might this mean you have reconciled yourself once more to participating in the discovery of natural history?'

'As long as you won't tell,' said Thea, dropping the chisel into the satchel she had bought for the purpose. Her heart thudded as she observed Martha, wondering if this was the moment she should summon her bravery.

'As your chaperone I am permitted to turn a blind eye to some deviances.' Martha's eyes sparkled almost mischievously for a second, but then Thea caught the moment she realised her words may be misconstrued. They hardened once more, leaving Thea bereft of the playfulness. She cast around to retrieve it.

'It may mean I have to give up painting.'

'That would be a shame.' Martha kept her expression impassive, but Thea was delighted to see the gleam return to her eyes. She sought to nurture it.

'My works are now quite unique, I am considering donating them all to my chaperone to thank her for her encouragement in Scarborough.'

Martha's eyes were soft and her lips twitched up a little. 'That is excellent news, the one with the boat will go excellently in my water closet. The one in the north wing where nobody goes.'

'Seagull,' noted Thea, and dared to give Martha a small nudge on her shoulder. It drew a laugh from them both, and when their eyes met again the look was loaded with too much unsaid. All of a sudden it felt too heavy, and Thea dropped her gaze back to the ammonite she still held between them, her resolve deserting her.

'You know I would treasure them.' When Thea looked up again Martha still looked straight at her eyes. She could only swallow and nod.

A breath snatched into Martha and she stepped back, glancing nervously around them. 'You have decided that it was not the collections after all?'

Thea checked around too, ensuring there was nobody in earshot. 'I have decided that it doesn't matter. That facts are facts and there are some truths which cannot be tempered by reason.'

'Perhaps you are right.' Martha was quiet. The playful mood had certainly taken flight. 'But at least we are able to determine our own response and are able to temper our actions with prudence.'

Thea looked back at the rock, her outward calm belying how her heart hammered within. 'And what if we should not wish our response to be prudent?'

She heard how sharply Martha inhaled, but didn't dare look up. 'I have to wish it to be, Thea, and so do you.'

'I thought I did.' Thea now smoothed her fingertips over the fossil, taking comfort in its cool solidity. She dragged her eyes up to Martha's. 'But what if it isn't possible to be too curious? What if we are meant to feel and experience, knowing this thing is a part of us, part of how we were made and therefore part of what we must strive to understand?'

Seducing Martha with science. It was too bold, she knew. Martha's eyes widened in shock and she moved closer again, her eyes flicking around them, betraying her disquiet. She kept her voice low so as not to be heard above the waves. 'But that is not the way, Thea – I thought we agreed?' Her eyes darted between Thea's own, finding no confirmation. 'The risk, you can't understand.'

'Do you think I don't?' Anger rose inside Thea, at how patronising the words felt. 'You might remember that the situation has not always been kind to me, Martha.'

'And you should remember that it never will be.'

They stared at each other, challenging, until Martha gathered herself. 'I am glad to see you collecting again.' She turned to leave, stepped off the rock and then turned back, her voice low. 'I am sorry, Thea, truly I am. I would do anything I could to lessen this pain for both of us.'

'And you are quite resolved that you will not let me try again on your behalf?' Mr Constable leaned forward eagerly on the table they shared with Mr and Miss Constable and Captain Morrison. 'I really cannot believe that the society have rejected the idea outright.'

Martha held up a hand to stop him. 'I thank you, Mr Constable, but I beg that you wouldn't.' Her tone was kind, but firm. 'Mr Grimston assures me that he corresponded with the highest orders in the society and they are not yet ready to further the proposal of publication.'

'I really must stress that there is no reason why they would not, given the nature of the discovery. I have seen the proof with my own eyes and am certain that if I could only explain–' he went on as Thea observed the interaction with interest. The letter from Mr Grimston with news of the proposal's rejection had arrived earlier that day and hadn't seemed to surprise Martha at all. She had taken the news with a dogged resignation, unlike Mr Constable who was more exercised than Thea had seen him in their short weeks together. Tonight was their last night with the jovial group which had now become firm friends – Thea was sad they were to part, but there were plenty of promises of future meetings and she felt she had learned so much from the avid collectors.

Her mind wandered as she observed the group in animated discussion. She didn't know if she was looking forward to being alone with Martha, or not. Since her boldness on the beach they had not addressed the topic of their relationship, nor spoken of anything more complex than how they might spend their days. The atmosphere sat heavy between them. Part of her yearned to address it once more and discharge the tension but the other part feared the distance such a discussion may bring. The tension between them meant they hadn't spoken of publication since Martha's reticence on the topic at Burton Constable, and Thea was surprised at how determined she remained.

'And with your drawings, Lady Foxmore,' Captain Morrison now interjected. 'Think of the beauty of the piece.'

'And the stir it would create!' Winifred was the last to speak up. 'To document the perceptive power of vegetables! You know Linnaeus himself is convinced that it is impossible and you have proved it beyond doubt.' The three of them leaned into Martha, their eyes shining with excitement. Thea watched as Martha straightened her cutlery so it lay perpendicular to the edge of the table.

'While I do appreciate your concern I have thought of it in significant detail I assure you. There will be an alternative route to sharing the knowledge, the discovery will not go to waste.' Martha was polite but curt. 'You must excuse me.'

The gentlemen rose from their seats as Martha left the table. Winifred looked after her and leaned sideways into Thea. 'She is spectacular, is she not, Miss Morell? If I had more guts I would...' In the time it took for Winifred to raise her glass to her lips and take a sip, a jealousy had risen inside Thea so violent it made her nauseated. She turned to Winifred with fire in her eyes, just in time for her to lower the glass. '...I would snap up the chance of publishing if I ever had the chance. Imagine what it would be like to have your work immortalised forever.' She placed her glass on the table, her eyes dancing, and Thea swallowed her anger. 'If my brother writes to them also they must take on the publication with two recommendations. I do hope you can convince her to let him, Miss Morell. I am certain that if anyone can, it is you.'

That would have been the case once, thought Thea, and wondered if it ever would be again. Nothing was the same between them, not now the knowledge of longing hung in the air, and every glance was laden with warmth, hunger and guilt in equal measure. They skirted around one another keeping a respectful distance as if each were afraid of where a physical or intellectual closeness may lead. In truth, Thea was afraid, but her fear was chased closely by a curiosity she knew couldn't be assuaged. But she also knew she may be the only one who could convince Martha to share her valuable discovery.

By the time Martha returned the conversation had moved on, and soon midnight and the end of the evening approached. With goodbyes said and promises made, Thea and Martha made their way back to the grand lodgings they had taken on the west cliff. They walked, as the night was bright with the moon and the journey up the cliff took in the gentle curve of the harbour and the estuary which rended the town in two. As they rounded the corner to ascend to the clifftop and the houses overlooking the sea, the far-off rumble of the waves told Thea the tide was out.

'What a beautiful night,' she murmured, almost to herself. The moon glinted on waves, wet sand and the windows of the houses above them, almost all of them in darkness. It was quiet up here, any revellers remaining in the town, only a handful of wealthy families able to afford to lodge in the grand row of villas with sea views. They had set off from the assembly rooms at Martha's usual brisk pace, but now they slowed. The atmosphere between them felt delicate, as if the Constables had been a splint splicing them together and now they must discover if they would hold their form alone. Thea glanced sideways at Martha whose gaze was fixed on the stone flags in front of her as they walked.

'What is it?' She kept her own gaze cast down but was determined to break the silence.

'What is what?' Martha didn't raise her gaze from their path.

'Why are you so dead set against publishing? You can't possibly think Mr Grimston gave a good account of the research as it came from a woman.'

She felt Martha shrug at her side. 'Perhaps he is correct. The world of print belongs to men.'

The surprise made Thea raise her head. 'Your gender is not something that you usually allow to stand in your way.'

'Don't I?'

Thea stopped abruptly. 'You know you don't. This whole episode feels like you are trying to sabotage the opportunity yourself, otherwise you would allow Mr Constable to advocate for the validity of the discovery.'

Martha now stopped two paces ahead but didn't turn back. The few seconds of silence felt leaden. 'There is no guarantee that it would go off anyway, these things often don't come to fruition.'

'I have never known you let a fear of failure put you off.'

Even from the back Thea saw Martha's jaw harden. 'I can't risk it.'

'What if the risk was worth it?'

'People would know.'

'They don't have to.'

'They would know, Thea, they would ridicule my work and throw it out and I cannot have that happen to the study I have worked so hard on.'

'But then how will you ever know?' Thea wasn't aware she had raised her voice until the words were out and Martha turned towards her, her lips a thin line and brow stern.

'For God's sake, Thea, you are determined to pull this out of me. We cannot simply do everything we wish. Even if it is the dearest wish of our hearts, sometimes it is impossible. If you must know I am scared. Scared of failure and scared of consequences.' She hesitated for a second. 'But mostly I am scared of hurting you.' Martha broke off, her breathing rapid and her gaze not leaving Thea's. They both knew they were no longer talking about publishing and Thea's resolve softened at the fear she saw deep in Martha's eyes. 'I'll see you back at the house.' Martha set off towards the beach and Thea stood. She wasn't sure if she should follow, but as she watched Martha descend the path cut in the cliffs, she realised there was no way she could leave her alone on the beach after dark.

She set off after her, watching the moving shape of Martha's elegant dress catch slivers of light at each long stride. They were yards down the beach and past the end of the row of clifftop houses far above them before she managed to make any ground on her companion.

'Martha,' she called, but the figure continued. She hurried forward as best she could. 'Martha,' she called louder this time and Martha stopped.

'Go back to the house,' she said as Thea haltingly approached, stumbling a little as her shoes sank into the sand.

'I'm not leaving you on the beach.'

'I am fine.'

'No you aren't.' Thea could hear the worry threaded through her own voice and saw how it made Martha catch herself. The hum of the waves filled the space between them and as Martha looked out to where they broke it felt like an admission.

'Thea, I am sorry, but I simply cannot bear it. We can't go on like this if you insist on asking more than I can offer.'

The frustration inside Thea rose. 'You can't bear it? What about me?' Martha looked back at her, surprised, and the emotion built again – surging too violently to be contained, everything she had wanted to say since the day of the assembly. 'Do you have any idea what it is like?' She took a few steps in, closing the gap between them, seeing Martha's cheek twitch. 'What it is like knowing you and watching you every day – your cleverness and kindness making me finally begin to admit the depth of my feeling for you and being able to do nothing about it?'

Martha was silent for a time, shock written in the moonlight glinting off her wide eyes but her jaw still set. She glanced around to check they were alone and kept her own voice low. 'Of course I know. All too well, Thea, believe me.' The pocket watch at her waist glinted as she ran a finger over it. 'But people get hurt.'

Although the beach was deserted Thea was nervous having this conversation outside of the house and knew Martha would be too. An outcrop of rocks jutted from the cliff into the beach just to their left, and she stepped towards it, urging Martha to follow. Martha tentatively stepped in and soon they stood, within a deep fissure in the rock, safe from any disturbance. Thea stood with her back pressed against the cool surface, aware of how close their refuge brought them. Now she saw the worried crinkle in Martha's brow and could hear her breath over the gentle murmur of the waves.

'I know that as well as anyone. I know where it can lead and the pain it can cause, but we don't know anything about what this could be, Martha. Are we really willing to nip the bud before it breaks?'

'I really don't see any alternative.'

'Do you not? What if it were worth it?'

'What if it went wrong?'

'What if it didn't? What if it was incredible?' She knew she shouldn't push, but she couldn't help it, not anymore, not with terror and determination settling inside in equal measure. Martha deserved to know, even if she chose not to act. But at the glimmer of suggested hope she saw Martha's gaze cloud a little and her breath become shallower.

'You can't know that.'

'I can't. But if it did go wrong, then we would deal with it together. In full knowledge and understanding like we always have.'

Now Martha shut her eyes. 'I am so scared of letting you down.'

'You could never.' Thea stepped in, tentatively taking Martha's hands in her own. 'Martha, you could never. I respect whatever you decide and I will not press you further nor mention this again if it is your wish that I shouldn't, but I need you to know that I understand the risks.' She knew Martha would want to shoulder the responsibility, and she couldn't, wouldn't let her. 'I am willing to take those risks –

if you ever feel that you could too. Now or in the future.' They were now so close she could feel Martha's breath and clung to her hands as if they drifted together in the roaring waves.

'What are you asking of me?' Martha's voice was small and her breath frayed, but her eyes were so questioning that Thea's heart leapt with hope for the first time.

'I don't know. I honestly don't know what I can ask or what I can offer.' She dared move a little closer. 'But since you told me how you felt I can't shake the thought of what might be possible. I so desperately want to know the truth. Our truth.'

Martha's brow puckered. 'I fear this is at once the easiest truth to know and the hardest to realise.' She closed her eyes against the clarity forming between them and Thea squeezed the hands she held tight in her own.

'I can't exist in this life being afraid of myself. You said yourself that we can never gain the truth whilst being limited to societal mores. I want to understand what it is like to love you. And now I have wondered, I cannot conceive of never knowing.' She could feel Martha fighting her own resolve as she leaned in and laid her forehead against Thea's, her eyes still screwed shut.

Thea slipped her arms around the form in front of her, drawing them close, holding Martha firm. Martha was tense against her, but her hands slipped to Thea's waist, her fingers pressing into the whalebone of her stays. Nestled in Martha's neck Thea breathed in the soothing scent of cedar and sandalwood and closed her eyes, relishing their closeness, aware it could shatter with a whisper. But then a long, heavy sigh left Martha, her head angled in and breath caressed Thea's ear.

'Dear god, do you have any idea how you undo me?'

The words seeped through Thea's skin and into her bones, turning them liquid. She wove her fingers into Martha's hair, need making them press firm. 'Let me,' she whispered against her, the hope making her weak.

There was a pause, before Martha retreated. Thea felt the loss keenly but then they were cheek to cheek, the very corner of their mouths touching. Martha's moved, and Thea's responded, so hesitantly that each could have claimed it was accidental. Thea shifted so they were nose to nose and she could feel Martha's quick breaths meeting her own. She kept her eyes tight shut, feeling Martha against her and the skitter of anticipation down her spine. She wouldn't do it, she had to allow Martha, if she wished.

After seconds that seemed to stretch, she felt Martha seek her. She leaned in, cautiously, and was rewarded with a soft, gentle brush of lips. There was another, more definite before she felt able to deepen the kiss herself, capturing one of Martha's lips between her own and tangling her fingers further into the chestnut hair. Martha made a noise – a muted note of longing that resonated deep inside Thea, split her apart and drew an answering whimper from the cleft left behind.

They broke away, long enough to catch their breath and register the certainty in each other's eyes before Martha pressed her back against the cool rock, her lips delving and tasting as if her reservations had been swallowed wholesale by the sea. Thea felt hands firm against her, exploring her, and she explored back, a hand running up Martha's bodice, the tantalising feel of a breast through layers of fabric and stays. Martha let out a sharp sigh and froze. Thea pulled back. 'Sorry. Slower. We can–'

But Martha had grabbed her hands. 'Not slower. Not if you want...' her voice was thready and her eyes dark. 'But... not here.'

Thea clasped her hand and led her back down the beach.

CHAPTER 21

As they began to ascend the cliff Martha took the lead with an urgent pace. They dropped hands in case anyone saw them, but as Martha looked back the hunger in her eyes set Thea aflame. She was hardly through the great wooden door of their lodging house when Martha took her hand once more and practically pulled her towards the stairs. Anticipation rose as they clattered upwards – but then a commotion from the landing commanded her hazy attention. The door to Martha's room opened revealing Mrs Jenkins. They froze. Suddenly Thea's mind cleared.

'Ah, you're back, my lady, I've just popped in a warming pan as it was getting late...' Mrs Jenkins trailed off as she raised her head and registered the two of them, Thea almost on top of Martha, their hands clasped together, wisps of hair trailing and faces no doubt flushed. Martha dropped the hand and tidied her skirts while Thea stepped away. The ripple in Mrs Jenkins' brow was almost disguised, as was the upwards twitch of her lips that followed as her eyes flicked between them. 'On second thoughts it is a fairly warm night, perhaps you don't need it.' She disappeared into the room leaving them staring at one other in horror on the stairs. The pan appeared back round the door first, followed by the round form of the housekeeper. They stepped to the side to let her down the stairs. 'There's water in the room, my lady. I'll be downstairs if you need anything but that's me done for the night.' She actually fake yawned. 'I've got a stew on down there and it is a noisy boil. Anyway, listen to me yabbering on. Good night.' As her candle disappeared into the darkness both Thea and Martha stared after her until they heard the downstairs door click shut.

'We can trust her.' Thea knew Martha was right.

'Yes.'

But a trickle of caution had seeped in at the interruption. Martha turned on the stairs and took Thea's hands. 'Are you sure about this?'

Thea took in the form in front of her – hair mussed, chest rising and falling rapidly above the firm hold of the stays but still somehow regal. She was overwhelmed by the hunger curling throughout her, and how strongly she felt this was right. Stepping up so they were on the same level she took the fabric at the top of Martha's skirts in one hand, pulling her closer.

'Enough, now,' she muttered, swaying close enough to feel Martha's warmth.

A spark lit in Martha's eyes, ignited by relief and fed by desire. She plucked the hand from where it clutched at her hip and grasping it firmly walked backwards, leading Thea through the heavy door. They didn't take their eyes from one another as Thea reached behind her and pressed it shut, the click of the lock confirming their sanctuary. Before she could quest further into the room Martha was on her, cupping her face in strong hands and capturing her in a soft, tender kiss. Thea returned her fingers to Martha's hair and sank into it, sighing against Martha's lips as they insistently explored her own. Hands began to wander over Thea's back, creating electricity where they touched. Encouraged, Thea's hungry hands untangled themselves from the hair and tracked down Martha's spine, a thumb following fingers, tracing the dip of the back to its conclusion and then lower. Feeling soft flesh through layers of fabric, Thea instinctively pulled Martha closer until they were pressed hard together.

Martha's tongue halted the path it had been tracing across Thea's lip as a breath caught in her throat, and then Thea felt herself pushed backwards, an almost-growl emanating from Martha as she pressed her hard against the wall, one hand pinning her firmly in place at her hip and the other wandering, first to run a thumb over the curve of a breast, next down the full length of her to graze her thigh. Thea dropped her head back against the wall and gasped at each touch, her head hazy and nerves on fire.

With some effort she pushed Martha off her and stilled her enough to unbutton the dress. Martha held herself on outstretched arms, framing Thea with her hands flat against the wall. Thea felt quick, hot breath on her skin as Martha's eyes roamed over her lips, neck and eyes. As she turned her around to loosen the lacing the air between them was alive with intensity and impatience. When Martha was free of her dress, stays and petticoats she undid Thea in the same way, discarding the garments carelessly on the floor. The satin shifts were shed last and then they stood with nothing more between them, the shadow of a self-conscious smile tinging Martha's lips, only making Thea's pulse rise further.

Full of anticipation, Thea stepped in towards Martha, her fingers tracing a path round the dip in her waist and feeling a shudder in response. She leaned in to kiss the soft skin of her neck and shoulder, breathing in everything she could and lost in her senses. Their bodies met gently and Martha groaned into her ear, pulling her closer with sure hands. The second seemed to last an age, every nerve in Thea's body alive as she drank in each sensation from her hands, her lips and her skin.

Suddenly out of patience, she placed both hands on Martha's hips and pushed her back until they found the bed. Martha pulled her down and Thea eased herself on top, her eyes raking the length of the smooth, athletic form beneath her. She dropped her lips to a soft breast and taking the bud in her mouth watched Martha arch upwards, her long, elegant neck fearlessly exposed and her head thrust back into the sheets. Feeling Martha's hips cant upwards she pressed a thigh in to meet them. The pressure drove hot and soft against bare skin and need flooded Thea as Martha's lips parted and she groaned in desperate pleasure. Thea slipped her hand lower, tracing the curves of the body underneath her but wasting no time. As her fingers traced a soft thigh she reached up and kissed Martha hard.

'May I?' she asked as she broke away, hearing how thready her voice came out.

'God, yes,' breathed Martha. Thea kissed her again and replaced her thigh with her hand, slipping straight into the melting warmth. Martha cried out into her mouth and the sound lodged itself somewhere inside Thea, driving her on. Martha pushed hungrily against her and Thea increased the pressure, rhythmic and firm.

Their bodies moved together, Martha arching and flexing to remain in as close contact as she could, sighing as she dug fingers hard into Thea's back. Thea revelled in watching her squirm when Martha's eyes opened and settled on hers. As their gaze held, Martha slipped a hand between their bodies and slid it lower, delight lighting her eyes when her fingers met their target. Thea growled as the sensation shot through her and she bore down against delicious resistance.

Martha kept wide eyes on Thea's as they heaved together, entirely at the mercy of their pleasure. They each fed on the other's desperation and it wasn't long before Thea felt Martha's breathing shift, her pace quicken and the insistent sounds from her throat climb higher. She kept her pressure steady until the body under her became taut and rigid, the convulsions tearing through Martha suddenly tipping Thea over the edge. Martha held her firm as flames burned through Thea over and over until she was certain that when they abated there would be nothing left but a charred husk.

As they both came to, breathing hard, Thea held herself up with the little strength left in her body and lost herself in the eyes that flickered with smouldering embers. 'You are truly remarkable,' she breathed, placing her forehead on Martha's and drinking in the sweet scent of her glowing skin.

Martha ran her hands all over Thea's body, savouring every moment and then slid a hand up Thea's arm, over her shoulder and traced the line of her jaw. 'Good Lord, I missed you.' Thea leaned in and stole another gentle kiss before feeling herself flipped and her back pressed against the bedclothes. Martha soared above her, her eyes dark and a mischievous smile playing at her lips. 'Apparently... experiments... must... be... repeatable,' she muttered haltingly, in between the kisses she placed down the body under her. An involuntary smile curved Thea's lips, her eyes closed and she lost herself to curiosity once more.

Thea cracked open heavy eyes and a smile crept across her face as the evening's events flowed back into her mind. She turned, and found Martha propped up against the pillows, teacup in hand and smiling down.

'Morning.'

'Morning.' Thea shuffled closer and buried her face in the crook of Martha's arm, sliding a hand across silken skin and earning a shudder in response. Martha sipped her tea.

'Hang on,' she said, her voice muffled against Martha, 'where did the tea come from?'

'Mrs Jenkins.' Thea could tell Martha was smiling as she spoke. 'Made a great show of clomping up the stairs and clearing her throat outside the door. When I opened it to reassure her she informed me that she had made these buns as she hoped they would be "fortifying".' Thea raised her head as Martha reached out and offered her a crumbly roll laved in butter, it smelled divine and she stretched up for a bite.

'We're lucky,' she mumbled between chews as she settled herself into the pillows. The heady flavour of caraway seeds burst on her tongue.

'Very much so,' said Martha, her eyes darkening briefly with concern, before she passed the bun to Thea and poured her a cup of tea. Their eyes met as she turned back and suddenly everything that had happened last night fizzed between them. The cup rattled a little on its saucer and Thea felt her pulse leap into her throat.

'How are you feeling this morning?' She both craved and dreaded the answer.

'A little nervous,' admitted Martha softly, 'but mostly happy. You make me happy.' She dropped a gentle kiss onto Thea's lips, somehow keeping the cup and saucer upright.

Relief drew a wide grin out of Thea, she sat up properly and took the tea, before placing it on the bedside cabinet, trailing a finger across the delicate skin of Martha's collar bone and claiming another soft kiss that made her scalp tingle. 'I can't believe I get to do this with you.' As soon as she said it she realised just how true that was – how astonishing that the deviant feelings that had plagued her for so long were shared by someone like Martha. A knot of emotion tightened in her throat and she caught Martha's eyes. 'If you'd have told me a year ago...' But nothing else would come out.

Martha caught Thea's hand and pressed a kiss to her fingertips, 'I know,' she muttered, her eyes never leaving Thea's. 'So different, and yet – still the same, outside these walls.'

Thea let herself stroke a finger down Martha's cheek. 'Don't think of it. Not for now. For now we are here and finding out, and we can do as we like. Let's not look too far ahead.'

Martha turned her head to kiss Thea's palm. 'I'll try,' she said, but there was still a note of caution in her words.

The weight of it, thought Thea – she had known the pressure had been becoming too much, how did anyone bear that heaviness of emotion with no outlet? 'Did you ever think of it?' she asked, softly. 'Did you ever imagine this could be?'

A small shake of the head. 'I could never even allow myself to hope. Before...' She caught herself and stopped.

'What?' asked Thea, gently.

Martha turned her face into Thea's hand, hiding her eyes. 'Before – when I heard about you and Ella. I couldn't bear to think that there were things she knew about you that I never could.'

'I want you to know everything. And I want to know everything about you. Every disgusting, painful and filthy thing. Not that I imagine there are any.'

'I'm sure we can find a few,' smiled Martha, 'and I am honoured to share myself with you.'

Thea turned to retrieve her cup and sat up cross legged on the bed, facing Martha, an old question raising its head. 'I hate to ask,' she said tentatively, 'but I did hear that you might have had something to do with Harriet's marriage. I know things are different with me, but why go to those lengths?'

Martha's face showed concern. 'It's true, I did,' she said, but then put out a hand to still Thea's further questions. 'And it is true that she only met the man once previously, but frankly, it appears they were soul mates of a sort and they are currently on the continent having a mutually fulfilling tour of observatories.'

Thea's jaw became slack. 'You mean she married an astronomer?'

'Astronomer, mathematician, musician, boxer,' said Martha, and Thea knew instantly there was a further story to be had. 'He is a good man and they are more alike than you may think on the romantic front, also. But that is all I will say on the subject.' She looked at Thea pointedly.

'Oh!' said Thea, realising her meaning. 'And I have been feeling sorry for her all this time.'

'It was an unfortunate situation,' said Martha, 'but nothing is above a solution with the appropriate application of thought.'

Thea smiled, but she had so many questions. 'And I'm sorry if this is not the time, but there is one other thing I've been wondering.' Martha looked at her expectantly and patiently. 'I have known you most of my life, but such a big part of who you are – missing from my understanding of you. Since you told me... how you felt, it has seemed sometimes like I may not even know you at all?'

Martha's hand roved reassuringly over her thigh. 'Do you think Ursula knows you?'

'Of course, more than anyone other than you.'

'Then there you are. This is only one aspect of you, Thea. It doesn't define you. A great number of virtues fuse to make you, you.' Thea nodded and resolved to spend as much time as she could finding out about Martha's virtues. Other questions would resolve themselves, in time, but there was another thing that bothered her.

'You and Lord Foxmore, you always seemed so close, from what I remember?'

Martha shifted a little. 'I really should have expected this of your curiosity shouldn't I?' Thea looked a little sheepish but Martha smiled. 'We were. I did love him, Thea, and he loved me. This is simply different – neither diminishes the other.'

'I see,' said Thea, even though she didn't.

'You've never felt anything for a man?' Martha laid a reassuring hand on Thea's bent knee. She shook her head. 'Some don't, it seems,' said Martha, in a tone that suggested she was more worldly on this matter than Thea had ever considered. But there would be more chances to understand. Ones when Martha wasn't laid out in front of her with nothing on but bedclothes, for example. She shuffled closer.

'What would you have done if the spa waters had cured me, Lady Foxmore?' She dared a mischievous grin. 'Wouldn't that have been a shame?' She sipped her tea and licked her lips, indulging herself in satisfaction as Martha's gaze flicked to her tongue and her eyes darkened.

'I don't think it works like that, Miss Morell, I would never advocate anything that would make you other than you are.' Thea twisted and placed her cup on the bedside table before once again claiming those lips for her own.

'Coo'ee, Lady Foxmore! Miss Morell!' Thea and Martha's heads snapped round in unison at the familiar voice. August was progressing, wildflowers were blooming and trees glowed deep green in the intense sunlight. It was Monday and they were taking a walk on the beach before heading out early for a day's botanising along the coast. The past week had been spent alone – they had walked, picnicked and revelled in the joy of each other. Thea was pleased that Martha's reservations seemed to be dissipating and she smiled and laughed more than she had ever seen. Sometimes, when nobody was around, she couldn't help just staring at her. Martha would smile, raise a mocking eyebrow and kiss her gently on the head, or the lips, or the neck. Away from society they were free to indulge themselves as they pleased and if she had ever been happier, Thea couldn't remember it.

The two figures now hurrying up the beach, bright blue and gold in the sunlight, thudded Thea back to reality. 'Oh no,' muttered Martha, 'it can't be? Did they say they were coming to Whitby?'

Thea glanced sideways with a wry smile. 'I thought you found Mrs Simmons – what was it? Interesting and diverting? Perhaps you will learn more about Skipton society?' Cecily scurried across the beach as fast as the soft sand would allow, leaving her mother trailing behind.

Martha shot Thea a withering look as the two ladies joined them. 'Good morning, Mrs Simmons, Miss Cecily.' Martha inclined her head generously and Cecily fluttered around the group.

'What wondrous luck to find you here, we didn't realise you were coming to Whitby did we mother, and you just disappearing from Scarborough without a word of goodbye, oh it is so long since we have seen you!' Thea watched in awe, wondering if she would ever pause for breath. 'What shall you do today? I think we must join you as I am so bored by the beach already and I cannot bear to spend another day in so little company.'

Thea kept quiet, the idea of their blissful day being invaded by Cecily felt horrifying. It seemed Martha thought the same. 'We plan to go on a long walk for some botanising, Miss Simmons – I fear that you would find it extremely dull. Perhaps we could arrange a short engagement for another–'

'Botanising? What on earth is that?' Cecily was not to be put off.

'We will look at the wildflowers, identify them and collect them.'

'What for?'

Martha took a composing breath. 'To create a taxonomic record of the flora of the world.' Thea stifled a smile and watched Cecily carefully. Surely a mention of taxonomy would dampen her enthusiasm?

The young lady paused, blinked, and then grabbed Martha by the arm with both hands. 'I *love* flowers – and collecting them!'

Martha cut back in quickly. 'And mosses. There are many interesting mosses around this part of the coast. It may be that we concentrate on those. In fact I think we shall today.' If that wouldn't do it, nothing would, thought Thea.

'Oh, mosses!' Cecily clasped her hands under her chin and performed a delighted little bob that made her shimmering skirt puff out voluminously. 'So fluffy! We *must* pick the fluffiest mosses, Lady Foxmore. We shall go with them, mother, shan't we?' Her mother only nodded with a wan smile and Thea suspected that she was simply pleased to have Cecily's incessant chatter directed anywhere else. Cecily didn't falter in her stride. 'I do think that the Scarborough waters are magical, don't you, Lady Foxmore? We have brought some with us so we can take them until we return.' Martha opened her mouth, but Cecily left no conversational space for a response. 'I feel so much revived since taking them every day and mother says I am calmer beyond measure, don't you mother?' She turned to Mrs Simmons who only nodded weakly again before Cecily skipped off towards the cliff.

Martha dared a fleeting glance in Thea's direction, who leaned into her ear. 'Serves you right for trying to find me friends I won't flirt with.' Martha pursed her lips and Thea fought to suppress the mirth that threatened. This could be a trying day.

Cecily scampered along the clifftop travelling twice as far as anyone else. Unexpectedly, she had embraced the task at hand and ran backwards and forwards between the clifftop meadow and their small group, bringing pieces of plant for them to identify. It kept her busy, so Martha and Thea didn't mind as they combed through the tufted grass, looking for rarities or species Martha may not yet have in her herbarium. A rhythm emerged and persisted for almost two hours. Cecily would return with a sample and Martha would look up briefly and identify it, usually with an additional snippet of knowledge. Cecily had listened intently to Martha's observations on the purpose of their trip and had resolved immediately to make a collection of her own. She turned out to be reasonably good at collecting representative samples and Mrs Simmons was becoming increasingly burdened with armfuls of foliage and flowers.

Martha and Thea were on their hands and knees perusing a particularly interesting patch of harebell when their new student bounced into view, clutching a ranging tangle of foliage with purple flowers now flopping at the ends.

Martha raised her gaze to it. '*Vicia*, known as tufted Vetch, pea family.' Thea smiled to herself, scanning the ground. Her eyes lighted on a dandelion and she picked the flower in bloom, turning to Martha with a smirk.

'Is this of any use?' she asked, expecting Martha to give her that exasperated grin she found so endearing. Martha came over and knelt down next to her, studying it.

'Actually, I will have it,' she said, getting a small trowel underneath it to ease out the root, there may be some geographical variation.' Thea rolled her eyes as Martha cleaned off the specimen with a brush and went on. 'A very important early plant for the bees. Common does not mean uninteresting.'

'I do like their tiny parachutes,' said Thea, half teasing Martha as she picked a ripe clock from another plant. She blew on it and watched them dance off in the wind.

'Off on their own adventures,' said Martha, watching them go. 'Taken by the wind on a journey entirely of providence. They will achieve their purpose, even if it takes them some time to find it.' She smiled at Thea fondly who almost forgot herself until quick footsteps approached. Martha twisted and looked up at Cecily from where she knelt. '*Corydalis*, poppy family, not native to Britain.'

Cecily's eyes widened. 'You mean it's rare?'

Martha didn't even look up. 'Certainly not, it is a garden escapee and gets everywhere. Pretty though.'

This satisfied Cecily who heaped the yellow mound on her mother and bounded off again. Thea crawled over to Martha and muttered so her voice didn't travel as she ran her hands through the rough groundcover.

'You know I find it irresistible when you do that? Always have, now I think about it.'

Martha flicked a pleased glance at her. 'When I do what?'

Thea's response was interrupted by Cecily, clutching a bunch of round, pink baubles on sticks atop a dense tuft of foliage.

'*Armeria*, known as thrift, or cliff clover – enjoys the coast.'

Thea fixed eyes on Martha as Cecily exited. 'That.' She placed a hand next to Martha's and brushed a finger gently across her wrist. Martha was about to respond but as she raised her head their eyes met and the words caught on her tongue. Thea's insides melted and she pressed a shoulder into Martha's. Their eyes danced over each other before Cecily bustled back into their reverie.

'This one looks like a happy little face!' With some effort Martha dragged her eyes from Thea's and made to provide a quick identification.

'Where did you find that?' She quickly stood and Thea tipped sideways as the shoulder on which she leant disappeared. She rolled her eyes, supposing she would have to get used to plants taking precedence, sometimes. Martha's voice had that tell-tale edge of collector's excitement. 'It's *Ophrys* – a bee orchid, are there more?' Martha followed Cecily and Thea trailed behind them, but on arrival had to admit that the find was particularly impressive. Small spikes of intricate flowers, each looking like a perfect, tiny, purple bee with a huge grin on its face.

Martha was on her knees again in the grass. 'I've never seen these before, we'll take one and press it immediately – I can return and draw them later.' Cecily was not at all upset to cut short their trip after making such an important find and they made back towards the town at a fair clip.

Back at the lodgings they worked on their new specimens until tea, Martha with *Species Plantarum* open and comparing and labelling her specimens, Thea with her new collection of fossils and a pamphlet she had bought locally. Martha put down her snips, proudly surveying the weighted pile bursting with botanical treasures and picked up a piece of Mrs Jenkins' delicious gingerbread.

'I am delighted you've taken up your interest again.' She nodded to the fossils arranged on the table as she took a bite. 'Even if it hasn't distracted you from your strange pebble fetish.' It was true, Thea thought, the pebbles were lining up on the fireplace again, Whitby ones just as good as Scarborough.

'Everything has its place.' Thea peered at a belemnite through the magnifying lens. 'However ordinary or peculiar as you said. You have your dandelions and I have my pebbles.'

'I am delighted in any case,' said Martha, closing the book. 'You are exceptionally grumpy when you have nothing to occupy your mind.' She stood and began to tidy the vegetable waste from the plant pressing. Thea feigned mock horror, rolled up a piece of scrap parchment and threw it at Martha.

'I'm grumpy! What about you?' She adopted a lower tone and a more cut glass accent than her own. '"*Miss Morell, you conducted a sordid and entirely inappropriate affair. It is not to be tolerated".*' She raised a challenging eyebrow and Martha's cheeks coloured.

'That was different.'

'That's a shame, I was looking forward to being sordid and inappropriate with you for quite a while.'

Martha's lips twitched upwards, but then her face darkened. 'You know we return home in less than two weeks.'

Thea's stomach twisted. At the beginning of their journey it had seemed that the two months would last forever. The thought that this might come to an end made her head swim. 'But – surely not so soon? We can't, can we?' She could hear the dismay in her own voice and knew she sounded feeble.

Martha's lips twitched again. 'I hoped you might say that. I took the liberty of drafting a letter to your mother.' Martha rounded the table and produced a piece of paper from the dresser. Thea raised a brow.

'And what does it say?'

Martha pulled Thea from the chair by the hand, took her by the waist and pulled their bodies together, pretending to read the letter over her shoulder. 'It says that you have been extremely bad, that I do not think it proper that we return so soon, and that I require more time to deal with your attitude with an extremely firm hand.'

Thea shuddered and smiled, running a hand up Martha's side and over her shoulder. 'I shall resolve to make the best of it.' Thea could feel her eyes bright with happiness. 'How long are you suggesting we stay on?'

'I have informed your mother that you are quite transformed and that I am delighted by your progress, but that we would like to explore further through Yorkshire and will be back at the beginning of November for the London season.' She suddenly looked nervous, as if hopeful it wasn't too greedy. 'Is that alright?'

Thea's insides leapt with joy. 'That's almost three months from now!'

Martha's eyes shone. 'Do you think you can bear it?' She trailed her fingertips up Thea's thigh, who quivered but halted them with her own hand.

'I will stay on one condition.' She grinned cheekily. They both knew it was a lie, but Martha played along.

'Any request will be met with enthusiasm, my lady, of course.'

Thea regarded her carefully, unsure of how her request would be received. 'Let me write to Mr Constable and ask him to propose your paper.' She held on to Martha as she felt her recede a little. 'Whatever it is, whatever scares you, Martha.' She traced a finger down Martha's jaw. 'We can manage it together. We are stronger now.'

Martha's eyes flitted between her own before the tension she held eased a little. 'Perhaps,' she said quietly.

'I believe in you, and I want to see your work recognised, even if it is through father.' She pulled Martha into a deep kiss that made them both gasp. 'Please? Do it for me, if you won't for yourself.'

'Well, if you put it like that.' Martha's voice was hazy, and she stared at Thea's lips, who took the opportunity.

'I will write to him tomorrow. So, what now?' she asked, placing another gentle kiss on Martha's neck. Martha looked at her with lidded eyes. 'I was thinking perhaps we should go for a swim?'

The gentleman on the beach walked them to one of the bathing machines. 'Will this one do, ladies?' It was essentially a wooden hut, about six feet by eight, supported on four wheels and with a bench and hooks inside. They agreed that it would. 'Very good, ladies. Do you want a woman to undress you?'

Thea felt Martha bristle next to her. 'I beg your pardon?'

He looked at her quizzically. 'For the swimming, my lady, we can provide a woman with the machine at a very reasonable price–'

Martha coloured for the second time in an hour and drew herself up. 'Thank you, we will manage ourselves just fine.'

Thea swallowed a laugh and bumped Martha with a shoulder while their host set off to fetch the horse. 'Touchy.'

Martha gave her an embarrassed smile as they ascended the steps and waited on the bench as the attendant harnessed the horse and led them into the sea. His voice filtered through the door as he walked. 'There's napkins in the back to dry yourselves with, they're new for every client, not like some of the outfits running machines down here.' Thea wrinkled her nose as the horse and the hut moved deeper into the waves then turned back towards the beach, facing the door at the back into the open sea. 'How long would you like, ladies?'

Martha was quick to respond. 'One hour and a half please. Or we'll call when we're done.' He nodded as he unharnessed the horse.

'Very good, ma'am. I'll pop the hood down for you.' He waded round to the back of the machine and opened the door onto the expanse of open sea before slipping open catches on a large gathering of material which framed the opening. It folded downwards, almost to the sea itself, creating a small, private swimming area within a tent. 'So you may bathe in complete privacy, ladies, if you wish.' He made his exit and walked the horse through the waves towards the beach.

Thea stared at Martha and at the waves. The afternoon sun was waning and the sea breeze chilled at her ankles. 'An hour and a half? I shall be frozen by then.'

Martha shot her a devious grin. 'I have absolutely no intention of bathing for so long, and equally no intention of you freezing.' She raised an eyebrow, and Thea felt her own eyes widen. 'Shall we hop in?'

The cold water made Thea gasp as she descended the steps dressed only in a satin shift. They laughed as they bobbed and swam in the gentle rising waves, and before long gained the confidence to exit their private hood and swim in the open sea. As they got used to the cold they splashed each other, their feet never too far from the soft sand below and exclaiming as slimy seaweed tangled in their ankles. Most of the other bathers had retired for the day, the evening light was lowering over the sea and there was nothing but joy between them.

After around half an hour they made their way back to their tiny sanctuary, bobbed under the hood and ascended the steps into the machine. After helping one another take off their dripping shifts, they came together in a gentle embrace, their bodies hot where they touched against the nip of wet skin. The sudden cold and exhilaration of swimming in the open water had set every one of Thea's nerves on edge. She felt every point at which their bodies met, and the slight chill where Martha's breath cooled the droplets on her shoulder. It warmed again as Martha sighed into her.

'You make me feel young again. And free.'

Thea ran a hand across her waist and up to the curve of her spine, salt water shedding in rivulets ahead of the caress. 'You are both.'

Martha pulled back and nestled her nose against Thea's damp cheek. 'Yes.'

She placed a hand on Thea's shoulder and pushed her down onto the bench, setting her crackling nerves alight.

A little while later, Martha sat on the edge of the bench, wiping away the remaining salt water with one of the provided napkins. Thea still lay in a state of happy disarray. 'I hope you will excuse me for raising the subject, Lady Foxmore, but you are exceptionally good at that. I suspect that this isn't the first time you have disgraced yourself with a lady.'

Martha offered her a sly smile as she ran the cloth over her shoulders and around her neck. 'There may have been one or two dalliances, in my youth.'

Thea threw an arm behind her head and propped herself up, grinning. 'Nothing more serious than a dalliance?'

Martha's gaze dropped and the napkin slowed. 'Just one. For about three years.'

Thea sensed a change as Martha's eyes met hers and her next question was more gentle. 'That's a long time.'

'It was.' Martha nodded. Her face was suddenly sombre.

Thea sat up and placed a tender hand on Martha's thigh, worried she had pushed too far. 'She hurt you?'

Martha thought for a few moments, the cloth clutched tight in a hand. 'We hurt each other, in the end.' Suddenly she turned to Thea and cupped a cheek in her hand, her face serious. 'Thea, this is a dangerous game. You know there is no circumstance in which we can be happy together. Not in the long term.' Thea was taken aback at the sudden change in demeanour, clearly wounds were still raw and she knew better than to press for the details.

She took Martha's face in both hands. 'We both know that, but we must take our happiness wherever we can, Martha. We have the opportunity of this time together, let's not waste it, whatever happens.' This was a different person to the Martha she felt she had known so well. The confident, formidable scholar who could hold her own in any debate, the society lady who quietly compelled those around her. Martha, the lover, was broken. Would she mind if she never knew why? 'Let us not consider the future until we must. There are those who can honestly say they have never experienced true love or passion in their lives – we shouldn't waste this chance.'

Martha relaxed a little and the anxiety in her eyes began to dissipate. 'You are right, of course.' Thea kissed Martha tenderly until at long last she felt her body settle.

CHAPTER 22

The days passed pleasantly, walks, boating, botanising, swimming and reading filling their days, revelling in the utter freedom. Thea's paintbrushes were now dry although Martha lamented the loss to high art, earning her a playful thump on the shoulder. They couldn't escape a little more botanising with the Simmons, but Cecily was such an enthusiastic student that by the end, neither of them minded. At least her attention was distracted from the gentlemen of the north and she found little to complain about. Mostly, however, Thea and Martha spent time with each other. Twice they attended the Whitby theatre and guiltily held hands under their cloaks in the darkness.

Her collecting spirits restored, Thea searched for insects, fossils and geological curios whilst Martha sketched plants for her collection, taking pieces back to their lodgings to dissect and record in more detail. The surfaces were filling up with samples tied with string and labelled, and Martha had ordered two new plant presses from town. Thea's collection of pebbles now filled the mantlepiece and stretched to the dresser next to it, pride of place taken by a beautiful, shiny black one which reminded her of their first swim in the sea. What a perfect night it had been, the sun dipping low over the golden sands, the sky clear and the air still warm from the heat of the day. After the swim they had carried their shoes and felt the sand press through their toes at every step, walking in the shimmering band between land and sea, splashing through the receding waves and dodging leathery patches of seaweed which clung to their feet.

'I thought you disliked my pebbles?' Thea had asked, as Martha had picked up the perfect handful, washed it in the sea and dropped it into her palm.

Martha had looked about to offer some sort of snarky remark, but then their eyes had lingered. How it had made Thea feel so complete, when Martha had said, 'I will always respect your choices.' Now Thea stared at it from her chair in the parlour, reliving the moment again, pretending that when they returned to Thornbury the rest of her family would feel the same.

Regular correspondence kept her close to home – Thea ensured to write to Ursula often and was delighted to hear that their father's health was much improved. He was excited to hear about the coastal wildflowers and the fossils of Whitby, as was Edgar, who she missed almost as much as her family. Now she provided him with detailed accounts of their collecting trips and delighted in the descriptions of his mad experiments sent by return. She knew her father had informed him about the letter when she received a line which read, '*I am sorry to hear Lady Eleanor is gone away. I hope you will resume your friendship on your mutual return.*' It would be foolish to commit an explicit response to paper and so she hoped he would understand her meaning when she wrote, '*I have not much hope of being reacquainted with Lady Eleanor in the year she travels to Germany. I am pleased that Lady Foxmore and I have renewed our friendship and her society continues to improve and gratify me.*' She smiled to herself as she sealed the letter. She was confident it would both delight and surprise Edgar.

On a morning in August came two notes. One from a subdued Ursula and one from a particularly excited Jane Ashby. Thea opened Jane's letter first and even the hand it was written in seemed to glow off the page. It was peppered with more exclamation marks than Thea dared to count. It was the news Thea had been hoping for – that Jane was finally engaged to Thomas Harker. Jane described how they had taken a trip to Emsworth harbour with a group of friends and he had contrived to see her alone. When they emerged from the dunes their friends were ready with a picnic and banners to celebrate the union. Thea was delighted for her friend and resolved to write back the same day, demanding more details and a date for the wedding.

The note from Ursula brought the sobering news that their father had mortgaged the house again to pay for the outstanding balance on the new library. He had confided to Ursula after she heard the ruckus from their mother. It was only temporary, he said, until he was truly back on his feet and could get the estate working to its potential and his investments with the bank came to fruition.

Martha furrowed her brow at the news and put down the pencil she was using to sketch. 'I hope he does have a series of good investments and the income from the estate is substantial. It is at least six times the size of Denbury so should bring him a reasonable amount. Does Ursula say anything else?'

Thea threw the letter on the table. 'Only that mother is already setting up dinner dates with strategic families in London. I'll be paraded around like a rouged cow at a market. We can only hope that nobody hears of father's troubles in advance.'

'Certainly,' said Martha, 'that would stymie your chances somewhat.'

Thea caught her eyes across the table. 'I wish we didn't have to talk about this.'

'But we do,' said Martha with a gentle but sad smile. 'There is no sense in us ignoring it. This is the truth we were so keen to explore.'

'Mmm,' agreed Thea. 'You know that on my return I am going to have to be everything my mother wants me to be. She will be frantic.'

'Yes.' Martha nudged the pencil until it was perpendicular with the edge of the table. 'And there can be no more rumours about your impropriety. Otherwise you could find yourself in an extremely difficult situation. And you may not be so lucky...'

'...as Harriet, I know,' said Thea. 'It has not escaped me that I was so fortunate last time. Had the thing not been so contained mother would have married me off in a heartbeat.' She caught Martha's eye across the table, who paused a little too long. 'Oh my,' she said. 'It nearly happened.' Martha still said nothing. She didn't have to. 'And you talked her out of it?' The reality of what could have been hit hard.

'It wasn't easy.'

'I bet it wasn't. Who... who was it?'

'Ralph Jefferys was the favourite,' said Martha, still not meeting her eye. 'But there were several names mentioned. You would have withered, Thea, in such small-minded company. I couldn't bear to think of it.' Now she looked up and Thea saw the moisture glisten in her eyes. She reached forward and took Martha's hands across the table.

'But you saved me, and I will be forever grateful.' This, at least drew out a small smile. 'How?'

'I agreed with her on all counts and told her that I would personally attend to your re-education. That the scholarship causing your deviance would be a thing of the past and I would impress on you the importance of finding a husband.'

Thea looked around her at the fossils, the plants, and down at her chaperone's hands which now softly caressed hers. 'This looks like success to me.'

At least Martha managed a wry smile in response. 'I had forgotten to ask you with – everything – but you really don't have any idea who sent the letter? The one that caused all the mess.'

Thea shook her head. 'No – initially I thought it may be Tabitha, but it wasn't.'

'She was my first suspect,' said Martha, 'why are you so sure?'

'I confronted her about it.' Thea shrugged. 'She pointed out that if I continued the relationship and ran away with Ella then the estate would go to her when she married. The letter put a stop to that.'

'And she was right of course,' said Martha, her eyebrows raising, 'she's not as stupid as she–' Martha broke off and pink rose in her cheeks. 'Sorry, I didn't mean to–'

Thea laughed. 'No, she isn't, clearly. I have thought about it at length and I can't deny Ella and I were a little indiscreet. There are a number of people it could have been, of course Mrs Jefferys is a possibility, or one of the servants.'

'I read the letter.' Martha's pink face now paled on recollection. 'Whoever wrote it knew your relationship was physical. Without that, it would have been a harmless romantic friendship. It would have been risky for Mrs Jefferys to accuse you as she could so easily have been wrong. Who could have known about the two of you?'

Thea put down her pen. That certainly narrowed it down. 'Edgar knew for certain, as did Mrs Phibbs, but I suppose people in the house could have suspected if they'd lingered round the door.' Her burning cheeks now felt bright against Martha's pallor. 'Father was ill and Ursula couldn't move around the house alone. That leaves Tabitha and the servants but most of them couldn't have constructed a letter so eloquently. There's always Agnes, I suppose but Mrs Phibbs tried to keep her away.'

Edgar knew?' Martha's brows pulled together. 'You don't think he might have told anyone else? Even in conversation? Mr Grimston maybe?' Her eyes had taken on an edge of agitation.

'I'm sure he wouldn't, he knew of the need for discretion of course.' Thea thought back to Edgar and his eccentricities. 'But I suppose it isn't out of the question.'

'Hmm,' said Martha, tapping a pencil on her lips. 'You do appreciate the need to keep our situation to ourselves don't you?' Thea squirmed in her chair a little as she thought about the letter to Edgar. 'He knows already, doesn't he?' said Martha, reading Thea like a book.

'Sorry,' said Thea quietly, 'excitement got the better of me.'

'No matter,' said Martha, 'Edgar is a good friend but we can't be too careful, we must impress on him the need for discretion on our return.'

She went back to her sketching and Thea pushed away the letter filled with Jane's happiness feeling unjust, but unable to reconcile herself to it while it was so raw. Martha looked up again at the rustle of paper across the table and gestured to the mound of fossils. 'How will you manage this on your return?'

It was a question that was still exercising Thea, and one for which she had no answer. 'Ursula's last letter says my mother has had the collection covered and the door locked. I doubt she is planning a grand unveiling on my return. I shall have to smuggle them in.'

'How ridiculous that she could think it has anything to do with – well – this.' Martha gestured between them again.

'You really don't think there's anything in it?'

'I do not, no.'

'Then why do people say it?'

Martha thought for a moment. 'I know that study makes those who do it more interesting and aware of the world. Some people find that intimidating, not to mention dangerous. Scholarship for women was almost encouraged in your grandmother's day but when they started getting too clever it became problematic.'

'I always wondered how she managed to be so learned,' said Thea, thinking back to the inspiring things her father had told her about the matriarch of the family and the formidable woman she remembered from her childhood. 'Father always said that grandpa encouraged her.'

'And Harold supported me,' said Martha, smiling. 'Without the support of a man it is difficult for us, especially now. Women have quick wits, subtle conceptions, clear understandings and solid judge-ments. Nevertheless, it is easier to keep others inferior if they can be convinced they do not, and cannot, ever know as much as you.'

'I wonder that men are clever enough to come up with it,' said Thea, wryly.

Martha smiled. 'It does not always happen through collective design but does become a social habit. And it is amazing what people can be led to believe, if lies are repeated often enough – the ones about lady's constitutions and how their brains just can't cope with too much knowledge.'

Thea took Martha's hands across the table. 'I think ours are coping alright.'

Martha regarded her. 'You were willing to give up the collections because you thought it would make you' – she paused but kept Thea's eyes – 'change. Would you still want it to be different, if it could be? Now that you know.'

Thea's mind flicked back to that electric kiss with Meg, the first time she had really understood, even if she hadn't been able to comprehend what it meant. How scared and alone she had felt. And now she took in the gentle eyes in front of her, nervously awaiting an answer. Eyes which belonged to a person who inspired so much feeling within her that she sometimes felt she might burst, a person who had caused such pain with her absence, and such joy on her return. Now she knew what it was like to be close to Martha, and she had someone who knew *her*.

'I worry about being different, but how could I wish that?' she asked, finally, keeping her voice gentle.

Relief softened Martha's features. 'I am glad. This time with you has been the greatest joy I could ever know.'

'You took enough convincing.' Thea chuckled and poked Martha under the table with a toe.

Martha poked her back. 'As hard as we may try to order the world, it seems that who we fall in love with is destined to remain both unquantifiable, and uncontrollable.'

Thea was about to respond, but then sat up. 'Wait – who we what?'

Martha raised an eyebrow. 'I believe you heard me.'

'You love me?' Thea felt tears begin to prick at her eyes.

'Did you not know?'

'You've never said it.'

'I didn't think I'd have to.'

Thea rose to her feet, grabbed Martha by the neckline of her dress and pulled her into a messy kiss across the table.

Later that day, Thea and Martha sat on a blanket on the beach. A picnic was spread and their shoes and stockings sat in a pile next to them. Thea raised her glass of punch and waited for Martha to do the same.

'A celebration!'

Martha's glass dropped a little and she made a play of rolling her eyes. 'Don't tell me...'

'To the fact that Martha Smilgrove, Countess of Foxmore' – Thea leaned into Martha and whispered – 'loves me. Did I mention it?'

'Once or twice,' laughed Martha trying to look aloof and failing miserably. Once Thea had got over her tears she had barely shut up about it until Martha had thrown up her hands and demanded they go somewhere public so she would be able to talk about it less. Apparently it hadn't worked, but the hamper that Mrs Jenkins had put together was excellent and there was something about being around the waves that amplified the whisper of potential within her and made life's possibilities seem endless. She knew she could get very used to this, with Martha, even though the chance of it seemed remote. For now she relaxed and watched life happen on the beach from their cosy position near the cliffs. Bathing machines preserved swimmers' modesty, carriages trundled to and from Sandsend and the *beau monde* promenaded along the golden expanse of sand.

A black page boy, clad in fancy livery and a turban was summoned from behind his mistress at the need of a parasol. He dutifully opened it, handed it to her, bowed and stepped back. A wave lapped at his foot and he hopped away. 'To think that could have been Scip's life,' said Thea, thinking of his original position in their household. 'He could have been running after mother and handing her parasols in a ridiculous outfit.'

'Mmm,' agreed Martha, swallowing a piece of dried fruit. And the plant movement research would be the poorer for it. Scip has been invaluable.'

'Surely Captain Morrison can't be right?' asked Thea, grappling with the thought that had been nagging at her since Burton Constable. 'It can't be true that blacks have no civility or want to work. Look at Scip – he works from dawn to dusk and often beyond and is one of the most sensible and civil people I know.'

'But he grew up in the plantations under a British hand,' said Martha. 'It isn't a fair comparison.'

'Has anyone made a fair comparison?' challenged Thea. 'Or are we simply to believe what we are told about people we have never met?'

'A fair comparison is not encouraged,' said Martha, leaning back on her arms, 'as you well know.'

Thea looked down at the box of sugared oranges in her hand. Scip had never spoken about his life and she hadn't asked. She had heard stories about the lives in the Indies, but they had always seemed so far removed from life in Sussex. It was beginning to seem so wrong. 'The Harringtons own plantations. Do you think they keep slaves?' Martha only looked at her incredulously. 'I knew it was a bad business,' said Thea, 'but I keep thinking about Captain Morrison and the slaves on his ship. To think that could have been Scip. I'm glad that our families, at least, have no part of it.' Martha blinked at her but said nothing. 'What?' asked Thea, immediately concerned.

'Thea, you know where your family's fortune came from?'

Thea screwed up her face dismissively. 'Of course – my grandmother, and her mother before that. They made good investments.'

'In?' asked Martha gently.

Thea's throat snagged as she realised she had no idea. 'Not...'

'The Royal African Company.'

'Which traded in...'

'Yes. Among other things,' said Martha softly, while Thea's mouth hung open. She banished the wave of disgust that lapped through her body.

'But not now. We cashed the investments.'

'True, but everything your family now has is built on that.' The wave of revulsion returned.

'You must think that's awful.' Thea peered at Martha carefully, but Martha only shook her head. 'Not you as well?' Thea asked.

'Harold had shares in ships.' Martha gave a small shrug and offered a smile that only curved one side of her mouth. 'It's how we built Foxmore Square. And I only have my independence because of them.'

'What do you mean?'

'Harold knew he was ill and wanted to provide for me. His distant cousin was set to inherit so he convinced him to sign over the property to me in return for the lion's share of the investments. It was a good deal for him, of course, the stock has soared.'

'The lion's share?' Thea had noticed the slight tick when Martha said it.

'The Denbury estate is relatively small,' said Martha, cautiously. 'It provides next to no income of its own.'

Thea leaned back, stunned at the history and present of the wealth of both of them. She sought any glimmer of redemption. 'At least my family has given it up. The Harringtons own directly and are still profiting heavily.'

'Mmm,' said Martha again, pursing her lips and looking over the sea. 'And at least we put the money to good use, rather than spending it on wallpaper.'

Thea poked her with a bare foot. 'Jealousy doesn't suit you.'

'It's not jealousy,' said Martha, looking back. 'Nobody can deny that the fortunes our families made have enabled growth and advancement. We spend it on science.'

It was Thea's turn to look incredulous. 'You can't approve?

'Of course I don't approve. But how many schools have been built? How much knowledge generated and how much progress gained?'

'And grand houses built, portraits painted, wine drunk, ladies of the night enjoyed.' Thea tucked her feet underneath her. 'Can you justify offsetting progress with the loss of liberty and life? You would choose science over humanity?'

'Calm down.' Martha laid a hand on Thea's arm. 'I am not justifying anything, I am merely saying it is a complex issue.'

Thea shuffled away. 'It is a matter of fundamental human decency.' She had a mind to storm off, but the sea was so soothing and there wouldn't be many more days to enjoy the late summer sun.

Martha gazed at her through heavily lidded eyes and shifted a hand to quickly entwine their fingers before pulling away. 'Let's not argue.'

'No,' she said, 'but I want to know more. It feels – wrong. What would happen if you gave up the shares?'

Martha thought for a while. 'There would be money for a few years, and then I would live more meagrely off the estate, or could mortgage, depending on how much I was prepared to risk.'

Thea only swallowed. She couldn't tell Martha what to do with her money and her security, but after the revelations at Burton Constable this felt too uncomfortable. Martha obviously saw it written on her face.

'I'll look into it when we get back to London,' said Martha, 'if that's what you want.'

'Perhaps just to know the possibilities?' asked Thea, gingerly. Martha nodded. As the lady and her page slipped out of sight down the beach Thea settled down and popped another sugared orange between Martha's lips.

'Apparently Henry VIII stayed here once,' Martha mumbled up from the pamphlet she clutched in her hand. She had carried it around for the two weeks they had spent exploring the nurseries, history and society of the city of York. Now she looked up, affecting a bright smile. 'With Catherine Howard.'

Thea attempted to match the smile, but her heart wasn't in it. Two months had passed since their declarations of love on the beach. Rust-coloured leaves now settled around their feet as they stood at the base of the ruined city wall at York. The city was the final leg of their journey, and this was their final night in it. Thea's heart ached at the thought of returning, and the letter she clutched in her dress pocket burned to make itself known as they stared up at the King's Manor and its pleasantly piecemeal brickwork.

Thea knew Martha was trying to distract her, but they both knew that it wouldn't work. She had become increasingly sullen over the past week, reality beginning to weigh heavy. They had extended their stay in Whitby, keen to keep their liberty for as long as possible. What a halcyon time it had been, full of laughter, fun and freedom. They had laughed since they had been in York, but not as much. Once Martha had tried to broach the subject of what might happen once they were back, but Thea had parried with the suggestion that Martha should be busy publishing her article, they had gone to bed grumpy and not revisited it the next morning. Then Thea had found the letter on Martha's dresser a week ago. Loathe to discuss it and risk a disagreement, she longed for Martha to raise the subject, but she hadn't.

Now she attempted a smile at Martha's mention of the historic Royal Family, took her arm and they continued over the river. It was over an hour later, and well past dusk when Thea spied York Minster and realised they had almost completed a whole circuit of the city. She had to gather the courage.

'When were you planning on telling me?' she asked quietly.

Martha looked at her, confused. 'Telling you?'

Thea extracted the letter from her pocket. 'You aren't pleased.' She knew Martha couldn't be, or she would have spoken of nothing else. The news that Mr Constable had been in touch with the Royal Society and they could not be more excited about publishing Martha's work in the *Transactions*. But Martha clearly did not share the enthusiasm.

Martha had the grace to look abashed. 'No.'

'Can I ask why?'

Martha's eyes closed. 'I can't risk it, Thea. Grimston knows, of course. The thought of the ridicule, of it being thrown out if anyone finds out it was done by...' She trailed off.

'A woman.' Thea was sanguine. By now, she almost understood and would respect Martha's choice. But it didn't make the truth any easier to accept.

'Exactly.'

They walked slowly, but steadily, the understanding quiet between them. 'What will you do now?' asked Thea. 'Will you continue with the research?' She knew that this decision must take the excitement out of Martha's work.

'I will,' said Martha, determinedly. 'And I will enjoy watching your collection grow. You are brilliant, and you may be braver than me, one day.'

Thea felt Martha's presence at her side keenly. She knew she would be disappointed by what she was about to say, but could think of no other option. 'I have to give it up,' she said quietly as they stepped carefully along the uneven cobbled street. Martha turned sharply to her in question.

'The collection,' Thea qualified, 'scholarship. I have to give it up when we return.' She was grateful they were walking and she didn't have to see Martha's face.

'Why?' asked Martha, her silhouette moving smoothly against the fluttering leaves of the trees.

Thea took a steadying breath. 'Because it is the only way I can think of to protect us.' No longer did she feel the coltishness and awe of the lecture room when Meg had sent the spark to her lips. She knew who she was and what she wanted, but her family would accept neither. 'My mother sent me away to give up scholarship and what she thinks of as my deviant tendencies. You were sent to ensure it. I have done neither. If I go back and continue collecting she will know we have been complicit. And she would be right. She wouldn't let us near one another, Martha.'

They turned at the northwest corner of the wall, giving a new perspective on the magnificence of the Minster. 'But the collections.' Martha squeezed her arm where they walked together. 'You love them, Thea.'

'I do,' said Thea, gritting her teeth, 'but I love you more and I cannot have both.'

'I can't let you do that.' Martha pulled Thea into the base of a tower from which half the stone had been robbed, away from fellow wanderers. 'You mustn't give it up for me, it is part of you.' They stood side by side gazing up at the Minster, chilled in moonlight, but Thea knew Martha's attention was entirely on her. Nobody but she could make this decision. The daunting anxiety of being unable to reconcile the awareness of her mind and her body was gone, replaced by the disquiet of an unknowable future. All she could do was to protect what she could, for as long as possible.

'I'm not asking you to let me,' she said, more surely than she felt. 'I have always had to pretend to be something I am not. I don't know what made me like this, but I no longer care. I can give up the collections, but I cannot pretend not to love you.'

'Thea, you must.'

'Of course I will in public, I can do that, but I can't pretend when it is just me and you, and I never want to be without that.' She prepared to voice the feelings that had been growing within her for the past few weeks. 'If we are clever, you and I will be able to hide in plain sight.'

Martha turned to her and took her arms, Thea kept her gaze turned away, into the city. 'I am sorry you have to bear this burden, Thea, whatever happens next has to be your choice and I will respect it as I always said I would.' Martha's voice was soft and her eyes kind, but Thea could feel her tension through the hands on her arms. 'I don't doubt what your heart tells you, but I am well-prepared that you may choose a different path. A more' – she hesitated – 'conventional one. I expect it and would, of course, support it.'

A hollow laugh escaped from Thea's throat. 'And then what? How do I spend my life? As the property of a man for whom I have no regard? Having his children, playing hostess to his friends?' The feeling of disquiet slipped from mind to body, as intense a hold as she had ever felt. Her pulse raced, her head swam and helplessness rose in her throat over and over until she felt she might choke.

'It would be easier.' Thea looked at Martha for the first time, ready to hiss her anger at the thought, but the look of helplessness tinged with hope in those eyes unravelled her.

'You were right,' said Thea, bringing shaking hands to grasp Martha's wrists, 'I wanted to know the truth about the world, and now I do. I know what the truth is for me. But like you said, knowledge leaves a mark. It is impossible to unlearn – impossible to cease a curiosity once it has taken root.' She looked into Martha's eyes. 'How can I settle for anything less now I know how it feels to be with you? The happiness of loving and being loved by you?' Darkness squeezed her chest and she turned back to the wall, gripping the cool stone with white fingers, 'Perhaps it would be best if I had never learned any of it. That I had remained ignorant on both counts. Perhaps then I could have been happy in my intended place.'

There was a pause before Martha's voice came, small and resigned. 'Do you really wish that?'

Thea turned back to her, the pain her hazel eyes breaking her heart. 'Of course I don't. How can I? It is only that now it seems impossible to let it go.' At the thought of it, fear made her start and rebellion rose in her stomach. She took Martha's hands in her own. 'I can't let it go. And I won't.' Her voice was not steady, but she was resolute. 'I know I have never been ordinary, but only the truth matters.' She took Martha by the waist and searched her face. 'I finally know who I am, but that person is not acceptable to society. Nevertheless, I will not be unfaithful to it.'

Martha cupped Thea's face in her hands and planted a kiss on her forehead. 'Forgive my reticence. You know how ardently I love you, but this is not a decision to be taken lightly. It is easy to make a resolution when we are out of society, but I have to ready myself for the possibility that you may feel different when you return. How we feel about one another may be the truth, but it is not a purpose for you, and you need that.'

Thea closed her eyes against reality. 'Then I will find another, but even if I could live without you, I don't want to.' She grasped Martha's wrap in both hands and pulled her closer. 'Please say we'll try.'

Martha gathered her in her arms. 'Of course, if it is what you want, but Thea, we must be nothing but careful. There is still someone close who has their eyes on you. Someone who is not afraid to make the situation known to your family. You were lucky the last time. Your mother will not be so forgiving the next and neither would society if it were found out.'

Thea gritted her teeth. 'Then we must be wary, but I will not cower. I will have you, Martha.' She buried her face in Martha's shoulder and held her tight, the energy of panic solidifying to a staunch resolution that she would make a life with the woman she loved.

CHAPTER 23

Milford, November 1758

'**S**he'll never know we're in here.'

The key clicked in the lock and Thea giggled despite herself. Ursula swung open the door and pushed herself into the cabinet, Thea following. Between them they lifted aside a few of the covers obscuring the collection. A number of familiar, hollow eyes gazed accusingly at Thea as she placed the best of the Whitby fossils on the geology shelf.

'I can't deny it,' she said, sighing. 'I will miss it.' How wonderful it was to be amongst it. Now she was back she realised just how much she had missed her sister, and her father – and Scip and Mrs Phibbs. The reunion with Tabitha and her mother had been more muted.

'You're set on it then?' Ursula's face betrayed her surprise. 'I thought once you were back here you might change your mind?' A memory of the last night in York thrust into Thea's thoughts – after their walk on the walls when she and Martha had retired to bed; the hunger, passion and desperation as they held and sated one another, almost until it was time to leave. They had been back for two days and still every minute was vivid. She gulped.

'I am set,' she said, with conviction. 'I have to protect what matters as best I can, and you know how mother would be.'

'I do.' Ursula picked up a fossil and interrogated Thea's labelling. 'But she doesn't have to know. And father is very apologetic. He wishes he had stood up to her earlier. Both he and I will cover for you – he got me these.' She jangled the keys in her hand.

Thea shook her head. 'It's kind of you, but I can't risk it. If I so much as look at a mollusc with interest I'll be married off in a heartbeat.'

'So there was nobody who turned your head in the north?' Ursula put down the fossil and turned to scrutinise her sister's face. 'Gentlemen *or* ladies?' Her mischievous eyes spoke of nothing but curiosity.

Thea saw Martha's smooth curves ahead of her, writhing as she was devoured. 'No.' She tried to keep her voice level. 'We engaged with society a little, but mostly kept to ourselves.'

'It didn't take Martha long to come around then?' asked Ursula.

In Thea's mind Martha's hands tangled in the sheets above her head, her whole body convulsed in ecstasy. 'Not too long, no.' She shook her head to banish the image. 'I must tell you about Mr Constable's walled garden,' she said, casting around for a change of subject. 'He has it laid out *as* a collection – in taxonomic order in the beds.'

That did it. Ursula froze. 'In the actual garden?'

'Yes.'

'In the beds themselves?'

'Exactly.'

'That's brilliant. We must replan. I'll talk to Scip first, obviously.'

Thea fought to suppress a grin. 'And father?'

Ursula waved a hand dismissively. 'Of course, he'll be delighted. He's having to allow others to take some responsibility now.'

Thea nodded. Their father was much improved, but a return of the dropsy was always a risk and he occasionally had to medicate with digitalis. 'If anyone can do it, you can.'

'And you could, Thea.' Ursula scoured her with a gaze, more seriously this time. Thea twitched beneath it.

'Martha was offered a chance to publish, and she turned it down. What would be the point of me going on anyway? I've always thought that perhaps if a woman made a discovery – despite all the obstacles in her way, that they would have to sit up and listen. But it wouldn't be owned by Martha, it would be by someone else, and she's scared, Urs. Scared of them finding out and ridiculing it. Through my life she has been the one person who hasn't been scared of anything. But this is too raw and too close to her to risk them belittling everything she feels she has ever achieved. And I understand.'

'Me too.' Ursula softly took her hand. 'Some things are too precious to us to risk to the censure of others.' Her lack of judgement made tears prick in Thea's eyes. 'But couldn't you be happy doing it for yourself?'

'I don't think so.' Thea nudged a couple of fossils into a more pleasing display. 'I want to spend my time doing something that could make a difference. And anyway, I have to find a way to lead a more acceptable life, don't you see?'

'More acceptable to whom?'

Thea gestured expansively with an arm. 'The world I suppose, I must find another way to occupy my time.'

Ursula inclined her head, seemingly unsatisfied with the decision. 'Like what?'

'I thought maybe painting.'

'You're dreadful at painting.'

'I did some while I was in Scarborough.'

'And was it better than last time we tried out on the downs with Mr Fenwick?'

Thea thought back to her efforts and a smile quirked her lips. 'No.'

Ursula tapped her fingers impatiently on her chair arm. 'Not that then. What else could you do? Maybe embroidery.'

Thea stared at her, non plussed. 'If I took up sewing I should like to make something useful – like Mrs Milne does at the drapers – exquisite dresses that enhance the form.' She raised an eyebrow at Ursula, who pursed her lips.

'Thea, you can't go into business, that's worse than collecting. And you aren't supposed to be useful, you're supposed to be a lady. And anyway' – she raised an eyebrow back – 'clearly you aren't to be trusted around ladies in any state of undress.'

Thea feigned shock but couldn't keep the snort from escaping her. They both collapsed in giggles.

'Embroidery it is.'

Martha had protected their time in the north so carefully that Jane Ashby's wedding came less than a week after their return. The day dawned bright but cold. Thea stepped out of the family carriage by the church and grinned at Thomas who stood nervously by the arched doorway, being fussed over by his brother. As her feet hit the path she felt a firm hand on her arm – it was Martha, in a deep burgundy gown that set off her eyes. They had seen each other only once since they arrived back in Sussex and Thea craved her. 'Oh, you–' she said, but her voice trailed off as she saw the grave look on Martha's face. 'What is it?' she asked, suddenly worried.

'This came this morning.' Martha produced a letter from her pocket and handed it to Thea, glancing nervously around her. The seal was unbroken.

'And?' asked Thea, not quite following. 'Do you not want to know what it says?'

'Look at it, Thea,' hissed Martha through gritted teeth as she guided Thea to a quiet spot underneath the churchyard yew. Thea did, and her heart bucked. The letter was addressed to *Lady Foxmore and Miss T Morell*.

Thea's skin chilled. 'Who can know already? You don't think..?' She didn't dare say it, but it was a sobering reminder that there was someone close they must be wary of.

Martha kept her eyes. 'I thought we should find out together.'

Thea slipped a finger by the seal and popped the wax from the parchment. Reaching into the envelope she pulled out a piece of card. As her eyes tracked across it relief flooded through her. 'It's an invite,' she said, feeling a little unsteady. 'To Cecily Simmons' wedding.' Immediately she saw Martha's muscles slacken and a nervous laugh escaped them both as Thea passed her the card. 'That was quick work,' she said. 'Cecily was only chasing gentlemen in Scarborough three months ago.'

Martha gave a small shrug. 'Or she was chasing gentlemen to try and avoid a match with the Neville Knatchbull of the invite?'

Thea's heart sank for the second time in as many minutes. 'She was always too keen. Poor girl, that must be why – desperate to find another.'

Martha gave a wan smile. 'Let's just hope she fell madly and swiftly in love with him on her return from Scarborough, shall we?'

Despite the anxiety of the morning Jane's ceremony was one of the happiest Thea had ever known, with both bride and groom beaming from ear to ear. Most of the village had turned out to wish them well and showered them in rice as they emerged triumphant from the ceremony.

True to form Edgar had been late and Thea ran over to him during the first break in proceedings. As she eyed him outside the church it struck her how old he was getting. It had only been six months, but the skin sagged off his face a little and his shoulders were hunched. She tapped him on one from behind. 'I see you have not yet entirely maimed yourself, Mr Pickles.'

He turned to her, delight spreading across his face and the years dropping away. 'Thea!' They embraced warmly and nattered incessantly as they walked through the cobbled streets of Thornbury to the assembly halls.

'So,' he said eventually, after glancing around the hall to ensure they weren't overheard, 'if I interpreted your letters correctly, you have directed your affections at another willing recipient?'

'Perhaps,' she grinned. 'I imagine you think it a little surprising?' She knew Martha wouldn't approve of the subject being discussed, but somehow couldn't help it.

Edgar shuffled himself round so that Martha was also in his view. 'I have to admit that now I think of it, I am far from surprised. You two are so wonderfully well-suited.'

Thea followed his gaze to Martha, perfect and elegant while she engaged a group with tales of the north. She sighed the kind of sigh that only happens in novels and didn't even feel ashamed of it. 'I believe so. I am determined there must be a future to it – I am happier now than I can ever remember.' Caution pricked at her. 'But you will keep it to yourself, won't you?'

He looked a little affronted as they were ushered into the reception. 'Of course I will, Thea – you know you can trust me. I could not be happier for you both or imagine a more suitable match between anyone. I do have a bone to pick with you, however.'

'Oh yes?' she asked, knowing what was coming.

'Martha tells me you have given it up. The collection. I'm afraid I cannot believe it, but she is very concerned.'

'Well, I am afraid that it is true.' Some of the indignation went from her. 'It has to be, Edgar, I don't want it to be, but I see no other option.'

'You are too good.' Edgar's generous brows became one. 'I cannot bear to see your brain idle, it is too sharp for that, and, for that matter, an idle brain is not good for *you*.'

That she could definitely agree with. 'It doesn't matter.' She dropped her voice and glanced over at Martha. 'I can't afford to risk everything we have for a field in which I can make no mark.'

He laid a hand over hers. 'You have always doubted yourself. And I do wish you wouldn't.'

She shrugged. 'Whatever collection I build will never be valued, whatever I say will not be heard. I weary of pretending and obfuscating in society because my activities are so distasteful to others. I'm tired of being the strange one trying not to talk about dead fish.'

Edgar allowed himself a sympathetic smile. 'Then perhaps the answer is finding more people who would like to talk about dead fish, rather than changing yourself to meet the expectations of those around you?'

'It is a beautiful thought and I would expect nothing less from you, Edgar,' she said appreciatively, 'but it is an academic point. I am not in control of where I socialise – my mother will see to that this winter – I have no collection of my own and no means of beginning one and anyway, what does it matter if none of my study would ever make the light of day? Martha is the cleverest person I know, man or woman, she has made a discovery in her field, and yet dare not publish. Why should I delude myself that I could achieve anything more, when she cannot.' They both looked over at Martha, confident and laughing with the group she entertained.

'I see,' he said, one of the brows now higher than the other. She took it as assent.

'I have to face it, Edgar,' she said more quietly. 'Serious science is not something I am able do. That has to be conducted by a man working under his own terms with no restraints of duty or sex, and without the scorn that would be poured on me for speaking out. I can never engage with this meaningfully in my situation. I realise that now.'

'I see,' Edgar said again, brows level.

'So it is time,' said Thea, 'to find a new kind of employment. One that isn't about distraction and that will not jeopardise the thing that is most dear to me.' She looked across at Martha again.

Edgar opened his mouth to respond but then Thea felt a hand on her arm and turned into the face of the bride. Edgar excused himself and shuffled off towards Martha, but not before giving her a look of stern reprimand.

Thea turned to Jane and looked her up and down. 'Look at you,' she said, taking one of Jane's arms and holding it out so she could assess the dress properly. 'You are a vision.'

'I wouldn't care if I were in muslin,' mused Jane, taking Thea's hands. 'I could not be happier – look at him.' She gestured to her new husband, happily chatting with Reverend Oates who knocked back another glass of wine. Thea also spied Edgar and Martha, already deep in conversation by the fireplace, her heart jumped a little and she suppressed a sigh.

'You are lucky, Jane, I can't wait to see your new house – what a life you will have together.'

'You next, Thea,' said Jane, giving her friend a stern look.

'Mmm,' said Thea, avoiding her gaze. 'Are those dianthus in your bouquet?'

'Yes,' said Jane, 'I knew if anyone would comment it would be you. Our housemaid made them up – she's such a talent.' She nodded to a black lady who moved deftly through the crowd carrying a trayful of glasses.

'I didn't even know you had a maid,' said Thea, thinking how much had changed since she had been away. 'Where did she come from?'

'We have two,' said Jane, 'Betty and Lucy. They came through a contact of Thomas's in the Quakers. They are doing good work there. The two of them have had a dreadful time of it although they work like trojans and I have yet to find anything they aren't good at. Lucy is at home with the children.'

'The children?' asked Thea, astounded. 'You took in children too?'

'We had no choice,' said Jane with a slight shrug. 'They are *their* children. This is Lucy's first but Betty has lost two in the plantations and was forced to leave her other in the Indies. Had we not taken them they would have been separated again. I can't imagine.'

'No,' said Thea, shocked. 'They separate them to sell?'

'Of course they do,' said Jane. 'Children fetch a high price. Thomas's Society of Friends is active in London and America. The things I could tell you. The things *they* could.' She nodded to Betty, now stoking the fire with more coal. She moved closer and dropped her voice. 'Thea, both children were born eight months from their landing in London. Neither has any idea which one of a dozen sailors the father is.'

The wine Thea had drunk almost made a reappearance as the blood rushed to her head. 'That's abominable. If only everyone was as good as you, Jane.'

'If only everyone was as good as my husband,' said Jane, savouring the word slightly. He is an excellent man and I love him so much more for this.'

Thea smiled at her, then shifted her gaze to Thomas over the expanse of the room and noisy bodies. 'In law, everything you are is now controlled by him,' she said, wondering. 'Do you not mind?'

Jane joined her in her gaze across the room. 'I don't – he is a good man and I am convinced of his character. We are a partnership.'

'You are sickeningly delightful, the two of you,' said Thea, raising a smile.

'And you deserve to be just as happy,' said Jane, with that mischievous twinkle in her eye. 'We have yet to discuss the potential gentlemen in your life.' Thea groaned and Jane looked at her sternly.

'You aren't telling me you spent five months in the north and no man turned your head?'

'I am saying that,' said Thea, pleased to be able to be honest with Jane at least this once.

'Seriously, Thea,' sighed Jane, 'think about it. You could have this too and you will never hold as much power as you do now, before marriage. You are free to make a choice.'

Thea actually snorted at the thought of the choice she wished for, set against the one she had to make. 'Women never hold power, Jane. And what choice do I have?'

Jane shrugged, refusing to be put off. 'Agency then, call it whatever you like. It is yours now, to choose the person who will live by your side – after that, you will be his. Choose someone you love or if you don't find him in time then choose someone you can tolerate and who will let you be, well' – she gestured in the direction of Thea with both hands – 'you.'

Before she had time to ask Jane what she meant the wedding banquet was immediately called and the two of them were whisked away. They ate, danced and drank into the night, celebrating the union of two earnest and good people very much in love.

A month later, and two weeks before Christmas she found herself outside Montagu House in Bloomsbury Square. A light dusting of snow made the courtyard shine and the grand, seventeen-bay building look fresh and new. For the beginning of the London season Thea had spent most of her time with Martha but had taken a few nights at Hanover Square to spare Ursula's sanity. Thea had thrown herself into her new pursuits, socialising and taking tea with Mrs Morell and Tabitha as well as the dinners and parties and of course attempting embroidery and poetry reading. Martha had stopped asking her to join her in visiting collections and even Ursula had stopped hassling her. She had to admit, though, Edgar had been right. Without the stimulation of books and objects her mind was getting restless. She had been glad of the distraction of a note from her father, asking them to pick up Ursula and meet him here.

'Good afternoon, ladies.' They spun round as one to find Mr Morell standing behind them, done up in a smart grey three piece and spreading his arms afront the grand building. 'Welcome to the new British Museum.'

'A museum?' asked Thea, pushing Ursula alongside her father and Martha as they approached the tall entrance between cones of topiary. 'Whose is it?'

'It belongs to the nation,' said Mr Morell excitedly. 'Sir Hans Sloane left it with strict instructions on his death. Tens of thousands of specimens, forty thousand books, three hundred and thirty-seven volumes of dried plants, for goodness sake. All open to anyone! By appointment, obviously.' Thea glanced at Martha and smiled as she saw her eyes shine.

'And what are we doing here?' she asked, suspicious.

Mr Morell stopped short outside the door and they gathered around. 'What better venue, I thought, for a piece of news I have been dying to share with you. You remember that you put me in touch with William Constable, Thea?' She nodded. 'Well, he introduced me to the secretary of the Royal Society, Douglas Thistleton. He is a trustee here as well as being involved in the Royal Society and, well, you are looking at the society's newest member.' He puffed himself up while they congratulated him.

'Amazing, Ben,' smiled Martha, clapping him on the arm, 'and what a wonderful idea to celebrate here.' Her eyes darted involuntarily to Thea and back to him. Subtle, thought Thea.

'Indeed,' said Mr Morell as they shared a glance, 'your mother won't mind, Thea, on this occasion. Not that she knows.'

Thea nodded, resigned. 'Shall we go inside?'

'Mmm, yes,' said Mr Morell, but hesitated. 'There's something you should know before we do.' They looked at him expectantly as he twirled his hat around in his hands. 'Mr Constable recommended me due to the work on the plant experiment. They want it as a paper at one of their meetings and published in the Transactions, but I said I could do no such thing without the agreement of the person behind the study.' Mr Morell's eyes settled on Martha and Thea felt her tense next to her. Momentarily worried that she would actually leave, Thea placed a hand on the small of her back and squeezed.

'You mean he's...' started Martha.

'Waiting for us, yes,' said Mr Morell. 'I will not press you, Martha, but I would love to introduce you and for you to hear what he has to say.'

Thea, watching intently, saw her swallow. 'Does he know?'

'Ah, Morell, you made it!' came a cheerful voice from the door. Mr Thistleton was tall, round and smooth. A brown wig topped ruddy cheeks and he beamed at them all. A tall, skinny man with a neat white wig perched precariously on top of his pointy head stood sour faced behind. 'This is honourable member Ephraim Herbert who has agreed to be a second proposer for you.' Mr Morell shook Mr Herbert's hand. Mr Herbert ignored the three ladies, and Mr Thistleton made no moves to include them. 'Do come in, won't you,' went on Mr Thistleton, 'I'm sure your team, as you call them, can join when they get here.'

'I suppose he doesn't know,' muttered Martha.

Thea, Martha and Ursula turned to Mr Morell as he licked his lips nervously but drew himself up. 'We are all here, Mr Thistleton, Mr Herbert,' Thea heard him say. 'Martha Smilgrove, Countess of Foxmore who led the experiment, and my two daughters Thea and Ursula Morell without whom the collections at Milford would be a tired mess.' He beamed at them all proudly, and they waited for the reaction.

Mr Herbert's expression did not change, and, to his credit, Mr Thistleton did well to hide his surprise. 'An honour to meet you, ladies.' He bowed to them all in turn. 'Many of our members would be very little without the administrative assistance of the women in their lives. Do come through.'

He turned and Thea bristled as they stepped inside. 'Administrative assistance? How dare he? Didn't he hear father say you led the experiment?'

Martha shushed her. 'It can be difficult for people to see past what they know.'

'It shouldn't be, if you're a natural philosopher,' muttered Ursula, sounding as grumpy as Thea felt as she pushed herself into the large hall.

Their attention was suddenly taken, however, by the scale of it.

'Others have added to the collection since Sloane's generous bequest,' said Mr Thistleton, standing with his hands on his hips and gazing around himself. 'It took five years to find a suitable home for such an important museum but we are pleased.' It was, indeed, impressive. Shelves lined the walls of the huge central room, tables in the middle bursting with curiosities, and rooms off the side showing tantalising glimpses of the knowledge within.

'Perhaps you would care to wonder at some of our treasures, ladies?' Mr Thistleton gestured to the shelves. Thea gave him as generous a smile as she could muster in the face of his condescending tone as they moved into the gallery.

'It *is* grand,' muttered Martha to Thea as they were led to one of the first cabinets.

Mr Thistleton reached up and retrieved a jar from a high shelf. It was filled with liquid and a small reptilian form. 'Could this be one of the only baby dragons ever to grace the shores of England?' he asked, flourishing it in front of them and shooting a knowing glance to Mr Herbert.

The annoying thing was, it wasn't an enquiry. Thea had seen that expression many times, mostly on the face of men who had decided to have a little tease with the ladies. She sagged a little inside, but it made her almost pleased to have made the decision to give up collecting. There would be less of these situations where she had to feign ignorance. Or, at least, where she couldn't muster the courage to speak up. 'May I look more closely, Mr Thistleton?' she asked politely.

'Of course, Miss Morell.' Mr Thistleton nestled the jar in her outstretched hands. 'But no sudden movements, we don't want any unwanted explosions do we, however small!' He laughed at his own joke. Thea managed a simpering titter.

It was, unmistakeably, a specimen of *Draco volans*, just like Mr Constable's. As she turned it round in front of her face the words rose up in her throat, ones that would inform Mr Thistleton coolly about how the patagium informed on its manner of gliding, and how the yellow dewlap said this was almost certainly a male. She felt Martha's eyes on her, wondering how she would respond. But she remembered the shame of the times she had spoken up, and the scoffing which would no doubt arise from both Misters Thistleton and Herbert if she did so now. The well-trained politeness within her dragged her informed words back down.

'Quite unbelievable,' was all she said as she dropped the jar back into his hands. She felt a little ashamed of herself, but Ursula looked at Mr Thistleton with barely disguised contempt. A little nervousness ran through Thea. She had seen that look before.

Oblivious, Mr Thistleton pressed on, warming to his game. She saw him give the unmoving Mr Herbert a little nudge as he passed. 'How about this,' he said, opening a cabinet and retrieving a smooth, solid object with regular sides. It looked heavy, while he held it out proudly. 'They say this is one of the rare thunderstones. An amulet that derives from where lightning has struck.'

'Who says that?' asked Ursula, wheeling herself over and peering at it.

'Well. It is just *said*, I suppose,' said Mr Thistleton, haltingly, and looking at Ursula for the first time.

'Can I see it?' asked Ursula, holding out her hands. Thea saw Martha turn away to hide the beginnings of a smile as their host tentatively passed it down to Ursula. She tested its weight and studied the butt end of it, as well as running a thumb over the curved ridge where the object flared. She held it up. 'Mr Thistleton, can I ask if you truly believe that this is the product of a lightning strike?'

'Um,' he said, 'it has been folklore for many hundreds of years.'

'Indeed it has,' said Ursula, 'but we gather here in a space of science, not witchcraft. I can only assume that you are still cataloguing the collections and will come to this in time, but if we stick to the facts I believe it will be less embarrassing for us all.'

'Ah,' said Mr Thistleton this time, and pulled at his collar a little.

'I believe this is an ancient axe head,' went on Ursula, weighing it in her hand. 'Although I suspect you know that already. For context I would recommend that you read Lafitau's work comparing the customs of ancient, primitive and contemporary diverse peoples. It is in French, but I am sure you can employ the administrative assistance of a woman in your life to translate.' She fixed him with a stare that even Thea and Martha shrank away from.

'Of course,' said Mr Thistleton. 'An excellent suggestion. Perhaps the next cabinet?' He fled, but Ursula followed, systematically critiquing the labelling and classification systems with a flawless knowledge. Thea and Martha trailed after, watching the back of his neck progressively bead with sweat. Thea wished she was the reason for the pride etched on Martha's face. To deaden the shame she nudged Martha forwards.

'Save the poor man,' she whispered, 'Ursula is on a roll and she's furious, we'll be here until next week if we don't stop her.'

'The ordering would be better though,' muttered Martha back to her, but stepped in and placed a hand on Ursula's shoulder. Mr Thistleton looked up at her with panic in his eyes. 'There are the ingredients here for quite the most progressive assemblage.' Martha smiled kindly at Mr Thistleton, who gulped, nevertheless. 'I am sure you have plans to bring the classification of it into the thinking of the day – we do appreciate that it is difficult when you are battling with the legacy of a bygone era.' By now the poor man looked utterly exhausted and Mr Herbert had strategically faded into the arachnid case, presumably finding it less uncomfortable.

'Perhaps we should speak about publication, Mr Morell?' squeaked Mr Thistleton, sidestepping to safety.

'Indeed we should,' said Mr Morell kindly, and Mr Thistleton's shoulders settled a little. 'But not without Lady Foxmore of course, it is her expertise we require most of all.' Thea shoved Ursula into a room of Peruvian artefacts before they could both burst out laughing at the look of horror on Mr Thistleton's face.

Thea and Martha were still laughing as they walked back to Martha's house through Windmill Street.

'Did he do the thing men do where they talk to father instead of you?' asked Thea as Martha recounted the conversation.

'Of course,' said Martha, laughing. 'Constantly. Your father kept directing him back towards me. He began to understand after it happened for the sixth time.'

'You'd think a man of science might learn quicker, wouldn't you?' Martha only laughed and took her arm as the snow began to fall once more. It disguised the dirt of London which for once looked warm and homely in the gaslight. It wasn't always safe for two ladies to walk alone, Thea knew, but she also knew that Martha kept a knife down her stocking for just this purpose – a fact that sent a little thrill through her whenever she thought of it. 'And what did you say to him?' asked Thea when Martha offered no further elaboration on the conversation with the two men. She was almost nervous to ask, but Martha smiled kindly.

'I didn't commit, if that is what you had hoped,' she said, pulling Thea a little closer to her as they walked. 'I am sorry if it disappoints you.'

'I'm only suggesting that you think about it,' said Thea. 'Father won't push you to publish if you would rather not and his place in the society is not dependent on it, but do it for you, Martha. You have worked so hard on it.'

'I did tell them I'd consider it,' said Martha, pulling her cloak tighter around her as they emerged into the fields around the waterworks, 'but if others find out about my part in it and the whole thing is discredited, it would be such a shame.'

'Just send Ursula in,' smiled Thea. 'She'll take them apart like she did Mr Thistleton.'

'She is impressive,' grinned Martha.

'And so are you.' Thea squeezed Martha's solid forearm, their hands concealed by the cloaks between them. 'Your work deserves to be known. If you are so worried we needn't even mention your involvement. It could all be on father – it wouldn't be fair, but at least it would be out.'

'But people would find out.' Martha sounded dejected. 'And then he would be tainted by association.

'There are only a tiny amount of people who are aware of your involvement,' Thea said. 'Mr Thistleton is unlikely to tell after today. Nobody else but Grimston knows the scale of your input and he doesn't even believe women have the capacity to think.'

Martha cast a glance at Thea. 'I'll think about it. Honestly I will,' she said quietly.

Thea squeezed her again. 'I'd like that.'

They slowed to a stop overlooking the ponds. There were no gas lights out here, but the reflection of the moon on the snow lit the long grass and the trees that peppered the meadows between the paths. Martha looked around to ensure nobody was near, and then quickly nuzzled into Thea's hair before pulling back. 'Edgar told me that you were giving it up because of me. Because you feel that if I can't make any headway, you can't either.'

Thea shrugged. 'That's not why I'm giving it up, but it is why I feel I am able. If there was a chance I could contribute perhaps I would think differently, but I just don't see that there is.'

Martha turned to face her. 'You shouldn't base all your decisions on my actions, you are your own person and have so much to offer. I watched you in the museum today. You lit up like you haven't in weeks.'

'Until I allowed Mr Thistleton to spin me a yarn which was untrue because I have no courage.' She felt a little smaller even saying it. Allowing herself to be trodden down. Neither Martha or Ursula would have allowed it, but she could feel any fight she ever had leaving her.

Martha's head spun to face her and the moonlight highlighted a momentary crinkle in her forehead. 'Because you are cautious and I understand why. You have been conditioned to be, but you could still pursue knowledge, Thea. In private if need be.'

Thea gave her a defeated smile. 'But you are the strongest and cleverest person I know. If your knowledge gets you nowhere, I have no chance.'

Martha turned back to the fields. 'Sometimes people aren't as capable or as strong as they appear.'

'But you are,' said Thea softly, reaching out and turning Martha's face towards her own. She was desperate to kiss her but didn't dare in public.

Martha opened her mouth to say something, and then closed it again. 'I saw a poster for Dr Gibson's lectures, you used to love those – why don't we go?'

Thea shook her head. 'If mother knew...'

'She won't know. You have to exercise your mind one way or another, we're all worried about you.'

'Who is?' Thea looked at her in shock.

'Your father, Ursula and Mr Pickles. You are struggling, Thea.'

'No I'm not.' It came out petulantly, and she knew it was a lie.

'You can't keep your anxieties from me, Thea,' said Martha, ignoring her tone. 'You were not in a good way at the Bringstone's last week.' Thea recalled it well. She had needed to leave whilst Mrs Bringstone had droned on about silk and her daughter had incessantly played at the harpsichord. Martha had followed Thea and silently calmed her in the corridor, but they hadn't talked about it, until now..

'I'm happy with you.' Thea gritted her teeth. She was trying not to admit it even to herself, but she knew she couldn't ignore it forever.

The threatening darkness she felt inside curled throughout her like smoke, dampening her senses. She could forget when she was with Martha, the loss felt dulled.

'Not truly you aren't, not without study. Honestly you have a brain that needs to be occupied and there are only so many embroideries that you need.'

'Actually,' said Thea, 'I've found a new way of running the thread and building it up so that it looks like...' She stopped, as Martha looked at her incredulously. 'Look, we'll figure it out somehow,' she sighed, taking Martha's arm and setting off across the fields. 'I have everything I need.' She snuggled into Martha's side as they made for Foxmore Square, wishing she believed her own words.

CHAPTER 24

Thea felt a little numb as she sipped from a glass of wine amidst a throng of bustling bodies. It was the day of Cecily's wedding and she and Martha stood together in the assembly rooms at Holborn, lost for conversation. It hadn't been the most joyful of days. The preparations were impeccable, the decoration sumptuous and the food faultless but it was a rainy January day and the happy couple looked almost as radiant as the weather. Thea could see Cecily trying, but it was abundantly clear that the gentleman by her side at the altar was not the love of her life. For a start, Neville Knatchbull looked almost forty years her senior, if not more. He reminded Thea a little of a ferret – tall and wiry with a pointy face. Now, after the ceremony and the food everyone was celebrating a new start, but for Thea the thought of a life lived for convenience and arrangement was a little too close to home. Judging by Martha's quiet she felt exactly the same.

To make matters worse, the only other people Thea and Martha knew at the wedding were the Jefferys. It turned out that Mr Jefferys had business with the groom in the midlands and they'd hung around Thea and Martha all day, commenting snidely on the food and the drink and the outfits of the guests and anything else they could find to critique. Thea had long since stopped trying to make conversation and allowed Mrs Jefferys to become part of the background hum.

'And the vulgar tea house the Fortesque's have thrown up in that silly little garden by the Thames,' she was saying as a girl stopped by to offer more wine. She held out her glass for more but as the girl went to fill it she became animated again. 'I say tea house but it is more of a palace–' As she spoke she raised her arms to make the point and both the wine glass and carafe went flying.

'Fool!' screeched Mrs Jefferys, mopping wine from her dress. The girl looked utterly panicked and immediately dropped to her knees to clear the mess, mumbling apologies. 'When Mrs Jefferys was satisfied the wine wouldn't be seen on her dark satin she turned her anger to the girl on the floor and shoved her with a foot, knocking her over. 'Watch what you're doing, girl – you could have caused me an injury. I'll be having a word with your master and I hope he teaches you a lesson.' A chill spread throughout Thea as the words settled. Looking down at the girl she noticed an ugly gash in her dark skin from where she had leant on broken glass in an attempt to break her fall. Blood mixed with wine on the floor. Mrs Jefferys averted her eyes. 'I can't even look at the mess she's making.'

Thea knelt and pulled out her handkerchief, but the girl flinched away, terrified. 'I'm sorry, my lady,' she muttered.

'It's ok,' Thea said softly, trying not to think about the flinch. She took the hand and inspected it gently before looking in in the girl's eye where she saw only fear. 'There's no glass in it, but you should deal with it before you go on out here.'

'She should not,' said Mrs Jefferys' voice from above. 'She should clean up this mess. What's the point in keeping them if we have to stand in dregs and bodily fluids?' Her lip curled and she stepped back, shifting the hem of her dress in a move rooted more in theatrics than practicality.

'She needs help,' said Thea quietly.

'She needs discipline,' said Mrs Jefferys. 'I think she's one of Neville's – at least he knows how to deal with them.'

Thea helped the girl to her feet. 'We'll need another handkerchief,' she said to Martha, through gritted teeth. Blood was beginning to seep through the one Thea had wadded in the girl's palm. Martha produced one and handed it to the girl before flicking her eyes to the door by way of dismissal. The girl hurried off after a shaky bob of thanks. Thea thought of the women Jane had employed and their desperate story. This girl couldn't be more than fifteen and she belonged to Neville. And Cecily now, she supposed. She hated the thought that Cecily had married someone who was apparently well versed in disciplining his slaves.

Anger rose within her at the casual acceptance of it and she wiped her hands on a second handkerchief passed to her by Martha. 'It costs nothing to be kind,' she said, keeping her eyes on her hands as she worked. 'It must be hard for – for people like her.' She wished she could be more eloquent, but the anger had muzzied her thoughts.

Out of the corner of her eye she saw Mrs Jefferys scoff. 'Hard for people like her? Don't tell me about her hard life.'

Now Thea looked up. 'You?'

Mrs Jefferys fiddled with an earring. 'A lady is always at the beck and call of men. No autonomy, no independence. I have had all of it and more.'

'You are not a black woman,' said Thea, knowing she shouldn't. She cast her eyes back down and a harsh, emotional edge tinting her words. 'And you are not owned. I can't even begin...' She felt Martha's hand reach the small of her back as her voice cracked.

'I think we all had a bit of a shock, but I am sure the girl will be fine. Let's enjoy the wedding, shall we?' She looked at Thea pointedly, who now looked back at Mrs Jefferys, staring daggers at her.

'Of course,' she said, through gritted teeth.

'When are we to have the pleasure of attending your nuptials, Miss Morell?' Mrs Jefferys' voice was sickly sweet again and both Thea and Martha tensed at the pointed question.

'I am not sure that is quite on the cards,' said Martha quietly.

'Oh, I am sure Miss Morell will choose well.' Mrs Jefferys took a small step forward, now keeping her eyes on Thea. 'She will repay the kindness of her mother in allowing her the freedom to remain out for so long.' Thea thought she might have been about to say something else, but her eyes flicked to Martha and she thought better of it.

'I have been lucky to have so much liberty,' said Thea pointedly.

'And exercise it, you have.' Mrs Jefferys pointed her chin. 'I was a little surprised at Earl Axbury's attentions to you at the Crowe's new year ball, Miss Morell, but even more surprised at your returned enthusiasm.' Thea's heart skipped. She noticed Martha's attention pique and muttered something she hoped was dismissive. 'You danced three with him, did you not, in addition to offering your hand to most of the gentlemen in attendance?' Mrs Jefferys now smiled a toothy smile and Thea's insides shrank. It wasn't a memory she was keen to dredge up and certainly not with Martha here. It had been a miserable way to begin a new year. She had drunk too much wine and with her mother's assertions about the worsening state of her father's fortunes and his still precarious heath ringing in her ears had been forced to maintain her future prospects by dancing with all the men put her way. Martha had stayed at home – she said as she was feeling off-colour, but Thea knew there was no joy in seeing her beloved offered up to every gentleman in the room.

'I danced with them as my mother ensured it, Mrs Jefferys.' Thea tried to keep her tone light.

'If I were her I would be ensuring more than that.' Mrs Jefferys flashed a toothy, sweet smile which contained no kindness. 'There is little time left at your age. I know she favours the wealth of George Crowe but he has his pick of the ladies.' She looked Thea up and down, pointedly.

'Indeed,' muttered Thea through clenched teeth. As Martha took a breath to speak they were interrupted by the bride who bounced into their gloomy corner.

'Are you all not dancing?' she asked, her eyes bright. 'Is the music not to your liking?' The entrance jarred after the tense and rude exchange, but Thea was pleased to be offered the respite from Mrs Jefferys.

Thea mustered a smile for their friend's sake. 'Perhaps later, Lady Foxmore and I are currently too full from your generous spread. Thank you so much for the invitation, Cecily.'

Cecily's grin was honest, but she was a more subdued version of herself than they had seen in Scarborough. 'How could I not invite the two people who introduced me to my new hobby? I am now quite taken by pressing plants and they provide excellent subject for my poetry.' Thea saw Mrs Jefferys roll her eyes.

'Of course,' said Martha, trying too hard to sound jolly. 'Nature is good for the soul. It provides solace and can't help but make us better people.' Thea noticed how she couldn't help a flicker of a glance towards Mrs Jefferys.

Thea forced similar cheery tone. 'It was a beautiful service and Neville seems – professional,' she tried. 'I hope you have had an excellent day?' She realised later she should have expected nothing less than complete honesty from Cecily.

'It is lovely to see everyone of course, and to celebrate. And look how happy my mother is.' Mrs Simmons was mid-flight in a reel, dancing as if her life depended on it. Thea and Martha both fixed Cecily with a knowing eye. The other girl smiled generously. 'I know what you are thinking but you need not worry – it doesn't matter.'

'Doesn't it?' asked Thea, surprised.

'Of course not,' said Cecily, matter-of-factly. 'I am an only child and quite without prospects. Neville has been a friend of my father's cousin for a long time and when my father died it became a prudent match. He is quite aware of the convenience of the arrangement. He owns a factory in the midlands but has recently bought a small estate in Berkshire and we shall move there. Anyway, you never quite know how a young man will turn out – this way in all events I am well informed of his character with all its blessings and failings.' A morose expression briefly clouded her face but it passed in a second. 'I will do what women do and engage myself with my friends and bear him children who will inherit the estate. There are worse lives, you know.'

Thea felt like the breath had been sucked from her body, grateful that Mrs Jefferys took up the conversation on the wonderful things she had heard about the estate from her husband. He had stood mute throughout. Thea had never considered that Cecily Simmons could be more sensible than her, but here she was, in front of them and pragmatic about a life with a man she didn't love. Because she had to be. Because that was her duty. And because she had made a rational choice.

Cecily soon moved on to greet other guests but Thea couldn't shake the bleak feeling for the rest of the evening. Mrs Jefferys rattled on but Martha was as sullen as Thea felt. As if by mutual agreement they made their excuses as early as maintained politeness and called the carriage.

They didn't speak for some time, Thea stared out of the window at the dark streets, mulling over Mrs Jefferys' spite and Cecily's unhappy situation. She had managed to keep the worsening financial situation and George Crowe's interest away from Martha until now. It had to surface at some point, but she'd hoped she could delay it for longer.

'I'm glad Cecily has started pressing plants. It'll give her something to do.' Martha broke the silence, but her tone was strained and Thea wasn't sure where this was leading.

'Mmm.'

'It's good to have a distraction from life's inevitabilities.'

'Apparently,' said Thea, not sure how to expand.

Martha turned to her. 'You didn't tell me about George Crowe.' It wasn't accusatory, but there was something in her voice that made Thea's heart seem to fold up on itself.

'I didn't know what to say.' Now she stared at her own feet. 'It's just hard, Martha.'

'Did you expect this to be a walk in the park?' Now Martha's tone took her by surprise and she looked up to find hard eyes.

'No, but at least I expect you to understand.'

'I understand that you are flirting with eligible gentlemen. Of course, I suppose that is your right.'

'It isn't my right, it's my duty.' They both sat rigid, but as they held one another's gaze across the carriage Thea saw Martha sag a little, and she allowed herself to do the same. 'I am sorry I didn't tell you. I just can't bear to voice it.'

Martha nodded. 'I know. I have no business being frustrated. I am sorry.'

Thea moved over to sit beside her and took her hand. 'It is inevitable.' She watched Martha's gloved fingers trace her own. 'Father has borrowed more money. He says the financial situation will pick up with the new growing season but everything feels so fragile.'

Martha's fingers halted in their caress. 'Why didn't you tell me?'

Why hadn't she? To stave off the inevitable conflict? To pretend things were different? 'For the same reason I didn't tell you about George Crowe.'

'What will you do?' asked Martha quietly, and the helplessness in her eyes nearly broke Thea apart.

'I don't know.' A chill washed through her from her feet to her fingers and she swayed, closing her eyes for a second. When she opened them Martha's were softer, probably due to the tears forming in her own.

'What do you want to do?'

'I want to run away with you and live happily ever after.' She'd said it, at least. The fantasy that had been flitting round her head for the past six months.

Martha considered her for long seconds. 'If that's what you really want, we will. But there are financial considerations and you know what the implications would be for your family.'

Hope and joy flooded Thea, but it left as quickly as it arrived. Her voice was now a whisper through the threatening tears. 'I know.' Martha's mention of her financial situation sparked a memory of the beach at Whitby. 'Have you given up your shares?'

Martha shook her head. 'Not yet. I knew it was our only chance to live comfortably together if you chose that path. But...' She left the word in the air.

'You found out more about the investments?'

'Yes.'

'And?'

'The worst kind of ships, Thea.' Martha's eyes were full of sorrow. For those like the girl Mrs Jefferys had so cruelly abused tonight, Thea knew, but also for what it meant for them. She closed her eyes to not see it written on Martha's face.

'Even if – even if that was what we decided...'

'We couldn't build a life on that,' finished Martha. Thea nodded, unable to say anything else against the lump in her throat. 'I'll sell them if you agree?'

'I do,' said Thea, pleased at Martha's empathy and the change in her views since Whitby. In Thornbury they had spoken to Jane about her experience with Betty and Lucy. Thea had watched Martha's rational mind assess and overturn the views that had been settled in her head since childhood. She knew it was right for Martha to give up the shares but with them went much of her financial independence – and their chance for an independent life of scholarship and society. If Denbury was sold there was still the outside chance they could hole themselves up in a cottage somewhere, but to do what? Would Martha be able to be happy without her plants and her study? And that was before any consideration of the financial security of Thea's sisters and the social disgrace it would bring the whole family. It would be the end of Milford and disastrous to the Morells. Her eyes lifted to Martha's and she saw the same conflict reflected back. She nestled into her neck and Martha pulled her close.

'I'm sorry it's so hard,' Martha whispered into her hair.

Thea contained a sigh. 'I am sorry I ever convinced you to embark on this. We knew how impossible it was.'

Martha dropped a gentle kiss into her hair. 'Never be sorry for us. We will work it out. Although Thea, you should know...' She paused and Thea's heart skipped.

'I should know what?'

Martha shifted uncomfortably. 'I can't be your mistress, Thea.' Thea couldn't deny she had considered it. To take an indifferent husband and move Martha in as a companion, but she knew it was impossible. Martha could never come second.

'I would never ask it of you.'

It was a visible relief. Martha pulled Thea back towards her and held her tight, whispering against her temple. 'You have difficult decisions to make and I will absolutely accept whatever they are, but Thea, we have to be honest with one another.' Thea only nodded and wrapped her arms around Martha, a weight lifted at Martha's understanding but a new uncertainty sitting heavy within her. She buried her face in Martha to contain the emotion that threatened to burst out.

She thought about Cecily and her new husband, forged from necessity. She thought about her own deviant tendencies and how she had felt they somehow marked her out from the hundreds of women each year who made prudent matches for title or for money. Now, while she felt the damp of one of Martha's tears trickle through her hair a terrible realisation hit.

She had been so taken up with being different that she had forgotten she was exactly the same as everybody else.

The next morning Thea blinked open her eyes to see the familiar drapes of Martha's bed, framing the bright sunlight. She reached out a hand and Martha rolled over at feeling the touch. 'Morning.' She shuffled over and nestled into Thea who wrapped her in her arms and held her tight. She shifted so they fit snuggly together and despite the continuing ache a wicked grin spread across Thea's face as her mind flashed back to the night before.

'God, last night–'

She felt Martha grin against her collarbone and a soft, sleepy kiss pressed to it. 'Quite acceptable.' Thea smiled. Through all the uncertainty and hurt there was a little more easiness. At least now they understood one another and would deal with their problems together.

Martha nuzzled her neck and kissed her gently. 'What shall we do today?'

'Anything with you. I have to...' *Make the most of you*, went unsaid.

Martha placed a gentle kiss on her lips. 'Won't you come to that Dr Gibson lecture with me? It's the first night of a new show.'

'But my mother...'

'I don't care what your mother thinks, I care about you, and Dr Gibson's lectures always cheered you up.' Martha's hand ran up her bare stomach.

'But if someone sees me and tells her it could... hang on.'

Martha sat up. 'What is it?'

A mischievous grin spread over Thea's face. 'I have an idea.'

'What on earth are you wearing?' Martha stood frozen in the doorway, her eyes wide with shock. Thea had left the house after breakfast, refusing to say where she was headed. On her return she had slipped upstairs, requesting the assistance of Mrs Jenkins and entreating Martha to join her in the bedroom in a quarter hour.

Thea grinned cheekily and raised a brow. 'Do you like it? Sometimes, when I wanted to sneak to Dr Gibson's lectures by myself, I would go like this.' She stood, arms out, inviting critique of herself in the old footman's casuals retrieved that morning from the outhouse at Hanover Square. 'I thought, perhaps, I could dress like this tonight.'

Her confidence faded a little and her arms dropped as Martha's surprise didn't wane. 'I mean, I thought we could go as a couple. Together.' Martha still remained silent. Should she keep talking? 'In public. Together. I mean, nobody has ever guessed I'm not a man. It's always been fine.' She was gabbling now, her earlier bravado evaporated and nerves seeping in as she shared her secret. If kissing a woman was socially dangerous, impersonating a man was significantly worse. She wondered if she had finally found the end of Martha's liberal streak.

The silence extended. A long pause seemed to draw out a taut thread in Thea's insides. Finally Martha spoke. 'Are you mad? Thea, you can't go out like that.'

Of course not. The thread broke. How reckless. Again. She opened her mouth to speak when Martha cut across her. 'If I am to be seen with a male companion he will at least be well-dressed and respectable. Wait there.'

CHAPTER 25

They arrived at the lecture in good time. Thea was nervous but felt resplendent in her new outfit. With nothing more than an amused smile Mrs Jenkins had dug out some of Lord Foxmore's old attire which, with a little pinning and tucking, fit Thea remarkably well. The deep blue jacket and waistcoat crowned light breeches and a shoe with a flamboyant buckle. The wig and felt hat hid her head of hair and she still wore less makeup than some of the actual men in the room. She proudly took her place next to Martha at the front of the lecture hall to ensure a good view and smiled as she noticed Martha stealing more glances than usual in her direction. The hall's familiar scent of musk and timber sent a frisson of excitement through her, intrigued to learn.

The lights dipped and Dr Gibson stepped onto the stage. He circled an object taller than himself, the cloth covering betraying glimpses of a machine beneath. 'Ladies and gentlemen!' He threw his arms wide. 'Welcome to the first night of my new show!' The crowd cheered. 'Before we proceed with tonight's experiment,' he went on, 'I would like to encourage you to think about the world that surrounds you, and that which caresses you even in this very room.' He chuckled and moved to the front of the stage as some of the audience shifted uncomfortably, glancing at their neighbours. He was so close Thea could see the sweat already beading on his face.

His eyes scanned the front row and he reached out a hand to Martha. 'My lady, if you would be so kind?' His eyes rested on Thea's. 'I shan't keep her for long, sir.' A frisson of nerves and excitement thrilled Thea as she nodded and Martha stepped up to the stage. He couldn't tell. Her eyes settled on Martha, elegant and regal as Dr Gibson strode around her. 'My lady, I wonder if I may trouble you to extend a hand directly in front of you, and to close your eyes.' Martha flicked a wary glance at him and to Thea but did as she was bid. The Doctor stopped his striding behind her and spoke over her shoulder so the audience could hear. 'Tell me, my lady, what do you feel, with that graceful, outstretched hand?'

Thea saw Martha's brow furrow momentarily. 'Nothing.'

'Nothing!' exclaimed Dr Gibson. 'My lady, are you absolutely certain? Perhaps try a slight wave of the appendage, and tell me again? What sensations do you encounter?'

A slight twitch of Martha's lips told Thea she understood. 'Air, Dr Gibson. I feel the air.'

'The air!' Dr Gibson clasped his hands together. 'My lady, I hope all of my future participants are as fleet of mind as you. I thank you for your assistance.' And with that, he helped her back to the bench seats before returning to the stage with a flourish.

'Tonight, ladies and gentlemen,' he boomed, 'we are to interrogate the properties and necessity of air! Meg, some assistance if you please!' Thea stilled as Meg appeared with a wide smile. She and Dr Gibson billowed the cloth at the centre of the stage with a flourish, theatrically revealing a large machine to the onlookers. Thea couldn't focus at first, she was too taken with the Doctor's assistant. She hadn't seen Meg since the electrical venus kiss, and while she smiled passively those deep blue eyes seemed to dart around the room with a startling intensity. She wore a gunmetal-grey dress with strappings of dark material seemingly trussing her in shoulder to hip. A dark silk scarf accentuated a high collar, gilt buttons dotted each side of the gown giving it a rakishly masculine edge and the line of her cut was sleek, showing off a slim waist and straight hips. It was a look a lady could only get away with on the stage, but Thea loved it. Her breath hitched as Martha turned to her.

'An air pump – like Edgar's!' Martha was beaming and clapping with the rest of the audience. Thea recovered herself and nodded keenly, belatedly noting the large glass vessel atop an elaborate mahogany stand, the pump cylinders only feet away from where they sat.

With his usual flair Dr Gibson presided over the evening's experiments while Meg strode around the apparatus, deftly loading the glass vessel with item after item and cranking the pump handle to expel the air. She extinguished candles, made mercury rise up a tube and expanded and shrunk a bladder. Thea couldn't help but be impressed at the adept way she handled the machinery. She felt a squeeze on her arm and snapped her eyes guiltily back to Martha's smiling gaze. 'Enjoying the show are we, Mr Morton?' she asked, amused, as Thea reddened. She had jokingly given herself the name of Tobias Morton in the carriage, but even he shouldn't be caught ogling the assistant.

'It's not that, it's just...' She trailed off, what was it? She couldn't quite put her finger on it. There was something that captivated her about Meg, something that wasn't attraction that continued to evade her.

Her musings were interrupted by Dr Gibson's striding gait calling her attention back to the stage. He clutched in his hand another cloth-covered object which he extended towards the audience.

'Now, ladies and gentlemen, for the grand finale!' With his free hand Dr Gibson grasped the cover and pulled it free with a flourish, revealing a bird cage and one very startled looking lark.

Thea's mind tripped over itself as it caught up with the implications. She looked up at Martha whose face betrayed the same alarm. 'He can't, can he?'

Martha glanced at her. 'Let's watch.'

This time it was Dr Gibson who lifted the glass vessel and gently placed the bird inside, before setting it atop the stand. The bird's wings fluttered against the walls of its prison until it settled, but Thea could see it leaning against the glass with its open beak panting in panic, such was her proximity. She didn't feel much calmer than it looked, although suspected the next few minutes were going to develop better for her.

Dr Gibson was now sweating profusely, fired by the excitement of the audience. His voice was quiet and more measured than before but still cut across the hush of the room. 'Ladies and gentlemen, we now see how essential the air around us is, to life itself.'

He began to crank the handle of the pump, turning slowly at first, and becoming gradually more vigorous. From the corner of her eye Thea saw Martha's breath quicken, her eyes fixed on the glass vessel and its stricken inhabitant. She turned her head away for a moment and her eyes caught Meg, standing just out of the wings, fists balled and tense and her eyes flicking from the unfolding scene to the audience that witnessed it. Thea saw her gasp as a delicate but urgent flutter seemed to fill the auditorium. The bird had sagged to the base of the vessel, and was twisting itself, convulsing as it visibly gasped. The audience was becoming restless.

The shout came from Thea's left. 'For goodness sake, stop it, won't you?' It was Martha. Her eyes were wide and incredulous fury filled her face. The footsteps came from Thea's right, Meg had stepped onto the stage at Martha's interjection, so close she was almost within touching distance.

'Never fear, my lady,' boomed Dr Gibson, his frenzied hands still winding at the crank with a sickening rapidity, '*that* is only a bird, but *this* is science!' Thea looked away to spare herself the sight of the bird flopping over and over on itself in desperation, and her own eyes met others of a deep blue. Meg was staring at her. She was unquestionably agitated, but there was something else. Her eyes flicked quickly to Dr Gibson and back again. 'Please?' she murmured so quietly only Tobias Morton could hear.

All of a sudden Thea understood and nodded at Meg before drawing herself up, hoping to affect a convincing resonance. 'Good God, man, spare the bird. An audience can't stomach this.' A murmuring of agreement swelled from the subdued crowd and Dr Gibson's face spun to hers and hesitated. Her eyes bore into his. 'You have proved your point, Doctor,' she said quietly. 'A fascinating display all round.'

The winding stopped and she saw the frenzy slip from his face. Dr Gibson could pass Martha off as a hysterical woman, but Thea now understood Meg's plea. The male voice must be recognised for authority and reason. There was an almost imperceptible nod as Dr Gibson stood and pressed a lever to allow air back into the chamber. With a flurry, the bird stopped its convulsing and righted itself, fluttering to smooth its wings. The peak of the tension slipped from the room, and Thea felt two bodies exhale near her, Martha's, and Meg's. She took Martha's arm and squeezed it, but her eyes were drawn to the Doctor's assistant, who stared at her, unwavering. The intensity of those azure and turquoise eyes that seemed to bore into her soul. That brow flicking in recognition, the tiny twitch of the lips and the nod of appreciation. God, how did Meg always know?

Dr Gibson was busy gathering his pride and concluding the lecture with a flourish as Meg stepped toward her, their eyes locked together. 'Thank you,' whispered Meg, barely audibly. Thea saw her draw breath to speak again, but suddenly the crowd was up and leaving and Dr Gibson strode towards them. As he passed Thea he nodded acknowledgement, but the gloss of performance was gone and he wiped his brow as Meg took his elbow and steered them away to the side of the stage.

'I did say.' Thea was still so close she could hear the accusation in Meg's voice. She took Martha's hand to stop her leaving as she stilled to better hear the muted words.

Dr Gibson inclined his head. 'You did, but this is science, Meg. Sacrifices must be made.' Thea was surprised to hear an almost pleading note in his voice.

'No.' Meg squared and looked him directly in the eye, steel and determination writ on her face. She poked an index finger forcefully towards the audience. '*This* is entertainment. I will not have that spectacle again.'

Dr Gibson half turned away and back again, his hands on his hips. 'So the show goes your way again.'

Meg's fierce gaze didn't waver. 'As soon as you have any valid contribution of your own to share then please do. Until then, the bird goes.'

Thea stood stock still, mesmerised. This Meg, assertive and with a sonorous, rich tone to her voice was a far cry from the assistant who tripped, ladylike around the apparatus, who languished by the static machine to offer an electrified kiss to hopeful punters. Suddenly Thea understood. Meg was the brains behind the lectures.

The realisation hit her full tilt. For all her admiration of Meg – her eyes, that kiss and that *spark*, it had never once occurred to Thea that Meg could be the driving force. *That* was what captivated her. She wanted to *be* like her. To have a purpose, to have strength, to be part of something tangible that people could respect for more than wealth. Dr Gibson was the frontman, the performer, the assistant to *her* endeavour. And yet she played that role, night after night with the grace to endure it because that was her path to success. She had *made* it a success. A small exclamation escaped her at the realisation and both Dr Gibson and Meg glanced up, catching her staring. Meg smiled before Dr Gibson strode off into the wings and she followed. What grit she must have, thought Thea. What fierce intelligence and relentless determination to fight for this position. A man's voice may hold more power in the immediacy of the moment, but Meg was proof that a woman could triumph quietly and decidedly in the fullness of time. She was proof that a woman may dictate the cut of her own cloth if only she believed. Thea looked between her on the one side, and the strong woman who captivated her heart on the other. *If only I had the mettle of either of them*, Thea thought, as she clung to Martha's hand and followed her out of the hall.

CHAPTER 26

Thea awoke with a knot in her stomach, part nerves and part excitement. She was back at Milford and today she would see Martha for the first time in two weeks. Martha had stayed in London to oversee the installation of running water at Foxmore Square but had promised to be back for today. Today was why Thea was nervous – a dinner with the Duke and Duchess of Hartford, and their son, George Crowe. Her mother had insisted that she return to Milford to prepare and had fussed over Thea for the entire two weeks. While she had managed to sneak away to see Jane and Edgar once or twice, she had mostly been primped and prepared. What she was going to wear, how her hair would be done, how she would borrow some vermillion blush from Tabitha, even how she must stand and where she and Lord Axbury must sit together. Thea did her best to bear it with good grace as she knew her mother meant only the best for the family. The one slight relief was that the Jefferys were also invited so half of Mrs Morell's attention was invested in her other daughter. Ursula commiserated with her, as did her father, out of earshot of her mother.

Today she had been bathed, dressed and done up by Agnes and Miss Walters – her mother's ladies maid who had been drafted in to help. Her dress was a rich textured silk in light gold, an intricate pattern embroidered in black thread winding out from its edges. The stomacher was embroidered with copper, gold and black flowers - even to her it seemed positively luxurious. Her hair was piled impossibly high and her face was powdered white like Tabitha always wore it. Much to her consternation she also detected the off whiff of clove from her own eyebrows. At the due hour she took her place in the hall as instructed to welcome the guests.

It wasn't a large party, only twenty in all, and she welcomed them graciously and warmly. The Jefferys were as joyless as usual but Tabitha flitted around Ralph enough to bring enthusiasm to any corner of the room. The Crowes arrived in a very grand carriage. Eldest daughter Helena was lately married and youngest Cassandra still in London, so the party consisted of only the Duke and Duchess of Hartford and George Crowe. As he stepped down from the carriage in a deep plum three-piece Thea had to admit that he was exceptionally handsome.

She dipped a curtsey as he took up her hand and kissed it. 'I am delighted to see you again, Miss Morell, thank you so much for the invitation to your beautiful house. It is full of character.'

He flashed her a smile laden with perfect teeth and she inclined her head generously. 'I am delighted you like Milford, Earl Axbury. I understand Hawkdean House is quite its equal.'

'Indeed I have always found it quite agreeable, but I hope that you will have the chance to judge it for yourself sometime.' He smiled again and caught her with an intense stare. Thea met it with what she knew was a slightly goofy grin but hoped for the best.

He was soon moved on and she looked around to find Stanhope Grimston next in line. 'Mr Grimston,' she said. 'What a delight to see you again.'

'Mmm,' he muttered, feigning politeness. 'It must be at least six months.'

'Eight, I think,' smiled Thea, falsely. 'Although Lady Foxmore and I did talk of you with Mr William Constable of the Royal Society when we visited the north. I assume you are aware of him.' She couldn't help herself and fixed him with a knowing stare. She was desperate for him to know that she could see through his lies. He muttered something about Mr Constable being a good man and wandered off.

Before long all guests were sipping wine in the drawing room, but one was missing. Martha was yet to arrive and Thea was beginning to worry – lateness was one of Martha's pet hates but anything could have happened on the journey from London. The minutes ticked past and no word came. They delayed dinner for as long as possible but eventually moved through to the dining room in order that Mrs Smeaton's duck in orange wasn't spoiled. Thea's heart was in her feet. Either there had been a misfortune or Martha had thought better of the visit. For all their promises, perhaps this was too much? Thea solemnly took a seat on Lord Axbury's left-hand side just as there was an almighty clattering of hooves on the driveway. She jumped up at a commotion in the hallway and a figure burst through the dining room door. It was Martha, dressed in a deep green riding habit which complemented the gold of her hair. She had tied her scarf like a stock to keep out the cold and peeled off her leather gloves, finger by finger as she stood over the room.

'I'm terribly sorry everyone, carriage broke a wheel at Ashtead. I had to ride in the end – wouldn't have missed it for the world.' She addressed the room at large but spoke only to the woman she was here for. Her eyes locked on Thea's whose heart turned over in her chest at the sight of her. Everyone who had jumped to their feet in welcome began to take their seats once more as Martha took her place, her eyes never leaving Thea's.

George Crowe chatted incessantly during dinner. The more she tried to engage others across the table or on her left, the more insistent he became. She didn't dare stare too hard at Martha, although her eyes kept wandering. Instead, she revelled in the times Martha spoke so she had an excuse to rest her eyes in that direction. On the brief occasions when their gaze met it was electric.

As George continued his monologue she shot a look of resignation at Ursula, who then looked at their father. She was sure she saw him nod, slightly.

'My sister is too modest, Lord Axbury,' said Ursula loudly, commanding the attention of the table, 'but you must ask her about her greatest passion and the subject in which she is held in high esteem.' There was silence for a few seconds. Mrs Morell's fork paused, her eyes wide, and Thea saw Martha hide a smile while George regarded Ursula, and then Thea with interest.

'Indeed I must,' he said gallantly. 'I have danced with her in London and engaged her for this past half hour and yet she has mentioned nothing of it.'

Thea paused, unsure of her approach. 'Embroidery!' came the frenetic shout from across the table. They all turned to look at Mrs Morell, who at least lowered the fork to her plate and inclined her head graciously to the Earl. 'My daughter enjoys embroidery and is,' she paused, 'very good at it.'

'And science,' said Mr Morell clearly, from the opposite end of the table. The look his wife shot him could have punctured steel. Thea pressed her lips together and pushed an orange segment around her plate

'Is that so?' asked George curiously, turning to Thea and actually looking at her, possibly for the first time, she thought.

'She collects natural history,' said Ursula, warming to her subject. 'Insects, fossils, fish, animals, that kind of thing.'

'And her knowledge is among the best in the county,' interjected Mr Morell. 'My daughter is quite the scholar, Lord Axbury.' He fixed George with a gaze which was at once full of challenge and pride, and it was all Thea could do not to leap across the table and hug him. The silence stretched on as George turned to Thea once again, sat back and considered her carefully. Martha's head was angled down but her eyes were on him, hawk-like. Mrs Morell simply had her eyes shut.

'I would love to hear about your insects, Miss Morell,' he said, smoothly, 'how on earth do you keep them from wandering off?' And with that, Thea found herself talking about butterflies as George listened intently.

Eventually dinner was complete and the party repaired to the drawing room. Usually, the gentlemen would split off but Mrs Morell had suggested a recital on the piano to keep the party mixed and her girls in the way of the eligible. 'Ursula will play and Thea can turn,' she announced, scowling at them both as they trooped through to a warming fire and more wine poured by Mr Wade and Mr Croft. Thea dutifully took up her place by the pianoforte – her role was no accident. She knew her playing was unlikely to impress and her figure would be better showcased in standing by the new instrument, purchased especially for this dinner. She drew herself into her most elegant posture, thinking only of Martha. Tabitha had Ralph Jefferys pinned in a corner and Mr Grimston held the rest of the family so Martha sat with George on the couch facing the piano, where Mrs Morell had artfully suggested he settle.

As hard as she tried, Thea couldn't prevent an occasional glance in their direction. There was some chat between them but mostly Martha sat and watched, a commanding presence with her legs crossed and her arm spread across the back of the seat. Every time Thea raised her eyes Martha was staring, brooding and beautiful. Thea longed to go to her, to get her alone and to tell her how desperately she had missed her. Martha had raced to Milford, against the events of the day to be here for her and to support her. She felt truly loved. Heat rose inside as dark eyes bored into her, roaming her figure as she leant and turned the pages as Ursula played. She resolved to extract Martha at the next opportunity and take her away – anywhere, so they could be alone, even just for a second.

There were only two pages remaining in the piece. Thea's glances became ever more frequent and her breath crescendoed with the tempo of the reel. She could see Martha's fingers white from gripping the soft fabric of the couch as she stared over, the intensity between them sucking the breath from her. Finally the last page was turned and as Ursula held the concluding note Thea strode over to the couch, her heart beating as fast as her feet took her.

'Lady Foxmore, I wonder if you would join me in the library? There is something I wish to discuss.'

Martha's eyes shone as she stood, never breaking her gaze with Thea's. 'I would be delighted, Miss Morell.' The words dripped out like warm honey and Thea's insides melted with them.

She nodded and went to turn, but George stood quickly. 'I wonder if I might trouble you for an audience also, Miss Morell? I would dearly love to see the collection I have heard so much about. When you have finished with Lady Foxmore of course.'

Thea stared at him, having almost forgotten his presence and had to gather herself. Before she could speak Mrs Morell pushed in front of her.

'Of course you must see it, Lord Axbury,' she trilled, 'We would be delighted to show you, but Ursula has another piece she has been dying to play for you, don't you Ursula?'

'I do?' Mrs Morell shot her a warning look. 'Oh yes, I do.'

She began to play, Thea reluctantly returned to the piano and the party took their seats once more while Mrs Morell bustled out of the room casting sweet smiles at George Crowe. Thea was pleased that Ursula had chosen a spirited jig – it almost distracted from the shouts and the crashing coming from the direction of the cabinet and Mrs Morell's shouts to Mrs Phibbs and Mr Wade, rudely drafted in to unlock and uncover the collection, she assumed. Despite the racket Thea couldn't take her eyes from Martha, who only gave her a wry smile.

As Ursula held the final note Mrs Morell slipped back in the door, slightly out of breath. 'How wonderful, Ursula, and quite worth the wait I am sure you would say, Lord Axbury?' He graciously agreed.

'And now Thea will take you to the collection herself.' She gave Thea a small shove in the direction of the door.

'I'll come too.' It was Mr Grimston. Then, the Duke and Duchess and the Jefferys decided to join and before long they were all crammed in the old library and perusing the shelves. Thea still didn't dare to speak in front of the group at large, but did answer the polite questions from the Duke, the Duchess and George, whilst being careful to not show too much intelligence or enthusiasm. She was almost pleased at Grimston's loud pontificating on many of her curiosities – even though he was mostly making it up.

Eventually the group ran out of wine and repaired back to the drawing room. Thea made to intercept Martha, but as she left the room a waiting George caught her arm and led her to an alcove by the library. 'I thank you for showing us the collection, Miss Morell, it is particularly diverting.'

'It is?' she asked innocently, suspecting she knew where this was going.

'The collections, and the – old fish – and suchlike. When you speak of it, it is as if I have known it all my life.'

She had often wondered if she might panic in this moment, or bolt. But now it was here and delivered with such false solemnity she felt unexpectedly calm. She crossed her arms in front of her. 'Is it?'

Her direct and confident manner made him falter. 'Uh, yes,' he said, swallowing, clearly not used to being questioned while he attempted charm.

'Is it the fish that you find so interesting,' she asked, 'or is it the prospect of renewing your inappropriate advances of the Harrington's ball?'

At least he had the grace to look uncomfortable. 'I can assure you that is not my intention on this occasion, Miss Morell, and I apologise for my behaviour on that night.' He did seem relatively contrite, she thought, as he checked over his shoulder at the empty corridor.

'And so what is your purpose in detaining me?' she asked, more calmly than she felt. 'I have guests to entertain, Lord Axbury.'

He regarded her carefully, the stare almost uncomfortable. 'Despite my reputation,' he began, now with a little more conviction, 'I am not a stupid man.' She inclined her head in acknowledgement. 'It is difficult to endure the number of London seasons we both have without gaining an insight into the character of those you most frequently encounter.' This, certainly, was true. 'And we cannot deny the obligations that you and I feel as the heirs to our family estates.'

'I cannot argue on either count,' she acknowledged, now almost keen to see where this conversation would lead.

'Even though your father has declined to take a title, the Morell name is still extremely well-renowned and your estate is among the biggest in the country. And I flatter myself that, for many, a match with my family is not undesirable.'

Understated at last, she thought. She remembered her mother and sister's raptures at the thought of his wealth. Numerous estates including rich coal seams, banking and building. His fortune was significant and secure. She almost felt guilty about not telling him about the mortgage, but he was right about the size of the Morell estate and managed well it would be lucrative. 'Indeed it is not,' she agreed again, 'and so I do wonder, Lord Axbury, why it is you are not yet linked to another family by marriage?'

He let a small smile escape. 'Wealth and the Hartford name have been kind to me,' he said honestly, tucking a thumb into the pocket of his waistcoat. 'I have been lucky to be able to... enjoy my time as a bachelor and I have been loath to move into the next phase of my life which I am aware may be more...' He searched for a word. 'Limiting.'

She cocked her head to the side, still unsure of his meaning. 'And you are now ready to be limited, or you are under too much pressure from your family to be so?'

'A little of both,' he acknowledged. 'It is time that I marry, and I have appreciated your frankness over the years we have been acquainted. Now that I understand you and your interests a little better I hope that you will appreciate mine. I wish to have a partner in managing the numerous estates and I believe you are rational and pragmatic.'

'You have come to this conclusion through seeing my dead fish?' she asked, genuinely interested in what had piqued his resolution.

'In part,' he said, 'your clear independence and quick mind would certainly be an asset to our union. I have thought for some time that you would be a good match – you are principled and I believed I may have mishandled the opportunity by my approach to you at the Harrington's ball. I had not dared to think that you would consider my offer, but I believe you regarded me with something bordering interest during your sister's recital and I dared to hope once again.'

How she regarded him during Ursula's recital? With a start she realised what he must mean. She certainly couldn't tell him she had been enchanted not by him, but by the woman next to him. 'Ah,' she said, thinking quickly. 'I may have been experiencing a little digestive discomfort.' Right. She would have preferred that some other words had presented themselves, but they were out now. Could she save any pride? 'I find the acid of the oranges can cause some reflux.' No. Clearly she could not.

He looked more cowed than shocked. 'I see. Then am I to assume that you would not consider a proposal favourably?'

She thought for a moment. Certainly, it was not what she wanted, but in the absence of any long-term plan which saved the prospects of her family, she should hear what he had to say. 'I would be interested to hear your thoughts,' she said, resting a hand on the marble pillar beside them.

He nodded. 'Thank you. Quite simply, I would propose marriage to you. Our families would be pleased at the advantageous union and desist with their ongoing campaigns towards us. I would gain a sensible wife I could tolerate and I believe we may even have interests in common. You would provide an heir to both the Hartford and Morell estates.' He paused and she was about to ask if there was anything else for her in this arrangement, before he held up a finger, and went on. 'I had been considering what else I could offer to make this agreement attractive to you, and tonight I think I have settled upon it. You are entranced by your collection of dead and old things, and your mother believes that this is not conducive to a good match, am I correct?'

Perhaps he was more perceptive than she thought. 'You are correct,' she confirmed.

He nodded once. 'And she is right in many cases. But I would be happy to personally support the continuation of your hobby and provide the finances for you to do so.' Although she bristled at the word "hobby", she thought it best not to correct him, at least until she had time to mull over the implications of his offer.

She considered him carefully. There was the hint of a wary look in his eye. 'Is that all?' she asked. 'You get support with the estates and an heir, and I get to pursue my interest in natural philosophy?'

He looked as if he were considering whether his next point should be vocalised. 'Almost,' he said, casting his eyes to rest on a floral arrangement across the hall. 'I do wish to start on the best terms with you, Miss Morell, so I will be honest. I enjoy women, and do not wish to give them up entirely on marriage.' She blanched a little at the candid nature of his request. 'I am sorry, I have shocked you,' he said.

'A little,' she said, honestly. But if only she could say the same thing to him, she would. 'Why tell me now? There are plenty of marriages which operate on this principle and certainly without prior agreement. We both know that if we married and you chose to take other women, I would have no recourse.'

'True,' he said, turning back to face her. 'But ladies have their ways of making their displeasure known and I should not like to deal with histrionics or moods on a regular basis. It is best that it is part of the arrangement.'

She acknowledged this. 'And what of my relationships? Would you be happy that I were to do the same with other men?' She was teasing him and they both knew it. It was common for men to take other women within marriage, almost expected. It would be a reputation-shredding scandal for a woman.

'I admire the boldness of your enquiry,' he smiled, 'but while it would be best that you act with discretion I will not limit any activity within reason.'

'Within reason,' she said, not willing to give up this prime bargaining tool. 'I would wish to be able to socialise with ladies of my own choice on a schedule of my own. Appreciating, of course, the need for unity between us in society.'

He thought for a moment. 'That would be acceptable.' She held his gaze, matching his resolve. 'Can I dare to hope we have an agreement?' he asked, and she smiled.

'Your proposal is intriguing, Lord Axbury,' she said. 'But you must give me time to consider it. You offer much I could enjoy but you have to know that this also asks a great deal of me and I do have alternatives to consider.'

'Of course.' He stepped back. 'My proposal will remain open unless either of us becomes otherwise engaged, however, do be aware of the pressure that we are both under from our families. I will await your word at your earliest convenience.'

At her nod of assent he lifted her hand and kissed it. 'I can be a gentleman, Miss Morell, and I promise faithfully that I would not come between you and your dead fish.' He flashed her a smile as he stepped backwards into the hallway and she had to admit he was amusing, when the moment took him.

Once alone she leaned back against the wall, gathering her breath. As she composed herself and smoothed her dress Martha emerged from the drawing room. Thea grabbed her and they wordlessly darted into the library before any further distraction could occur. Once in, Martha pushed Thea swiftly up against the door, clicking it shut and planting a deep kiss on Thea's lips in one deft movement.

'Am I glad to see you,' mumbled Thea as they broke away.

'Did he ask?' Martha's eyes flitted between hers.

'Yes. A considered proposal. He was not as disagreeable as I had imagined but one could certainly hope for a more auspicious start to a marriage.'

'And what was your response?' asked Martha, nervously.

'I have delayed him, for now.' Thea ran a finger down Martha's cheek who closed her eyes and leaned into the touch.

'You know I can't offer you anything that he can.'

Thea dropped a chaste kiss on the line of her jaw. 'You give me more that I want.'

Martha grasped Thea's wrists and made her meet her eyes. 'Nothing of substance. Security, independence, any standing that will give you a platform to achieve the things you have always wanted. Space for collections, a grand estate, money to spend on your scholarship. I can provide none of that.'

Thea freed her wrists from Martha's yielding hands. 'You don't have to offer me anything other than yourself.'

'You know what I mean, Thea.' Martha's face was pleading.

'Look,' said Thea, running a hand round the back of Martha's neck. 'I cannot know what will be, and neither can you, but for now, I am glad you're back.' This, at least drew a smile from Martha.

'I have missed you.'

'And I might only have five minutes with you before we have to rejoin the party.' She placed another gentle kiss on Martha's lips, but Martha shifted away with a knowing smile. 'What?'

'How do you feel about coming home with me?'

Thea groaned. 'Oh don't tease. I'd give anything for that.'

'It's cleared with your father.' Martha's eyes shone. 'I told him you were helping me to record the changes in my plant collections since I've been away and that we'll need a few days at least. He was delighted that you have renewed your interest and your mother is, of course, happy with it now that George is. I told them you have to come now as I was so late back we can't wait until tomorrow as I need to unpack the most delicate samples in their carrying cases before the morning.'

Thea grinned. 'They agreed to that?'

Martha shrugged. 'As long as we wait until the Crowes have gone. Apparently I'm a good influence on you.'

Within two more hours the Foxmore carriage had returned to collect them. There were more kisses on the journey back to Denbury – charge coursed through Thea's body and she longed to get Martha alone and upstairs. She followed her lover helplessly out of the carriage then into the house and the library, her head fogged with desire.

Martha stood over the boxes of specimens. 'Right, which ones do you want to take?'

Thea stared at her, and then at the plant samples in front of them. 'You really mean to do this now?'

She received an apologetic face in response. 'They'll spoil if we don't.'

Thea grinned and rolled her eyes before gathering a handful of sheets.

Martha straightened up and kissed Thea's unimpressed lips. 'Just the most fragile, my love, and I promise I will take you straight to bed.'

CHAPTER 27

T hea woke to spring light streaming through the windows and looked up to Martha in a blue and gold silken robe, pulling open the curtains. 'Morning, sleepyhead.'

Thea stretched and took in the boxes all around her. She was still in the library, on the couch. 'Oh, what hour is it?'

'Almost nine.' Martha smiled tenderly. 'A matchmaking dinner and cataloguing in one evening is too much for anyone. I have only just woken myself.'

'You slept here too?'

'Of course.' Martha lowered herself to the seat next to Thea, their knees touching. 'How could I be parted from you again so soon?'

Thea pulled her in and kissed her gently until there was a knock at the door. Martha sprang up and Thea tried to look unruffled. 'Yes?'

Mr Fletcher entered and they relaxed. 'Sorry to disturb, your lady-ship, a letter just arrived by express.'

'Thank you, Fletcher.' Martha opened it quickly as Thea sat up, concerned. Letters arriving by express were rarely good news. Thea relaxed as Martha's face softened and a wry smile curved her lips as she read. 'It's from Mr Pickles, there's an experiment he's been dying to show us which requires a thunderstorm, and one is due tonight. He requests our company from seven for dinner and afterwards for some "electrifying entertainment".'

Thea smiled, 'That sounds terrifying, if I know Edgar!'

'Indeed,' said Martha, 'Your father and Ursula are invited too so at least good sense should prevail. Oh, and Mr Grimston.' Her face darkened. 'Twice in two days, lucky us. Anyway.' She held out a hand to Thea as she stood and a smile reappeared on her lips. 'Breakfast?'

They arrived at Pook End as storm clouds burgeoned on the horizon. Edgar welcomed them warmly. 'Ah, my dear friends, welcome, welcome to what should be a truly enlightening evening! Lady Foxmore, it is a delight to have you back with us, you look radiant, my dear, as do all the ladies in the party. And Thea, I cannot tell you what a wonder it is to welcome you back to where you belong – the laboratory!' She smiled warmly, very glad to be back. What the future would be for her interests she still wasn't sure, but with the immediate danger from her mother now dampened due to George's interest, she was pleased to be amongst the collections. 'Let us waste no time,' continued Edgar. 'To the laboratory, where I shall explain.'

The party dutifully followed him down the winding passages to the brightly lit room. Thea looked around for a new, grand machine – but there was none. In the centre of the room was a kite, propped against a telescope. A long string, extended from its base with a key attached close to the bottom. Edgar buzzed around it with excitement as his audience looked expectant.

'Tonight, my friends, we will recreate one of the most spectacular experiments ever undertaken by man. Or woman.' He made a nod to the ladies of the group. 'It has been recently completed by Benjamin Franklin in America to great success. Tonight, we draw electricity out of the sky!'

The group looked a little more concerned as Edgar continued. 'Of course, this is not just any kite, the iron conductor at its top will gather a charge. The electrical fluid will travel down the string, and the key will spark when a human finger is placed near it. Tonight, this will be my finger.' He glowed with pride as he stood, the object of their collective attention.

For a little while a reverent silence fell, broken only by a snort from Mr Grimston. 'Don't be ridiculous, man. This was brought to the Royal Society two years ago by Peter Collinson – on behalf of Franklin. It was laughed out of the room even then.'

Thea saw a spark of delight in Edgar's eyes. 'I was hoping you might mention that, Grimston,' he said eagerly. 'The London society did not like it, but the French did and my contacts have informed me of relevant developments. Tonight we will recreate it on English soil and bring ourselves in line with the continent. Can't let the French get away from us can we, eh?' He winked at Mr Grimston, drawing a huff and folded arms. As pleased as Thea was to see Mr Grimston's argument go up in smoke, she was still concerned Edgar might do the same.

'Um, Edgar. Do you remember that tree at Milford, which was struck by lightning–?'

Edgar grinned. 'I do, Miss Morell, and I would expect no less caution from a brain like yours, but fear not! The lightning does not strike the kite, the electricity is gathered from the clouds themselves.'

The flaw in the plan seemed too obvious. 'But what if it does strike the kite?' Ursula asked, warily.

'Then I shall be standing under cover and holding this end of the string which is made from silk and does not transmit the force. Don't you worry yourselves, ladies, the plan is foolproof!'

Thea did worry, and so did everyone else judging by their expressions as they were ushered through to dinner.

Conversation was of the London season, the excitement of Mr Morell's election to the Royal Society, and of course an account of which parts of Mr Grimston's collections currently enthralled its president. Edgar rolled his eyes at Thea across the table. When they were fully satisfied and waiting for the storm to commence in earnest,

Martha, Ursula and Mr Morell went to investigate some new equipment of Edgar's, and Mr Grimston poked around the collections by himself. Thea cornered their host and tried to talk him out of the experiment, but he would have none of it – he was determined and there was nothing to be done with an experimental philosopher in this state.

'My wonderful Thea, do not worry.' He patted his large stomach. 'You know, I have spent my life collecting – and what do I have to show for it? A messy room full of stuff. This is my only chance to make any kind of mark on the page of natural philosophy – a science that will change the prospects of humanity in ways that we cannot yet dream of!'

Thea couldn't help but smile at his enthusiasm, but his words brought her familiar anxiety rising to the surface. He must have seen her face fall. 'Come now, Thea, you are not still having doubts? I heard of Ursula's triumph at the British Museum and understand you, once again, hid your light under a bushel.'

She shuffled her feet and looked up into his concerned eyes. 'I dare say my mother would allow me to engage again, but like you say, I don't just want a room full of stuff. Natural philosophy may change the world,' she said, folding her arms in frustration, 'I simply cannot see my part in it. Nobody of note will listen to a woman.'

'Then you must alter their perceptions,' said Edgar. 'Nothing changes unless people like you stand up and make fusty old men think differently. You have the ability.'

'Do I?' she asked. 'I have no collection, no money of my own and no value in the world of knowledge. Even if I did, I cannot muster the confidence to defend it in front of those I know will dismiss me, despite how ardently I wish I could.'

Edgar's face folded into its most kindly crinkle. 'Then change their minds. You can, Thea. You are phenomenal.'

She blinked against the moisture in her eyes. 'I will try to share your confidence, Edgar, I truly will. But currently I have only two great loves in my life, and it is likely that I will be able to fulfil or enjoy neither. Certainly not both.' Tears pricked now, for a different reason.

Edgar took her gently by the arms and pulled her round to face him. 'Thea, I have watched you since you were young and you are quite without equal in my acquaintance. You and Martha are formidable – both together and apart. You have determination in spades and I have never doubted you – not once. Opportunities will present themselves. I would only plead with you that when they do, you must have as great a faith in yourself as I have.'

She gave him a weak smile and a strong hug. 'I promise I will try.'

He drew her close. 'You will observe, reason, and draw conclusions, Thea.' He still held her tight. 'Because that is your nature, and because it is what you have been taught. The light will get brighter and the picture will clarify, I promise you.'

Thea grinned weakly and wiped away a tear. 'I will try.'

'Of course you will,' he said, beaming. At that moment a boom of rolling thunder filled the air and rain battered the windows. Edgar's eyes lit. 'It is time. Remember, Thea, without risk, there is no progress. Believe in yourself!'

He grabbed the kite and its peripherals and turned to the room. 'My ladies and gentlemen!' His resonant voice was punctuated by cracks of thunder. 'Please join me outside for the climax of tonight's sizzling entertainment!' He ushered them towards the garden and dashed into the howling rain. Thea ran through the door and into the back porch of the house. She followed Edgar into the weather but stumbled back under cover when the rain drenched her within seconds.

Martha appeared at her side at a run. 'He's not actually doing it is he?'

When Thea met Martha's gaze she saw her own fears reflected back. She nodded. 'And there's no trying to talk him out of it. He's deter-mined.' Mr Morell pushed Ursula fast through the door, followed by Mr Grimston who lingered at the back. Almost the whole party was now squeezed under cover, inches from the thunderstorm.

It wasn't easy to make out the figures in the darkness, but the regular lightning illuminated vignettes of activity. Edgar and his butler making for the stables, the kite held aloft above the meadow. Edgar taking the tension and running backwards towards the stables' overhang while the butler jumped and threw to aid the launch.

The thunder was coming more regularly now and lightning forked from the billowing clouds. Edgar pulled on the rope and watched the kite soar, caught easily by the wind. He laughed with delight and let out the string to increase the altitude until the key was about two feet from his hands. The tension and the clean, astringent smell of lightning and spent electricity returned Thea to Doctor Gibson's – or should she say Meg's – electricity lectures. She could almost hear the click, click, click of the metal chain on stone, and she felt the tension rise and her heart pound. She was wound so tight she jumped as she felt a pressure on her waist, but then reached round to grasp Martha's nervous hand, squeezing it tight.

The party watched wide-eyed as the kite danced in the gale and the hemp string began to bristle, just as Ella's hair had that day – a day that seemed a lifetime ago – when she touched the electrical machine. Edgar watched the static progress down the string, inch by inch, until it reached the key. He moved forwards into the elements and extended a slightly shaking finger. Everyone held their breath.

When the finger came around two inches from the key, a spark suddenly shot out and arced across into his body. It was brilliant and blue against the dark of the night. Edgar jolted, and then looked back at them with delight writ large on his gnarled face. They all cheered and clapped with relief as he strode forwards out into the weather and held his arms aloft in triumph.

The audience's gaze collectively shot to the heavens as a deafening clap of thunder cleft the air. In a split second the fork of lightning had hit the kite and travelled down the string. This time it didn't stop at the key, or at the silk which had become wet in the driving rain. Edgar was thrown like a ragdoll, his limp form bouncing as it hit the ground and his large stomach protruding above the grass in the meadow. Thea's shout was taken by the gale as she and Martha ran out into the storm, racing to their friend as the charred remains of the kite danced away in the turbulent air.

In the days that followed Edgar's death, Thea spent a long time out of doors, either at Milford or Denbury. Her head was full of the potential of natural philosophy and the risk it posed filled her mind. There was still a nip in the spring air, but it helped to numb the loss and confusion. The first spring flowers tentatively showing their hand reminded her that there was still hope to be found in the world, and moving, whether walking the estate or planting out with Scip or Martha avoided endless idle hours to think. Both her mother and Scip protested at her working the soil, but the dirtier she got, the better she seemed to feel.

She spent as many nights as she could with Martha and a day at Pook End helping to organise the house and the staff. The estate would go to a cousin of Edgar's – nobody had even known that he had one – but Edgar had specific instructions about his moveable property which would take a few days to arrange. While the papers were with the attorney in the village there was little more to be done and so Martha and Thea resumed their garden endeavours.

As the days passed her grief turned to an unresolved desire for action. She needed to express how she felt but there were no words, needed to honour his memory but wasn't sure how. They had written to Mr Franklin in Philadelphia to inform him of the outcome of the experiment. It was important to record results, positive or negative, and they earnestly hoped that awareness of Edgar's sacrifice would help to avoid future tragedies. A last, handwritten legacy distinguishing the prolific man of letters. She reflected long and hard on that last conversation with Edgar. She wanted to believe in herself as he had urged her to – the problem was that she just didn't.

One morning, a week after the fateful event, Thea, Ursula and Martha sat in the library at Milford. Samples of spring flowers were strewn around them waiting to be pressed, but no one could quite muster the enthusiasm. Suddenly Thea was startled out of her torpor by shouts coming from the driveway. The three of them dashed out of the library, Martha bringing Ursula, and rounded the corner to see Stanhope Grimston barging through the grand entrance to Milford, glowering at Mrs Morell and Mrs Phibbs who blocked his path.

'Where is she?!' he shouted, his face purple with rage.

'Mr Grimston, calm yourself for heavens sake,' said Mrs Morell, stepping back while Mrs Phibbs stood her ground. 'Who can you mean?'

He spotted Thea who had put herself in view, closely flanked by a protective Martha. 'Her!' he bellowed, pushing past Mrs Phibbs and brandishing his cane in Thea's direction. 'That opportunist! I am here to demand what is rightfully mine, and I will have it.'

Mr Morell and Scip raced in from the garden. Thea's father drew himself up against the assault on his family. 'Grimston, what is the meaning of this commotion in my house?'

Mr Grimston rounded on him. 'Your daughter, Morell, has done me out of my inheritance, no doubt through her disgusting, manipulative ways.'

'Do you know what he's talking about?' Mr Morell shot a cautious glance to Thea.

Thea shook her head. 'Not a clue.'

'Would you care to elaborate?' Mr Morell asked the red face in front of him.

'Edgar Pickles has *apparently* left the entirety of his cabinet collection to your daughter.' Mr Grimston took a breath. 'All of it! As if a female will appreciate it or could even comprehend its importance!'

Mr Morell stifled a smile and turned to his daughter. 'Did you know about this, Thea?'

'No.' She didn't bother to hide her own smile and had no wish to express her actual level of surprise in front of Mr Grimston.

Mr Morell gave a nonchalant shrug in the direction of their visitor. 'Well, Grimston, if it is as you say I fear there is nothing to be done. If the will is clear, the collection is Thea's. I'm sure she will use it well.'

Mr Grimston's face was now almost entirely puce. Thea almost worried that they may lose two of their number in one week. 'She will not! I am his oldest friend and I know he always meant it to be mine. Apparently the change in the will was recent. I demand she forfeit it to me directly.'

'And why would I do that, Mr Grimston?' Thea moved closer towards him and didn't break eye contact. Martha, Mrs Phibbs and Mr Morell protectively moved within reaching distance. Mr Grimston's eyes flicked between the three of them and he pointed a fat finger in Thea's face.

'You have manipulated him! Inveigled yourself into his affections with all your prettiness and girliness.' He waved his hands in the air as if trying to be feminine. The effect would have been comic if he wasn't also spitting in anger. 'He would never have considered this otherwise. That collection is rightfully mine and wasted on a woman. And don't think I don't hold you partially responsible.' This time he poked a finger towards Martha, who flinched but stood her ground.

'Well, that is a shame,' said Thea. 'The collection will just have to sit here and rot away, for clearly I am not equal to it and yet Mr Pickles wished I should have it.' She gave a theatrical sigh as a whisper of potential and a gratitude to Edgar spread through her. 'Anyway it was nice of you to bring the news, Mr Grimston, unless father needs you Mrs Phibbs can show you out.'

Mrs Phibbs smiled and Mr Morell indicated that he required no more of Mr Grimston's time. Their visitor gaped like a fish, saw there was nothing more to be done, turned on his heel and stormed out of the door.

The black-clad party encircled the grave as Edgar was lowered into the earth. Thea's tears had created a wet patch on Martha's shoulder as she drew comfort from the arm around her. Despite her coolness in the face of Stanhope Grimston, Thea was, in reality, stunned by the revelation about the Pickles collection. It was a great honour for her to think that Edgar trusted her with his precious apparatus but she had no idea how she would do it justice. Martha had been delighted for her, although Thea suspected the death had hit her harder than she was letting on. She had been quieter than usual over the past few days.

Thea stroked Martha's arm and squeezed her in reassurance as the first soil was scattered, the final words were spoken and the party began to dissipate. She looked up with red eyes and saw Mr Grimston glowering at them from the other side of the grave.

'Don't look now,' she muttered, 'but I think Mr Grimston wants us.'

As Martha glanced over she dropped Thea's arm and shifted her weight. 'I'll go and see – I don't want him near you.'

As Thea turned she saw a figure that made her start. It was Samuel Harrington and he was looking straight at her. If there was one thing she didn't need today it was a discussion about her past indiscretions, but he was already making his way over and there was no polite way to evade him.

She curtseyed. 'Viscount Stockwood. What a delight to see you again.'

He bowed deeply. 'Miss Morell, the pleasure is all mine. Sam. Please.' They made light conversation of the kindness of the weather and the appropriateness of the reverend's words fitting to Edgar's untimely end. After a short while she could bear the forced politeness no longer.

'Sam, please do speak your mind if you wish. I deserve every charge levelled at me with regard to your sister.'

He looked directly at her with only kindness and concern on his face. 'Miss Morell, please do not worry yourself. I can assure you I wish to level no charges at your door.'

She looked directly at him, surprised. 'You don't?'

He shook his head, but shuffled his feet awkwardly. 'I hoped to speak to you on two matters, Miss Morell. The first is to give you news of my sister, if you would wish to hear it?'

Thea gulped. She had tried to banish thoughts of Ella and her betrayal over the past few months but the pain still pricked when it was roused. 'I should be very glad of it. I do hope she is well. And call me Thea, please.'

Sam nodded his thanks. 'Ella has spent a diverting time in Germany which has introduced her to new society and she is to be married to our cousin in Dorset, this summer. He is an upcoming politician.' Sam smiled wanly. 'She does tolerably well, but' – his words faltered – 'but I have observed in her the same melancholy which plagued her prior to our arrival here at Stanbourne last spring.'

Thea didn't need reminding of how miserable the two of them had made one another, particularly not today. 'I am sorry, Sam, I fear that is partly my doing.'

Tears pricked her eyes and he looked alarmed. 'No, no, that is not my meaning. I cannot deny my sister was indeed extremely upset after – well – after the letter came last summer, but that is not your doing. I have spoken to Ella at length and I believe with all my heart that she engaged in the connection with you both willingly and independent-ly.'

Thea stared at him in disbelief. 'You do?'

He still looked awkward but had a determination about him that made her consider that this was the true object of his conversation.

'Moreover, I have never seen her as happy as in the short months she spent with you. My mother and father, despite their obvious reservations, are at least willing to acknowledge that point.'

Thea wasn't sure how to respond. She had known he was the most generous of men but hadn't expected this level of toleration with regard to his sister. It was also surprising to hear of Ella's happiness – they had had a good time, she supposed, whatever Ella's intentions. 'I do hope, for her sake, that she may find contentment,' she said, choosing her words carefully.

He smiled. 'Thea, I wonder if you would be willing to see my sister again?' His eyes made their way back to her and she saw how desperate he was for Ella to be happy.

'You should know that I can't in any way reinstate–'

He raised his hands in concession and kindly cut her off. 'No, not that. It is only that Ella feels very keenly that she said things she should not have and let you down at the end. If she could just explain to you in person, I have hope that it would help her to come to terms with... what happened.'

Thea so desperately wanted to please him and to do anything she could to help, but she certainly wouldn't arrange to see Ella without first discussing it with Martha. 'This is something of a surprise, Sam. Would you grant me leave to think about it?'

He smiled, relief evident on his face. 'Of course. I shall await your word.' He shuffled again and Thea remembered there was more. 'I said there was a second matter.'

She nodded. 'You did.' She waited expectantly, but he pulled at a short twist of his hair and strode over to the old yew in the churchyard.

'You know that most of a yew tree will kill you, but the red bit won't?' he asked, pointing at the vibrant berries that punctuated the deep green foliage.

'I'm sorry?' asked Thea, perplexed.

'The seed inside will make you terribly ill and so eating any of the plant is certainly inadvisable, but the red aril is simply unpleasant, not deadly. My sister taught me that. She has become quite the botanical scholar since meeting you.'

Thea furrowed her brow a little in confusion. 'Is that the second thing you wanted to tell me, Sam?'

'No. It isn't.' He spun around, slid his hat off his head and fiddled with it in front of his waistcoat. A spring of reticence bubbled up in Thea's veins. 'You will remember, I do hope, that I expressed my feelings to you. Once before. At Stanbourne during the assembly. I am sorry that this is not the correct time or place, but I cannot hesitate any longer after seeing you in the crowd today.'

His delivery was halting and the alarm crept further through her body. 'Of course I remember, you were very kind. I hope that events since then have served to assure you that my reluctance was not out of any lack of regard or affection, Sam.' This, at least, elicited a smile.

'Indeed I am grateful to hear it. I think we understand one another far better now.' She couldn't deny that they did. Probably too much for the conversation which seemed upon her once again. He went on. 'Although the situation has been not as either of us would have hoped I must admit that my regard for you is higher than ever. You have conducted yourself with integrity even though I know that events must have been as distressing to you as they were to Ella.'

Her eyes implored him to stop, but he would not be put off. 'However, Thea, neither are my sister's feelings any less keenly felt, than my continued affection for you.'

There it was, but it seemed inexplicable. 'Sam, surely within the circumstances you must know that this line of conversation can have no favourable conclusion.'

He stepped forward, licking his lips nervously, turmoil evident on his ordinarily assured features. 'Thea I know it seems madness. But I can only assume that you will eventually be required to marry by your family, the same as my sister. My feelings for you have only grown over these twelve months and no sport, society or amusement has been able to distract me from it. I had hoped that despite past events I may be able to convince you that I could be the gentleman to share your life.'

He was such a good man she dared to step towards him, run a hand around his arm and offer a gentle caress – as much to buy herself some time to think as to reassure him. 'Your sister once told me that you hoped to marry for love, Sam.'

His eyes showed a glimmer of hope, tinged by a sadness that suggested success was not expected. 'And I love you, and I hope that you could one day learn to love me. In your own way. From what I understand from my sister, Thea, if you marry, then someone will be deceived. Why not me, with knowledge and acceptance of the situation? You deserve to be loved–' His delivery faltered and Thea's heart bled for him.

'As do you, Sam. But this is not the love you wished for, or that you deserve.'

For all his affability Sam was not as easily dissuaded as she had hoped. He took her hands in his own. 'But it is the love I want. Thea, I have never felt about anyone the way I feel about you. Your endeavours make you so much more interesting than any other lady of my acquaintance.' She made to respond but he silenced her with a look, his jaw set firm against emotion. 'Please do not reject me outright – at least give me the honour of consideration. You cannot think that I would suggest such a thing without resolving in my own mind that it was my preferred course. If your answer is no I will of course respect it, but please – consider it.' He moved towards her in a resolute show of affirmation. 'Thea, believe me when I tell you that this is what I choose.'

Finally he stepped away from her and the taut tangle of her nerves eased. There didn't seem to be any point in arguing so she nodded her assent. 'Of course.'

A glimmer of a smile flitted over his lips. 'You do me a great honour. Now, we should return to the party.'

'I'll follow you,' she said, needing time to think. With a small nod of satisfaction he took his leave and strode off through the church-yard, cutting a handsome figure all in black. What a man he was, she thought, he would make someone a fine and fair husband.

Should it be her?

CHAPTER 28

B oxes littered every surface in the Milford corridors, in the hall and on the driveway. Despite her bluster to Mr Grimston Thea was shocked that Edgar had bequeathed her his collection. And there was a lot of it. Her father had taken her aside, apologised for not encouraging her and pressed her to take it up once more. Her mother had weighed in and insisted that she display the collection in the blue room so that George would have more to look at 'if he ever popped by'. Eventually Thea had agreed, although she was still too confused. She had meant what she said to Edgar – she wanted to do something with her time that made a difference, but she still couldn't see how she could, even with his vast assemblage at her disposal. She felt disloyal for even having the thought, however, so despite her turmoil she thought it couldn't hurt to occupy the blue room for now.

As she arranged objects on shelves the note from Edgar was tucked into her bodice – *I hope you feel that this may be of use in whatever way you see fit, but it would be a shame if it failed to reach its potential.* It was dated December of the previous year – shortly after she had confessed to him that she was having doubts. Keeping it close made her smile, to think that he believed in her, but also at his dogged stubbornness that she would continue her scientific endeavours.

They had hired men from the town who now struggled through doors with heavy cases while Thea directed their movements. She had personally supervised the packing at Pook End and knew precisely the contents of each box. She opened one of the cases perched atop a marble side table as it arrived in what was now to be the blue museum room.

'Urs, have you started unpacking these already?'

Ursula turned from where she was checking off the boxes at the other side of the room. 'No, why?'

Thea put her hands on her hips. 'There's a vase missing out of this one. It wasn't nice, but I stuck it on top so it could go at the back.'

Ursula shrugged. 'Maybe the box was too heavy and they moved it elsewhere?'

'Mmm.'

It was a tiring day but by the evening everything either had a place or was checked in its box and ready to display or store. Thea had noticed a handful of other missing items which weren't where she expected and which hadn't turned up anywhere else. She assumed they had been left behind in the move but it was dark and she wanted nothing but dinner and her bed, so resolved to head to Pook End in the morning.

After breakfast she rode there on her horse, Frederick, and strode up to the door. By now Mr Roberts the butler was used to her and let her in with a smile. He would have to find a new position before too long but for now was coordinating the dissemination of Edgar's possessions.

'Six tall vases?' he asked.

'That's them,' said Thea. 'Have you seen them?'

'I have, Miss,' he confirmed. 'Lady Foxmore came to pick them up the day before yesterday. Said she was taking them on first as they were delicate and she didn't trust the men with them. Have they not turned up?'

Thea's brow furrowed. 'Not yet, Roberts, but thank you – I assume she's just holding them at Denbury. I'll ride over there now.' She smiled and left but in reality wasn't sure why Martha would take the vases – particularly why she wouldn't have said anything. Martha had been strange since the funeral. More distant. Thea had begun to worry that she may have overheard the conversation with Samuel Harrington. Martha had been evasive towards her for the rest of the day and had made a point of heading back to her own house, alone, for the night, saying she had work to do. Since then Thea had been so taken up with the movement of Edgar's collection that she hadn't pursued Martha but neither had Martha pursued her.

She mounted Frederick and rode off, heading for Denbury. As she rode up the drive ten minutes later she saw a familiar figure heading out – it was Mr Grimston, juddering past in his carriage. Catching her eye he grinned smugly out of the window and tipped his hat. *Odious little man*, she thought to herself as she proceeded past the canal and the greenhouse up to the front door.

As she rang the bell she heard footsteps coming apace across the hall behind it. 'I'll deal with this, Fletcher.' It was Martha's voice. Perhaps she had missed her, Thea considered, with a smile.

Martha opened the door, stepped around it and closed it behind her. 'Thea, how lovely to see you, I wasn't expecting you this morning.'

Thea faltered at the strange address. 'No, I hadn't planned a visit. Are you – quite alright?'

She regarded Martha, concerned. She looked as poised as usual, if a little tired around the eyes. 'Fine, thank you.' It was a brief reply.

'I just saw Mr Grimston on the way out, what did he want?'

'Nothing in particular,' said Martha quickly. 'Just a courtesy call.'

'When we were unpacking the collections I noticed a few items were missing.' Something about their exchange made Thea choose her next words carefully. 'You haven't seen them, have you?' She watched Martha's reaction closely and was sure she saw a little colour creep into the cheeks.

'No, no I haven't.'

Thea pursed her lips. 'Are you sure?'

Martha nodded. 'Quite sure, but now you mention it, while we were at Pook End I think there was some discussion of some possessions being entailed away to Edgar's distant family. Decorative items. Perhaps they were some of them?' Thea nodded and was silent. Martha went on. 'I am impressed that you have unpacked so quickly, I thought it would take you days to get sorted.'

'Well, you know what Ursula is like when she gets going.' Thea forced a smile. 'Perhaps you're right that they were alternatively entailed.' Martha returned the smile and nodded. There was an awkward silence between them and Thea made no move to leave.

Martha was the first to speak. 'Anyway I really must get on. Had a thought about the next stage of the experiment. Might we might see one another sometime later in the week?'

Thea nodded and stepped back as Martha vanished around the door, closing it swiftly. Thea mounted and set off back down the drive thoroughly confused. Martha had taken the vases and lied to her about it. That much was certain. But why? She was so consumed in her own thoughts that she almost didn't see the carriage waiting around the corner until Frederick swerved. It was Mr Grimston again. She stopped adjacent to his window. 'Is there a reason you are skulking around on Lady Foxmore's drive, Mr Grimston?'

He smiled that smug smile again. 'Just checking that you get off ok, Miss Morell. I admit that I expected you to be longer with the Countess?'

Thea could have snarled at him. Partly down to his arrogant smugness and partly down to her own disappointment that the visit had been so brief. 'Not today, Mr Grimston,' she spat back. 'Just a quick visit.'

She squeezed her heels and Frederick carried her off, just in time that Mr Grimston didn't see the tears beginning to form. What was happening? There was an obvious conclusion but it seemed too unlikely that the two of them had conspired to procure items from Edgar's collection. There must be a simple explanation. She would go home and tend to the collection until they could talk later in the week, just like Martha had promised.

One week later Thea gritted her teeth as she waited by the river for Samuel and Ella. Across the water the blackthorn bloomed white with flower and pops of spring green peppered the landscape. She had planned to discuss the meeting with Martha, but Martha hadn't visited. Not once. Neither had she sent a note. Thea didn't dare to go back to Denbury – being snubbed once was bad enough. She hadn't been able to delay a reply to Sam any longer and as the days went by she began to feel less guilty. Why should she be worried when Martha would not engage with her? When Martha had taken items which were rightfully hers. It seemed so strange and so unlikely but Martha had not explained and the week-long silence had been almost unbearable.

Without Martha Thea felt more alone than ever. She couldn't talk to her family and with Edgar gone the only person with whom she could confide was Mrs Phibbs. Sharing news on both George and Sam's proposals had helped a little, but she couldn't hide her tears on every day Martha had failed to be in touch. She began to doubt herself and everything she understood. 'What do you think?' she had said to Mrs Phibbs as the housekeeper opened up one morning. 'Why is she being like this?'

'I didn't like to say, Miss,' said Mrs Phibbs as she tied back the curtains, 'but I hear him talking about her, and it isn't always favourable.'

'Who?' asked Thea, stunned. She thought everyone loved Martha.

'Mr Grimston to your mother, Miss. He has some particularly nasty things to say.'

'But Martha is always trying to protect him,' said Thea, by now thoroughly bemused. 'You know what he's like, it must be because she's a woman?'

'So is your mother, Miss. I get the impression it runs deeper than that.' Thea had tried to question Mrs Phibbs but she would be drawn no further and Thea was in no mood to find out more unpleasant truths. While she knew the stories of good men turning to thievery and deceit to further their scientific endeavours, it had never once occurred to her that the same might happen to Martha, she had always seemed so strong and principled. But if there were another reason, why wouldn't Martha have spoken to her?

As the days passed Thea had written to Sam to accept his suggestion of the meeting with Ella. It felt like the least she could do. They had decided that to meet in public would be too risky and so Sam was to bring Ella to the meadow by the river on the Milford estate where few of the family ever ventured. Even if they were seen, he could vouch for them. Now the day was here Thea felt more nervous than expected and her stomach turned over as she saw both Ella and Sam ride approach along the river bank. They dismounted and he took the horses to allow them to speak alone.

Ella looked as graceful as ever, if a little anxious, as she stepped gingerly through the long grass to where Thea stood. She said only, 'Thea.'

Hearing her name again in those gentle tones did nothing for Thea's churning insides. She was still wary of Ella, after their parting. 'How delightful to see you again.'

Ella smiled and took a breath. 'I would like to thank you for being here. I don't deserve it after how badly I behaved.' She fiddled nervously with a handkerchief.

'You mean?'

'At our parting. I think of it all the time. That I left you with those cruel words after everything that had passed between us.' She paused. 'Everything that was still between us. But I was scared, Thea, and confused. I had been swept up in the moment and it had taken me so out of myself and what I knew that when it came to the letter, the others' reactions were too much. It confounded me to the point that I hardly knew my own mind.'

Thea shoved her hands into her dress pockets. 'I admit it was a shock. I did think we were more to one another.'

'Oh, Thea.' Ella looked like she wished to come forwards but didn't dare. 'Of course we were. I had to intimate to you I was only in it for the' – she looked around and dropped her voice – 'experimentation – but I hoped that you knew, somewhere inside, that it was more.'

Thea was still a little perplexed. 'Then why tell me that?'

The corner of Ella's mouth ticked up a little. 'Because even in those few, short weeks I learned how determined you are. I suspected that your feelings were as strong as mine and that you would not be put off, but all that lay ahead was more pain if we didn't give it up.'

'I see,' said Thea, trying to replay the conversation in her mind. The sorrow in Ella's eyes and the turn of her countenance when she had dismissed Thea did uphold this new version of events.

'I am desperately sorry for the pain it must have caused you,' said Ella softly, keeping Thea's eyes. 'I have thought of it so often and the dislike you must feel towards me. It has plagued my thoughts, after what we were to one another.' The pain in her eyes was so genuine that Thea could do nothing but believe her.

'It was an impossible situation,' she said. 'You are right that I would not have given it up, rightly or wrongly, and I understand you needing to protect yourself from that. We should neither of us bear the other any ill will.'

Ella smiled and her face lit as it had all those months ago. 'That would give me great comfort.'

There was an awkward pause and the nagging question popped into Thea's head. 'You never found out who sent the letter?'

Ella eyed her carefully. 'Do you not know?'

'You do?' Thea's heart turned over and Ella nodded sheepishly. 'Well, who was it?' Thea asked when Ella remained silent.

'If you are unaware it is perhaps best to keep it that way,' said Ella, but Thea's chest thumped.

'But if it happens again–' Thea broke off, conscious of what she was about to reveal, and Ella gave her a sly grin.

'I see.' She flicked an eyebrow. 'All you should know, Thea, is that there is no further risk. Believe me.'

Thea stared at Ella, wanting to pursue but saw in her face that she would get no further. 'Fine,' she said, raising her arms and letting them fall in an exaggerated show of frustration. 'I hear you are to be married to your cousin.' Thea searched her face. 'Is he a good man?'

Ella looked calmly over the swirling river. 'He is kind enough and believes in his work. He thinks perhaps he will be sent abroad as an ambassador, so there will be the opportunity to travel. The rest of the time we will live in Dorset and I will have the country and the coast to entertain me.' She looked back to Thea who knew her own eyes were full of concern. 'Please do not worry about me, Thea. I will make my own happiness and I can now rest knowing that you do not think ill of me.'

'I will always appreciate the time we had together,' said Thea quietly. 'And I am pleased that I can now think of it with genuine fondness and understanding.' As Ella's eyes filled she dabbed at them with a handkerchief but it dropped from a shaky hand. When she stooped to retrieve it a locket on a silver chain slipped from her dress and swayed from her neck. She grasped it and pushed it back in.

'Is that from him?' Thea asked kindly, as Ella straightened.

'No,' said Ella, quietly. She held Thea's eyes for a few seconds as if wondering whether to elaborate, then, in one fluid movement slipped the chain over her head and dropped the locket into Thea's palm. 'Open it.' Thea did, and there, gleaming emerald and sky-blue in the spring sunlight, was the piece of abalone shell she had given to Ella all those months ago. It took her breath away and she could only stare at it. 'There are things I need to remember,' said Ella, 'I had the locket made in Germany, especially to fit.'

Thea couldn't help herself. She dropped the chain back over Ella's head and drew the girl into a warm embrace. They held each other tight for long seconds – the goodbye they never had.

When they split Thea held her by the arms and looked into her eyes. 'Should I write to you?'

Ella's eyes flitted between Thea's own and when she spoke her voice was quiet and apologetic. 'I beg that you wouldn't. I understand that our feelings cannot be the same and while I have spent so long in repairing mine, seeing you reminds me that they may return a hundred times quicker than they can be banished.'

'I understand,' said Thea quietly.

Ella planted a soft kiss on Thea's cheek. 'Goodbye, Thea. I wish you all the happiness you deserve.' Thea muttered a goodbye through the lump in her throat and watched Ella walk away and mount her horse. Samuel nodded a thank you but Thea couldn't take her eyes from his sister as they rode off. What would her life be from now on?

And Ella knew about the letter. There was a revelation. Why was she so sure the author was no longer a risk? With a start she realised that Ella must mean Edgar. He was certainly of no further risk and it was just like Ella to be kind to his memory. But why would he have done it?

She pondered the situation as she watched the rhythmic sway of the Harrington's horses taking them away along the riverbank. When they were out of sight she turned to walk back up the hill and saw a figure standing regally atop it, staring down at her.

It was Martha.

CHAPTER 29

Thea cursed the dreadful timing as Martha turned on her heel and stalked across the hilltop. If she heard Thea's shouts as she ran after her she didn't stop. The distance between them was so great that as Thea rounded the house onto the driveway Martha's horse was already kicking up the dust of the gravel.

'Mr Croft!' shouted Thea, running round to the stables. 'I need Frederick, now!' But Mr Croft was nowhere to be seen. Thea dashed to the tack room herself, a bridle would do. She slipped the bit into Frederick's mouth, slid the supple leather over his ears and swung her leg over his back from the mounting block. It felt strange to ride astride with her skirts hitched up but side saddle was impossible bareback. Frederick responded quickly as she pressed her heels and set off after Martha.

As they galloped up the Denbury driveway leaving a cloud of dust in their wake, she spied a figure stride out of the back door and head for the greenhouse. She reined Frederick left and took him as far as she could before dismounting at a trot and then vaulting the iron railings to the garden. Running towards Martha across the lawn, Thea became aware of quick footsteps to her right and felt a hand close around her arm, stopping her in her tracks.

'Her ladyship has left strict instructions that she is not to be disturbed, Miss Morell,' Mr Fletcher growled.

Thea spun, astonished to be handled by a servant, but he held tight. 'Mr Fletcher, I have to see her.'

He made to respond but was interrupted by a shout from the scullery door. Mrs Jenkins clattered down the steps, hitching her petticoats above her ankles, and wheezed as she leant on the butler's shoulder. 'Let her go, Mr Fletcher,' she said, kindly but firmly. 'It'll help.'

The tall form of the butler still looked unsure, but a softer look crossed his face, he gave a slight nod of acquiescence, and released his grip on Thea's arm.

She thanked them quickly as she took off once more, moving so fast she was gasping for breath by the time she reached the greenhouse. Through the high windows she could see straight through to the calm, glassy surface of the canal beyond. Citrus, strawberry and coral trees crowded the glass, some leaves pressed up against the windows, half formed oranges and lemons pendulous and green on their branches. Amongst them a solitary figure stood, her back to the house, looking out over the water. Thea slipped inside and Martha turned with a start as the door clicked shut. She stared at Thea harshly, her chest rising and falling with quick, shallow breaths. 'What are you doing here?'

'What do you think?' Thea watched her carefully, still unsure what to make of the situation or how to approach it.

Martha turned back to the water. 'If you're wondering how I knew you were by the river, I found this note in your room.' She held out the note from Samuel Harrington, detailing the date and time of the visit.

Thea's anger bubbled over. First Martha stole from her, then she had been snooping amongst her things. 'What were you doing in my room?' she asked quietly.

'I needed to talk to you – if you must know I came to explain. Your mother told me that that's where you were – clearly you had deceived your family also. When I saw the note I assumed Viscount Stockwood intended to propose, but this, Thea!' Martha's measured delivery took on a tone of incredulity and she turned away. 'It didn't take you long.'

Thea couldn't think what she meant. 'What?'

Martha turned back to her, fury writ on her face. 'Bringing Lady Eleanor back into your life – or have you been deceiving me for longer?' Her jaw hardened. 'What a fool I was to think I could keep you when you were back in society with young ladies on offer! But I had not been gone a week!'

Thea was unsympathetic. 'And why were you gone?' Martha turned away and made no response, so Thea took a step closer. 'Samuel Harrington proposed at the funeral.. He also asked me to see Ella who has been struggling with her health after the manner of our parting. I wanted to speak to you about it, but you were not there to ask.' Martha turned back to the water. 'Perhaps you are only accusing me of it so that you have an easy way out – now that you have what you want.' Anger bubbled dangerously near the surface.

Martha turned back and looked her up and down with a curling lip. 'What do you mean?'

'I know you have the vases from Edgar's collection. I went to Pook End and Mr Roberts told me you took them before the collection was moved out. And then I came here and you lied to me.' Tears pricked for the second time that day. 'And now here we are in a position where you clearly don't trust me, and I cannot trust you.' She stared at Martha, defying her to challenge the accusation.

The seconds stretched on. Thea was too disappointed and she couldn't think what would come next. What she hadn't expected was that Martha would crumble the way she did. Whatever strength held her together suddenly gave way and her whole body sagged. 'Thea, I have no defence. I took the vases and I didn't tell you. Worse than that, I was not honest with you.'

Thea was thrown. 'Why?' she asked, joining Martha by the double door to the canal. Bright spring light streamed in from the south and reflected silver on the water.

Martha took a difficult breath. 'When Edgar's collection was left to you, Grimston concluded that you and I had conspired to deny him what was rightfully his. There were a few pieces that he coveted above others so he insisted that I procure them for him.' She hesitated. 'And I am ashamed that I did so.'

Martha paused and Thea screwed up her face in confusion. 'Why the vases?'

'They are valuable and of no scientific merit, you know what he likes. I took them because I knew you wouldn't care for them but he also wanted the vegetable lamb – I knew that would be valuable to you so I refused to take it. He is still cross and visited the other day to tell me so, you arrived just after he did and I was flustered.'

Thea was confused. 'Why not refuse?'

Martha sighed as if she had been expecting the question and ran a hand down the back of her head. 'Unfortunately, it is not quite as simple as that.'

'Why not?' Thea's feelings ran between anger, frustration and a desperate need to trust Martha again.

Martha looked upwards at the clouds out of the high window and drew in a shaky breath. 'Thea, do you remember that I told you that you were not the first lady with whom I had relations?' Thea nodded, an unease starting to settle within her. 'Well... my companion in that relationship was Mr Grimston's daughter.' Martha clenched her jaw. 'We enjoyed each others' company for three years. Perhaps we got a little complacent. He has never forgiven me for leading her astray, as he saw it.'

Thea was stunned. 'I didn't even know he had a daughter?'

When Martha turned her head Thea saw that tears were beginning to form, but she kept the emotion from her voice. 'You wouldn't know. He never speaks of her and so others respect that. She' – Martha paused and her voice shook for the first time – 'Rebecca – sadly passed away some years ago.'

'I'm sorry,' said Thea, seeing how difficult this was and beginning to think she may have been too hasty in her anger.

Martha stepped out of the greenhouse and began to descend the terrace steps towards the canal. 'Grimston has always held it over me but when his fortunes started dropping with the Royal Society he got desperate. His plan was to use items from Edgar's collection to save his reputation but when it was left to you he had no further options.' She stopped where the terrace met the canal and stared at the wispy clouds. 'Thea, he has been threatening to expose me – for all that I am – in your mother's favourite – the *Tête-a-Tête* column in *Town and Country* magazine. You know they leave nothing to the imagination. It matters little for me, but he has made his own deductions about you and I over recent months. The day of Edgar's funeral he threatened to implicate you too.' She looked back at Thea, eyes shining with sorrow, anger and helplessness. 'It would shatter your future, Thea. Since then I have done everything I could to distance myself from you. It was agony, but better than the alternative.' She took up one of Theas' hands – Martha's were cold and trembling. 'I hope you can forgive me in time, but please know I thought only to act in your best interests.'

Thea nodded her understanding. She had no doubt Martha was telling the truth, it would explain Mr Grimston's presence at Denbury and his hanging around to catch her out. 'Why wouldn't you tell me?' she asked.

Martha cupped Thea's face in her hands, stroking trembling fingers across her cheeks. Her voice shook with emotion and a tear slid down her cheek. 'How could I when I have been so unfair to you? I have exposed you to risk I vowed to never bring on another person in my life.'

'All you did was love another woman,' said Thea, still confused. 'In a mutually consented relationship.'

As Thea searched Martha's face for an answer it suddenly creased. She dragged her hands away from Thea's and held them to her face as a sob convulsed her body. 'Our relationship was ruinous for her. After we were found out Grimston cut her off. The shame of him knowing, the marriage to a man he forced on her ate away at her, bit by bit.' Martha covered her mouth with a quivering hand, almost shouting now. 'Thea, she took her own life. She jumped into the Thames and never came out.' As she spoke, tears engulfed her. Tremulous, wracking sobs that spilled years of contained grief. Thea gathered her gently but firmly in her arms as Martha leant on her heavily, trembling fingers desperately grasping at the satin of Thea's dress.

When the sobs abated, Thea stroked a hand up Martha's back. 'I can't believe you bore this alone. For all these years.'

'I almost didn't,' said Martha, quietly. 'I thought about following her. But then I considered the horror of her last moments and the pain left behind. I vowed to do what I could to honour her memory.'

'I'm so glad,' said Thea, desperate at the thought of how empty the world would feel without Martha in it. 'I really am, but why do you still defend Grimston?' she asked – she had always wondered and now it seemed even more perplexing.

'Rebecca left me a note.' Martha hung her head. 'She asked me to look out for him and so I have, for years.'

'While he made every effort to convince you of your guilt.' Thea was seething. Martha looked away. 'Martha, you must believe me. All you did was love her.'

Martha took one steadying breath and placed her forehead at Thea's temple. 'I once told you I was weak when I was with you.' The whisper wavered against Thea's skin. 'The depth of my love for you terrifies me, Thea. How could I tell you why I was so indebted to Grimston? That a life ended because of me and I, in full knowledge of that, put you at the same risk?'

Martha broke off as the tears came again and Thea held her tight until at last her breathing steadied. 'Martha, you are not responsible for her death.' Martha shook her head in disbelief, so Thea held her tighter. 'You are not. It is not your love she couldn't bear, but his hate, Martha. Tears still streamed down Martha's cheeks but a glimmer of understanding lit her face. 'I told you in Whitby that I was willing to take the risk and I am. I understand what the consequences could be and so do you. Whatever the future may hold we must not forbid ourselves love and happiness where we can find it.'

Martha's eyes flitted between Thea's before she pulled her in and kissed her with an intensity Thea had never felt.

They lay on the chaise in Martha's library and held each other close for almost a full hour. Occasionally Thea stroked reassuring hands across Martha's shoulders or touched a gentle kiss to her head, but mostly she knew that her lover needed to reassess her feelings now that they were shared. All of the reticence and worry finally slipped into understanding and Thea's heart ached with reflected pain. With a grief so stark multiplied by the pernicious and poisonous rhetoric of Stanhope Grimston, it was easy to see how the most tenacious resolve could crumble.

When Martha's breathing had regulated and the trembling stopped, Thea let her mind wander. Suddenly she sat up. 'What is it?' Martha asked, her nerves still on edge.

'That's why you helped Harriet and Emma, too?' asked Thea.

Martha nodded. 'I had to see them at least content with good men. The alternative was too much to bear.'

Thea planted a gentle kiss on her forehead. 'What was Grimston going to do with the pieces from Edgar's collection?'

Martha shrugged. 'Put them in his cabinet and show them off to his victims I suppose. And take some to the Royal Society to support his position for office.'

Thea nodded. 'We should let him have the lamb.'

Martha looked confused. 'Don't you want it? I have never seen a lamb like it.'

'It isn't a lamb. It is a fern.'

Both of Martha's brows shot up as she caught on. 'That would be cruel.'

'So is Grimston,' said Thea.

'He is sad,' said Martha, mustering more understanding than Thea ever could.

'He is also a bigot,' said Thea, 'and a cruel one at that. You are only giving him what he has asked, under the threat of being socially discredited. He is not your responsibility.' She grasped Martha's face in her hands. 'Free yourself from him.'

The smile began at the edges of Martha's lips and spread across her whole face. 'I may do just that.'

CHAPTER 30

Dinner at the Morell's was always a slightly frenetic affair, but tonight Mrs Morell and Tabitha were beside themselves. Ralph Jefferys had finally proposed over a game of cards that afternoon. Mrs Morell could talk of nothing but the dress and Tabitha wondered whether they would stay nearby in Sussex or go further afield for adventure. The Jeffery fortune was limited and certainly nothing that the two betrothed couldn't fritter away in a matter of years, but Tabitha seemed genuinely happy. Thea had hugged her sister and congratulated her warmly, hopeful of better family relations once they lived further apart.

By the time dessert arrived Tabitha was beginning to turn her attentions outwards and success in love had not yet tempered her harsh tongue. 'What about you, sister?' she asked, regarding Thea through a spoonful of jam roll. 'Another summer on the way, twice as many rocks but still no suitor. You must be delighted?'

Thea knew better than to rise to it. 'So it seems. Although rocks seem to be less trouble than most men, I flatter myself that my chances of a suitor are not completely nought.'

Tabitha raised a cloved brow. 'You want one?'

'Not especially, but I am considering it.'

Tabitha affected an air of superiority, gazing out of the window as if family matters were now quite beneath her. 'Well there's no rush, the longer you delay the more likely it is that Milford will pass to me and Ralph. I can rather see myself as the lady of the house, can't you, mother? We would lawn over the walled garden of course and replace the stove with a sun terrace, they are now far more the fashion.' *If there is an estate left*, thought Thea, considering her father across the table. He looked pale again and she hoped he had remembered to take his digitalis. The stress of an uncertain future for the estate couldn't be helping him.

As her sister went on with a list of home improvements Thea became increasingly delighted that this conversational strand had begun with the final course. Escaping as early as she could she made for her own room. Despite her bravado at dinner Tabitha's news changed things and a resolution on her part was already overdue.

Agnes had performed her duties and Thea was making her final preparations for bed when there was a knock at her door. At her reply Mrs Phibbs pushed Ursula to the side of Thea's bed, gave a brief furrow of the brow to indicate that something was awry, and left. Thea was relieved beyond words that she had been able to reassure Mrs Phibbs on Martha's character. She had managed to explain without revealing too many of Martha's secrets and had confided almost everything of her own feelings to the housekeeper. It had been quite the relief.

Now, Ursula sat next to the bed, looking across to the window. She said nothing, but there was no doubt that she was unsettled. 'Is everything alright?' Thea asked, turning around from her toilette table.

Ursula gave a small shrug. 'Fine. I just thought it would be nice to chat.'

Thea had spent enough time around ladies to know that "fine" meant anything but. 'How are you feeling about Tabitha's news?' she asked, selecting the most probable cause of disquiet.

Ursula's face brightened a little. 'I am very pleased – Tab could do worse than Ralph, and she likes him. I should hate to think of her unhappy.'

Thea frowned to herself in the glass. It wasn't that then. She placed her brush on its stand and padded over in bare feet to sit on the bed. 'Do you want to get up? It's warm in the day but April nights are still chilly.' Ursula nodded and Thea helped her onto the bed where they wrapped themselves in the bed clothes. Thea regarded her unusually subdued sister, afraid she did indeed know what was the matter. 'I always thought Tab would find one first. I suppose I better get on with it, hadn't I, before Milford is lost forever on a hand of piquet.'

Ursula remained quiet for a short time as her fingers traced the embroidered flowers on the quilt. 'That's why I'm here. I was surprised to hear you say you were considering marriage. Wouldn't you rather build a life with Martha?' Thea's gaze shot to meet her sister's and was met by a wise, knowing look. 'Thea you can't expect that I hadn't noticed, especially after Ella. It is obvious that you are in love and that she is with you.'

Suddenly Thea's mouth was entirely devoid of moisture. So much for being careful. 'Aren't you cross?' she asked carefully.

Ursula moved a hand across the quilt and laid a reassuring hand on her leg. 'Of course I'm not. I thought about what you said before you went off to Scarborough and it all made sense. Everything I knew about you since we were young.' She gave Thea's leg a playful poke through the thick layers of cotton. 'It fits you. The two of you together are unstoppable.'

Thea gave a wry chuckle. 'Sadly not, it seems. We could be, I think, but our sex are unfortunately hobbled in so many areas.' Ursula regarded her for a short time, opened her mouth to speak and then thought better of it. The playful moment had passed and there was the worry again, as much an imposter on her kind face as a nettle in Scip's tan beds. 'Urs, what is it?' asked Thea, growing ever more concerned.

Ursula gripped the quilt between two fists and turned to face her sister straight on. 'There's something I need to tell you.'

Thea rested an arm on the bedhead behind her sister in order to face her more comfortably. 'You can tell me anything, you know that.'

Ursula fiddled with the sheets between her fingers. 'You might not think so.' As Thea only looked at her expectantly, she took a breath. 'Here it is. I sent the letter to Lord and Lady Swanham. The one about you and Ella. I am so, so sorry, and of course if I knew what I know now, I never would have, ever. I understand if you hate me, but I never thought it would be so serious.'

Her voice shook throughout the confession and now she raised the bed sheets to her eyes and broke down in tears. Thea was stunned. It had never occurred to her that the author could be her kind, thoughtful sister. What she was sure of, was that the reason would not be spite or jealousy. She absorbed the shock inside herself and kept her voice steady. 'Why would you do that?'

Ursula sniffed and raised puffy eyes. 'I heard mother shouting at father about mortgaging the house – you know how she always forgets I'm there. I wasn't too worried but then father became ill, Tabitha was in love with Ralph and you only had eyes for Ella. If you were found out and discredited my fortunes would be entirely dependent on Tab, and you know how she thinks of me.' Ursula's face crumpled briefly and Thea's heart broke as she saw her sister fight to right herself. 'I thought that if our parents knew first, that others might not and there would still be hope for the future. I'm so sorry, Thea.' Ursula sobbed back into the sheets as Thea enveloped her in her arms and held her tight.

'Oh, Ursula, I'm the one who should be sorry.' A vice gripped her chest. In all her deliberations she had thought about all of their future prospects, but never about how helpless Ursula must have felt when her security was so out of her own control. She should have had never considered what may have come of Ursula if her fate was left to Tabitha – it certainly wouldn't have been favourable. Thea felt disgusted by herself for not looking at it from Ursula's point of view.

'What have you to be sorry about?' sniffed Ursula. 'You were just being you and I went and spoiled it all with my own selfishness. If I had known how you really felt about Ella I promise I never would have, Thea. I have felt so guilty ever since. After we spoke I sent her a note to tell her it was me and to try to bring her back for you, but the damage was done.'

The perplexing discussion with Ella now made sense – but recalling her earlier conversation with Martha there was one thing that still did not. 'The letter was only effective because it intimated that the relations were' – Thea paused – 'physical.' She eyed Ursula carefully. 'How did you know?'

Ursula shrugged. 'I didn't. I knew it was more serious than a usual romantic friendship and took a chance. You and Ella both confirmed it when they questioned you.'

Despite herself, Thea was impressed. 'Crafty,' she said, but Ursula only looked embarrassed. Thea leaned away and tilted Ursula's chin to look into her eyes. 'Ursula, you have done nothing wrong. Please don't be sorry. It is my responsibility to look after the future of this family and I have failed you and everybody else. I have delayed what I know must be through a desire to have it all my own way. I will put it right.'

Ursula grasped at her arms. 'No, Thea, you mustn't. I have had time to reflect since then. My happiness is no more important than your own. You must follow your heart and not act because of me.'

Her goodness would be her downfall, Thea thought. 'Urs, this is not your happiness at stake, it is your safety.'

'I could live with you and Martha?' said Ursula hopefully. 'I needn't get in your way.'

'You know it isn't as simple as that,' said Thea gently, wishing with all her heart that it was. 'Society would turn their back on us all and if anything happened to me and Martha you would be left alone. Without fortune or standing...' She trailed off. They both knew the impossible situation of those immobile and alone.

'There must be a way.' Ursula hugged her legs. 'Tabitha would have to look after me, whether she liked it or not.'

'Don't you worry,' said Thea, sounding more confident than she felt. 'I have been putting serious thought into this as you can imagine, and I do have options.'

'Do you?' asked Ursula, more hopeful.

Thea drew in her sister and kissed the top of her head. 'Lord Axbury certainly has fortune enough for us all.'

Ursula started. 'You never said.' The smile on Thea's face was wary. She hadn't told Ursula anything about George's advances and suddenly felt terribly guilty. In fact, she hadn't told anyone apart from Martha and Mrs Phibbs but she couldn't keep it to herself forever.

'You know if I told mother she would have me back to London, buying a dress before I could even write the date on the parchment to respond. She's convinced that she heard his father cough more than usual when they came to dinner and that George may be Duke earlier than we thought.'

Ursula gave an understanding smile. 'What has he said?'

Thea weighed up her options but Ursula demanded only the truth. 'On his visit here he outlined his intentions for us to marry. He made a pragmatic but compelling case.'

'How terribly romantic.' The dryness of Ursula's delivery almost made Thea chortle. 'How did you respond?'

'Enthusiastically enough to keep him engaged, not enough to commit.'

Ursula's lips curved up a little. 'I always thought it would be Samuel Harrington who proposed.' Thea felt herself colour. 'He *has* proposed?' Ursula's face was a picture of shock and amusement. 'As well as George Crowe? Oh, Thea, how have you kept this from me?'

Thea squeezed her sister's fingers kindly. 'If I'm honest I haven't known what to do with it. It is only I who can make the decision, and it has come to the point where I can delay no longer.'

Ursula took her hand. 'There is no decision to be made. Your heart belongs to someone else.'

Thea smiled despite herself. 'Ursula, how have you been dealing with this by yourself?' she asked, appalled that she had allowed Ursula to worry alone. She was relieved when her sister shook her head.

'Scip has been very good to me. He took the letter of apology to Ella and I had to tell him what it was. We talk sometimes.' Thea pulled the covers around them, relieved that the gardener was more perceptive than she. 'Do you want to stay here tonight?' she asked. Ursula nodded and they settled down to sleep. Or at least Ursula did. Thea lay awake for hours, thinking of nothing but how terrified her sister must have been to send a letter betraying a member of her family, and that no matter what she had said tonight, the predicament was still no different.

The following morning Thea stood bleary eyed while Mrs Phibbs fastened her stays. She knew the housekeeper had come to dress her in case Thea needed to talk, but she was at a loss for words. Her head was fuzzy after a night of little sleep and the look on Ursula's face as she had admitted how scared she was kept appearing, time and again before her eyes. Mrs Phibbs caught her eye in the mirror and slowed as she fastened the petticoats. Thea's pulse quickened and she drew in a shallow breath, but she still couldn't form a sentence. She let out the breath and looked down at the weight in her hands. She had absentmindedly picked up one of the Scarborough pebbles from her dresser. They had lain there since her return, the black pebble which had been dropped into her hand by Martha sitting proudly atop the pile. Their surfaces were dulled in the absence of the gloss of moisture from the waves, but holding their smooth forms in her hands usually rekindled fond and soothing memories – today it might as well have been mocking her.

Behind her, Mrs Phibbs held up three stomachers. 'Which one today – the green, ivory or plum?'

Thea spun to face her, away from the glass. 'I can't decide.' She knew the panic was both visible in her face and strung tight through her words.

'They all suit you well,' said Mrs Phibbs, her brow creasing in concern and eyeing each triangle of fabric in turn. 'Do you not have a preference?'

'Of course I have a preference,' blurted Thea, 'but it isn't up to me, is it.' She turned back to the glass, her throat tightening and a creeping chill crawling down her spine as she watched understanding register on Mrs Phibbs' face.

The housekeeper put down the stomachers. 'Ah.'

Suddenly the words couldn't come fast enough. 'If I choose Sam I am dishonest and break his heart, if I choose George I am dishonest and break my own, and if I choose Martha I will break everyone's other than my own and bring disgrace and destitution on my family.' She closed her eyes, dropped her head, and ran a hand up to squeeze the back of her own neck, an attempt to release the cloying tension that now seemed permanently present. Within a second she felt Mrs Phibbs' firm but bony hand close around her upper arm.

'Why now?' the housekeeper asked quietly.

Thea raised her head, blinked at the light and found Mrs Phibbs' worried eyes in the mirror. 'Ursula sent the letter,' she whispered, 'because she was so scared of her future in Tabitha's hands if Ella and I were found out. She told me last night.'

Comprehension dawned on Mrs Phibbs' features for the second time and Thea felt the grip tighten sympathetically around her arm. 'Do you know what you will do?'

Thea only shook her head. 'But I must decide soon.' Anger rose inside her as she stared at the pebble nestled comfortably in her hand. 'God, it's so unfair.' It wasn't a shout, but her voice was high and seemed to reverberate around the room. She threw the pebble force-fully across the floor and it skittered under her wardrobe.

They both watched it go and then Mrs Phibbs' hand shifted to rub her gently in the small of the back. 'I think the plum, perhaps,' she said gently, and began to pin the embroidered fabric firmly onto Thea's satin stays.

After breakfast Thea took a walk in the garden to clear her head. The morning was bright with sun and the grass lush after a balmy but damp spring. Shoots emerged from the soil in the walled garden and vegetables thrust out of the ground in neat rows, every one in their place. However gloomy she felt, the relentless optimism of nature never failed to lift her spirits.

The clarity it offered helped. She and Martha had agreed to be honest with one another, and so she must discuss it with her. It would be heartbreaking, but people counted on her and she couldn't let them down. She was rounding the stables to call for Frederick when the object of her thoughts cantered into view, a broad smile lighting her face when she saw Thea. She dismounted and strode towards her, tugging off her gloves on the way and dropping a kiss onto her cheek.

'Just the person I wanted to see.'

'Funny you should say that.' Thea's insides withered a little. 'I was on my way to see you.'

'Great minds,' whispered Martha into her ear as she turned her round and headed to the garden. 'Do you have a minute, then, I wish to speak with you.'

'Of course,' Thea gulped.

There was a confidence to Martha's smile today. Not that she wasn't always assured, but now she seemed to fit more comfortably in it, as if she'd relaxed a little into her skin. There was a joy that lit her eyes and a sparkle in them that spoke of good news. *Disaster*, thought Thea. This was going to make the inevitable conversation more difficult.

'Where are we going?' asked Thea as Martha steered her into the meadow.

'Just somewhere we can talk without being overheard,' said Martha, looking around to ensure no one was in earshot. Finally satisfied, she turned back.

'I have given it some thought, and have decided to go ahead with the paper to the Royal Society and publish in the *Transactions*.' Her eyes settled on Thea's and she smiled warmly. 'I couldn't continue to let my own demons affect you, Thea. I know one of the reasons you are so cautious about the collections is that you feel you can make no headway. I hope that this will prove to you that you can.'

Thea stared at her open mouthed, and then started forward, enveloping her in a tight hug. 'That's wonderful news.'

'It is,' said Martha, 'I have informed Mr Thistleton who has confirmed it can go to the next meeting in a month's time. I am preparing the illustration plates for the printers now.' She took Thea's arm as they walked through the paths cut in the long grass. 'I should thank you, Thea, I reflected on your words and you are right, I would never have been able to do it with such guilt hanging over me.'

Thea turned to her as they walked. 'He's why you wouldn't publish – Grimston!'

'Yes.' Martha's eyes followed the track of the river. 'I felt like I had to ask him first as I knew what he would say. When he wrote back to express his outrage, as I knew he would, I knew it was best to abandon the whole thing. He hadn't even written to the society of course, the response came back so quickly.'

'And that's why you still wouldn't go ahead, even with Mr Constable's affirmation and father's encouragement?'

'Yes. There was always a chance that Grimston would discredit it of course, but also I felt bound by the limitations he placed on me. I realise now I need to stop letting him define my actions. You helped me with that.'

'So – now?'

'Now I am happy to be associated with the research, whatever reception it gets. Your father will have to present of course, and I need to ensure that he is happy with the approach. I am hoping that the lamb will go some way to attenuating Grimston's impact as it will be presented at the same meeting.'

A grin formed on Thea's face. 'Of course. We should go and tell Scip.'

'We should,' said Martha, matching her grin.

They found Scip in the stove pricking out lettuce seedlings. He wiped his hands on a rag at his belt and turned to give them his full attention. His smile grew as Martha imparted the news, he knew as much as she did what it would mean to have their work recognised.

'Just think, Scip,' said Thea, still giddy with happiness, 'your name in print.'

He almost guffawed. 'I don't think my name will be associated, Miss.'

Thea looked at Martha, questioningly, some of the brightness she felt seeping away. 'Martha?'

'Neither Scip's or mine, Thea,' she said, quietly. 'Just your father's.'

'But that's not right!' Thea looked between them, 'I can understand him giving the paper, but for you not to be credited at all…'

'Is standard, I am afraid,' finished Martha for her. 'Nevertheless, the work will be out, which is what we wanted. Thank you both for your efforts in getting us to this point.' She threw a genuine smile of gratitude to each of them and slapped both gloves into one hand. 'Now I must go and speak to your father, Thea. Scip, I will be back and we will talk about the next phase, I have a number of ideas and I would appreciate your insight to build on what we have already achieved.'

'Of course, my lady,' he smiled.

Martha went to exit the stove, but then turned back. 'Oh, Thea, you said you had something to discuss with me?' Thea swallowed. 'It can wait,' she said – there was no way she was ruining Martha's mood today. Her heart skipped as Martha winked at her and closed the stove door with a firm click.

Scip had returned to pricking out the seedlings. 'I hate that you have to accept this with such equanimity,' she said, incredulous. 'You and Lady Foxmore have done the lion's share of the work.'

He turned to her with something approaching amusement as he carefully extracted another seedling, pinching its delicate leaves between a strong finger and thumb. 'I have little choice in the matter, Miss.'

Of course he didn't, she thought, it had been a stupid thing to say. He deftly dropped the seedling into the hole, firming the compost around it before selecting another. She leant on the side of the tan bed and picked at a piece of lichen which hugged the brick. 'Scip, I would like you to know something.' He turned to face her, but she still picked at the brick. 'I am sorry about – about the reason you are here.'

'The seedlings, Miss?' he asked, confused.

'No,' she said, hating how awkward she felt.

'To do the garden?'

'No.' The frustration at herself was evident in her voice but she managed to look up. 'The... reason you are in England.'

'Oh,' he said, understanding dawning. He placed his dibber on the bench and looked almost as ill at ease as she felt. 'I am not sure it was down to you, Miss.'

She cleared her throat, knowing she was making a hash of this conversation. 'Nevertheless – Lady Foxmore and I are doing what we can to distance ourselves from the trade. Financially and for the future.'

She was grateful that he tried to spare her blushes and a genuine smile curved his lips. 'I appreciate that, Miss.'

'And when I have independent funds of my own I will be supporting the Quaker's efforts in London to help... your people.' She was even more embarrassed that she didn't have the language to talk about this with him without potentially causing offence. She wished she had spoken to Jane and Thomas and educated herself.

He now allowed himself to look a little amused. 'I don't know them all personally, Miss.' She coloured and he smiled again. 'But I am pleased that you are willing.'

'I wish I could do something about your name on that paper,' she said. 'It really isn't fair.'

A gracious smile again. 'It will take more than money to achieve that,' he said. 'And we should avoid talk of fairness.'

She looked at him, astonished. 'We should?'

'Not in principle,' he qualified. 'In principle it is always a goal. But in practicality it will not be achieved for too many, and dwelling on that eats you up inside.'

The futility of his words reached deep inside her. 'Then what is the answer?'

Scip shrugged. 'Facts. Life for many is about what is – not what we think it should be, or what we would like it to be.' Thea faltered. How could he be so pragmatic? He broke the silence, regarding her carefully. 'Logic and reason apply as strongly to society as to science. Somebody once taught me that you should change what you can and live with the rest.'

'But why can't we change it?' muttered Thea grumpily, looking back at him. 'I mean, your work should be recognised.' She mumbled again, as his eyes searched her face.

He turned and leaned against the bench, folding his arms. 'There are lines which society will not yet cross. There are those who will work for change and eventually it will be achieved. The world will change by degrees and slowly, as generations form new habits. But for now, nobody will put my name on that paper.'

'I will ask them to,' said Thea quietly.

He picked up his dibber again. 'Thank you.' They both knew it would make no difference.

'I am sorry,' she said, at last.

He shook his head. 'There are victims. I am lucky I can choose not to be one of them, but many are not. I am proud of the part I play here and I know what I have contributed to this experiment. A word on a page written by a wealthy white man makes no difference to that.' She stared at him, open mouthed at his resolve.

'What is important is in here.' He tapped his temple with a composty finger. 'To survive sometimes we must consider what is fact over what is fair. And I made my choice.'

CHAPTER 31

London, June 1759

'If you're still interested,' said Martha as she handed Thea the package. Thea grinned. The present was large and rectangular, and she could smell the familiar leather as she ripped open the paper to reveal volume seven of Diderot's *Encyclopédie*. She hugged Martha and thanked her. This year the birthday party was just Thea, Martha and her father at Hanover Square. The Royal Society meeting was tomorrow, the paper was prepared, and all that was left was for Mr Morell to deliver it. Thea and Martha both knew it by heart – he had practiced it all the way to London in the carriage and at least twice a day on each of the three days since they arrived. They knew it would be a success and had hatched a plan to support him in person. It had involved a trip to the haberdashers and a very confused looking tailor, but a few shillings extra had put him at ease and Martha was more than delighted at her new three-piece suit in sage green.

Tonight he looked more relaxed than he had since the start of the journey as he handed Thea a second present. 'To do with as you wish.' He had a sly grin on his face and she was immediately intrigued, carefully removing the wrapping to see what lay within. When it fell away, she was confused to see a small, glass jar. She weighed it in her hand and held it up to the light.

'Oh,' she said. 'It's from the collection.'

'It is,' said her father. 'It's the thing that came out of a shark's stomach.'

'You've found out what it is?' she asked, excited.

'No.' He was grinning, so she lowered it and gave him a look of amused exasperation.

'Then are you going to tell me why you felt the need to drag it all the way to London to wrap up for my birthday?'

He stood and kissed her on the head, taking it from her. 'Because you care what it might be and have the temerity to explore and find out. Because you will do more with it and its cabinet companions than I ever did.' She could only stare at him. 'The collection is yours, Thea, to do with as you wish. With that and Edgar's you have the start of something potentially transformative.'

With no words she stood and wrapped her arms around his neck, gratitude welling within her. 'Are you sure?'

'I am,' he said. I have the plants, as long as we manage to keep hold of Milford. 'And I will not live forever.'

She pulled back and furrowed her brows at him. 'You have enough time left in you yet, but – thank you.' She meant it, and he knew it. He hugged her again before they sat down once more, Thea with the *Encyclopédie* and unidentified shark-stomach contents before her. Knowledge and practice.

As her father and Martha chatted she flicked through the pages, marvelling at the wealth of insight within. Never static, constantly shifting, knowledge progressing through the actions of people like those in the room with her right now. She felt privileged to be a tiny part of it, whatever that would be. A whisper of potential curled within her.

Knowledge wasn't the only thing that shifted. How different she was to the Thea who had opened volume six of Diderot, only a year ago. She would be different again by the time they left London. The thought chilled that curl of optimism. Two weeks had passed since

Ursula's confession and her conversation with Scip. That was when reality had hit her with a force which felt almost physical. She met Martha's eyes and her stomach twisted. Martha now knew about Ursula and the letter, but not about Thea's decision. For all of their promises of being honest and navigating difficult waters together, it was easier said than done. Martha was so happy it wouldn't be fair to discuss her decision before the meeting. How could she spoil the moment that Martha had waited for all her life, with the news that the person she loved was soon to be betrothed to someone else? They would talk about it afterwards, she had decided.

For the past three days Mr Morell, Martha and Thea had dined together at Hanover Square, a comfortable party who sought collections and collectibles in the day and enjoyed each others' conversation at night. Now, the day before the Royal Society meeting, Mr Morell was to eat with a group of society contributors and so Thea and Martha were to be left alone. Following presents, a walk and another run through the paper, Mr Morell left and Thea and Martha headed upstairs to change for dinner. Martha pushed the door shut behind them, a clear sign to Mrs Phibbs that they were not to be disturbed. 'I may have more presents for you,' she said, her lips curving into a smile.

Thea grinned and hutched herself up onto the bed. 'Ones that I couldn't open in front of my father?'

Martha raised an eyebrow. 'Perhaps.' She produced two more parcels from under the bed. One large and flat, the other small and square. 'This one first,' said Martha, handing her the large package. Thea carefully ripped off the paper and held the framed picture at arm's length in front of her, laughing out loud when she realised its subject. The painting looked for all the world like one of Martha's botanical drawings, but it depicted a fluffy lamb, attached to a growing mass of foliage by a stalk, with a look on its face of particular confusion. The caption underneath the painting read 'Vegetable Lamb of Tartary,' and around the illustration were various amusing captions including 'umbilical stalk' and 'hirsute coating: reduces desiccation.'

Thea ran her fingers appreciatively over the frame. 'When did you have the time?' Her eyes smiled as she looked up. It was a beautiful reminder of Edgar and his collection, but she knew it was more than that. As they had agreed over a month ago, Martha had given the vegetable lamb to Stanhope Grimston who still planned to present it at the Royal Society meeting the following night. To Martha the lamb meant freedom from the torment that had plagued her for so many years. It was a reminder that hate would never win.

She smiled. 'I managed to grab a few moments over the past month when you weren't at Denbury.'

Thea kissed her soundly. 'I love it, thank you.'

'And now this one.' Martha handed her the small package which, when unwrapped, revealed a small box. Pressing open the lid on its hinge Thea gasped. Inside was a beautiful necklace – an ammonite, held in a solid silver clasp on a delicate chain.

She looked up into Martha's hazelnut-brown eyes, alive with expectation. 'Is this from–?'

Martha nodded. 'From our visit to Whitby. I know you're not usually one for jewellery, but I thought this might prove an exception.'

Thea threw her arms around Martha's neck and spoke into her ear. 'It's perfect, thank you.' Her voice cracked a little. Emotion was never far from the surface just now. The ring she had bought for Martha was neatly tucked under her pillow. It was inlaid with a line of jet from Whitby – great minds, she thought. She planned to give it to Martha after the lecture, in a quiet moment. Before she told her about her decision.

Martha's gentle touch on the small of her back brought her back to the room. 'I hope you will always think of me, when you wear it.'

Thea gripped the silk of Martha's dress like her life depended on it. She breathed in the familiar scent and closed her eyes until she trusted herself to get out two words unaccompanied by a sob. 'Of course.' They held on until Thea's breathing settled. She placed a hand behind Martha's neck and planted a single, tender and lingering kiss on the waiting lips. 'You have spoiled me today. I don't deserve you.' Tears threatened again. If only Martha knew how true that was.

Martha's eyes flicked between hers and she seemed to think for a minute before she pushed Thea down on to the bed and kissed her so intensely that it drew any remaining breath from her body. As Martha broke away she gripped Thea's shoulders, the playfulness fled from her face, and her look was raw. 'Thea, we have to talk,' she said, her voice tight.

Thea froze. *She knows*, she thought. Nothing else would have caused that sudden shift. Nothing else would fire the desperation she now saw etched on the face she loved, but she couldn't bear to talk about it today. Not before the culmination and triumph of Martha's research. 'We do,' she said, taking Martha's face between both hands and gently stroking her cheeks, 'but not now.' Martha made to protest but Thea slipped a thumb over her lips. 'Please.'

Martha let go of the breath she held but slid a hand from Thea's shoulder and caressed her cheek with the back of a finger. 'Of course.' But the hand slid to the back of Thea's head and grasped into her hair so hard it was almost painful. 'Just promise me you will never doubt how I feel about you.' The desperation was still written in her eyes and Thea felt a surge of emotion threaten. Words stuck in her throat. 'Promise me, Thea.' Martha's eyes flitted between Thea's, demanding an answer.

'I promise,' whispered Thea, tipping her head sideways to kiss the soft skin of Martha's wrist while artfully hiding the impending tears.

CHAPTER 32

M r Morell's nervous gaze was transfixed out of the window as the carriage juddered along the cobbled streets of London. He looked pale and Thea worried that he may be in need of his medicine.

'Father?' she tried, concerned. But he didn't hear.

'Involuntary movement,' he mumbled, jiggling a leg up and down. She smiled and leaned forward stilling his fidgeting knee. 'Father, you know it off by heart, and you will be fabulous.'

His smile was weak. 'I just don't want to let anyone down.' His eyes dropped sideways to Martha who tutted. It gave Thea an excuse to look back at her. They would never be allowed in as women, so they had been creative. Martha's outfit was impeccable. A deep, sage-green, three-piece gentleman's suit with a high collar and cream piping, topped off with a brushed leather tricorn hat. It defined her figure perfectly, accentuating her slim waist and her broad shoulders. Martha had also insisted on a cane and Thea suspected she was rather enjoying herself. Now Mr Morell received a sharp tap on the shin with it.

'Don't be ridiculous, Ben. Even if your delivery is dreadful the paper is excellent. Half of them will be asleep or drunk anyway.' Martha grinned cheekily, but this seemed to relax Mr Morell and he brightened a little as the carriage drew to a halt.

Thea pressed a felt hat onto her head and kissed him on the cheek. 'You'll be brilliant, papa, we'll be with you in spirit.'

He gathered himself and strode purposefully down the steps as Mr Croft opened the door. Thea beamed with pride, he looked every inch the scholar and was about to address some of the most learned in the land. She let Martha exit the carriage ahead of her, adjusting her own breeches and pulling Lord Foxmore's newly adjusted jacket around her. She felt in her pocket for the ring box. The ring she had made from Whitby jet and silver – that she would give to Martha to celebrate the presentation of her own research. And not long before she would find out if Martha's name was on the paper. Thea had written to Mr Thistleton to request it – not as herself of course, she couldn't ask, but Tobias Moreton could. And Mr Thistleton didn't have to know that M. Smilgrove was a woman. A clever, generous woman who deserved every bit of recognition. Pride swelled inside her as she stepped onto the cobbles.

Mr Croft nodded to them both and grinned as he shut the door. 'I will see you later, sirs.' Thea was trying not to look at Martha. It wasn't done for a gentleman to stare so longingly at another. Her heart quickened as they approached the entrance and she saw Martha reach for her pocket watch nervously. Nobody cared how you were dressed at a public lecture when you paid half a penny for entry, but the Royal Society was a more select crowd. As they strode through the entrance the clerk on the door looked up. 'I'm sorry, I don't recognise–'

Mr Morell drew himself up. 'It's Morell. I am a new member speaking tonight, and these are my guests.' He gestured to Thea and Martha as they tried to hide their faces by pretending to discuss the carvings around the door.

The clerk dipped his quill and held it poised over the book. 'Names?'

'Tobias Morton,' said Thea, keeping her voice in a low register.

'And Lord Foxhole,' said Martha. Thea tried not to grin as the clerk looked up sharply at the title.

'An honour it is to have you at our meeting, my lord.' As he spoke his gaze travelled up Martha's outfit. Then back down again, and back up. Thea was sure she saw his pupils dilate as he leapt to his feet and smoothed his wig. 'Do let me know if there is anything I can assist you with this evening, my lord. Anything at all.'

Martha stepped towards his table and leaned in a little. 'I will do just that.' The colour in the clerk's cheeks shone through his white powder and he dropped his quill on the page, splattering ink on the names. Martha shot him a dazzling smile, turned on her heel and strode up the stairs, flicking her cane with each step.

'Flirt,' whispered Thea, grinning as she caught up with her.

Martha met her with a devilish smile. 'And why shouldn't I, I am dashing tonight.'

'You are,' snorted Thea as they hit the landing.

On entering the upstairs room they took a seat at a back table and each ordered a coffee as Mr Morell went to find the convenors. The wainscoted walls and dark floorboards were lit by high windows. The air smelled of bitter coffee, pies cooking at the inn next door and old sweat. Thea considered that if this was what learned meetings were like, perhaps she was happy to be excluded. Thea's eyes found Grimston in the crowd and gritted her teeth against the disgust that rose within her as he held forth to a group which looked collectively bored. When she saw Mr Morell shake the hand of another man the chatter of shared knowledge and clatter of cups became a little overwhelming and she sat down to sip her coffee. Martha joined her, the two of them trying to meld into the background as Martha clasped her hands nervously in her lap.

Before long the talks began and despite her nerves Thea found she enjoyed them. One on experiments attempting to ascertain the specific gravity of living men, and one on the discovery of a baby dragon. *Draco volans* again, she thought, no wonder the society was so worried about its reputation if claims like this got a hearing.

'Tell me again why men find themselves so superior,' Martha whispered in her ear as the man waxed lyrical about the emergent fireglands he claimed he saw at its throat. 'You have ten times their knowledge – remember that.'

Before Thea could argue the room animated into a smattering of applause, and the dragon man sat down. She held her breath as the clapping died away and Mr Morell took to the lectern, but she needn't have worried. Once he had breathed through the first few lines he grew in confidence and seemed comfortable in his subject. He described the movements of all three species of plants and handed around examples of the plates which would accompany the published paper. Low and appreciative murmurings skittered around the room as he explained the difference in stimulus of movement between the sensitive plant (touch) and the telegraph plant (sunlight). Thea glanced across at Martha and noticed her mouthing the words along with him, willing him to succeed.

The room fell silent as Mr Morell produced the plate of the *Dionea* – the venus fly trap. There was much interest in these little plants and Mr Morell was enjoying himself by now. 'Gentlemen, I now come to one of the most startling conclusions of the research – that the fly trap possesses the power of perception and can indeed count!' The room erupted in denial. Of course they couldn't, how could a plant know numbers, they didn't have a brain like animals and only humans (and then not all of them), were clever enough to count. Thea smiled at her father across the room. He had expected just such a reaction and was prepared. He produced two fly traps from the side of the room along with a small stick, and asked the president to join him at the front. A number of interested parties rose from their tables and moved to see more clearly. Soon there was a crowd around Mr Morell and the gasps and exclamations that ensued reassured Thea that Mr Morell had indeed convinced them. While his hand was shaken, his back slapped and the room distracted by the break for coffee she leaned into Martha.

'I am so proud of you.'

Martha smiled back, her eyes steely with concentration and analysis, but undeniably pleased. 'I can't tell you how delighted I am. If this gives you the confidence to go on, that is all that matters.'

Thea looked back to the seething group, crowding around the tiny plants. 'I wish it could be you, up there.'

Martha shook her head. 'It doesn't matter. We all take our place and make our contribution, however we can.' Thea nodded and gulped. Soon she would take hers. But this was Martha's time.

She glanced around furtively and squeezed Martha's hand under the table. 'I'll go and get us some coffee – we'll raise more brows by sitting here in the shadows.' Martha nodded and Thea made her way between groups of sweaty, chattering men – most of them discussing the excitement of the counting plants. She retrieved two cups and was on her return when she heard a slightly desperate Mr Thistleton in conversation with the dragon man and a few others surrounding a table by the window. Glancing over at Martha she saw that she had been joined by Mr Morell, who narrowly avoided kissing Lord Foxhole on the cheek and gave her a hearty handshake instead. He had a pot of coffee for them both, so Thea allowed herself time and positioned herself to hear more about the "dragon".

'I mean no offence but I must enquire of you how this specimen came to be presented at the meeting today,' said Mr Thistleton. 'We do know, do we not, that dragons do not exist.'

'Do we?' came the prickly response. 'I realise this has been the dominant opinion of recent years, but this juvenile seems to prove otherwise, do you not think?'

'I do not think so,' said Mr Thistleton firmly. 'Dragons do not exist.'

'Then what is your interpretation?' A third voice. 'It has wings, Thistleton. What on earth else could it be?'

'Well – I...' Mr Thistleton faltered. 'I admit I am not certain of the exact identification but I am sure a thorough...'

I know, thought Thea, still standing quietly.

Guffaws sounded around the table. 'If you are to refute a hypothesis you surely must propose a an alternative other than the fact that you do not believe in the subject.'

'Dragons are myth!' Mr Thistleton's voice was rising now. 'They are *not real*.'

The group exchanged amused glances at one another as Mr Thistleton struggled for a more compelling argument. A surge of potential rose within Thea and suddenly she couldn't hold herself back. She joined them at the table and set down the cups, the group turning to her as one. 'An impressive specimen, gentlemen,' she said, more calmly than she felt. 'Would you mind if I take a look?'

The dragon owner indicated that he would not, passing the jar to her. She brought it near to her face and squinted at the specimen. It was more ragged than Mr Constable's, but still unmistakeable.

'I enjoyed your presentation very much,' she said, addressing the dragon man directly, 'and you are quite right to hypothesise based on observation – remaining open to the infinite possibilities of the world is vital for the advancement of science.' Beside her she saw Mr Thistleton sag a little, as the dragon man exchanged pleased glances with others around the table.

'But I am afraid that on this occasion I have to present an alternative interpretation.' She placed the jar on the table, turning it to give the group a clear view. Mr Thistleton's interest roused and he half turned to face her. 'The structures you refer to as wings do, in fact, emerge from the side of the body rather than adjacent to the spine, even allowing for development into adulthood. I believe this is a patagium more fitted for gliding than independent flight.' She indicated the relevant details of the specimen as she spoke, then retrieved the jar and peered at it again, tapping on the glass near its throat. 'Equally I understand your identification of fire glands, but I believe these are throat lappets which assist with balance in flight. Don't you agree, Mr Thistleton?' She looked him dead in the eye.

'Well, yes,' he said, sweating a little. 'That would seem to make sense.'

'Indeed it would,' she said, growing in confidence at the awestruck stares now turned her way. I would say that what you have here, gentlemen, is a relatively well-preserved specimen of *Draco volans*. Extremely impressive. Described in the new Linnaeus. Page eight hundred and twenty-four.' She placed the jar purposefully back on the table and smiled around at them. 'Probably a male, judging by the yellow dewlap.'

She prepared for them to scoff or to dismiss her, but instead they looked between themselves and the dragon man picked up the jar. 'You know, you might be right, sir, I do see the difference in the gliding apparatus.'

'Now I come to think of it, I perhaps did see it in Linnaeus,' said another. The look they gave her contained something bordering on admiration, and she swelled a little with pride. A small frisson of excitement rolled through her as she realised what she was about to do.

'I believe they have a well preserved one in the British Museum which you are able to view by appointment,' she said, and then turned to look directly at Mr Thistleton. 'I am sure Mr Thistleton would be pleased to show you, and, I am told, he also provides informative tours for the ladies in your lives.' She didn't lose his gaze for a second. To his credit, the only external sign of recognition he showed was a rippling of the brow and a slight bulge of the eyes. She could see the point he almost exposed her as his mouth opened, and then the realisation that he would have to admit he had been vindicated by a woman as he shut it again.

'Indeed, gentlemen,' he said, turning back to the table. 'Do make an appointment, we would be glad to receive you.' They nodded, and then leaned into the specimen, discussing its detail.

Mr Thistleton turned to her. 'I suppose I owe you thanks,' he said, his pride almost visibly raw.

'Not especially,' she said calmly. 'But we can't have people going out of this room believing they have a baby dragon in a jar, can we?'

As she met his gaze she didn't know if he was furious or frustrated. Eventually he let a small smile creep through. 'Well, credit where credit is due.' He held out a hand, and she shook it.

'There is something I wanted to ask you.' She took a sip of coffee, trying not to grimace at the bitter taste. Mr Thistleton nodded his assent. 'I wondered if I could take a look at the proofs of my father's paper?'

Mr Thistleton rummaged in a leather folder on a table nearby and retrieved three printed sheets, handing them over with a confused glance. Thea took them up eagerly, wondering if Tobias Morton's request for Martha's name to be added to the paper had been accepted. What she saw made her head snap up to meet Mr Thistleton's gaze.

'M. Smilgrove and S. Morell are both listed as contributing authors?'

'Indeed,' he said, looking panicked. 'Is that not correct?' She suspected she could tell him anything at this moment and he would believe it.

'It is,' she said, 'but I only wrote to you to ask about M. Smilgrove. How did you know to add Scip? I mean, S. Morell,' she corrected herself.

A wearied look crossed Mr Thistleton's face. 'You are Tobias Moreton?'

'I am afraid so,' said Thea, with a sly smile.

'I received letters from both you and a Lord Foxhole,' said the president with an air of resignation. 'His asked for S. Morell to be added.' Thea couldn't resist an amused glance over at Martha who was deep in conversation with Mr Morell. She hadn't asked for Scip's name as Scip had made it clear that wasn't something he valued, but she was glad it would be there, nonetheless. Mr Thistleton went on. 'I checked with your father on both names, of course. I assume I have been outsmarted once again?' Thea was relieved he looked resigned, rather than angry. She gave him her most charming smile.

'Only a little, Mr Thistleton. I can't help thinking it is only right that all contributors will gain the recognition they deserve.'

'And who am I to argue?' At least he was smiling now. 'I apologise that I underestimated you.'

'Most people do,' she returned, with more confidence than she had ever felt. She picked up the spare cup and handed it to him. 'Coffee?'

The room hushed once again as Mr Grimston took to the stand. Still alive from her discussion with Mr Thistleton, Thea felt herself bristle for a different reason. That Grimston was able to address these men and Martha was not technically permitted in the room filled her with disgust, although she had to admit she was curious to witness the reaction to the vegetable lamb. She glanced at Martha who was staring intently and looked apprehensive. Every encounter with Grimston now made Thea realise what power he had held over Martha. How she had always doubted herself because of him – he had chipped away at her confidence, bit by bit, and that would take a long time to heal. Thea stared at him, hating him for it.

'Is it that Grimston fellow?' muttered a voice on the table next to them, not quite quiet enough to be furtive. 'What is it this time?'

Mr Grimston cleared his throat. 'Gentlemen, I do have a comment to make about the most recent presentation.' He glared at Mr Morell from across the room and Thea and Martha glowered back. 'But first, I present an item to you this evening which I know will both astound and delight.'

'The tail of a mermaid!' piped up a voice from a middle table. A titter diffused around the room and then faded, like ink dropped into the ocean.

'Aha,' said Mr Grimston, colouring a little, 'the barnacle goose was just my little joke for you all, I do hope the learned society appreciated it. What I have here today is something entirely new to natural history, and quite genuine.'

'Please, Lord, not another lumpy bird,' muttered the voice next to them. Thea stifled a smile and glanced at Martha, who shifted uncomfortably.

'Today I present to you,' went on Grimston, 'the Vegetable Lamb of Tartary!' He held up the brown lump that Edgar had introduced to Thea over a year before, and that Grimston had demanded from Martha whilst threatening her honour. Thea saw her draw herself up and set her jaw.

'Oh dear God–' The gentleman on the table next to them had his head in his hands. A murmur rose and fell in the room like a gentle wave offshore.

'This organism begins life as a plant. The lush foliage sprouts forth a sturdy stem with a bud at its apex which transforms into a lamb. On maturity the lamb detaches and lives life as an independent mammal. This, my friends, truly spans the void between the vegetable and animal kingdoms.' He held the lump aloft and awaited the applause.

Someone took a noisy slurp of coffee amidst the silence. 'Mutton chops, two pennies,' came a muffled shout from the street below.

The man on the table next to them looked up from his hands. 'More ridiculous than the dragon. Get him off,' he shouted.

Doubt shadowed Grimston's face for a second. He started to protest but was drowned out by the swelling tide of noise in the room.

'Giving the society a bad name!'

'Where's that counting plant man gone?'

'I have something to say about that paper,' shouted Grimston against the din, 'it was partially conducted by a...' but his words were swallowed by the noise of the crowd. He stared around the room, challenging every member of the audience and losing each in turn.

Eventually he snatched up the fern, stalked through the baying crowd and stormed out of the door.

Mr Morell leaned into Thea. 'Wasn't that in Edgar's collection?' Her eyes confirmed it and she shot him a guilty smile. Would he be cross? Only a warm grin shone back at her. 'That'll teach him to underestimate my daughter.' She smiled with relief and turned to gauge Martha's reaction, but the chair was empty. Out of the corner of her eye she saw the green tail of a coat disappear through the door. She followed it just in time to see Martha clatter down the stairs after Grimston and bark his name into the void of the entrance hall.

He turned. 'What, man? Can't it wait?' Now she had his attention Martha stalked elegantly down the stairs and stopped two from the bottom. She drew herself up in front of him, chin high, expression defiant. Holding his gaze she reached up and pulled the hat and wig from her head, allowing her ashen hair to fall in waves around her shoulders. Thea's heart already beat wildly and at this it jumped too far up her throat for comfort. The clerk on the door stared at Martha, open mouthed.

Grimston staggered backwards. 'You!' he exclaimed. 'What on earth–?' He looked Martha up and down, lost for words as a laugh erupted from deep within her.

'Did you think I would miss your moment of triumph, Grimston? I am delighted to say it didn't disappoint.' She looked down at him, still and regal.

Grimston's face took a few seconds to register his understanding. 'You *knew*!' He spat the words. 'The lamb.'

Martha didn't deny it. 'You demanded it of me under threat. What was I to do?'

He snarled at her. 'I'll tell you what *I* am going to do.' He stalked around the door and shouted for his footman. 'Mason! Get a boy to *Town and Country*. I have left a story with them – see that it goes in the morning edition.' Mr Mason nodded and ran. Grimston had stared at

Martha as he delivered the last line of his instruction. His face betrayed only shock as she stepped towards him and smiled.

'Don't think for a second I didn't expect it. Do as you wish, Grimston. By the time that paper is in the hands of the gullible public I will be out of the country – on a ship bound for the South of Africa and all the botanical treasures it possesses. Print what you wish and let them know the truth. You no longer hold anything over me.'

Thea barely registered it when Mr Grimston stalked off. She hardly felt her father's hand close around her arm. Time seemed to slow as Martha turned from her adversary and looked upwards, straight towards her. She saw Martha's eyes widen and a hand cover her mouth. 'Oh, Thea.' Martha started up the stairs but Thea was already racing down them at speed, headed for the carriage.

Mr Croft leapt down and flung the door open as she approached. She shot into the dark interior and Martha clattered after her. The two of them sat awkwardly and Thea's heart thudded in her ears as the door was held for Mr Morell. 'I'll walk, actually,' he said, pointing down the road with a slight raise of the brows. 'Nice evening, would be a shame to miss it.' Mr Croft nodded, professionally impassive, and closed the door. Once alone and the carriage jolted into motion, Thea's eyes settled questioningly on Martha's which looked wary and anxious.

'Thea, I'm–'

'Is it true?' That was all Thea wanted to know. She didn't *want* to know. But she had to. A wave of nausea washed over her.

Martha dropped her head. 'Yes.' It was a whisper which spoke of resignation and surrender. 'Thea, I am so sorry, I was going to tell you.'

Thea stared at her. 'When? By letter when you arrive in *Africa*?' She spat the last word.

Martha pressed her hands to her breeches as she leaned forward. 'I did try. I would have tonight. I have begun to tell you too many times, but whenever I started I knew it would break your heart and I couldn't. Not before our success tonight.'

The look Thea gave was nothing short of incredulous. 'And you think this is better?' Martha shook her head and looked lost for words. However painful, Thea had to know more. 'How? When?'

Martha took a breath. 'With Captain Morrison, to the Cape of Good Hope. Tomorrow.'

Thea thought her eyes might jump out of her head. 'Tomorrow! How long have you been planning it?'

'Hardly any time at all.' Martha's knuckles whitened on her knees. 'He asked me when I met him in London in the winter season – after you had returned to Milford.' Thea took a breath, but Martha raised a hand to stop her. 'I said no. Because of you. But then, over the past month' – she looked searchingly into Thea's eyes – 'you resolved on your future, I think. Captain Morrison had said there would be an open place if I changed my mind and I thought it would be easier this way.'

The understanding settled like autumn leaves in Thea's mind. She had suspected Martha knew of her plans, but not that long ago. Martha had tried to tell her last night, but Thea had stopped her. The knowledge did nothing to calm her. 'Easier for who? You didn't have to do that with Grimston – you could just have let him go and you could have stayed.' Tears of anger and desperation pricked her eyes. Her throat was thick and her heart beat so fast she thought she might faint. It was too much, to think she might lose Martha so suddenly and without warning.

Martha shook her head. 'He was never going to let this drop, Thea, I just thank god that he won't implicate you because of your father's success with the society. He has no such qualms about me of course. I knew he would go to the press. But let him publish, let the world know who I really am. Now it won't matter.'

An involuntary sob rose through and out of Thea's body. 'But you are also saying that *we* do not matter.'

Martha shook her head and took Thea's hands from across the carriage. 'No. Of all things that could never be. The past two weeks have made me realise how terrified I am of losing you. But Thea, I am more terrified of losing half of you. Of watching you slip ever further away, me fluttering around the edges of your new life and landing occasionally if, and when I could. It couldn't be borne, and so I must do it quickly.'

The pool of grief froze into anger inside Thea, making her whole body shudder. 'You must do it quickly.' She was surprised at her own voice, it was full of bitterness and regret. 'What about me? My feelings don't matter?' Thea regretted the words as soon as they were out. The look that hit her could have shattered stone.

'Your feelings have always been the only ones that matter to me,' retorted Martha angrily.

Thea gritted her teeth against the rising emotion. 'But you have decided for us.'

'You were about to decide yourself!' Martha shouted and Thea couldn't deny it. But she also couldn't comprehend the fact that Martha was leaving her. Tomorrow and without warning.

'I have no choice!' Thea's fingers gripped white on the seat of the carriage as it lurched around a corner. 'My family's security, particularly Ursula's safety, depends on me, how can I ignore that?'

'You can't,' said Martha, waving a hand in dismissal. 'Of course you can't. I just wish you'd told me.'

'Yes, well,' said Thea, the fight seeping from her. She had been guilty as much as Martha. 'So do I.'

'And I wish I'd told you too,' said Martha, huffing back into the seat. She slackened a little. 'You know I have always been willing to stand by you, whatever you chose. You have decided on a secure future for her and the rest of your family which is the right and brave course.' They stared at one another, unspeaking as the carriage drew to a halt and Thea looked out to see Martha's home at Foxmore Square. The carriage was parked outside with trunks loaded.

'You're going now?' Fear and fury rose inside Thea once more. At least she hadn't waited until her wedding night to break the news.

Martha nodded and her eyes flitted over Thea's, hopefully. 'To temporary lodgings before we sail at sunrise. You could come with me, tonight?'

Thea sat back and fixed her with a firm gaze. This was too much. Being near to Martha felt as necessary to her as air or water. How dare she take it away in a matter of hours? The emotion was too much and she needed to be alone. 'I can't. I wish you a safe voyage.'

Martha stared at her, the unsaid crackling between them. 'As you wish.' She stalked out of the carriage and into the house without looking back.

Thea tapped on the carriage wall. 'Home, Croft.'

Once at Hanover Square Thea dashed up the stairs and straight to her room, ignoring the welcome of Mrs Phibbs. She slammed the door and let out a painful, breathy sob, followed by another, and another. For once she allowed them to overwhelm her. She paced up and down furiously, and then threw herself on the bed in a manner she felt befitting to the heartbroken.

She recalled telling Martha that she was willing to take the risk of heartbreak. Today cast an entirely new light on the glib declaration. Now she understood. There was the pain of losing someone you loved, of course. That was the worst part. But at the same time the wrench of losing something much more profound. She couldn't quite put her finger on it. A way of being, gone. Like part of the essence of who you were, slipping away without hope of rescue.

After a few minutes of self-pitiful sobbing she reached under the pillow. There was the ammonite necklace, proudly arranged in its box and awaiting her. She had placed it there for after her discussion with Martha. The conversation about the fact that she had to marry soon, the conversation that said things would never be quite the same. The necklace was under her pillow so that whatever happened she could return to the room and remember that Martha loved her – that she would always love her, no matter how different things might be. Thea was disgusted at herself for being so angry with Martha for doing something she had been about to do herself, but still couldn't shake the feeling of betrayal and resentment.

Suddenly there was a knock at her door. She shut her eyes. 'Can it wait?' Her father opened the door a crack.

'Are you decent?'

'Yes,' she mumbled.

'Then no it can't, I just made it back.' He stepped around the door and she hurried to sit up and dry her eyes.

'How are you, my little one?' He placed himself next to her on the bed, slipping an arm around her. She buried her face in his shoulder, willing it to still the squall within her. They had never spoken about what was between her and Martha – he probably suspected, she thought, but certainly not the extent of it. She chose caution.

'I'll live, probably.' She hid her pain and sniffed into his shoulder.

'How was Martha when you left her?'

Her chest tightened. 'I – I don't know.'

'You don't know?'

Thea sat up, unsure of where this was heading. 'We didn't part on the best of terms.' She looked abashed, and then a thought crossed her mind. 'Did you know? About her... trip?'

He shook his head. 'Not a peep. Where is she going?'

'To the Cape of Good Hope. Tomorrow, at sunrise.' The details were etched in her mind.

Her father raised a brow. 'She is going on a long sea voyage, and you didn't part on the best of terms?'

Thea glowered back defiantly, but the words she was about to utter sounded ridiculous even before they came out. 'She didn't tell me.'

To her father's credit, he only squeezed her tighter. 'But you love her. And she loves you.' Thea could only stare at him. 'Of course I know, Thea, the woman is infatuated with you. Did you expect her to wait around for you to find a husband?'

As Thea blinked, still in shock, she felt a solitary tear slip down her cheek. 'It just seems so unfair–' She checked herself, remembering the conversation with Scip, and understood for the first time how the feeling of injustice could overwhelm a whole life.

Her father pulled away to look at her, his comfortable, familiar face lined with concern. 'Undoubtedly so. But Thea, Martha has had to seek happiness wherever she can for her whole life. She has always wanted to travel and this is her chance. The business with Grimston's daughter was terrible for her and she hasn't been the same since, until recently.'

Thea's eyes widened. 'You knew?'

'Edgar and I figured it out.' He squeezed her hands. 'We have looked out for Martha these years but I knew you could only be good for one another in Scarborough. For the first time Martha has confidence in herself – you helped her to gain that and she did the same for you.' Thea shut her eyes and rested her head against him once more, appalled at herself. 'Perhaps you would like to have a think about how you choose to part, when she will be away for so long?'

Thea sat up. 'I have been abominably selfish. Again. And I don't know where she is.'

'She's gone already?'

'Everything was waiting when we got to Foxmore Square. I don't know where she's staying or where she sails from. She'll be gone and I was so awful to her.' The tears rose again, but suddenly the door shot open. It was Mrs Phibbs, standing tall and defiant.

'It wasn't that we were listening at the door, but I believe we can help with that, Miss Thea.' The housekeeper stepped sideways allowing Mrs Jenkins to appear alongside.

Thea looked between them, astonished. 'Mrs Jenkins, what are you–?'

'I came to plead with you to reconsider your position, Miss. Lady Foxmore was not in a good way when you returned and I would hate to see her going off like that. After everything that has happened, and how you have been.' She fixed Thea with a knowing gaze. 'She has been so different and so happy, Miss, and to lose it all at the last minute–' Her voice trailed off and Thea saw Mrs Phibbs raise moist eyes to the ceiling and set her jaw.

'Do you know where she is, Mrs Jenkins?' asked Thea, desperate to be off, but Mrs Jenkins shook her head.

'She was so upset she wouldn't say, Miss, but I do know that she sails from Greenwich in the morning. We won't find her lodgings but a ship should be hard to miss.'

A thought crept through Thea that solidified in resolve as soon as it hit her veins. 'Then that gives me time.' She flew out of the room and down the stairs, pursued by the two housekeepers. Thea shouted to Croft for the carriage and waited impatiently on the pavement.

Mrs Phibbs and Mrs Jenkins appeared beside her. 'We'll help.' It wasn't a question. Thea looked between them, allowed herself a small smile and jumped into the carriage almost before it had stopped. When the carriage jolted into motion she shared her plan with her formidable allies.

As she stepped through the door of the *Town and Country* magazine office Thea thought how out of place she must look in this part of London. Then she looked down and realised she was still wearing Lord

Foxmore's clothes, her hair had come loose and tears still tracked her cheeks. She would even look out of place on the stage. She felt for the ring, still secure in her pocket – that was what mattered.

Rapping on the counter, she waited impatiently. 'Too late for tomorrow's paper,' came a shout from behind the office door.

She rapped again. 'I wish to speak with someone. It is urgent.' A greasy looking man in a shirt streaked with black ink stepped languidly through the door. As it opened the deafening clatter of printing presses filled the air. He wiped his hands on a rag trailing from his belt and looked her up and down.

'Are you lost' – he regarded her more carefully – 'sir? Perhaps I can help?'

'Perhaps you can, my good sir.' She drew herself up, hoping to salvage a little dignity. 'I understand that you have a piece from a Mr Stanhope Grimston for the morning edition. I wish to replace it.'

He smirked. 'Ah. I've been expecting you. You're not a disappointment I must say.' He ran a hand through oily black hair as his eyes wandered over her frame, making her insides shrink away from his gaze. 'No can do I'm afraid. That piece Grimston has is a juicy piece of gossip and carries some useful morals on the place and position of a lady. It's dangerous when they get out of hand, wouldn't you agree, sir?'

Thea kept his gaze defiantly and threw a bag of coins on the desk. 'I'm sure this will help.'

He laughed, a patronising guffaw. 'You'll have to do better than that. Gossip's worth its weight in gold in this business, and that paper back there is pretty heavy.' He placed both hands on the counter and jerked his head in the direction of the door to the press. 'The people love a Countess brought down when she's got above her station. It's a public service to keep everyone informed.'

Thea's lip curled. She was not about to let this slippery man best her. 'I'll sue you for libel. You are printing untruths.'

His eyes lazily wandered her suit-clad figure once more. 'Am I now? Anyway, you are welcome to do so – *sir*.' He savoured the word as a threat. 'We'll add you to the wall.' He nodded to a row of notices pinned up proudly, each one announcing a fine. 'We take more in paper sales. It's mostly good advertising.'

Anger boiled over within her. 'Now look here. Either you pull that piece or I'll–'

He leaned over the counter and grinned at her, exposing brown teeth. She could smell his rank breath and see the grease slicking his face. 'Or you'll what?'

Thea hesitated. What would she do? She had nothing else. She gritted her teeth and was about to turn on her heel when the door burst open.

'Or I'll tell your mother, little Timmy Walters.'

His greasy face receded as he started back from the counter. 'Aunt Althea.' His mouth remained open in shock.

This was a surprise, but Thea was happy to let Mrs Phibbs take the floor. 'Indeed it is, lad. I'm sure your mother would be interested to know that you've been printing unverified information which could land my good friend Mrs Jenkins here unemployed, wouldn't she?' His eyes were still wide as she gestured to the defiant form beside her. 'And that is what will happen to Mrs Jenkins if the Countess loses her standing. I suggest you retract that article immediately.'

The man looked as if his shirt were suddenly too small as he pulled at his collar. 'I can't, Aunt Althea. I have a contract with the gentleman – he made me sign 'cause he knew someone would try to pull the piece.'

She raised an eyebrow and leaned over the wooden surface towards him. 'Then I suggest you make space in your paper and print the qualifier that Miss Morell is about to provide for you.' Thea had never seen such an intent gleam in her eye. 'Ready the presses, lad. This won't take long.'

Thea awoke to her elbow being shaken and paper sheets waved in her face. The chattering of the presses was deafening, how had she slept in the office? Mrs Jenkins and Mrs Phibbs sat alongside her, alert and eyeballing Little Timmy Walters as he sweated over her. 'Here you go, Miss,' he gulped, 'the first copy off the press, just as you requested.' The paper shook a little as he held it out.

Thea jumped up and snatched it from him, not caring how crumpled she must look. 'Thank you.' She ran out of the door and into the waiting carriage, followed closely by two housekeepers. 'To Greenwich dock, Croft,' she shouted, waking the sleeping footman. 'Fast as you can.' They sped down Cannon Street, scattering pedestrians ahead of them and causing an oncoming carriage to swerve and scrape down the side of a building. Thea hung out of the window and looked ahead. 'Which way will we go?' She had to shout to be heard against the rushing wind.

'Over Tower Bridge, Miss,' he yelled behind him, 'I know a short-cut.' It had been dark when she awoke, but as they sped through overhanging buildings the sky began to lighten. They clattered over cobbles as the warm, orange glow was punctuated by a prick of yellow light, swelling as it flooded the Thames and announced the dawn. The ship sailed at sunrise. What if it was gone when they arrived?

As they neared Greenwich Thea frantically craned her neck to catch a glimpse of any departing ship. She spied two vessels moored on the south bank at the trading docks. One was a clipper being loaded with crates and bundles by a large crane. The other was more substantial – already prepared and beginning to slide away from its wharf, tugged by two small boats out in the swelling river. Mr Croft steered the horses close and brought them to a screeching halt. 'Sorry girls,' he bellowed as their hooves clattered on the cobbles, 'it's for a good cause!'

Thea flung open the door and jumped out, hotly pursued by Mrs Phibbs and Mrs Jenkins. 'You, man,' she hollered to a porter coiling a rope around a bollard, 'which of these ships is bound for the Cape of Good Hope?' She prayed with every fibre of her being he would indicate the one being loaded. The man turned and pointed to the larger ship – the one making its way slowly but purposefully away from the wharf. The bow was headed to the sailing lane, the stern pivoting and beginning to open a gap between itself and the rickety structure.

Thea's heart sank. Surely after all her efforts she had to reach Martha before she left, she had no idea when, or even if, she would see her again. As she glanced back to Mrs Phibbs and Mrs Jenkins she saw the eyes of both glistened with tears. Somehow their understanding confirmed her resolve.

'Not like this,' she muttered under her breath, and started to run. She heard the ship creak and groan, the timbers twisting as it manoeuvred. Closing in she started to slow. The gangways were long since brought in and the deck too high. Then she saw it. A ladder, of rope and wooden slats hanging from the stern. A split-second decision and judgement. She picked up her pace and ran as fast as she could. By the time she reached the edge of solid ground a gap six feet wide gaped beneath her. She planted a foot firmly on the edge of the wharf and leapt.

CHAPTER 33

T hea stood amongst the commotion around her, men winding ropes, shouting orders, gathering sails. They were too engrossed in their own work to pay her attention. All she could see was the stately figure ahead of her, standing at the bow of the boat and looking out into the expanse of freedom that awaited. A breeze caught the hem of a steel-grey travelling habit under a redingote tailored jacket of the same colour, and a tricorn, brushed leather hat sat regally above the hair gathered in a messy knot, slicked with gold from the sun behind.

Thea moved swiftly through the bustle and to the relative quiet of the bow deck. Suddenly and with terror she realised that Martha may not want to see her after she had been so petulant at their parting. Her pounding heart made her light-headed and her voice didn't seem like her own when it fled her lips. 'Martha.'

The figure turned sharply and blinked twice in disbelief. 'Thea! What the–'

Thea stepped forward, doubt flooding her veins as she proffered the copy of *Town and Country,* hot off the press. 'I thought you should at least see this, before you go.' Martha took the paper, a wary frown on her brow as she read the segment indicated. Her face became ever more grave as her eyes took in the defamation of her character, the accusations of sapphism and the lies surrounding the number of sexual partners she had taken, even within her marriage. As ever with the odious gossip columns of *Tête-a-Tête* she was not named, but from the description there could be no doubt she was the subject. She looked up at Thea, uncertain of her motives after the virulence of their most recent exchange.

'Did you have to show me?'

Thea nodded to the paper, trying to keep her eyes soft, but she couldn't keep the worry from creasing her brow. 'Turn back a page.' Martha stared uneasily but flicked the paper over with a graceful finger. It was a single page, prefacing the *Tête-a-Tête* piece, with only a few words in the centre. The typesetters only had time for a short passage, but Thea thought it did the job perfectly.

A gentleman of wonder is harmless, truth be told,
Until challenged by a Countess, both scholarly and bold,
With printed words he strikes against her greater skill,
Dear reader, on the following, do interpret as you will.

As Martha read, confusion spread over her face. She looked up. 'Who wrote this?'

Thea raised an eyebrow and mischief shone through her grief. 'I confess that it was mostly Mrs Jenkins, but I put in the bit about greater skill.' She stepped forward again. 'And Mr Thistleton has confirmed that you and Scip will be named on the paper, Martha. We both wrote to him, as it turned out.'

Martha exhaled a breath that it looked like she had held for weeks. 'Oh, Thea—'

Thea interrupted her. She had formulated her speech in the printers before sleep had taken her and was determined to get it out. 'Martha, I am as sorry as I could possibly be. I have been utterly selfish.' She gripped the fabric at the sides of the suit she still wore, desperate to reach for Martha but not daring. 'We both knew that what we had couldn't last forever. You are right that I had made a decision and I had no right to react so disgracefully to yours.' They were still feet away from each other, the rail of the ship at Martha's back and the sunlight flooding around her form. The ship moved imperceptibly slowly, advancing to the sailing lane.

Martha hugged her own arms tightly to her as if trying to protect herself from reality. 'I was wrong, Thea, I should have told you, I was only greedy for our time together and couldn't bear that it would end any sooner than it must.'

Thea dashed away the apology with a shake of her head. 'This is what you have always wanted. You will bring back knowledge that will transform our understanding of the world. You will be immortalised in your drawings and natural philosophers and botanists of the future will base their work on your observations. I could never stand in the way of that. It's just that I don't know how I–' her voice tailed off and her eyes filled with tears as the reality of a future without Martha set in. '– I just don't know who I am without you.'

As her head dropped and the tears came again she felt Martha's soft hands on her face, imploring her to look up. She opened her eyes to meet those she craved most desperately. 'Of course you do,' said Martha, firmly. 'You are a strong, independent woman with a bright future. Not only as a dedicated part of your family, and goodness knows you will need all of your resolution for that, but as a natural philosopher in your own right. We are all shaped by those around us but it does not mean we are nothing without them.' She ran a finger across the line of Thea's jaw. 'You will have to work ten times, or twenty times as hard as any man, but you have brains and determination.'

Thea twisted her head to the side and nestled into Martha's palm, eager for the reassurance while the chance remained. 'I know you're right. I'm just scared.'

Martha looked at her kindly, but with a good measure of the steely determination that Thea knew so well. 'Good, or you aren't doing it right. Without adversity there is no progress.'

Thea smiled to herself as Martha echoed Edgar's words. 'Perhaps Grimston was right.'

Martha blanched. 'I doubt that very much.'

A nervous chuckle managed to find its way out. 'I mean when he said that female curiosity is dangerous. There is a danger. That we might learn exactly what is possible.' Martha's eyes softened as her jaw hardened and she took both Thea's hands in hers, Thea saw a thousand words on her lips. Words that would never find form, but that spoke of the injustice and oppression that led them here. 'What if I'm not ready to let you go?' she asked quietly, the sound of her own heart in her ears louder than the words.

Now Martha looked confused. 'I thought you were marrying?'

'I am,' confirmed Thea, 'and I know you said you couldn't be a mistress, but the decision I have made gives me more independence than I once hoped. What if you and I could have a chance? It may not be what we would choose, but we could make it our own. Just to know it was possible...'

Martha looked away towards the slowly shifting bank of the river. 'I do admit I have been reassessing my earlier statement, ever since the thought of losing you became real. I did think I couldn't be a mistress, but then I also realised I couldn't be without you.'

Ever since Thea had made her decision she had nurtured a delicate kernel of hope, but at Martha's words it took root. Tears of pride, sorrow and possibility massed in her eyes and she grasped Martha's hands more firmly. 'I don't quite know how yet, but I know we can do it.'

There was a light in Martha's eyes now, one of prospect and opportunity. 'We will find a way, I am sure of it.' The hope began to unfurl. Thea couldn't wait any longer. She dropped Martha's hands and flung her arms around her neck, realising how much they both were shaking. As Thea sobbed Martha held on to her firmly, as if physical strength would keep them from being parted. Then she pulled back and looked seriously into Thea's eyes. 'Would you rather I didn't go?' She indicated the expanse of the Thames with a thumb thrown over her shoulder. It seemed like such a simple gesture to encompass the vastness of the world that lay before her. 'I will stay, if it will make it easier for you?'

Thea shook her head. 'Absolutely not. I have to take steps which would be harder with you here. And more than that, I want you to experience the world as you have always wished to. Only think of the things you are going to see that thousands never will. We are strong enough to survive this time apart.'

Martha's eyes tracked over Thea's face, taking her in, and a thumb grazed her cheek. 'I think I could survive anything, knowing you were waiting.'

'I will be,' said Thea quietly. 'How long?'

'A year, perhaps a little more,' said Martha, looking at her with concern. 'Is that alright?'

'Anything is alright as long as I know you will be mine on your return.' There was certainty now. Now that she knew there was a future the parting had lost the cavernous desperation of finality. Hope bloomed within her. She knew that tears still tracked down her cheeks but they held potential as well as pain.

'I will write,' said Martha, 'and I will let you know where you can write to me, as long as there are planned landings and friendly ports.'

'I already can't wait to hear about your adventures.'

Martha's eyes danced but then flitted to the tall masts above them. 'You better spend your time making that cabinet into something special. Who knows what treasures will return with me on this ship, and they will need a home. I am not sailing for the likes of Stanhope Grimston, Thea, anything we bring back will need to be subject to a proper analytical process.'

Thea smiled at the stirring within her – something hot like molten metal that seeped through her veins and right to her fingertips. It solidified into a nervous determination. 'Then I will be ready.'

Martha nodded in satisfaction and then looked awkwardly at her hands. 'Speaking of which – Thea I know this isn't really the right time, but there won't be another. My plants. I couldn't tell anyone I was leaving until the last minute so there are no plans. I have written to the household and McCarthy of course – he will keep the collection at Denbury in my absence – but your father should take the plants he wants and so should you, if you choose to do so. I think you have been coming round to them, over the past year.'

The laugh bubbled out of Thea through the thick wetness of her sorrow. 'Are you more sad about leaving me, or your plants?'

The tenderness in Martha's eyes betrayed her, but she shrugged nonchalance in a last act of defiance. 'Difficult to say.' For a second there were no words as the reality that moments like this – tender, caring, teasing moments – would be gone until they resumed an arrangement that would be quite different.

Thea shook it out of her head. 'I will lavish your plants with the attention I would prefer to lavish on their owner, and they will be dead from smothering within six months.' She sighed. 'I think perhaps, despite myself, I fell in love with them at the same time I fell in love with you. There is such potential.' She had never quite shaken the fact that without a plant, her father would likely be – well, it didn't bear thinking about.

Martha stepped closer and Thea trailed a finger across the scar below her eye, one last time. Martha caught her hand. 'Knowledge leaves a mark on all of us. That is good, as long as it is managed. Some of it will enable you to thrive. Some is more difficult.'

'I am determined,' she said, realising how true that was. 'How can I do anything other than honour Edgar's legacy and be here for what comes off that ship when you return?'

Martha looked deep into her eyes. 'We can change the world.'

Changing the world seemed rather daunting, but Thea's new-found mettle carried her through. 'We will.' She took a parcel out of her jacket pocket and offered it to Martha who cradled it like it was the most delicate glass. 'I was going to give this to you after the lecture, to always remind you of what is possible, when you are free.'

She sniffed and looked around her with another weak smile. 'Not that you need it now.'

Martha slipped off the paper and opened the small box inside. She gasped at the ring. 'Is that–?'

Thea nodded. 'Jet from Whitby. I am so proud of you, Martha.'

Martha didn't even bother to try to stem the tears falling from her face. 'Thea, I could never have done this without you. The doubt had got the better of me, and you knew. You have breathed new life into me, transformed me, given me the confidence to have desires and to follow my ambitions. You have unlocked something that I scarce knew was there myself.'

Thea gave a wet laugh, through a sob. 'The physical laws of the world are so equitable. If only we could apply the same reason to matters of the heart and soul.'

Martha wrapped her fingers around Thea's, trapping the ring between their palms. 'They will take longer to see the light, but please know that I regret nothing about what has happened over the past year. Our love may never be conventionally accepted, Thea, but that makes it no less sincere.'

Thea ground her teeth to stop the raw emotion bubbling up her throat and out of her chest. While there was a future, the next year at least did not have Martha in it. 'Perhaps we relish it more, knowing it must take hardship to endure. I will miss you.'

Martha's face was crumpling but she took Thea's face in her hands and looked deep into her eyes. 'I am utterly in love with you. Never forget it.'

Thea's throat hitched. She was seized with a sudden desperation. She drank in the face in front of her and held on to Martha as the emotion overwhelmed her. Retrieving the ring from their palms she slipped it on to Martha's finger. 'And I you. Remember me. Remember me everywhere you go and take me with you. I will be here, waiting.'

Martha nodded through the tears, cast a glance around them and pulled Thea into a gap between the mast and a fold of sails. They devoured each other tenderly and ravenously, twining fingers through hair, tracking curves and soft skin. Thea closed her eyes and grasped at Martha with a fierce determination, committing every touch and sensation to memory, knowing it would be a source of solace in the coming, difficult months.

The air felt different as Thea stepped into the hallway of Hanover Square. The house wasn't different of course, but she was changed within it. Mrs Phibbs and Mrs Jenkins had met her on the quayside and sat with her as she rode out an overwhelming conflation of emotion. A desperate, heavy grief that the source of her most ardent happiness was gone, but delight at the shared understanding and hope for their future. She felt every emotion keenly. Mrs Phibbs said that it would pass, that it would morph and change and make her grow stronger. She started to believe it.

She had been given a lift off the ship by a lighterman, Scip's words ringing in her ears as they made their way silently back to shore. No, the situation wasn't fair, but she must control what she was able. And Jane had been right, this was a time when Thea held the cards. She would approach life as a science and base her decisions on facts and reason rather than the ideal and wonderful. If she couldn't control what she felt in her heart, she could dictate what was written on the blank sheet of her mind, and that would be something spectacular, she decided. She would curate her own happiness through the pursuit of learning, inquiry and progress in all aspects of natural philosophy. She would take the opportunity presented to her, as Edgar had implored her so passionately.

It was strange, standing there in the hallway of her family home, to feel certain for the first time in her life. There was a calm about the situation – a relief that she had decided on a path – a determination about the future. What's more, she felt like she had a purpose. The strangling dread that she may spend her life flitting from tea, to balls, to children was at least one thing she could quell – that life may be inevitable, but she would also make it her own. Edgar's collection would be the basis for her future endeavour of collecting the world. It was what Martha demanded, and what Thea now earnestly desired. The fresh, reassuring understanding that her efforts in life may make some small imprint on the future seemed to make her shoulders lighter, her breathing easier and the choice she was about to make almost bearable.

To succeed she would require a husband who would enable her vision through fortune and freedom and allow her to indulge her curiosity. One that would allow her a greater purpose than being a wife. Her union would secure the future of her family, of Milford and, most importantly, the wellbeing of her sister. As much as Ursula had tried to reassure her, Thea knew this was the only way to be certain.

She strode through the hallway, holding herself tall and confident in her resolve, her boots clicking rapidly on the solid marble. Her father dashed out of his study to meet her. 'Did you see her?' She nodded and smiled. His tension gave way to relief. 'I am so glad.'

'So am I.' She meant it with every fibre of her being.

'What now?' he asked. She looked around her at the Morell house, the crest above the fireplace, pointed firmly out at the wealth of the capital.

'Now,' she said with an assurance that sent a frisson of electricity from the top of her head down to her feet, 'I am to marry.'

Her father knew better than to express the surprise he must have felt. There was a steel about her that shouldn't be trifled with. 'Do you know who?' She nodded slowly. Two choices. The way she preferred that would ultimately break another heart. And the way she must choose.

'I will marry George Crowe.' Although she had known for a fortnight, saying it out loud helped to confirm it to herself. She knew she could never offer the union of body and soul that Sam so deserved.

Mr Morell's expression was a mixture of relief and concern. 'Does he know?'

Her assured smile went some way to calming his apprehension. 'Not yet, I shall inform him immediately.' She kissed her father deftly on the cheek and strode off to the library for paper and ink.

WHAT HAPPENS NEXT?

What excitement awaits for Martha? Can Thea fit all her fossils in her new house? Will they get to snuggle again? To be the first to know what happens on Thea and Martha's next adventure, sign up for the Curiosity Club newsletter. It also offers information, news on progress and upcoming releases, and competitions. You can unsubscribe at any time.

suzannemoss.co.uk/signup

In the meantime, if you'd like to know what Martha got up to on her travels there is a FREE short story available. *An Account of a Voyage of Curiosity* awaits, simply visit the link below.

suzannemoss.co.uk/Martha

You can also purchase Observations gift boxes and other curiosity and book-related items as gifts or as a treat for yourself. You deserve it. This was a long book.

suzannemoss.co.uk/shop

ABOUT THE AUTHOR

Dr Suzanne Moss is a horticultural education professional and researcher in eighteenth-century gardens and collections. The history of gardens as scientific collections is a particular interest and was the subject of her PhD and subsequent post-doctorate research fellowship. The history of sexuality has become a recent fascination while trying to write this book. A background in both archaeology and horticulture means she can dig a really excellent hole, both literally and metaphorically.

Sue lives in Hampshire, UK with her wife Milly and dogs Wilma and Pheebs. She is originally from Yorkshire and misses it. In her spare time she's renovating a house, doing the garden and writing books – it really sounds quite wholesome doesn't it.

She finds writing about herself in the third person weird.

To download free short stories in this series and to keep up to date, sign up for the Curiosity Club newsletter at

You can connect with me on:

Web: suzannemoss.co.uk

Twitter: twitter.com/DrSueMoss

Mastodon: @DrSueMoss@mastodonapp.uk

Facebook: facebook.com/SuzanneMossBooks

Instagram: instagram.com/drsuemoss

Printed in Great Britain
by Amazon